THE DARK FABLE

THE DARK FABLE

KATHERINE HARBOUR

BLOOMSBURY

NEW YORK   LONDON   OXFORD   NEW DELHI   SYDNEY

BLOOMSBURY YA
Bloomsbury Publishing Inc., part of Bloomsbury Publishing Plc
1385 Broadway, New York, NY 10018

First published in the United States of America in January 2024 by Bloomsbury YA

Bloomsbury books may be purchased for business or promotional use. For information on bulk
purchases please contact Macmillan Corporate and Premium Sales Department at
specialmarkets@macmillan.com

Library of Congress Cataloging-in-Publication Data
available upon request
ISBN 978-1-5476-1374-8 (hardcover) • ISBN 978-1-5476-1375-5 (e-book)

Book design by Yelena Safronova
Typeset by Westchester Publishing Services
Printed and bound in the U.S.A.
2 4 6 8 10 9 7 5 3 1

To find out more about our authors and books visit www.bloomsbury.com
and sign up for our newsletters.

This book is dedicated to you, my readers

We are La Fable Sombre, the Dark Fable.
We are spirits of revolution and revenge.
We are the thorn in your side, the bitter in your cup.
We are the ink spilled over the stories of tyrants.

THE DARK FABLE

Beginning

It's not a memory anymore. It might be a nightmare. Because how could it be real?

I am eight years old. I'm standing in my room streaked with rain shadows, listening to my dad arguing with my mom. Thunder crashes.

I peer through the half-open door. I see the monster. I see the bones twisting in a crown from its head, its white skin scarred with symbols that make me want to cry, to hide. Only its eyes are beautiful, a burning blue. When it comes to kill me, it wears my dad's face.

It doesn't take me. I don't let it. (It isn't my dad.)

It moves toward my little brother and sister instead. (It isn't my dad.)

I can't protect them. I can't save them.

I've been living with that nightmare ever since.

PART I

Amusement et Jeux

Chapter One

Initiation

Evie's favorite color was black. Black was as comforting as shadows, as night, and, like an ink spill or a fall of darkness, it changed the rules. It was the color of magic and elegance. Of alchemical transformation. Of the mysterious spaces in the universe before stars or stories were born.

Gazing at her galaxy of black clothes, she reached into her closet for her uniform. She slid the white dress and the pinafore on over her slip; the catering company preferred their employees to look as though they'd stepped out of a silent film. She glimpsed her pale face in a darkened mirror. The bruises beneath her eyes were tragic.

Shrugging into a jacket, she hurried from the attic of the apartment building in which she'd been illegally squatting for over a year. It was raining, but the Plaza La Mer, the hotel where she was working tonight, wasn't far, so she ran through the neighborhood, past pawnshops and raggedy palm trees.

The hotel—ebony and chartreuse, all Art Nouveau decadence—stood at the end of the boardwalk. She pushed through the employee entrance. As she wound through the kitchen dense with the aromas of salty preserved meats and ancient cheeses, she spotted her supervisor, Tyrone, a lanky figure in white, wrapping an apron around his waist. He was eighteen like her, majoring in physics, and holding down two part-time jobs.

"Evie. You're late." Tyrone pointed to the trays scattered with appetizers. "We can't let these rich folks wait." Lifting two platters to shoulder height, he glided past her, the light gleaming pink on his black braids. "Good luck." He pushed through the doors, into the party, a gala for the Silver Cove Museum, where the California elite pretended to care about art, fossils, and dead civilizations.

Evie swept the snaky tendrils of her short, dark hair into a clip and lifted the appetizer platter, the antique rings she wore on each finger clinking against the silver. She followed two other servers into the huge ballroom gleaming with satin cocktail dresses and silk ties. She offered appetizers to people who didn't even look at her. One woman, arms banded with gold bracelets, flicked her fingers, shooing Evie away.

Another woman straight out of French *Vogue* stepped onto the dais. She wore a jet-black sheath dress, her golden hair coiled. A gorgeous necklace snaked across her cleavage, all gold and black opals studded with sapphires—a cobra, its head resting above her heart. She began to speak, her words revealing a faint accent. "Welcome, all of you. I am Lila Pearce. My husband loved the museum we are here to support. Thank you for coming, and for your generosity. Our first piece for auction is the Queen Cobra." She touched her necklace. "Once worn by the Egyptian queen, Cleopatra, and donated anonymously . . ."

Evie turned and collided with someone. Pink champagne splashed over her pinafore.

She met the amused gaze of a young white guy in a perfectly tailored black suit, his dark brown hair swept up like a 1960s idol's. His silvery eyes looked her up and down. He set his empty glass on the tray without a word to her and continued walking.

As Evie stood there, fuming, champagne dripping from her skirt, she imagined chucking a wine bottle at the back of his head. Her temper was a problem—last month, a man had flung a hundred-dollar bill to her as a tip, and she'd ripped it to pieces in front of him. She'd spent an hour taping it back together later that night and cursing herself for her careless anger.

She made her way to Tyrone, who was leaning against a wall, arms folded as he supervised.

"Hey, boss." She set down the empty platter.

"Look at these people. You can see the old money, over there. Near the window, those are the self-made bastards. The ones circulating barely got in and are trying to make nice with the popular kids. And the people not mingling, but just observing? They're trying to figure out who's going to be the most useful. Social engineering is like chaos theory. You can control something if you figure out its patterns. I'm figuring out which ones'll tip."

"And her?" Evie nodded to the blonde woman wearing the snake necklace. She was speaking to a man with a silver beard.

They stood out, all stylish arrogance, in the mosaic of Rolexes and old pearls.

"Lila Pearce. She owns a lot of resorts around the world. This is her shindig."

"I hate everyone here, Ty. It's my break time."

"Enjoy it. Please come back."

Evie began to work back through the party as a brunette in a white gown and a fancy rabbit mask produced several small spheres of pink paper and tossed them into the air. The pink paper unraveled, and glitter shimmered down. Another person, in an expensive suit and tiger mask, tossed other paper spheres into the air. More glitter misted over the crowd. People laughed in surprise. There was a delicate round of applause.

Evie narrowly evaded the shower of glitter as she headed for the powder room. Inside, she dabbed at the champagne stain with paper towels and heaved in a breath. She wanted to scream. She always wanted to scream.

A girl in a silver cocktail dress and a cropped jacket of pink feathers entered. Her blonde hair, streaked with pink, glittered with diamond pins. As she began applying lip gloss in front of the mirror, she slid her black-rimmed gaze to Evie and said, "What big eyes you have."

"Thanks?" Evie thought the other girl had eyes like a wolf.

The girl snapped the lip gloss shut. She turned and leaned against the counter, flicked a glance over Evie's uniform. "You look like Little Bo-Peep in that getup." She leaned close, confidential, her wolf eyes sly. "I can see you're having a rough time."

"I'm kind of working, so yeah."

"I'm sorry. No one deserves that."

Evie stared at her. "Deserves what?"

"Indentured servitude." The girl tilted her head. "I'm Mad."

That was her name, Evie realized. "Evie." She wondered why a rich girl was bothering to speak to her. She wanted to retort that she actually liked this job.

"Here." The girl—Mad—slipped off the little jacket. "Take it. It'll cover that stain."

Evie reluctantly accepted the jacket. The designer on the label made her eyes widen. "You sure—"

"I've got lots. So, you do anything besides this?"

The girl must be bored. "I've got two other jobs." Evie suddenly felt ashamed. She shrugged. "I paint."

"You do?" Mad's uninterested expression faded into delight. "Do you know your art stuff? Go to school for it?"

Evie's throat tightened. "No school." Fiercely, she added, "But I *do* know my art stuff."

"That's perfect. The Pre-Raphaelites and the Surrealists are my favorites. There are some amazing films the Surrealists created." Mad checked a fancy watch on her wrist. She looked up. "Want me to smuggle you in a fancy drink and some goose liver pâté?"

"No, thank you." Evie laughed. In this baroque powder room, she didn't feel like the clockwork creature she became at most of her jobs. She checked her tousled hair in the mirror, her smudgy eyeliner. "I'd better get back."

"Suit yourself, pretty elf." The wolf-eyed girl glided from the powder room. She paused in the doorway and said, without looking back, "Tall, Dark, and Handsome is going to wonder where his wallet went. I hope you took the cash and ditched the crocodile skin." The door swung shut behind her.

Evie went still. She *had* ditched the wallet she'd lifted from the gorgeous jerk who'd spilled the champagne over her. The bills were tucked into her bra.

A text pinged on her phone: Ready for fun?

She squinted at the unknown number.

"Wrong number, weirdo." She set the phone on the counter and stared into the mirror. The thought of returning to that pack of entitled effers made her stomach clench.

She slipped back into the kitchen. It was empty. Where *was* everyone? She stepped into the catering area and lifted a platter. As she moved down the corridor, she heard a ruckus beyond the swinging doors to the ballroom. She slipped through.

And halted.

Mayhem had erupted among the guests. One tuxedoed man punched another, while two women in gowns crashed against a table of desserts. Spilled champagne glistened like rosy blood on the white marble. It was as if old grudges had risen like an evil spell, the fancy clothes and civilized conversation forgotten. Evie ducked a thrown bottle, a swinging arm. Across the room, two girls in masks—the rabbit and an owl—wove through the brawl.

The gorgeous young man who'd spilled champagne on Evie earlier leaned against a sarcophagus on the dais, pouring himself a glass of bubbly as security cut through the crowds.

Evie stepped back, avoiding a flying cake. She watched the melee with a sort of horrified hilarity, flinching as one of her fellow servers clobbered a shouting man with a silver tray.

The gorgeous guy near the sarcophagus straightened, set aside his glass, and pulled a metal dragon mask down over his face. He moved to Lila Pearce, who was yelling at everyone, and discreetly unhooked the Cobra necklace from around her throat. His gaze sought someone behind Evie. She glanced over her shoulder, saw the brown-skinned man in the tiger mask raise one arm.

The unknown number pinged on Evie's phone again. She glanced swiftly at the text: Success=Ur the best. Fail=U go to jail.

Dragon Mask tossed the necklace to Evie.

Evie, unthinkingly, instinctively, reached out and caught the necklace. It was heavier than she expected.

Lila Pearce shrieked, "The necklace!"

The four masked people had vanished into the fray.

Two fierce-looking young men in suits—security—pushed toward Evie through the mayhem. Evie panicked. She knew people like Lila Pearce—entitled, impatient folk who wouldn't believe someone like Evie, who didn't have the cleanest record anyway. She wondered how many years one could get for grand larceny. She thought, *Don't see me. Don't see me.*

Darkness ribboned around her like eels, as if an eclipse had come and hung over only her. She could see everyone around her, in monochrome, all color gone. She could hear sounds, but they were muted. And she was suddenly so *cold* . . . As the veils of shadow ebbed, she heard whispering she couldn't understand. She stood in an uncanny stillness, as if she'd stepped out of the world. What was happening? Was she having a panic attack? A stroke?

The two militant young men stalked past her without a glance—and she still clutched the Cobra necklace.

The shadows and cold slid away from her like a caul. The noise returned full blast, in a dizzying wave.

She jammed the necklace into a pocket and ran. Avoiding a pair of men grappling with one another, she clambered onto a table, picking her way through pyramids of shrimp cocktails and towers of little cakes. She jumped down and dashed into the hall.

And collided with someone, a young Asian guy, his suit bespoke, his spiky hair blue, his smile vicious. "You've got something that doesn't belong to you."

She stepped back, instinctively knowing this stranger wasn't security. He grabbed her arm. She twisted free—

The shadows coiled around her again—it was as if she were slipping deeper into a world beneath the skin of this one. Veiled in that cold and whispering darkness, bewildered, Evie fled.

In another hall, she slid behind a pillar, fighting to catch her breath, which misted in the freezing air. Opposite her was a mirrored wall.

She did not see herself in it. She stepped forward, raised one hand—

The blue-haired stranger appeared, slinking down the hall. Evie ducked back behind the pillar.

"I know you're here," he called. "I *know* you're here." He prowled closer. He said, "I get it. You're new. I'll walk you out of here before security gets you. I'll keep you safe. And that's something, 'cause people are usually running *away* from me—"

She broke from the pillar and raced down the hall. She heard a girl shout, "Knife, what are you *doing*?"

"Looking for that girl . . . ," Knife replied.

Evie bashed through the kitchen doors and crouched behind a counter. She reached for her phone, groaned, and pressed her brow against her updrawn knees. She'd dropped it somewhere.

When she heard a door open, her head jerked up. Tyrone sauntered in, wrapping his apron back around his hips. She snapped up, grabbed him, and dragged him down behind the counter. "Where *were* you?"

His eyes widened. "In my car, studying. *What* is all that noise—"

She lifted a finger to his lips. She rose, saw the outside doors sweep open to admit three figures in masks—the dragon, the owl, and the tiger. The girl in the owl mask looked directly at Evie.

Evie crouched back behind the counter. She whispered, "I think we're being robbed."

"We need weapons," Tyrone whispered back, frantically reaching for the knife drawer.

Evie smacked his hand away. "We're not knife people." She indicated the nearest cabinet. "*Hide.*"

They crammed themselves into the cabinet. As Evie closed the door and darkness folded over them, she heard a male voice speak in a Liverpool singsong. "How do we find her if we can't see her?"

The second male's voice was deep and velvety. "We don't need to find her yet. Just make sure Nara crew doesn't get her."

"This rivalry with Nara and Fenrir. It really needs to stop." The male with the Liverpool accent sounded irritated.

"Silence and Night say it keeps us on our toes." The girl's voice—Evie recognized it. *Mad.* The blonde girl whose jacket she wore.

"The Deer and the Wolves'll never beat us." Liverpool's voice was so close. "We cheat."

The cabinet doors flew open. Evie grabbed Tyrone's hand as the thief in the tiger mask peered in. Her skin iced. There was a weird buzzing in her ears. Her scalp prickled. Her vision blurred and a coppery taste filled her mouth.

The thief's gaze passed over them. Evie held her breath until he withdrew and shut the cabinet doors. "Nothing here."

She felt Tyrone's hand in hers tighten. She waited, her stomach churning, for the cruel punchline. Surely, the crook was just playing games. Any moment, the doors would open and they'd be dragged out . . .

The voices faded as the trio left.

Evie, opposite Tyrone, saw the gleam of his eyes in the dark. She didn't know how long they waited, scarcely breathing, wondering if they were going to die.

Then she heard the sirens, faint at first, growing closer. She breathed out. Tyrone finally exhaled.

They pushed open the cabinet doors. Blue and red lights swirled on the ceiling from the parking lot. The police had arrived.

—◆—

Evie's encounter with the Silver Cove Police Department was a blur of procedure and authority, two things Evie passionately disliked. But she had become a master of evasion. When asked about her parents, she replied, "They're dead." The female officer interviewing her seemed startled, then genuinely sympathetic, which only irritated Evie further.

"What happened?" Evie needed to know exactly what had transpired tonight. "Everyone went wild."

The officer glanced around at the police swarming the kitchen. Tyrone sat at the opposite end speaking with another cop. "Something in the champagne, they think. Won't be identified until the evidence goes through forensics."

No. It wasn't the champagne. Evie remembered the darkhaired girl in red tossing paper balls into the air, the glitter that had fallen. Her breath shook. The blonde girl—Mad—had *distracted* Evie while the pandemonium unfolded. It was an unnerving realization.

There had been four of them. And, for some reason, they had *selected* Evie. Even before the necklace was tossed right at her. And the strange texts on her phone . . . they had *targeted* her, made her an accessory.

The idea was terrifying. Like playing with a Ouija board for fun, then realizing one had actually summoned something hella dangerous.

Evie clutched at her seat with both hands as the officer sauntered away to speak with another colleague. Evie was still wondering why people hadn't been able to see her. It had been bothering her for hours. She couldn't figure out what had happened. How those security guards and then Knife and Tiger Mask had failed to see her. And that moment of terror when her reflection had been missing in the mirror . . . From childhood, she'd had a tricky relationship with mirrors . . . and with the shadow girl she sometimes glimpsed behind her while brushing her hair or her teeth. An imaginary friend that had faded as she'd grown older.

But . . . tonight . . . had it been the *necklace*? Had the Queen Cobra affected her in some way?

She *hadn't* become invisible.

Had she?

She spotted a young man speaking with the officer who had questioned her. The officer pointed to Evie, who frowned as the stranger walked toward her. His cashmere coat and shoes looked expensive. He moved with athletic grace and there was a formidable intelligence in his dark eyes. His name badge, on a lanyard, read "Jason Ra."

"You're Evie Wilder?" The smoky timbre of his voice glinted with a posh British accent. He sat in the chair the officer had vacated. Light gleamed in his dark hair, classically side-parted and sculpted to emphasize a somewhat hawkish face. Despite the curve to his lips, and a cute black freckle dotting one nostril, he radiated all the warmth of an icicle. "May I ask you some questions?"

"Ra." She played it cool. "The name of the Egyptian sun god."

"Everyone knows mythology these days." He studied her. "My last name's Korean, but I was born in London."

"Aren't you young to be a cop?"

"I'm not a police officer." He didn't look amused.

"What are you then?" Evie was suspicious.

"I'm a private investigator."

"Can you be a PI at your age?"

"I'm nineteen, and, yes, you can. My dad was Interpol. The officer who spoke with you—she's from LA. She knew my dad from a case involving her partner's car accident."

Evie narrowed her eyes. "Are we suspects? There are security cameras—"

"All the footage was scrambled. We've only got you and your friend as witnesses."

"I told the co—the officer—everything." Evie scrutinized her interrogator.

He smiled and it was breathtaking. "You don't mind speaking to me as well, do you? You saw two males. A girl was with them?"

"Yeah." Evie remembered the dark-haired girl who had tossed paper balls into the air. The glitter. She kept quiet about that.

Jason Ra produced a small notebook and wrote in it. "Didn't see their faces, just what they wore?"

"They wore animal masks. Fancy ones." Evie told him what the two males had said. "They spoke in some sort of poetic robber jargon."

His mouth curved, a slight, telling dimple. "No names?"

"No."

Jason Ra closed the notebook and returned that and the expensive-looking pen to a place inside his blazer. He studied her with remote interest. "You didn't exchange any words with them?"

Evie thought of Mad. "We were hiding in a cabinet. Why would I speak to crooks?" Aside from being evasive, she was also a good liar.

"Have you ever heard of *La Fable Sombre*?"

She blinked. "That French?"

"It means 'the Dark Fable.' They're a gang of thieves—some say nothing but an urban legend—who've been committing thefts around the world. Odd thefts, usually of obscure valuables and ancient objects."

Evie listened, her brow crinkled. The necklace slithered in her pocket. If they searched her . . .

"A necklace called the Queen Cobra was stolen tonight. It belonged to Cleopatra, a queen of the Ptolemaic dynasty. Its value is phenomenal."

"Huh. Maybe the museum shouldn't have advertised that they had it."

"It *was* an auction."

"Too bad then."

His gaze never left her face. Evie thought he could tell, he could *sense,* that she was leaving something out. She stood up abruptly. "Nice speaking to you, detective. But I've got to pee."

Evie brooded in the passenger seat as Tyrone drove his Ford Ranchero past the hotels on Ocean Avenue. The pink neon cross above a chapel, the red torpor of a liquor shop sign, contributed to the unsettling smoke-and-mirrors atmosphere of the evening. Silver Cove's downtown was seedy, its once glamorous Art Nouveau hotels rehabbed into grungy apartments. The glitz that had once appealed to 1920s' film stars and gangsters was now tarnished.

Tyrone pulled up in front of the apartment building Evie had dubbed the Pink Blight. On its hill, with the shops below huddled around it like courtiers, it reminded her of a decrepit queen.

"Evie," Tyrone said as she got out. He was gripping the steering wheel as he stared straight ahead. "We didn't die today."

"No. We didn't." She shut the Ranchero's door. "See you later, Ty."

"I think I'm looking for another job," he called after her.

"I'll miss you." She knew he'd be back in the morning.

She ignored the catcalls from a gathering of guys as she trudged up the Pink Blight's stairs. She didn't become invisible, which relieved and disappointed her. She was too tired to make decisions concerning reality versus fantasy.

The thieves would come after that necklace. La Fable Sombre. And, when they did, she'd need to be a damn good liar. She fumbled with the keys and stepped into the hall.

When she heard someone enter behind her, she didn't look back. In front of her, a girl was sitting on the interior stairs. Elegant in tartan leggings and a leather jacket, her dark brown hair sleek over one shoulder, she watched Evie, a cherry-red vape pen glowing between two fingers. Feline eyes, an upturned nose, and a wry smile gave her a roguish look.

"Hey." A male voice came from behind Evie. "I wanna speak to you. Snitch."

Evie's stomach dropped. It was her downstairs neighbor. Lanky and sneering, he slinked around the apartment steps with his minions at night. The Brute. She met the girl's gaze and saw amusement. The girl said, "I'd hurry if I were you."

Evie slid past her, up the stairs. She glanced back.

The Brute was blurred by a cloud of smoke that had come from the girl's lips. It was an unusual amount of smoke. He coughed and stumbled a little. The girl rose, vanishing into the bluish smoke, leaving Evie to fend for herself.

Evie hesitated. The Brute stopped waving his arms and glared up at her.

She whirled and ran. She reached the third-floor hallway and the stairs to the attic. She got her door open. She slammed it shut and shot home the bolts.

When the door shuddered beneath a violent blow, she stumbled back. She heard drunken laughter and obscenities. Fists bashed at the door.

"Bitch! You tell the landlord I bothered you?"

She couldn't do that—the landlord didn't even know she was here. She also didn't know who the landlord was.

As the door shook beneath more kicks, she sank down with her back against it, her arms over her head. If she closed her eyes, she could pretend she was floating in the ocean, in the night. Sometimes, she sensed another girl stirring inside her, a hidden part of her psyche, a self-defense mechanism born from ten years of precarious circumstances and uncertainty, whispering, *I will always love you. I will always take care of you.*

The lights flickered. She thought of her brother and sister—they'd be seventeen and sixteen now, if they hadn't . . . they weren't lying in an unmarked grave. She told herself that every day.

She lifted a hand toward the medallion she wore for luck, a lacquered image of a girl's face painted with a skull, her dark hair blooded with roses. *She will protect you,* Evie's mother had promised.

She touched the divot between her collarbones—the medallion was gone, lost in the chaos of this evening. Tears blurred her vision.

For most of her life, Evie had been in foster homes, in a recurring state of fight or flight, her only constant a caseworker named Amy Rodriguez, who had taken Evie shopping for school supplies and brought her to the doctor to get her birth control. What did Evie have to show for those years? No higher education. Dead dreams. Dead-end jobs. Just a future of wandering and luck. A future without seeing her brother and sister grow up.

The Brute eventually went away.

Evie looked around her attic. With its tiny half bath, it had once been an artist's studio, now forgotten. When it rained, she had to keep buckets in several places. And, sometimes, there were mice. But the electric and the water worked, and it was rent-free because only her neighbor Ava knew she was here. Well. Until now.

She rose and flicked on the lights, avoided her reflection in the one mirror she owned, a sunburst above the bathroom sink. The black walls and the few pieces of salvaged furniture were comforting after this evening's shock. She walked to the bulletin board pinned with Polaroids. She pressed her palm against the photo of Ezra and Juliet, who had been six and seven years old.

Evie's world had ended when she'd been eight, when her father had shot her mom and himself, and she'd never seen her brother and sister again. She hadn't come out of her room when it had happened, had been found curled in her closet, her arms over her head. Years later, those headlines were still burned into her brain: *Local musician, father of three, murders wife, dies by suicide. Two missing children assumed dead. One survivor.*

Three years ago, Evie had scraped together enough money

to hire a private detective who had been willing to listen to her. He'd believed her when she'd told him that a murderer had tricked his way into their house—

There were nights when she doubted, when she remembered her father's temper, and her mom weeping quietly in the bedroom. Her dad had never raised a hand to any of them, but there had been broken and repaired objects in the Los Angeles bungalow, hallmarks of his moods and her mom's stubborn resistance to them. Evie sometimes wondered if what the psychiatrists said had been true: *Typical dissociation—you replaced your father with a monster because you couldn't deal with the truth . . .*

She would do anything to see her little brother and sister again, to embrace them grown, even if they were strangers. Sometimes, she thought she'd been tricked, that the monster she'd imagined hadn't—

She drew the Queen Cobra from her dress with shaking hands and stared at it. She stood before the mirror in her bathroom. She closed her eyes. She willed the shadows around her, sought out some break in reality that would allow her to be unseen. Cold whispered across her skin.

Her eyes flew open, and she gasped as a shadow flickered behind her, vanished. Her reflection stared back at her with eyes that were all pupil. What was she doing?

The thieves, La Fable Sombre . . . she would have to be very, very careful when they came for the Cobra.

For her.

———

Ava Dubrowska always had tea and a scrumptious babka she bought from the Polish bakery around the corner. Evie wasn't quite sure of Ava's age, as she had the fine bones of a ballerina and the vibrant manner of a Bohemian. Evie loved wandering around her apartment with its teal wallpaper scrolled with silver flowers and peacocks, its antiques and objects from all over the world. The photographs of Ava when she'd been a concert pianist were absolutely cinematic. She had been teaching Evie how to sing.

"How are you doing?" Ava, seated in her chair, her silver hair in its usual elegant updo, added a sugar cube to her tea.

Evie told her: "There was a weird heist or something at the party I worked tonight."

Ava arched an eyebrow. "It was all over the news."

Evie turned back to the wall of photographs. "They only stole from the rich guests. One of my co-workers found a hundred-dollar bill in his pocket."

"How fascinating."

"There were a lot of assholes at that party."

Ava sighed. "Don't be savage, Evie. It doesn't suit you."

Evie thought it suited her just fine.

"Did they steal from the museum?" Ava asked.

"They took a necklace called the Cobra."

"No artifacts?"

"I don't think so."

"They wore masks?"

"Yeah. Animal faces."

"When I was your age, in Romania, there were rumors of a gang of thieves. They had stolen a crown from a Babylonian gravesite. They had thieved Greta Garbo's fox bracelets. I believe there was even an incident with the Prussian crown jewels. They called themselves La Fable Sombre. Anyone who crossed them regretted it. They were quite the bogeyman, slinking beneath all the other horrors of the war."

Evie pretended she wasn't listening intently. She tilted her head, gazing at a photograph of Ava with her husband when they'd been young. Ava wore a necklace of sapphires and silvery mermaids. "Your husband was a hottie, Ava. That necklace is fabulous."

"Alexander was a jeweler. He made that for me. It was a copy of my mother's, one I lost." She smiled wistfully. "He called me his mermaid."

Evie sat down and reached for a slice of cinnamon babka. Ava's cat, a sleek tabby, curled beside her. Evie petted it cautiously. She didn't have any pets, afraid to love anything. One of her foster moms, Betty Gordan, had had cats. She'd neglected nine-year-old Evie but not the damn cats. Although Evie had loved those cats. While sleeping in her curtained cubby at night, the cats had curled around her and kept the cockroaches away.

She glanced up at Ava, who spoke matter-of-factly: "The soldiers took all our jewelry when they came for us. My mother's necklace . . . it's in a museum in Austria now." She looked at the photograph. "At least I have these. And St. Stanislaus. Oh dear." She picked up a statue of some pretty saint and frowned at it. "He has a crack in his face. That's new."

Evie reached out and laid a hand over one of Ava's. She said, "Next time, could you teach me a song from the Roaring Twenties?"

"How old do you think I am?" Ava laughed. "I'll teach you a lovely tune I know. Something for young people."

Evie sat back, cradling her teacup. "I'm sorry, Ava. About those bastards taking your mom's necklace."

"It was only a thing."

Evie gazed down into her tea. She asked delicately, "How did you get through it? Being so powerless?"

"Powerless?" Ava smiled proudly. "I was not powerless. I watched. I waited. I learned. I found their weaknesses. I grew stronger. I am not a survivor, Evie. I am not a victim. I am a victor."

And Evie thought about being a victor.

—⁓—

Back in her apartment, Evie sat on a pink railroad trunk and studied her latest unfinished painting. It stood in a corner cluttered with mason jars spiky with brushes, canvases of all sizes stacked against the walls. The half-finished painting was of a boy with scarlet wings on a red background spattered with gold. Her figures emerged from chaos, from the mosaic of jewel-like colors she plastered onto canvases painted black. She'd discovered painting when she was thirteen. She loved the fury and the mess of the medium. And she'd sold a few of them as a side hustle.

She knelt beside the pink trunk. At least once a month, she opened the trunk to sort through the objects within, talismans from her childhood.

1. The nine albums that had belonged to her dad, including her favorite, Prince's *Purple Rain*.

2. Her dad's leather wallet containing a Hermes dime and a Polaroid of her parents when they'd been very young, the sun setting behind them and five of their friends. They looked happy.

3. A red-leather copy of Sun Tzu's *Art of War* with an inscription inked on the inside cover: *To Trick— LEARN THIS.* It was signed with a sharp and elaborate *B.*

When she dropped the Queen Cobra into the trunk's false bottom, the Cobra's eye glinted as if it were winking at her. She glanced out the grimy window, to the boulevard below. An old-fashioned Rolls-Royce was parked opposite the Pink Blight.

Apprehension whispered up her spine. She rose and crept closer to the window.

A figure in a suit leaned against the car. He lit a cigarette, cupping a match against the wind. The flame briefly lit the hollow of his cheekbone, the sweep of dark hair. He looked up.

Evie ducked down, her heart slamming. It was the gorgeous stranger from the museum gala.

A black envelope slid beneath her door. She scrambled back, staring at it. She reached up, opened a drawer, and fumbled out a pair of chopsticks. She picked up the envelope and tore it with one of the chopsticks. A piece of black parchment floated to the floor. The letterhead and the writing were silver. *Take care of the Queen Cobra. We'll be in touch. LFS.*

Evie curled back against her bed, the copper taste in her mouth returning. So. Her desperation *had* summoned something dangerous. She crawled to the light switch and flicked it off. She moved back to the window and peeked out.

The Rolls-Royce was gone. Hanging from the parking meter was the dragon mask the lead robber had worn, a lit cigarette stuck in its mouth like a flaming tongue.

CHAPTER TWO

Invitation

The gas station where Evie worked her third job—her second was the country club on weekends—had been around since the thirties. Located on the highway at the city's entry point, the building was all rusting chrome and fire-engine red. The restroom was a horror show that Evie avoided until 2:46 AM, when she entered, armed with a plunger and elbow-length rubber gloves, vowing to never work another graveyard shift. She lifted her gaze to the mirror over the sink and glared at her reflection. As if she were reciting an incantation, she whispered, "Don't see me. *Don't see me.*"

Nothing. She didn't vanish or fade. How did it work? *Was* it the necklace? Did she really become invisible or was the power something that diverted other people from seeing her? All those moments when she'd thought people were being rude or ignoring her . . . had she been fading out of reality without knowing it?

Or was it all her imagination?

When she stepped out of the restroom, she flung the plunger at the wall. Garth, the manager, stood outside by the ice machine, earbuds in, as he took one of his many smoking breaks. She slid behind the counter, hoping she hadn't gotten toilet water on her uniform shirt, and began sorting candy bars.

"Hello, luv."

Startled—she hadn't heard the entrance bell chime—she looked up and stared at a young man about her age. In a cobalt blue suit that glowed against his dark brown skin, his garnet tie rivaling his sunset-dyed buzz cut, he was out of place amidst the tacky merchandise.

"You." She stood dumbly. She recognized his voice as that of Tiger Mask.

"Me." He cast her a devastating smile, and the Liverpool lilt sang through his words: "I'm Devon. I prefer Dev—"

"Why are you *here?*"

"Well, it's a petrol station, innit, and we needed petrol." He leaned forward confidentially. His irises were a tawny hue, almost golden, and made him even lovelier. He had the lithe manner of a boxer who'd become a fashion model. It was very disconcerting. He continued, "And I was feeling snackie."

She gritted her teeth and rang up his items. He smelled like spice and cedar smoke.

"I see you noticed the fancy cologne." That smile again. "It's Clive Christian. You can have nice things too."

She shoved the magazine and the Twizzlers at him. "I think you should leave."

He opened the Twizzlers, offered her the bag. She glowered.

He shrugged and bit into one bright red rope. "A girl like you. A place like this. It doesn't seem right, does it? I believe you've got something of ours."

"*Dev.*" She tried his name as if it were a spell. "I'll give it to you if you promise to go away."

"You don't have it on you . . . you're smarter than that. When it's time to retrieve it, well, you did get our invitation, didn't you?" He smiled again and sauntered out. The store became dull when he'd gone.

Evie sank down onto a plastic crate and put her face in her hands.

The door chime buzzed. Someone approached. Without looking up, she said, "Can I help—"

"Open the fucking register."

She looked up into the barrel of a gun. The guy behind it was masked only by a bandanna. She said, numb with shock, "I can't."

"I *said,* open—" The robber's words cut off the moment she wished he couldn't see her.

Everything froze as an ominous cold enveloped her. Darkness folded around her, causing everything she saw to become black and white, like a silent film. She heard those voices speaking a language older than the stars. She felt suspended, caught between the skin of reality and the night of the impossible.

And she was terrified.

She glanced at the shop's reflection in the window—she didn't see herself behind the counter.

The robber lowered the gun, his gaze dumbfounded. "Where . . . ?" He looked around, raised the gun again. "Hey! Where'd you go?"

Evie stared at him. He really couldn't see her. Was she . . . ?

The door chime rang again. Evie and the robber turned.

The gorgeous guy from the Plaza La Mer gala strolled in, whistling. He browsed the chip aisle, not even looking at the robber, who aimed the gun with a shaking hand. The robber barked, "Hey, asshole."

The gorgeous guy turned. "It's Ciaran, mate." His smile made Evie's skin prickle. "Evie . . . I could use a little distraction."

Evie flung a pack of cigarettes to the robber's left. As the cigarettes struck the window, she ducked behind the counter. A gunshot cracked out, followed by the acrid bite of propellant in the air, and her heart slammed as the bullet shattered the plate glass. She heard grunts, things crashing. Then, silence.

The menace who called himself Ciaran leaned over the counter. "He's down."

She rose, shivering. He watched her. He had a split lip. The robber was splayed on the floor behind him. Gently, he asked, "You all right?"

She decided to be honest. "I don't know."

"Saw you blink out. Don't forget that." He pointed upward. "Video surveillance. You can't let anyone see what you can do, got me? Dev'll be taking care of it."

Evie clutched the counter. So it was true. "Why . . . ?"

"Ease up." His voice was soft. "Take a nice, deep true-'til-death." He inhaled and exhaled as an example.

Breathe. She breathed in, out. Calm poured through her.

"I'm here to get Twizzlers and something to drink and . . . whatever this is, 'cause it's damn cute." He plucked a Kewpie doll from the display of Kewpies dressed as old-timey film stars like Charlie Chaplin and Marilyn Monroe.

"I can't believe this." Hysteria rose in her again. "Is this happening?"

He eyed her. Then he jerked his head at the robber. "Call 911 after I leave." He strode out. He left the Kewpie doll on the counter.

Garth stumbled in at that moment, removing his earbuds. The look on his face was comical as he took in the strewn bags of chips, overturned racks of candy, the shattered window, and the robber on the floor. "What the *hell*?"

Evie glared at him. "Seriously? How did you *not* hear or see all that?"

A text *ping*ed on her phone. It read, Seven PM sharp tonight. Follow the clue.

With a shaking hand, she lifted the Kewpie doll Ciaran had selected. It was a Rudolph Valentino. In its heyday, Silver Cove had been a resort for movie stars and gangsters, when the boardwalk, with its sapphire blue roller coaster and gilded Ferris wheel, had been bright and new. There was a mural of one of Rudolph Valentino's films painted on the old Metro station downtown.

She had an entire day to decide what she wanted, to pretend she had a choice.

———∿∿———

Evie had researched, online, all the modern thefts laid at the feet of the elusive urban legend called La Fable Sombre. The stories ricocheted through her head as she strode down a neon-daubed street. She had a few more blocks to go before she reached the old Metro station. She passed a closed bookstore and some boutiques with spooky mannequins in the windows. It was late, but there were no buses, and she didn't have the money for a cab.

In New York City, a famous painting lent to the Met had been ghosted away, without any locks picked or windows broken. At a Monte Carlo resort, three people had disguised themselves as a limo driver and two wealthy young heirs, then disappeared—after every guest had been robbed of their possessions while they slept. At a fundraiser in Crete, two rollerskating girls in Greek goddess masks had made off with priceless statuettes from ancient Sumer. Two people in raven masks had scaled a high-rise in Dubai, cut a hole in a window, and stolen an Isis necklace of blue diamonds, a signature piece by Bulgari.

The exotic and sinister name *La Fable Sombre,* "the Dark Fable," had originated from a mythical society of thieves only hinted at in obscure books—a fact she had learned from an old article in the *New York Times.* And, although these modern crimes were speculated wistfully to have been committed by La Fable Sombre's latest incarnation, it seemed none of the people who'd written about the thieves actually believed they existed.

A pink Aston Martin glided past and halted. Evie stopped walking, suspicion prickling. The car crept backward until it was parallel to her. The driver rolled down the window. "Evie. It's dark and there are not-so-nice people around. Get in. It's a dangerous neighborhood. Hear that?"

Evie squinted at the driver, recognized the wolf-eyed girl.

Mad. She heard glass break, some excessive shouting down a nearby alley. She cursed. She strode to the pretty car and got in.

Mad, who now wore a short white raincoat and pink Converse, smiled at her. There were rosy streaks in her gold-white hair. "Nice to see you again."

"You're one of them."

Mad began to drive, gloved hands careful on the wheel. "One of whom?"

"Okay. Be like that." Evie sat stiffly as shadows and streetlights swept over her.

The old Metro station loomed with Cthulhuian elegance from the silent buildings clustered around it. The train station, built in the 1920s, had shut down in the eighties, replaced by a sleeker system elsewhere. The building, a soaring basilica of shiny stone hewn into vines and lilies, resembled an ebony kraken rising against the night. Evie got out of the car with Mad and gazed at the building, apprehensive. She couldn't see anything beyond the archway and shivered in the cold California night. Mad moved toward the shadows, hands in her pockets. "Follow me, Evie. Don't stray. Don't speak. And don't look afraid."

Evie hesitated. Mad, continuing on into the dark, said, "If we were going to murder you, we'd've done that a while ago." She turned, the shadows folding over her as her voice drifted back. "Come on."

Evie followed her into the station, imagining the shadows she'd glimpsed beyond the arch might give chase if she changed her mind and fled. As she emerged from the gloom, old-fashioned lamps scattered light from a huge chandelier that had fallen in the center of the Metro's lobby, the illumination shattering onto the figures waiting there. The place was a tableau of elegant decay: art deco murals depicting women with flowing hair were blotched with moss. Rust oozed from wrought-iron cherubs curled around the tops of pillars.

The leader, Ciaran, sat in a chair, watching Evie. "You know who we are?" He hunched forward.

"Yes." Evie's gaze skimmed the others. She wasn't surprised to find the regal brunette she'd seen on the stair in her apartment building; Dev leaned against a broken pillar, his buzz cut a smoldering red. They all looked dangerous. Evie spoke clearly, "You're La Fable Sombre."

Ciaran rose and walked toward her. He smiled. *That* smile was bad news; she knew it as surely as if it had been a blade kissing her throat.

"Evie Wilder," he said. "Who doesn't like to be noticed. Who can be invisible."

She laughed, a sharp spark. "I'm sorry. What?"

Mad lifted a pink cell phone so that Evie could see the screen. A video played, showing the Plaza La Mer's ritzy gala descending into mayhem and Evie standing amidst the chaos. Then she saw herself . . . vanish.

Of course, it was true. Had she needed that video to confirm it?

Mad raised her other hand and flicked a finger. "Dev."

Dev peeled himself from the pillar to hit the button on a film projector set up nearby.

Images in lush black and white jittered across a marble wall. Evie saw herself, a girl with smoky eyes, standing in line for a movie, ignored as people moved around her, a few even bumping into her. She lost sight of her image in the crowd. Then, a second clip, as she sat in a café. Two strangers took seats at her table, starting a conversation over their lattes as she stared at them indignantly—she saw herself fade from sight. In the next scene, she stood in her catering uniform in the center of a party as guests swanned past her. And then she wasn't there.

She remembered those times, all too often, when she'd felt ignored and isolated.

After she'd regained some control, she turned with a wrathful gaze. "You've been stalking me." And identifying an impossible, mind-reeling ability Evie had been using all her life without realizing it.

Dev swept up his hands. "I wasn't stalking you personally, luv. It was a team effort."

"Evie." Ciaran spoke gently. "You can make yourself invisible. When you fade out, do you feel anything?"

She recalled her lack of a reflection in the Plaza La Mer. Of Dev not seeing her and Tyrone in the cabinet. Had she also made *Ty* unseen? "Darkness. Cold. Tunnel vision. Everything goes black and white, and noises are muffled . . ." Terror and wonder were ripping the veil from the world she knew. "When it started, it was just the graying out and the cold. I thought they were just panic attacks."

Ciaran explained, "You instinctively make yourself invisible. You step out of this world, beneath its skin, so to speak."

"No. That's not possible."

Mad clasped Evie's hand as if pulling her back from a precipice. Her wolf gaze was direct. "We've all got something, Evie."

Voice hoarse, Evie asked, "What do you mean? *All* of you . . . ?"

"Dev, there, is our trickster. He can charm anything, anywhere."

Dev smiled and ran a hand over his sunset fade. "Anything. Anywhere. Anyone."

The brunette snorted.

"Queenie." Mad indicated the brunette in her shimmering silver dress—the girl who'd blown smoke at the Brute on the stair of the Pink Blight. "She's our alchemist, a purveyor of potions."

"She created the confetti." Evie realized. "That made everyone turn against each other."

"That's why I took you aside, so you wouldn't be affected." Mad grinned. She gestured to the leader. "And that's Ciaran Argent. Criminal mastermind and god of Doors. Doors with a capital *D*."

Ciaran walked to a door. He turned to Evie. "Name a place you've always wanted to visit. A real one. Not a fictional one."

"Please, no fictional ones," Dev muttered. "That was a bloody fiasco."

Evie had to play this game.

"Just say a place," Mad urged. "Just try it."

Evie flung out a desperate answer. "Paris then."

Dev groaned. "Why is it always fucking Paris, yeah?"

Evie had always wanted to go to Paris. Long ago, when she'd been happy, she remembered posters of illustrated Parisian ladies on the rose-pink walls of her parents' bungalow and a little Eiffel Tower that had held books. She still had a brooch that had belonged to her mom, an imitation Boucheron, with rhinestones instead of diamonds, a crown atop a circle. Paris had always seemed like a fictional place to her.

"Paris is a *goddess*." Mad turned on Dev defensively.

Dev shrugged. "It's overrated."

"London then." Evie didn't know why she was encouraging whatever this was.

"My hometown." Ciaran sounded approving. He knocked on the door three times. He looked at Evie, blue shadows edging his jawline. "Go on. Open it."

Evie found herself drawn to that door, a work of art in bronze, engraved with a woman in a swirling gown, her hair scattered with stars. She laid one hand on the doorknob and pulled.

Chill, damp air swept over her. Framed by writhing shadows was a city that glistened in the night. She saw a giant Ferris wheel and the obsidian gleam of a snaking river. Her heart jolted. *It's a trick.* But she could smell wet asphalt, car exhaust, the fug of that old river.

She set one foot over the threshold. Shadows swept across her. Absolute darkness. For an instant, she breathed scorching cold. Then London air kissed her skin as if the Thames was winding itself around her.

A hand grabbed her by one wrist. She glanced over her shoulder to meet Mad's gaze. Mad said, "Come back now."

Mad drew her back over the threshold. As the door shut, Evie marveled. "Was that real? *How?*"

"Any door. Any place. As long as it exists in the real world. I'm a Traveler." Ciaran walked Evie to a marble bench. She dropped onto it. Mad sat on one side and Ciaran on the other.

Still processing what she'd seen, Evie whispered, "I don't know how I . . . do it. I don't know how to control it. What I can do. I don't know what it is."

"It's you," Ciaran told her. "It's like breathing. You don't control it. No need to think about it. You're a natural."

"I'm not."

"You lifted my wallet, Evie." Ciaran laid one arm on the back of the sofa. "You got out of the gala with the Cobra. You were meant to be with us. Aren't you tired? Of dead-end jobs? Of having to rely on strangers? Of just scraping by?"

Evie kept very still, surrounded by these dangerous creatures. "How did you find each other?"

"Ciaran found us," Mad replied. She and Ciaran fist-bumped. "With the Doors. He wanted to locate others like us, so he asked the Doors. But you appeared when we came for a job. That was just kismet."

"Maybe our energy is making more of us." Dev sat on the arm of Queenie's chair, his white suit immaculate in the romantic light.

"That's not how energy works," Queenie told him. "I'm not explaining it to you again."

Dev gave her the V-shaped British version of the bird.

Evie forced the next question. "What is La Fable Sombre?"

Ciaran told her: "We're the successors of the original Dark Fable. Every decade, La Fable Sombre is reborn with a new crew."

"There were the Rogues in the 1970s. Vergil and Grace, from Michigan and Paris." Mad sighed. "They robbed the Montreal Museum of Fine Arts."

Ciaran stretched his arms over his head. "The Misfits in the eighties, a Texas girl and a boy from Colombia who purloined all those Aztec and Mayan artifacts from Madrid."

"The Sisters in Paris," Queenie said. "During the French Revolution. Stole Marie Antoinette's crown *and* her Book of Shadows."

"The Songbirds." Dev spoke. "A Navajo musician and a girl guitarist from Bangladesh. 1960s. Swiped a king's ransom of Hollywood jewelry. Stole a cursed ring of Charlie Chaplin's that came from the tomb of Tutankhamun."

"Wasn't Chaplin LFS?" Queenie was watching Evie.

"No." Dev looked thoughtful. "Harry Houdini was. And Marie Laveau . . . what other famous alumni? Wild Bill Hickok. Blackbeard. Until he got kicked out for being an absolute *nightmare*."

Evie was both awed by this secret history and skeptical. She wished she could read about these fabulous exploits. Ciaran seemed to sense what she was thinking. "Sorry, Evie. You won't find our scintillating predecessors described in any history books. Only rumors."

"What we can do . . . ," Evie whispered.

"We, each of us, had nothing once. Then we found out we had something. An ability, like." Ciaran watched her.

Dev hunched forward. "It's like we were all so fucked over by life we made ourselves special."

Queenie rested her head against the cushions. "Speak for yourself. I've always been special."

Dev cast a sidelong look at her. "And lovely."

"Obviously."

Mad twirled her hand, indicating all of them. "We're a

family, Evie. We look out for each other. We won't let you fall. We won't let you fail."

Evie realized she was every girl on every threshold to every magical world there ever was. "So . . . is it just all of you?"

"We're part of an organization," Ciaran told her with a smile. "You'll meet them later."

Evie had made her decision even before she'd realized she could trick reality. She curled her hands into fists so the others wouldn't see them trembling. "Do I have to sign something in blood? Get a tattoo?"

Ciaran sat back, the shadows slanting across his face so that only his eyes were visible. "None of that."

"There is a bit of a learning curve though." Dev looked meaningfully at Ciaran. "We'll be relying on what you can do. So, you need to practice how to use it."

"Why do you do it?" Evie asked, voice steady. Of course, there'd be a learning curve.

"For the thrill. For the money. Because we can." Mad was serious. "We all came from the dark. So did you. Can't you feel it, Evie? The power. Like a guardian spirit. I imagine mine as an owl with a girl's face."

"That's creepy," Dev murmured. "Mine's a tiger with Idris Elba's voice."

Evie looked at Queenie, who stared back at her. Then, the other girl shrugged. "A black rabbit."

"And Ciar's is a python dragon or something." Mad grinned. "So, what do you envision, Eves?"

Evie lied, "I don't envision anything."

"You will," Mad promised. "Now—you in or you out?"

Evie thought of returning to the catering service, the country club, the gas station. She thought of her dingy apartment on the third floor, the electricity turning on and off depending on the time of day. She should have a million more questions, but, really, no answers would change her mind. Finally belonging anywhere was enough. She flicked her gaze over the glittering group around her.

"I'm in."

Dev rose and approached her. "I'll be taking your phone, thank you."

Evie dropped the phone she'd retrieved into his hand. He flashed a smile, pocketed it, and said, "Don't worry, luv. You'll get a shiny new burner phone after I scrub the internet of your existence."

Ciaran held out a hand. "Now you establish our trust by handing over the Cobra."

Evie offered him the Queen Cobra. It shimmered like a real snake, twining over her fingers. He lifted it, laid it against her collarbones. She shivered as his fingers slid beneath the hair at the back of her neck to fasten the clasp. He said, "Wear it for a little while."

"How do you know it's real?" she asked, touching the necklace, fascinated. The sapphires seemed to hum with energy. It was a magic object snaking across her collarbones.

"It's real." Ciaran continued, "It either casts a glamour of beauty over the wearer or poisons them."

Evie scowled at him, but she didn't remove the Cobra. "That thug at the gas station—was he part of this?"

Ciaran shrugged. "A rando we hired. You needed a little encouragement after the initiation."

Evie didn't ask if the bullet had been real. She decided not to be angry. "Initiation. Right. That was the museum gala?"

"That's part of it," Mad told her. "Now that you're a pro, we should talk about your share."

As vertigo tilted the world, Evie breathed out. "What's my share and how and when do I get it?"

"A couple thousand." Dev sat opposite her. "First, you need to get on the payroll. Then you need to hide it. We've got people for that. I've got a family enterprise in Liverpool. Queens siphons money to her Inupiat community in Alaska. Your first paycheck'll be cash, so get a fireproof safe, or a safety deposit box at any institution of your choice."

Evie felt an overwhelming hunger that made her wince, as if she hadn't eaten for days. Queenie, observing this, said, "When we use our talents, it messes with our metabolism. You'll sleep all day. You'll eat a lot."

Evie studied each of them with the dragonfly swiftness she'd learned playing chess. Mad had a reckless, charming energy, but those lupine eyes hinted at menace. Dev's graceful and affable demeanor didn't conceal some rough edges. Queenie's proud façade glossed a trickster flicker. And Ciaran was the calm, dark center, a coiled threat behind a hero's mask. Evie asked, "What are we?"

Mad winked. "We're La Fable Sombre. And, now, Evie Wilder, you're one of us."

CHAPTER THREE

Owl Girl

The ride in Mad's Aston Martin was uneventful, with Mad singing along with the music on the radio as Evie gazed out the window and wondered how this was going to end. When Mad pulled up to the curb in front of the Pink Blight, Evie saw a few people sitting on the hillside stair.

"You want me to walk you to the door?" Mad asked as Evie slid out of the car.

"No. I'm fine." Feeling crackly, as if she'd stuck her finger in an electrical socket, Evie began her ascent up the stairs, fishing her keys from her pocket. She didn't know how Ava had obtained the keys, but she was grateful to have them. She glanced back at Mad, who hadn't yet driven away. Evie pushed the key into the door, her hand shaking. She was overwhelmed and exhausted. What had she gotten herself into?

Someone slammed a shoulder into her so violently, she fell, scraping her knees and the palms of her hands. Shocked, she looked up.

The Brute smiled down at her. "Hey, snitch. I'm getting evicted because of you."

"I didn't—" She avoided the kick he aimed at her and scrambled up. She jammed the key into the lock, yanked at the door. His hand shot past her to keep it open. But she slid in and dashed up the interior stairs. He raced after her.

She reached the top floor, glanced over one shoulder when she heard a sharp whistle, the kind used to call a dog. The Brute, now standing at the hall's end, turned to stare at the open window behind him.

Mad sat on the sill, swinging her legs and chewing gum. She smiled at him. "You're not much of a gent, are you? You're giving my girl there the heebie-jeebies."

"Wha . . ." The Brute sounded dumbstruck.

"You're not too bright either." Mad blew a bubble. The bubble popped. The Brute flinched.

"Mad," Evie whispered.

"You . . ." The Brute stumbled toward Mad. Bellowing with rage, he lunged for her.

Mad backflipped out the window.

Evie slammed her hands over her mouth as the Brute teetered, half over the windowsill.

He fell out, headfirst, with a shriek. Evie swallowed an upheaval of bile. After a moment, she walked slowly toward the window.

She reeled back as Mad appeared, sliding over the sill, lithe as an acrobat. The other girl glanced over her shoulder, out the window. "Ooh. He's not going to walk for a while. I'm thinking full body cast."

"We've got to call someone . . ." Evie remembered she didn't have a phone.

Mad fastened that wolf gaze on her. "Don't bother. A couple people saw him hit the ground. They're calling 911 or taking pictures or something."

Evie couldn't speak.

"Eves." Mad set her hands on Evie's shoulders. "He was a *bad* man."

Evie thought she should be shaking. She was frighteningly calm. She heard the distant whine of sirens. Blood trickled from Mad's left nostril. Mad slid to her feet, dabbed at the blood with the back of one hand, said, "Don't mind that. You have any booze at your place?"

"I think . . . maybe?" Wide-eyed, zombie-like, Evie moved to the attic door. Mad gathered up Evie's spilled satchel and sauntered after her.

As Evie flicked the lights on in her attic, Mad glanced around. Evie didn't move as the other girl prowled forward, halted in front of the alcove where Evie painted. Mad reached out to touch the painting of a cat-eared girl in a gas-blue gown. She studied the other paintings: a boy in a black suit, his face half a dragon's; a veiled figure in a flapper's dress, its clawed hands cradling a human skull. "These are *amazing*."

"Mad." Evie didn't know how she didn't shout the name, how it came out as a whisper. "How did you . . . you didn't fall."

Mad twirled to face her. Then she stood on tiptoe, arms outstretched.

She *levitated*.

It wasn't the spectacle of Ciaran's Door to London. Evie had been able to cope with that because the sheer impossibility of it had sent her into magical thinking, maybe, like temporary insanity. This . . . this was the laws of reality being obliterated before her. Evie watched in awe as the top of Mad's head touched the ceiling. Mad did a graceful backflip, like an astronaut in space. The lights flickered.

"Stop it." Evie abruptly sat down on her salvaged sofa. "Come down. Please."

Mad landed before Evie. She dropped onto the pink velvet sofa. "I hate coming down. I could do that forever."

"You can fly."

"It's more like . . ." Mad gestured as if she were the conductor of an orchestra. She'd glued a tiny glitter heart beneath her left eye. "Gravity has no power over me when I concentrate."

Evie kicked her shoes off and folded her legs beneath her. "When did you find out you could do it?"

"I wasn't always floating out of my window when I was a kid, if that's what you're asking." Mad poked at a couple of Evie's paintbrushes in a mason jar. "It's a boring story."

Evie didn't understand how discovering one could fly could be boring.

Mad moved to her feet and began wandering again. She halted before the bulletin board and gazed at the Polaroids of little Ezra and Juliet. "Who're these kiddos?"

"My cousins," Evie lied.

"Cute."

Evie changed the subject. "These things we can do—"

"Yeah. Neat, huh?"

"You don't think it's a little scary? That we're—"

"Different? You want to be like everyone else?"

"I guess I don't. What's next?"

Mad tilted her head. "What's next? Earning our trust, Evie. And that's not so easy." She sauntered to the door, opened it. "See you later, alligator." The door clicked shut.

Alone, Evie curled up, arms over her head, wanting to laugh and cry at the same time. She had summoned something dangerous and now it had her in its teeth.

CHAPTER FOUR

A Place to Belong

The Saint Street Café had once been a small church, its interior now scattered with tables and comfy chairs, the altar a performance space wreathed in lights shaped like miniature cherubs. As Evie stepped through the stained-glass door, she felt as if an electric heater switched on inside her.

She bought tea and a cupcake. She opened her brand-new laptop—no social media allowed with LFS, but she could still surf for information—and enjoyed the luxurious interlude while the sun set. The headline of the *Silver Cove City Herald*: "La Fable Sombre. Urban Legend Strikes Again?" caught her eye. She skimmed the article.

A fortune in items had been stolen in LA: serpent bracelets once worn by Rita Hayworth, a Lalique ouroboros ring once owned by Buster Keaton, a pair of diamond python earrings that had belonged to Marilyn Monroe. Evie realized La Fable Sombre must have accomplished the thefts on the same night as the Queen Cobra. After they'd left that invitation for her, the Dark Fable had traveled to LA for a crime spree?

As she was wondering if she'd just joined a gang of adrenaline junkies, Queenie entered. Dressed in a short green velvet jacket and embroidered jeans, she lowered heart-shaped sunglasses and glanced around before she sauntered over. Evie pushed out a chair with one foot. Queenie shoved the sunglasses back on her head and looked around, disdainful, as she sat. Evie shut her laptop. "Are the others here?"

"You'll see." So, Queenie had decided to be mysterious.

Dev strolled in, dressed in a pigeon-blue Yves Saint Laurent suit. A lotus the same dusk red of his buzz cut was tucked behind his left ear. His sleeves were rolled up to reveal tattoos: tigers twining along his brown arms. He cast Queenie and Evie one of his devastating smiles. "Is there a reason it's so hot in here?"

"My ears are ringing," Queenie complained.

Dev nodded. "It's like a sauna."

"What's wrong with you two?" Evie demanded, although she felt it too, a dissonance with the world and her body, similar to the dying-swan feeling that accompanied the flu.

Mad swept through the door, exhibiting vagabond chic in denim shorts patterned with hearts, a white tank top, and a black velvet jacket with a silver owl on the back. Her motorcycle boots clomped on the wooden floor. People stared at her as she sat opposite Evie.

Mad leaned confidentially forward, elbows on the table. "We're moving you."

Evie's pulse jumped. "Moving me where?"

As Dev strolled to the counter to order espressos for everyone, Mad sat back with a look of satisfaction. "To live with us."

"You don't have a choice," Queenie answered Evie's unasked question.

Evie closed her laptop and leveled a look at the other two girls. "Don't I?"

"Oh, come *on*, Evie," Mad pleaded playfully. "You'll love it. And we'll be your neighbors!"

"Won't that be fun?" Queenie asked wryly.

Dev returned with a tray of cups exuding a heavenly aroma of espresso spired with whipped cream. Snagging a cup, he said, "I don't like this place."

"I'm with you." Mad's whisper was exaggerated. "Everyone's staring at us."

Evie, who could see that they stood out like a jeweled menagerie, sighed.

Mad lifted an arm. "Hey. I'm breaking out in hives. Dev. Is there *honey* in this drink? You put honey in *everything*."

"Only sugar in yours, luv."

Evie drank her caffeine. It tasted like liquid ashes, as if something were dulling all her senses.

Queenie stretched to her feet, cup in hand. "Let's hoof it. Mad's driving, so say your prayers."

"This is a bad neighborhood," Mad complained. "Some guy fell out of a window here a few days ago."

As Evie opened the door and entered the attic of her apartment building, Mad, Queenie, and Dev followed, hauling folded boxes. Queenie cast a wary glance around. "What do you want to take?"

Evie had worked hard to find even the junkiest items for this place. She edged toward her pink railroad trunk, crouched down, and made certain it was locked without seeming to do so. "This. All my good clothes are in it." She stood up, watched as Dev collected her books from the homemade shelves and dumped the stack in a box. Queenie began carefully wrapping Evie's small collection of glass animals. Evie picked up a carton and headed for her bed. Mad trailed after. As they were clearing off her bureau, Mad picked up a glass globe containing a ballerina, shook it so that glitter fell around the dancer. "I wanted to be a ballerina. Took classes and everything."

"Why didn't you?" Evie discreetly tucked photographs of Ezra and Juliet into her carton.

Mad shrugged and set the ballerina globe in another box. "I fell. Wait till you see your new place."

Evie looked around. She heard distant sirens, an argument in the hallway below. This had never been home. She would have to come back and tell Ava. "Let's go."

―――✺―――

Mad halted the Aston Martin on a street lined with warehouses and rundown buildings. The lights were sulfurous in the evening, and the graffiti was all strange creatures and symbols, as if whatever lurked here influenced even taggers.

Dev got out and chivalrously opened the car door for Evie. He said, "Welcome to our lair."

Evie followed them toward a warehouse painted with a

mural of a girl flying through a night sky with stars in her hair. A pair of rusty doors loomed. Evie halted, realizing that, once she stepped through those doors, there was no going back.

Dev took out his phone and tapped at it. The doors opened by a mechanism, shedding interior light over the rain-slicked pavement. Mad slung an arm around Evie's shoulders as they followed the others inside. A trompe l'oeil mural of a warehouse space appeared before them. Queenie slid open trick panels in the mural, revealing a stairway, which they ascended.

"All the buildings are connected. We own this entire block," Mad explained. "Well. Our organization does."

"Your organization." Evie knew there had to be more to LFS than four charismatic and supernaturally gifted people. The people in charge, she suspected, would be older and scarier. "I'm going to learn more about them, right?"

"Oh, you will," Queenie promised as they stepped into an enormous chamber scattered with fancy furniture and a galaxy of light fixtures. Evie saw a spiral staircase, a floor-to-ceiling wall of bookshelves, old paintings in elaborate frames. Above, a giant round skylight of stained glass depicted a black animal— a hybrid wolf-dragon—curved on a ruby background. Three sets of paneled doors led into hallways also hung with paintings. An alcove contained a pool table, and sports memorabilia hung on the walls. A bar carved into images of ferocious beasts created an altar for a collection of expensive liquor.

As La Fable Sombre separated in the cavernous space, Evie found herself thinking, *I am home.*

—◊◊—

Evie's new apartment was located in a shabby brownstone above an esoteric shop called Quail Ridge Books. The building was attached to the warehouse containing LFS's lair. The apartment was a spacious studio with a peaked ceiling and a chandelier of red and green glass. The ivory walls were bare, the wooden floor glossy. When Evie saw the apartment, she had to blink away a few tears.

It was the most beautiful place she'd ever seen.

She sat in the middle of the floor, surrounded by boxes and the few pieces of furniture she'd kept. She heard birds singing in the walnut tree outside the cathedral window. Mad was seated opposite her. The last of the sun dripped from her blonde hair, over the little gold rings on her fingers. "You like it?"

Evie propped herself back on her elbows and tilted her head. "You're bribing me."

"I figured you'd prefer whimsy over swank."

Evie caught Mad studying her with calculation and steered the conversation in the direction she wanted. "So, what's next?"

Mad twirled one hand. "Thieves' Night. You'll meet Mother and Father and the rest of the Kingdom."

"The Kingdom?" Evie sat up straight. "And who are Mother and Father?"

Mad was still smiling, but her gaze was solemn. "The Plaza La Mer was a teensy-weensy test. Mother Night and Father Silence are the fences, the ones with connections to the Collectors. They're the *royalty*. You graduate to that when you don't want to be a thief anymore. You need to prove yourself to them, but don't worry. It'll be a piece of cake."

Evie ruminated on how dangerous a Mother Night and a Father Silence might be. "They choose the heists?"

"The three major ones of the year. We get the best ones." Mad beamed. She took Evie's hand and pulled her to her feet. "Come see my place."

"This Mother and Father." Evie allowed herself to be led. "Are they like us? You know . . . *gifted*?"

Mad glanced over one shoulder, lifted an eyebrow. "Of course."

As they climbed a spiraling metal stair, Evie imagined the darkness at the edges of the light whispering, shifting, following. In a hall where lamps painted with monarch butterflies flickered patterns onto their skin, Mad shoved open a pink door. "Home sweet home."

The apartment was a series of interlocking rooms. Evie could see all the way to the back. The parlor was painted scarlet, the walls decorated with silent film posters. *Metropolis. Nosferatu.* The furniture was curvy and plush. A little robot of painted tin stood on a bookshelf. Evie picked up a framed photograph of a blonde woman in a pink waitress uniform.

"My mom." Mad, coming up behind Evie, gazed at it. "She wanted to be an actress." She dropped onto the sofa, tugging her hair free of its pins. Evie set the photograph back as Mad continued, "She loved silent films. All those raccoon-eyed girls and men in lipstick. Theda Bara. Clara Bow. Lon Chaney. Rudolph Valentino."

"Your mom . . ." Evie hesitated over the question.

"Dead as a doornail."

"I'm sorry." Evie sat on the sofa beside Mad. She studied a poster of a dark mansion and the silhouettes of a boy and a girl standing before it.

"That's one of my fav silent movies. *The Beautiful Devils.*"

Mad nodded to the poster. She picked up a remote control, and a retro film projector behind them began to hum, casting images onto a white screen above the fireplace. A surreal story unwound, of a boy and a girl lost in a forest. They arrived at an abandoned mansion, where they were served a feast by invisible beings. While they slept, doors opened and weird creatures emerged: A man with a fox's head. A woman whose gown appeared to be a serpent tail. And other oddities, both whimsical and nightmarish. In the end, the lost boy and girl faded into the house—the boy into the patterned wallpaper, the girl into the drapes, only their faces remaining visible.

Evie felt as if she were disappearing into the sofa. "I need to splash my face with cold water."

Mad headed for the kitchen. "Bathroom is between the two bedrooms. Hot cocoa?"

"Sure." Evie ventured into a bedroom with a window revealing an old greenhouse on the roof. The bathroom separating the two bedrooms was black, with a moon-and-stars theme. Evie shut the door through which she'd come and stepped into Mad's bedroom.

Fairy lights were strung across the walls. Hung over a bureau was a painting of a woman gowned in scarlet, stabbing herself in the thigh—Evie recognized the painting and hoped it was a copy, suspected it was not. The floor was scattered with department-store boxes, clothes, and shoes. The vanity table was cluttered with perfume bottles shaped like skulls and butterflies. The mirror was plastered with photographs: Mad and Queenie posing in bathing suits and big hats; Mad in a polka-dot dress, with Ciaran and Dev kissing her on either side; Mad and a brunette girl in T-shirts and jeans outside of the Eiffel Tower; Ciaran and Mad, like a gangster and his moll, seated in a swanky club, their eyes turned red by the camera flash.

"Hey."

Evie turned to find Mad lounging in the doorway. The other girl said, "Swell. So we've got some trust issues. That's okay."

Evie gazed at the photographs, trying to decipher the nuances of Mad and Ciaran's relationship.

"We're like Sherlock and Watson. Ida and Cal." When Evie stared blankly, Mad clarified, "They were LFS, the Grifters, who, in the Depression era, robbed banks, posing as a Japanese princess and an heir of the Vanderbilt dynasty. As I was saying, we're like Butch and Cassidy—"

"Bonnie and Clyde?"

Mad primly tucked her hair behind her ears. "Bonnie and Clyde were *thrill killers*, Evie. Ciar and I are business partners. Nothing more." She gripped the door frame and leaned in. "Now, come get hot cocoa and gingerbread. Queenie made the gingerbread, and she's a culinary alchemist. What kind of music do you like?"

———※———

They lip-synched to Dean Martin and Etta James, Mad's collection of jewelry shimmering on their arms and throats. Mad piled the bed with clothes she'd never worn and told Evie to select whatever she wanted. She coaxed Evie into trying on Alexander McQueen boots embroidered with diamond birds-of-paradise and shiny black Gucci loafers with platform heels.

As they were lying on the floor, listening to music and

gazing up at the ceiling painted with a glorious sunset, Evie asked, "How do you think we became like this?"

"Bad things happened to us. Dev was locked in a closet when he was a kid. Queens was almost assaulted at fourteen by two boys when her parents were stationed at an air force base in Arizona."

Evie pictured a younger Queenie, in a red hoodie, stomping past cacti, pursued by two blond coyotes. She whispered, "Something bad happened to you too."

Mad sat up. She flicked her honey-gold hair back, her gaze hard and bright. "We evolved out of dark places. Do you know what La Fable Sombre means to me? Taking control, finally, after being tossed around like a rag doll in a hurricane."

Evie had let herself be passed around all her life while committing small acts of rebellion that only made life harder. She'd followed the rules, and how had that worked out for her? "Mad."

"It's Madrigal Jones, and I'm going to tell you what happened to me. Because Ciaran told me what happened to you. Your dad shot your mom and himself and probably, before that, your little brother and sister. Those kids in that photo . . . they weren't your cousins."

Evie shoved a shrieking memory back behind a mirrored door, but the grief clawing its way up from the darkest part of her brain overwhelmed her. She began to shake, and something between a gasp and a sob escaped her.

"Evie!" Mad whispered as the tidal wave of sorrow crashed through the mirrored door in Evie's mind. "I'm so sorry . . . it's okay to cry. Sometimes, it feels good, you know? When you cry yourself into a coma. You wake up and it's still the same shitty world, but there you are, tougher and stronger. See, I got that crying thing done when I was a kid."

I have no tears, Evie thought, aching. Not after all those nights in strangers' homes, all those times she'd been met with coldness or a kindness that wouldn't last. All her tears had long since alchemized into a venom that had slowly turned her heart into a vitreous knot.

Mad continued, her voice dreamy, "My dad wasn't cool like yours. He wasn't a musician. He wasn't anyone. He drank a lot. When my mom left, he threw me off a bridge. I was eight."

Evie sat back on her heels. *"Mad . . ."*

"That's when I learned I could fly." Mad's face hardened, and something prowled behind her pale eyes. "I stopped in midair. Boy, was my dad surprised. Did your parents love you, Evie? Then those are good tears."

Evie didn't tell Mad the tears, now, weren't for her parents, as Mad knelt before her, hands limp in her lap, as if she were that little girl again, discovering she could fly after someone she'd trusted had flung her off a bridge as if she were trash.

When Mad looked at her, her gaze was diamond hard. "But then someone found me, took care of me, gave me food and money. We talked about books. There was no funny business. He was a gentleman's gentleman. I was not a good person. I gave up on my mom. I hurt people. This man gave me back my soul. But, of course, I screwed *that* up . . ."

Before Evie could ask if she was talking about Ciaran, the door opened, and Dev stuck his head in. Evie's apprehension pricked when she saw his grim expression. "Mad. We need you.

One of those rich assholes from the hotel job is dead. Queenie's not taking it well."

Evie didn't think she'd heard him correctly. "You mean one of the people you *drugged* at Plaza La Mer?"

Mad glanced at Evie, half her face in shadow. "You're one of us now. Remember that."

"*What did you do?*" Evie had not signed up for murder.

"Evie." Dev addressed her. "We didn't do anything. We're not killers. We'll get an explanation from Ciar. Let's go."

Dread clawing at her, Evie followed Dev and Mad through the maze of hallways that connected the buildings. Dev pushed open a pair of metal doors, and they stepped into the main room, where Queenie sat in a wingback chair, head bowed. Ciaran was crouched before her.

"Queenie," Ciaran was saying, his tone soothing. "I understand, but it was my decision. You had nothing to do with it."

"I made the poison." Queenie drew her knees to her chin, wrapped her arms around them.

Ciaran continued, "Lila Pearce was a murderer. Vero is dead because of her."

Evie wanted to ask who the hell Vero was and why was she dead.

"We should have had a say in it, boss." Dev leaned against the wall, arms folded.

"None of you would have been okay with it," Ciaran said darkly. "This way, only *my* hands got bloody."

Evie sank down onto the sofa, noticed leftover takeout on the tables.

Ciaran rose. "We can't let anyone think it's fine to kill us.

We need to be more than thieves. La Fable Sombre has to be what it once was."

"You mean when it was a horror story?" Mad walked to Queenie's chair and sat on the arm, setting a comforting hand on Queenie's shoulder.

"Let me remind all of you of the video Dev found." Ciaran watched them. "The one from Pearce's penthouse apartment, when she had her thugs shove Vero out the window."

"Christ, Ciar." Dev looked ill.

"You killed Lila Pearce." Horror flashed through Evie. She quickly subdued it. "How . . . ?"

"His ring." Mad spoke quietly. "The tiny skull has a tiny needle. Poison."

Ciaran sat down beside Evie. "Pearce had a heart attack three days after the robbery. No trace. No evidence. Nothing to prove."

"It was a vendetta." Evie's hands shook. She understood the desire for revenge all too well.

Dev swept up his laptop, opened it, and leaned over Evie. "This is Vero. The one we lost. The one we loved."

On the screen was an article and a photograph of a dark-haired girl with a crooked smile. Vero Jordan. Evie skimmed the article about the girl's grisly death.

Ciaran spoke, his voice gravelly with fury. "Pearce made her murder look like an accident. A thief getting what she deserved. It took Vero two days to die, with every bone in her body broken and head trauma."

"Okay. I *get it*," Evie hissed. Dev closed the laptop. She hunched over. "What are your bosses going to say about this?"

Everyone, for a moment, was quiet.

Ciaran said, "They're going to understand."

Evie didn't like that at all. "What are we?" She cast her gaze around at each of them. "Not just thieves."

"Not just thieves," Mad agreed.

"Spirits of revolution and revenge?" Queenie suggested faintly.

"Once, LFS caused trouble for kings and queens." Dev was somber. "It was begun by a Moorish medical student, a highwayman, and a French courtesan in medieval Paris. They started a small revolution."

"And got rich while doing it," Queenie murmured.

"And looked good while doing it." Mad stretched her arms above her head.

"La Fable Sombre is the oldest crew," Ciaran explained to Evie. "There are other crews, but they can't do what we can."

"We're the tricksters," Dev told Evie. "We're mayhem."

Queenie was still huddled in her chair. "Spirits of mischief and violence."

Ciaran watched Evie, who couldn't meet his gaze. She didn't voice her opinion. The mischief, she didn't mind. But the violence, she did.

"I don't like the violence." Dev echoed Evie's thoughts.

"No more violence," Ciaran promised, his voice like honey. And, somehow, they seemed to believe him, becoming silent, introspective, still troubled. Ciaran effortlessly switched gears. "Now, you lot going to tidy up this pigsty?"

"Gotta go." Dev unfolded himself from his chair and left.

"No menial work after midnight for me." Queenie followed Dev.

Mad arched an eyebrow and looked at Evie. "Well, ain't that a kick in the teeth? Sorry, Charlie." She strolled out of the room.

Evie stood up, looked around, bewildered. "What just happened?"

"The rat bastards." Ciaran rolled up his sleeves. He bent to pick up two bottles and a Styrofoam container.

Evie gathered up a plate of chicken bones and was surprised at how steady her hands were, considering how off-balance she felt. Ciaran had *poisoned* someone in retaliation for the ugly death of one of LFS's members—she couldn't help but feel a sort of secret war had been waged.

She followed him toward the kitchen. He flipped a switch and blue light illuminated stainless steel and black marble. The kitchen was just as messy as the main room. Evie dumped the dishes in the sink. Ciaran tossed the bottles in the trash as she opened the dishwasher and found it full. She cursed.

"You didn't expect it to be empty, did you?" He began taking glasses out of the dishwasher. "At least someone turned this on." There were shadows beneath his striking eyes.

As he took plates out of the dishwasher, the kitchen's frosty light silvered a scrollwork of scars on his arms. Evie stared at the scars, then flicked her gaze to the water running over the sky-blue bowl she held. For a moment, she was overwhelmed by an alienating panic. "How long have you been doing this?"

"You're trying to get my story. Not yet, Evie. How about hot chocolate?" He lifted a gilded canister and shook it teasingly.

She wanted to know who Ciaran was. Was he the first in this crew? Why had he chosen this life? What dark event had happened to *him*? She studied him, the crisp white of his shirt against his bronze skin. No smudges, no wear in his clothing—simple, classic, a bit of flash in the silver cuff links shaped like serpents and that eerie skull ring.

She would get his story eventually, she promised herself, and hopefully it wouldn't be all lies.

"What's with you people and hot chocolate?" She wistfully recalled hot cocoa and blanket forts with tiny Ezra and little Juliet, the patio doors open to a summer night flashing with fireflies. "It'd be nice if we had a blanket fort to enjoy it in."

He leaned against the counter. "I've blankets."

She had to take a steady breath because he made that statement sound like an invitation. "You can tell me more about Thieves' Night while you make me hot chocolate. Forget the blankets."

"Right." He opened a cabinet, took down a saucepan.

"Mad told me about Mother and Father. What about the other crews?"

"They're ordinary. Fetch the milk and whipped cream?"

She opened the fridge, grabbed a bottle of milk and a whipped cream canister. The only other items in the fridge were a bottle of expensive champagne and an orange. She wondered who did the grocery shopping. "What do your bosses expect from me?"

"Evie." His smile was back, and so charming, it made the panic spill out of her skull. "You got the Queen Cobra. You're in their good graces."

"That was sort of accidental."

He looked at her, serious. "It wasn't accidental. It's in you, what we are. After a decade of heists, we're free to retire, make way for new blood." He poured the milk into the saucepan, added spoonfuls of the rich chocolate mix. His skull ring flashed, reminding her of how dangerous he was. "Two or three major jobs a year, a few minor ones, maybe. Not a bad deal, is it?"

"And if one wants to retire earlier?"

"If you want to go . . . now's the time. No one's going to stop you." He slanted her a diamond-hard look and she saw, there, the darkness that had poisoned someone. "But you'll never see any of us again."

It didn't register as a threat at first, but Evie felt a vertigo-like despair at the thought of returning to the Pink Blight, to nowhere jobs and a precarious future. To a life without La Fable Sombre. "These heists are dangerous?"

"You think we'd get all this if it was easy? Most assignments fit into one of four categories: Art, which is always a commission. Jewelry, which is taken apart and reassembled by some guy in Vienna and sold. Antiquities, which are easier to sell on the fly but which can also be commissions. Then there are the artifacts, which are unique. Our specialty. A saint's toenails. Da Vinci's paintbrushes." His smile was a flash. "Cerberus's dog dish."

"Thor's hammer? The Holy Grail?" Evie was relieved they weren't talking about her leaving anymore.

"Your sarcasm is bewitching. We'll be best mates, you and I. Yes, that last category is weird shit wanted by special people. And by special people, I mean Silence and Night's sanctioned Collectors. We present three items a year. Best thieves get best jobs. Luxury. Cash."

Evie hesitated with her next question. "Mad said you knew about my parents and my . . ." Her throat constricted with anguish. "My brother and sister. About the murders. How did you know?"

His voice was gentle. "I didn't. Mother Night and Father Silence told me what happened to you."

Her stomach plummeted. "They've been investigating me?"

"That they have. No secrets with that pair. 'S'all right. None of us go by our real names." He watched her. "They didn't give me details. I didn't ask. You are not that scared kid anymore, Evie."

She didn't tell him how her family still haunted her. How the color yellow made her sad because little Juliet had loved to wear yellow dresses. How anything space-related reminded her of six-year-old Ezra, who had been obsessed with astronauts and rocket ships. How she couldn't ever eat strawberries because they had been her mom's favorite.

Ciaran looked at her with a searching intimacy that made her stare defiantly back at him. Gently, he asked a question no one had ever asked her before: "What do you want, Evie Wilder?"

She wanted her family back. But what did Ciaran want to hear? She told him, "The usual. Money. Power over my life." She hesitated because she meant the next one. "A place to belong."

His smile was breathtaking, it was so genuine. "You have it now."

"So." Evie accepted her second cup of cocoa for the night and looked away from him. "Tell me how to *stay* in Mother Night and Father Silence's good graces."

—⁂—

Evie was returning to her apartment, Ciaran's smile and his eyes imprinted on her brain, when she saw Mad heading up the stairs to the roof. Evie followed. She attempted to wish the veil around herself, that otherworldly cold that meant invisibility. It didn't happen. So, she used stealth instead as she carefully stepped onto the roof, keeping to the shadows.

Mad sat on a cupola above, gazing at the city.

Evie heard movement, saw Ciaran walk across the roof to lean against the railing. The night breeze swept his hair into his eyes. She couldn't read his expression.

Mad floated down beside him. As she draped herself on the railing, he tilted back his head.

Mad said, "It's Valentine's Day tomorrow. We need to show Evie we're more than freaks. So she doesn't leave."

"She won't leave."

Mad tilted a little forward over the railing so that her hair hung down over her face. She let her toes leave the cement. "I want to go to our place. It's tradition. Traditions are important."

His elbows on the railing, Ciaran watched her. "We can go there anytime. How about the Moulin Rouge in Paris? That nightclub in Venice? Hot-air ballooning in Myanmar instead? Our usual place has become spectacularly boring with people who only want to get drunk or get into each other's intimates."

Mad straightened. "Do you know how *old* you sound?"

He addressed the universe above. "Do you really miss it?"

"Sometimes, yes." Mad continued, "Why didn't you tell me about the vendetta against Pearce? No secrets from each other, remember?"

"Was it a secret, Mad? You really expected me to let that go? Were *you* going to let that go?"

"I wasn't. Not after what happened to Vero." There was an

unexpected edge in Mad's voice. "What about Jason . . . what do you think he's after?"

Ciaran had one elbow on the railing as he regarded Mad. "What else? Revenge. Oldest story in the books. But it's not Pearce he's blaming, is it? Well, he can't. Because she's dead. So, he's going after us. You *know* what he's like."

Evie yearned to hear more but retreated back toward the stairs as neon light caressed her skin.

She needed to learn how to control her power faster, better.

Chapter Five

Alchemist

The next day, Evie ascended to the roof. She crossed to a glass door leading into a greenhouse, where she made her way through a jungle of potted plants and humanoid animal statues that looked like they belonged in Narnia. She came to a door with peeling red paint and knocked. Queenie called out, "Come in!"

Evie stepped into an apartment, where nearly everything was white but for some of the furniture. A taxidermy rabbit reigned on a mantelpiece cluttered with science fiction paperbacks. A counter beneath the window was cluttered with colorful bottles. Above a drum set was a blackboard wall scrawled with symbols and equations. Queenie, casual in denim cut-offs, a plaid shirt, and Belleville boots, stood in the aisle kitchen stirring something. She wore goggles and gloves. "What's up, Invisible Girl?"

"Why did you make the poison?"

Queenie shoved the goggles onto her head and fixed Evie with a hard stare. "Why are you asking me that?"

Evie dropped into a beanbag chair, setting aside a rabbit of raggedy black velvet. "You were shocked Ciaran used it."

Queenie stripped off her gloves, revealing the intricate black tattoos banding her fingers. She walked over and sat in the chair opposite. She stared down at her hands. "You want to know how I could poison someone?"

"You didn't. Ciaran did." Evie *wanted* to know if she'd just joined a gang of murderers. She needed to know who each of them was. She needed to learn their stories. "Why did you create it in the first place?"

"It was a challenge. Could I do it? With innocent plants? It was *pride*."

Evie understood pride. It was a rare and valuable commodity.

Queenie rose and walked to a red cabinet, opened it to display needles and vials, each a different color. She pointed to a green vial. "If I make a toxic agent, I always create an antidote. That's the one for the poison in Ciaran's ring." She closed the cabinet. "I've collected a couple of ancient writings, artifacts about alchemy . . . genuine witchy stuff. All with a basis in chemistry. Some of them are about poison."

"That stuff at the Plaza La Mer . . . they thought it was the champagne, but it was the confetti . . ."

"It was pollen. Dosed with a Wish of anger and a bit of cocaine. It's absorbed through the nose. I call it 'Ballroom Blitz.' Ciar doesn't like drugs, FYI, so if you're into them . . ."

"I'm not." Evie wanted to know more. "How did you learn to do this?"

Queenie shrugged. "I was always interested in chemistry, ever since reading about Cleopatra, the Greek alchemist. But the chemistry became . . . different, after my mom and dad . . . They were in the air force." Queenie stopped for a moment, her fingers twisting the two military dog tags she wore around her neck.

Evie realized both of Queenie's parents were dead.

"Chemistry was something I *worked* to learn. But . . . after my mom and dad . . . I began to see strange formulas, read between the lines. Information ran through my brain like a shadowy hare. I created a perfume that caused a fight-or-flight response in anyone sprayed with it. I made another that numbed people's muscle responses. I refined the potions with Wishes. And I see the formulas, like blueprints, in my mind." She frowned, as if puzzled by her need to share the discovery of her incredible gift. "I used one of those potions to terrify the two boys who had gone after me. I know Mad told you about it, but did she tell you I had a seizure that night that sent me to the ER? It was like blowback for what I'd done. So I never used what I learned to kill. Until Ciaran. Until the vendetta against Vero's murderer." Shadows filled Queenie's eyes.

Gently, Evie said, "You are the Alchemist."

"And you're the Invisible Girl."

Evie looked at Queenie's hands. "Those tattoos . . . do they mean anything?"

Queenie spread out her inked fingers. "My gran gave them to me. There's a story of a girl who takes up with a trickster. Her dad rescues her, but a storm wrecks the boat so that it can only carry one. Her asshole dad cuts off her fingers as she clings to the boat. She sinks to the bottom of the ocean and becomes the queen of the sea. Her fingers turn into ocean creatures, some of which eat people."

"So, those tats symbolize a girl who got screwed over by the world and became a goddess?"

Queenie's smile was as quick and fierce as Evie's own. "That's right, white girl. Any more strategic questions?"

Evie continued carefully, "Who is Ciaran?"

"I'm pretty sure Ciar was raised in a Dickensian orphanage and apprenticed to a master criminal, so this is just a way of life for him." Queenie reached over to a table and picked up a black box. She tossed it to Evie. "Here. A welcome gift."

Evie opened the box, stared down at a pair of gloves that appeared to be made of metallic green scales. "Um."

"This material . . . a little bit of heat and it melts. It's not silk." Queenie removed the shade of a lamp and held a piece of the material close to the bright bulb. The fabric melted into a rubbery goo that smelled like mint. She kneaded it between her fingers. "So, you stick it in a lock, like gum. It'll expand and break the lock. Even in water."

Evie was impressed. "NASA would kill for this stuff."

"Is NASA going to give me enough money to get my grand-folks a beachfront vacation home in Honolulu? A pair of one-off Louboutins designed especially for me? No. But La Fable Sombre will." Queenie rose, walking back to the kitchen. "You've got my story. You can go now. Make sure to close the greenhouse door. I don't want bugs getting into my plants, and it's the only place my babies don't wither."

Evie stood. At the door, she halted and asked, "So I know why you joined. Why do you stay?"

Queenie didn't hesitate. "They need me. They're my family."

CHAPTER SIX

Knight

La Fable Sombre planned a celebratory night out. Evie had chosen a tasseled black dress and strappy sandals. A headband of dark rosettes threaded through her tousled hair, courtesy of Mad. Seated in a luxury Cadillac, she glanced at herself in the rearview and saw a stranger with kohl-rimmed eyes and rosebud lips—Queenie's expert touch in cosmetics.

She studied her crew. Queenie shimmered in a gown of ice-blue silk. Dev was sleek in Brunello Cucinelli. Mad wore a dress of pink beads and had coiled her hair up with gauzy butterflies. Ciaran, in dark blue bespoke and diamond cuff links, was driving.

Mad grinned at Evie. "You look like an adorable strumpet."

Dev nodded. "That the look you were going for, Evie?"

"I was hoping more for dark goddess." Evie shrugged.

"Goddess of crooks and thieves." Ciaran's gaze met hers in the rearview.

"It's the Night Empress mascara and the Witch Apple lip rouge." Queenie was gazing out the window. "They've gone to her head."

"That really the name of those cosmetics?" Dev laughed a realization. "*You* made them."

Queenie pointed one black-nailed finger at Ciaran. "I also made Ciar's cologne."

"Ah, now you'll have to make a signature cologne for me." Dev straightened his tie.

"You're too particular."

"Make me a lip gloss that's everlasting cherry?" Mad paused. "Or a perfume that reminds everyone of their best childhood moment."

"I'm not the Willy Wonka of fragrances, Mad."

Listening to their banter, Evie became less anxious, even smiled a little.

Ciaran turned into an alley, heading for a pair of graffitied metal doors—which opened onto shadows and an otherworldly cold that cracked the window near Evie. They slid through darkness, toward a square of light. Evie saw a plain of black grass, thought she glimpsed figures in the distance.

The dark fell away in tatters as they emerged into a night city. Ciaran parked the Cadillac in a neon-spattered alley. He got out and opened the rear door for Evie and Mad. Dev emerged, extending a hand to Queenie, who bared her teeth and shoved him back. Dev laughed.

"The Howling Cat Club." Mad hooked an arm through Evie's as they walked through pools of crimson and absinthe-green neon. "My favorite place. It used to be a gangster speakeasy."

The club was a Gothic-looking building with spiky gates to either side. They moved into a hall where strips of pink neon led toward an arch of dark metal forming a cat's face, its open mouth the entrance. As they stepped into the club, Evie heard lo-fi music that complemented her mood. A girl in a gown of white feathers sang as a small band played behind her. Above pink leather seating, chandeliers dripped from a ceiling like a starless night. As La Fable Sombre wound through the patrons— all sophisticated, all young—toward a curved booth in the back, Evie ran her fingers across walls muraled with elegant cat people.

They sat, with Ciaran in the middle, his arms resting on the booth's back. The blue light etched his face into angles so that his beauty became almost supernatural. Evie watched him scan the club as if searching for someone.

"You need to drink more." Dev leaned across the table to pour Evie a glass of wine. His ruby cuff links caught the light.

"You're a bad influence." Mad, on Evie's other side, took the glass and drank it down.

Evie was strategically avoiding the alcohol. "You're all bad influences."

"It's not real alcohol." Queenie poured some into her glass. "You think we can ever risk being off our game?"

"So, it's this and mocktails." Dev lifted his glass.

"No booze. No drugs. And the smoking?" Evie teased.

"That vape pen was a prop." Queenie waved a hand.

"I don't smoke." Ciaran didn't touch his fake wine. "That night, when I left the mask, that was just for dramatic effect, like."

"We are very dramatic," Dev explained.

"Let's dance." Mad stood up and Evie wondered if she was levitating a little bit. Mad tapped her glass. "Dev, be a good egg and pour me another."

Dev tipped the bottle of expensive non-liquor over her glass. He said, "Remember not to Tinkerbell like last time. People here are so-phis-ti-cated. They aren't rubes. They'll notice a levitating girl." He rose, glancing at Ciaran. "Going to join us, old sport?"

Evie was beginning to understand that the old-timey slang La Fable Sombre used was their secret language, a ritual banter.

"Not yet." Ciaran continued to skim his gaze across the patrons.

What are you looking for? Evie thought.

Dev extended a hand to Queenie. "We're the best dancers here, Queens."

Queenie rose, clasped his hand. They drifted onto the dance floor, Mad following. As they moved out among the dancers, Mad twirled like a ballerina. Dev and Queenie spun together, obviously having a great time.

Ciaran leaned toward Evie. "You're not invisible here. Why are you pretending you are?" He rose with carnal grace, stretched out a hand. The silver skull ring seemed to wink at her.

"No." Evie shook her head.

"Evie." The way he said her name made her blind to everything around her.

"You're making a spectacle of yourself," she chided.

His smile was dazzling. "And you're not doing me any favors sitting there like I'm the devil."

"I don't dance."

"But can you move in a circle?" He gently clasped her hands and drew her to her feet. "Like when you were a kid, spinning?"

Grudgingly, she allowed him to lead. She wasn't going to let herself be swept away despite the swoony music.

"See?" he said, turning her. "Isn't this fun?"

"Not as fun as stealing jewelry and joining secret societies." If she kept the conversation going, she wouldn't have to think about Ciaran's hands in hers or how good he smelled. He spun her. It was so breathtakingly easy. He bent his head as he snapped her close to him—she had to slam her hands against his chest to avoid a collision she wasn't ready for.

He asked, "And where did you learn to tango?"

"From a Roller Derby queen." Evie didn't tell him how one of her foster moms, the cool Isabeau, with her vintage rockabilly chic and pagan beliefs, had betrayed Evie by marrying a man who didn't want kids, that it had been a wrenching separation at fifteen. She permitted Ciaran to slide an arm around her, then ribboned quickly out of his grasp. Dancing with him was like flying. She felt like a dangerous thing, a creature from subterranean depths.

Ciaran spun her again, caught her against him. She stopped breathing. The warmth of his fingers twined with hers, the power of his gray eyes, made her unsteady. Those eyes were the color of arsenic.

"How do you do it?" she asked, to break the tension. "The Doors?"

He twirled her away, back, whispered in her ear, "How do you not let people see you?"

"Being invisible isn't the same as opening doors to other cities."

"I was going through a bad time when I opened my first Door. Maybe that's what triggered it. Desperation. Fear. *Want.* I'll get you another drink. What would you like?" And, just like that, he twisted the conversation away from himself.

"Something hot." Everything seemed too bright, too sharp. But she liked it, liked this feeling of magic.

"Hot." The way he uttered the word made warmth bloom within her. "Be right back."

As Ciaran wove toward the bar, Evie spotted a familiar figure enter the club. She glanced frantically back at Queenie, Dev, and Mad, who had returned to the booth, lifting glasses and having conversations.

She looked back at Jason Ra. He was speaking with a slinky girl in a beaded dress. When he smiled, it was so natural and charming, it made Evie smile herself, wistfully. With his classic looks, his short, sculpted hair, he seemed like a ghost from the speakeasy's past.

She wound through the patrons, stalking him as he moved, alone, to one of the smaller booths. When she slithered into the seat opposite, he turned his head to regard her coolly.

"What do you want?" she demanded. "I already answered all the questions with the cops."

"You're with them." He indicated La Fable Sombre with a jerk of his chin.

"You following me or them?"

He studied her. "Did they dip you in glitter?"

She blinked her glittery eyelashes and scowled. She needed

to deflect his attention away from La Fable Sombre. "Most guys just ask a girl out. Can you tell from looking at me what my hobbies are and what music I like?"

The sweet curve appeared at the corner of his mouth again. She glimpsed someone who might actually laugh and play video games. "Not yet."

She set her chin on her hands. "I can tell stuff about *you* from looking at you."

"Is that right?" He sat back, skeptical.

She skimmed her gaze over him. She wanted to get under his skin, but she was aware of the danger of Ciaran seeing them together. She also needed to throw him off the scent. "Fancy threads. A little worn. That watch is expensive but old. Maybe an heirloom? You definitely don't cut your own hair. How am I doing so far?"

His head tilted. "Not bad." He suddenly leaned forward, his dark gaze capturing hers. "My turn. You prefer solitude. You hate rules. You're hiding something."

That hit a little too close to home. She deflected with a challenge. "What's my favorite song?"

He flicked his gaze over her. "'Paint It Black.' Rolling Stones."

Again, a guess that had veered in the right direction. She nodded and tapped her fingers against the table, not to be outdone. "Yours is 'Hallelujah.' Leonard Cohen."

His eyes widened for a second, and she laughed. "*No.* I was right?"

"It's a great song. Aren't you going to ask me why I'm here? To return this to you." With a sleight of hand, he produced a medallion on a silver chain. It twirled, revealing the painting of the pretty maiden death. Her mother's medallion. Evie snatched it from him, ran her fingers over the intricate, silver design like Celtic knotwork.

"How'd you know it was mine?"

"I didn't until now. You're lucky I found it, not the police."

"How did you know this is where we'd be?" She clutched the medallion against her heart.

"They come here every Valentine's Day." He removed a small silver Polaroid camera from his blazer. He aimed it at Mad and the others. "After their first heist of the year."

She wanted to smack the camera from his hands. "You can't take photos of us without our permission."

He clicked the Polaroid's button and a pearly square of paper slid out. He waved it idly, taunting her. He slid the Polaroid across to her. The slick paper had darkened into Evie, raven hair falling over eyes like black holes in her face. He raised the camera and clicked it again. "I got this camera from my dad. He loved antiques and artifacts because they were ciphers of the past."

"Ra." She affected boredom. "You're not going to find anything here except a group of friends having a good time."

"That so?" He raised the camera and clicked it again, fanned himself with the Polaroid. A picture of Mad, Dev, and Queenie dropped onto the table between them. "My dad's favorite quote was from Baudelaire: *La plus belle des ruses du diable est de vous persuader qu'il n'existe pas.*"

"Are you trying to impress me with your *French*?"

He smiled and she was distracted. The black freckle on

one side of his nose made his chiseled looks less intimidating. He said, "It means, 'the devil's finest trick is to persuade you he doesn't exist.'"

Evie leaned slightly forward and whispered, furious, "What are you trying to prove?"

"Did you know that Veronica Jordan was thrown from a penthouse high-rise in New York City? She was only seventeen." Something in his voice made Evie wary—a note of bitter rage. He continued, "If she hadn't been with *them*, she wouldn't have died."

Evie sat back. "You don't actually believe that *they*"—she pointed at La Fable Sombre—"are some mythical gang of thieves?"

His eyes were cold. "Now you're lying."

"You're not Interpol, Sherlock. Who hired you to stalk my friends?"

He said quietly, "No one hired me. I told you my father worked for Interpol. Last year, he was found shot in the head."

She was so cold, so suddenly, it was as if the invisibility had fallen over her. She waited, breathless and wide-eyed, hoping she hadn't just vanished before Jason Ra. He continued in a clipped tone, "My father was investigating an international crime ring. A gang of thieves whose thefts were flashy and impossible. Art. Jewelry. Antiquities. Never cash."

Evie spoke softly, "You think this gang murdered your dad?"

Something shaded his dark eyes. "Interpol agents don't carry guns. Interpol is a communication network for extradition. My dad didn't suicide."

My dad didn't suicide. She'd worn that look herself. She sat back. She glanced over at La Fable Sombre, her heart drumming. "They're not murderers." Now, *she* was lying.

"How long have you known them? Why did they choose *you*, Evie Wilder? Mystery girl?"

She laughed, quick and incredulous. He was trying to trap her? She retreated behind a cool façade. "I think you need to find a new hobby." She stood up.

"Evie." His tone halted her. "They're not what you think. The Dark Fable go as far back as medieval France. They are a shadow society. They're more than just thieves . . . they're not in it just for the money. They're in it for the *mayhem*."

She hesitated. He couldn't ruin this for her. She turned, demanded, "You said you find people?"

"I do." His look was suddenly intense. "Do you need someone found?"

Her lips parted. "No." She began to turn away.

"Evie. Look around you. At these people. Did Ciaran Argent tell you where he was taking you tonight? Where you are? He took you through a Door, into a *fiction*."

Everything became edged and dazzling as Evie studied her surroundings, watched a woman in a peacock silk gown glide past. A man in a fedora was speaking with the bartender. On the stage, the singer was mostly in shadow but for a bar of light across her eyes. Everything here was too shiny, the colors glowing. And the people . . . like facsimiles, perfect tropes from a film. She almost expected Jay Gatsby to swagger through the door.

No fictional worlds, Ciaran had said. Except this one, apparently. She turned to Jason, eyes wide, panic biting at her. "If that's the truth, then how are *you* here?"

"Evie." It was Ciaran's voice. "This gent bothering you?"

She concealed her dismay with a smile. "We were just talking about music."

Ciaran shook his head as he approached. "Don't cover for him. Jase and I have unfinished business, don't we, Jase?"

Jason didn't reply.

"So, I'll just sit right here." Ciaran slid into the seat opposite Jason. "I think we've some things to discuss, mate."

"Do we?" Jason's tone was chilly.

Sensing an epic confrontation, Evie stepped back. Without looking at her, Ciaran grabbed one of her wrists. "Stay. No harm in you listening to us chat."

Evie sat beside Ciaran, looked pointedly at his hand. He released her, watching Jason. "I thought you'd be tired of playing detective by now."

Jason told him, "I'm going to end LFS. For Vero. For my *father*."

The smile vanished as Ciaran's face became a feral mask. "I was wrong, Evie. Maybe you should leave us to hash this out, like."

"No." Evie wasn't leaving now. And she was absolutely freaked out by her surroundings.

Ciaran shrugged. Both he and Jason had their hands on the table, as if following some unspoken nemesis protocol. Ciaran spoke, continuing an old conversation. "Vero was an accident, mate."

Jason was gripping the table edge so hard, Evie thought it might crack in his grip. He said, "Vero told me everything."

"Did she? Anything you didn't already know? My favorite color? What a happy kid I was?"

"You weren't a happy kid. None of you were."

"Aw, Jase, that's a low blow. And you being a born-again White Hat or whatever. Evie, did Jase here tell you what a bad boy he used to be?"

Evie looked from one to the other, saw the matching fear-lessness—it was like sitting between two beasts ready to rip out each other's throats.

Ciaran sprawled back, both hands still on the table. "Remember our year of B-sides, Jase? Barcelona, Berlin, Buenos Aires . . ."

Evie stared at Jason, shocked by the revelation. "*You were one of them.*"

Jason was watching Ciaran, his expression calculating when he answered, "I got out."

Ciaran continued reminiscing, and it was, Evie thought, ruthlessly manipulative. "But Jaipur . . . that was the jewel in our crown, wasn't it? Bad luck dogged our heels, Evie. Mad got caught on camera, levitating. Dev almost got beheaded. I had to rescue Vero from the Basilisk—a Very Bad Man. Queenie and I distracted the villain with a tango in the yellow ballroom of a palace. And Jase saved us all, in a savage and diabolical fashion." He tapped a finger against the table and the skull ring flashed. "Do you know what an idée fixe is, Jase? It's an obsession, one that usually ends badly for the obsessed."

"That another threat, Argent? It's tiresome. *Mate.*"

Ciaran's eyes glittered. "You were an animal, Jase. And you gave that up for *this*?" He gestured disdainfully at Jason's ensemble. "Roleplaying a wannabe junior gumshoe?"

"I know what you're going to do, Argent. Bring out the darkness in her. I won't let you." Jason leaned forward. "What terrible thing happened to you, to make you what you are?"

Evie flinched as Ciaran's gaze eclipsed. "That darkness, Jase, is what has kept all of us alive. Not everyone was born with a silver spoon between their lips. Your mum had the dosh, did she? And your dad was the hero. What a legacy to follow. So, with that perfect life of yours, tell me," Ciaran lowered his voice in mocking confidence, "what terrible thing happened to *you* to make *you* what *you* are?"

Jason was silent, his eyes cold.

Ciaran hitched slightly forward, his voice almost tender when he spoke. "You keep this up and you won't just be my enemy. You'll be Mad's enemy. Dev's. Queenie's. *Evie*'s enemy."

"Stop," Evie protested.

Almost casually, Jason asked Ciaran, "Did Vero become *your* enemy? Is that why she's dead?"

Evie turned her head, wide eyes fixed on Ciaran.

Ciaran rose. "I'm taking Evie for a tour, mate. Care to come with?" It was a manipulative switch of subjects.

Jason also stood. "I'll come with you."

Evie set a hand on Ciaran's shoulder. "Where are we going?"

"Follow me." Ciaran led them toward a black door painted with stars. He opened a Door and pulled her through. Jason followed. Cold blistered Evie's lungs. Darkness brushed against her, whispering—it was the eternal chill of the otherworldly night that now draped her whenever she made herself unseen.

They stepped into a chamber that resembled a medieval hall, with stone walls and no windows, only a ceiling of green glass. Illuminated by spotlights, paintings in elaborate frames were hung on the walls. Display cases were filled with artifacts and jewelry. Jason's face was remote as he followed his former friend.

Evie halted before a tiny painting of two women in old-fashioned clothing, standing in a room with a chessboard floor. She breathed out when she recognized it. "*The Concert.* The stolen Vermeer."

"The Gardner Museum heist." Jason moved to her side, studying the masterpiece. "The museum still has the empty frames up for the paintings that were swiped."

"1990." Ciaran spoke with pride. "Silence and Night's predecessors, the Dolls, pulled that off."

Evie moved on to the next painting, a small watercolor by Degas. The painting beside it was a Rembrandt, also infamously stolen. She moved on, to *The Nativity with Saint Francis and Saint Lawrence,* reached out, her fingertips hovering over an angel's face. "Caravaggio."

Ciaran looked at her, hands in his pockets. "You know your art." He sounded appraising.

"The Elegants stole that one," Jason said softly. "Oruko and Astrid. In the Gilded Age. They were a musician and a girl acrobat. Stole a mill in contraband artwork from a New York City mansion."

"Jase knows all of La Fable Sombre's history." Ciaran turned his head from the painting he'd been admiring, to watch Jason and Evie. "Come on then. More to see."

As Ciaran and Evie continued walking, Jason trailing after, Ciaran explained, "This is the only vault I can get into because I've seen it. Can't go anywhere I haven't seen, with the exception of cities, as long as I've viewed a recent photograph." He stopped before a painting. It was a landscape of sulfur yellows and shadowy blacks, with a dark figure slouched against a wall, the sun dying behind it. The figure's hand was on a door. The plaque beneath read: *The Dweller on the Threshold*. "This one's my favorite."

Evie moved to his side. "It's a *Goya*, isn't it? I've never seen it before." She gazed at the painting with reverence. "But I recognize the style, the colors."

"It is a Goya." Ciaran looked impressed. "Not many know it even exists."

Evie turned, quiet with reverence. She wandered again, examining the way paint and varnish had been applied to canvas by the hands of masters. She saw the headless Winged Victory of Samothrace. *Odysseus and the Sphinx*. Jewelry that had adorned pharaohs and queens. Every room of artifacts was perfumed with the dust of ancient civilizations. The paintings seemed to move. If she looked out of the corner of her eye, leaves rustled. Waves swirled. She thought she saw the statue of a god tilt its head. The scent of magic smoked around her.

Ciaran slung an arm over Jason's shoulders. "Do you miss us, bruv?"

Evie glanced worriedly at Jason.

Jason shrugged Ciaran's arm away. "We're not brothers." Bitterness spiked his words. If Ciaran was a venomous thorn, Jason was a stinging nettle. And Evie felt as if she were a vine twining them together.

They walked silently, with Evie leading. She found herself thinking about how Ciaran had brought her into a world she never would have found otherwise. Without Ciaran, she would have been stuck in a life of servitude and hopelessness. It had been the same for Mad, Dev, and Queenie, she suspected.

What had he offered Jason?

Ciaran suddenly said, "We didn't kill your dad, Jase."

Evie winced. Jason halted. Evie turned, wanting to reach out to him, but Jason was like a stone as he said, "I know who told Silence and Night my father was Interpol."

"You think it was me?" Ciaran stepped closer to Jason. Tension snapped between them. "You think Silence and Night didn't suss you out the minute you hooked up with us? Let me tell you, Evie, about Jase. He isn't a fucking saint. When Vero fell, he was there. He was there when she hit the ground. He held her. He got up, all red in her blood, and walked into that building, took the elevator to the penthouse Vero had been shoved out of."

Evie reluctantly visualized everything Ciaran narrated.

"I'm sure when Lila Pearce's people answered the door, they had weapons. Didn't matter. Jase took them out. Three professional bodyguards. One ended up with a broken neck. One with a shattered spine. And one got flung out of a window. Jase is a knight, but that shiny armor's got some bloodstains on it."

Jason didn't flinch when Ciaran said into his ear, "Remember that it was *you* who persuaded Vero to join us."

Jason swung at him. Ciaran glided back, but Jason moved with lethal swiftness. Ciaran avoided a kick meant to break a kneecap. He lunged, grabbed Jason by his blazer, slammed him against the wall.

"*Stop!*" Evie was prepared to jump on Ciaran's back to drag him away.

Jason twisted free and hit Ciaran in the stomach. Ciaran doubled up with a choking sound. He laughed. Jason slammed a fist into his jaw. Ciaran's head snapped back. He spat blood to one side, smiled wickedly, curled a hand in invitation. "There you are, bruv."

Evie saw the viciousness for what it was—these two had been good friends. They were more alike than they cared to admit. Jason believed Ciaran had betrayed him; Ciaran was furious that Jason had left La Fable Sombre.

Evie thought of a phrase that had been a favorite of her mother's: *The virtue and the vice.* She saw in Jason the courage that she'd lost. She saw in Ciaran the darkness that had set her free.

As the two went at each other, crashing into a statue, tumbling to the floor, attempting to annihilate one another, Evie, avoiding the blood drops on the floor, walked calmly over. "Hey."

They both stopped to look up at her.

"Jason. I don't want to see you again." She managed a laugh that made Ciaran fall back from Jason and Jason stare up at her. "You really think I'm going to give all this up because of your white knight complex? Get over yourself." The words left her like venom. It was as if a serpent had its fangs in her heart. She finalized the execution. "Leave me alone."

Ciaran, wiping blood from his mouth, his gaze watchful, rose. He reached out a hand to Jason. "No hard feelings, bruv."

Jason stood on his own, bruises already forming on his face. His gaze on Evie, he backed away. She stood still, swaying on her feet, resisting the urge to scream at him, *I don't mean it!*

A silver pentacle appeared in the air behind him, a black hole behind it. He stepped through the pentacle, into the darkness.

Then he was gone.

"That's it then." Ciaran straightened his blazer. He led her to the Door. It opened back into the Howling Cat Club. As Evie stepped over the threshold, the darkness clung to her, whispering. The chill of the crossing was blistering. Then they were back in the light and the music of a fake world, a metaphor, Evie thought bitterly, for the world she'd chosen over reality.

The new knowledge felt like bits of shattered glass against her skin.

CHAPTER SEVEN

Thieves' Night

As the sun set like an ominous, bloodshot eye over the ocean, La Fable Sombre brought Evie to meet Mother Night and Father Silence. They passed through Ciaran's Door, an icy gloom enveloping them, darkness twining around their limbs. Briefly, to either side, was that night-drenched grassland and a violet sky. Evie thought she heard voices, an eerie hymn that echoed.

They stepped into a grand bazaar in Marrakesh, a crowded corridor flaunting a wonderland of glistening fabrics and blown-glass lamps. Topaz, fire blue, garnet red, and green flamed everywhere, almost surreal, as was the clamor of languages and sounds, the perfumed heat. The aroma of honey-baked pastries made Evie's mouth water. As Ciaran moved into the corridor of arabesque arches, Evie and the others followed, the chill shadows releasing them. They passed women in hijabs and men in Hawaiian shirts. Mopeds zipped through. *This is magic,* Evie marveled.

"So many shiny things." Dev slid a brand-new watch onto his left wrist and admired it against his tiger tattoos. He handed a hundred-dollar bill to the vendor. "That's a work of art, mate. Finest copy of a Piguet I've ever seen."

"You're gonna wear a fake?" Queenie eyed him.

He shrugged. "I'll wear it to places I don't mind it getting broken."

To one side, Evie saw a girl in black spinning fire. Somewhere, music was playing, a sinuous melody that spiraled into a Nirvana song Evie recognized as one of her mom's favorites. Hearing it in this amazing place caused a pang of sadness.

As they approached a man in a tuxedo performing tricks with a monkey, Mad gasped in delight and lunged toward them.

"No. *No.*" Dev caught her and hauled her back. "Never trust the monkey. Haven't you ever seen *any* adventure movie? Look, there's a henna artist." He pulled her toward a red-haired woman painting intricate designs on people's arms.

"I'm getting pastries." Queenie headed for a vendor.

Ciaran and Evie paused to watch a snake charmer in jeans and a Rolling Stones T-shirt. Ciaran crouched down, met the snake charmer's gaze. Evie saw the man's eyes widen in concern as the cobra—the freaking *cobra*—turned its hooded head and began to sway toward Ciaran. The man lowered his flute, spoke urgently in Arabic.

Ciaran lifted a hand, his attention on the cobra. Evie wanted to yank him away but remained still as the snake glided toward him. The snake charmer began to whisper what sounded like a prayer as the cobra twined around Ciaran's wrist. Ciaran spoke in another language, words that bit the air, that sent apprehension twisting through Evie. Ciaran lifted his arm and the cobra's hooded head swayed before his face. A wind swept through the marketplace, rattling pottery, sweeping woven rugs and colorful fabrics into the air. Ciaran gently lowered his wrist and the cobra twined back to the basket.

"Nice." Queenie punched Ciaran in one shoulder. He rose and laughed softly, said, "Let's get some mint tea, ladies."

Evie trailed Ciaran and Queenie, glanced back to see the snake charmer staring after them as if he'd seen the devil.

After the tea in a café, Ciaran led them out of the bazaar, through a series of hilly streets. On an avenue tangled with date trees, they ascended a steep stairway, toward a castle of black-and-white-striped stone. The dusk tinted its windows golden. Behind a scrim of vines and flowers, the building stood aloof from the rest of the neighborhood. Ciaran said, "That is the Palm and the Lotus. Home to Father and Mother."

"That's where they live?" Evie studied it.

"Sometimes." Ciaran glanced at her. "They have other homes. They're rich as sin, blackbird."

The nickname surprised and delighted her but she didn't let him see that.

"If it wasn't warded at every door and window, we could get a Door right *into* the place." Queenie looped an arm around Mad as Mad slipped on a pair of hand-painted slippers she'd delightedly haggled for.

Dev told Evie, "The Plaza La Mer caper was amateur night at the laundromat. This is Wagner's entire Ring cycle."

"You even pronounced Wagner correctly." Queenie was mock amazed. She leveled a gaze on Evie. "You'll do fine. You book us a nice hotel, Ciar?"

"For the evening," he said. "Until they come for us."

"We can take naps, swim in the pool, do a little shopping." Mad wrapped an arm around Queenie's waist.

Evie studied the Palm and the Lotus as fear and excitement sizzled through her. "So. We're the stars of the show?"

"We're their favorites." Ciaran shot her a smile, but his eyes were filled with darkness.

If we're their favorites, Evie thought, *why is their lair warded against us?*

Evie slept until late in the day, a dreamless, absolute slumber, from which she was awakened by Mad jumping on the bed. Evie lifted her head, craving espresso and a hot shower.

"Wake up, Eves. We have to get you ready."

Evie buried her face in the pillow exquisitely scented with lemon verbena. "Okay."

"First shopping. And then it's dinner with Mother and Father."

Evie raised her head again, blinking in the sunlight. Mad pirouetted across the suite. Beyond the half-open doors, Evie saw Dev pouring tea at a table, and Queenie, wrapped in a silk robe, peeling a hard-boiled egg. Ciaran, seated in a chair, flicked his gaze up from his phone and smiled at her.

How could a life of roaming and thieving be home? Evie thought, her heart a tender, bruised thing. It was dangerous ... how addicted to this she could become.

A silver Rolls-Royce arrived at the fancy hotel to pick them up. A young man with a shaved head and kohl-rimmed eyes unfolded himself from the vehicle. He looked as if he'd been time-swept from some Viking battle and placed in a nice suit. Ciaran strolled toward him and the two spoke like old friends.

Dev adjusted his ruby cufflinks. Queenie, in a gown of daffodil-yellow satin, moved to his side. Evie, who had chosen a black gown with yards of smoky gossamer, and silver serpent bracelets that twined around her upper arms, felt like a femme fatale.

"Everyone ready?" Ciaran gestured to the Rolls.

As Dev passed the driver, whose forehead was scripted with a tattoo that read "Life," Dev nodded to him. "You have 'Death' tattooed on your bum?"

The driver bared teeth that looked as if they'd been sharpened. Dev sighed. "You Batavi are a scary lot."

Mad smiled sweetly at the driver, who just looked at her, dark eyes cold. She shivered and ducked into the back in a froth of pink tulle. Evie and Queenie followed. Evie said, her voice low, "Batavi?"

"Mercenaries," Queenie answered. "Anyone in our world—Collectors, criminals—can hire them as guards or security. They have no loyalties."

"Well, they're loyal to *money*," Dev noted.

Mad looked wistful. "You gotta admire that."

"I'm so concerned about you." Queenie shook her head.

Mad patted Evie's shoulder. "Nervous? You're supposed to be. You're the ingenue."

Evie slouched. So. Not the femme fatale after all.

—*∿*—

The Rolls-Royce cruised through wrought-iron gates and wound up a drive lined with palm trees, the castle's palatial façade appearing from among a lush growth of hedges and trees. A grand stairway ascended to a pair of medieval doors. Every window emanated light stained blue, ruby, or green, depending on the glass.

As the limo stopped, Mad shoved the passenger door open and slid out. Following her, Evie didn't see anyone, not even a valet. Ciaran, Dev, and Queenie emerged, Dev straightening his white blazer.

Queenie handed out metal half masks. "Don't take these masks off until you're told to. It's etiquette."

Evie wrestled with an escalating panic that came at her like a horned monster lifting its head in the dark.

"Listen." Ciaran's voice halted all conversation. He was in shadow but for a light striping across his eyes. "We have the Queen Cobra. We needn't worry about what Night and Silence will think of Lila Pearce's unfortunate end."

Her poisoning. Evie winced and glanced at Queenie. The other girl's expression was serene, but a muscle twitched in her jaw.

"Are we doing any scarpering?" Dev ran a hand across his red buzz cut. "The Nara crew are always flashing diamonds."

"Not to mention a gold tooth or two among Fenrir." Queenie adjusted her bronze bracelets of interlocking rabbits.

"No scarpering. Honor among thieves and all that." Ciaran was completely at ease. "Keep an eye out for the Boy Detective."

Evie was unsettled by this mention of Jason Ra.

Queenie placed one of the metal masks over her face. "It's haunted—this desert place."

"You *know* I don't like it when you talk about ghosts." Dev shivered.

"I see shadows out of the corners of my eye." Queenie was stern. "Whenever I'm here."

As Evie studied the castle, Ciaran drew down his dragon-like mask of gilded copper, his mouth a lush curve beneath. "Follow. And, Evie, remember, what we can do . . . it doesn't work inside the Palm and the Lotus. Something mutes our swagger. Only Silence and Night's powers function within those walls."

So. Evie was walking into a dragon's lair without any magic tricks.

She felt the night snapping with magic and peril. At the doors, a man in a suit and black domino held up a scanner to each of their masks and Evie realized there must be ID chips in them. As he waved them into the foyer, Evie didn't need to see a gun to know he had one.

The Palm and the Lotus was saturated with mosaics of Byzantine saints and curdling with woodwork depicting ravens, eyes, dragons, an eerie motif of upraised hands, and lotus flowers. In the center of the entry hall was a statue of Mercury, the god of thieves. Evie almost wanted to curtsey before it.

Mad, her mask suggestive of an owl's face, looked at Evie. "You'll meet the king and queen after the ritual."

Evie adjusted her own mask, crowned with a tangle of silver serpents. She glimpsed herself in a verdigris-misted mirror. The mask's eye slits seemed to gaze back at her. "Rituals. No sacrifices, right?"

Mad made a zipping gesture across her lips as two young men in wolfish brass masks passed them. They cast disdainful looks at La Fable Sombre. Evie instantly disliked them.

"The Fenrir crew," Ciaran told Evie. "Absolute assholes.

Responsible for the down-and-dirty stuff—bank heists and casino stings. Toxic masculinity at its finest."

As they passed a door, it swung outward and two black-haired girls in deer half masks stepped out. One of the girls grinned. She said something in Japanese before she and her companion moved gracefully onward.

"Nara crew," Queenie told Evie. "The jewelry specialists. They were supposed to be backup for us at the Plaza La Mer. And that bitch said 'Good luck' because she meant the opposite. You never say good luck on Thieves' Night."

"You speak Japanese, Queens?" Mad sounded impressed. "I mean, I know you speak Inupiaq, Russian, Cantonese . . . Spanish. Too bad you weren't with us in Buenos Aires. Remember that, Dev?"

"I'll never forget it. The Diamonde family were *Gothic*. All those bewitching siblings." He sighed. He wore a snarling feline face of intricate brass. "A nest of pretty, poisonous psychopaths."

Evie, fascinated by this trinket of information from La Fable Sombre's past, heard classical music as they moved toward a stairway that twisted upward. The stained-glass window on the landing depicted two hands—one white, one black—holding a crimson lotus. They stepped into a black-and-gold ballroom, where more people in masks mingled in groups near tables stacked with ornamental treats and glasses filled with punch.

"These are the other crews," Mad explained to Evie. "Not like us. No super powers. But you have to admire the skills of everyone here." She indicated a group wearing weblike silver masks, an ebony-skinned boy reigning among them. "The Arachnae, over there, are cat burglars and high-rise climbers.

The Seraphim"—she nodded to a group in gaudy, tailored clothing and Harlequin masks—"the con artists."

"And they had to learn all that shit." Dev had a drink in one hand. He popped an hors d'oeuvre into his mouth. "I'll miss Circe, clever girl." He told Evie, "She and her crew, the Sirens, were scuba divers and experts at nautical theft."

"And where are the Sirens?" Evie looked around, intrigued.

"Not here," Ciaran's voice was low.

"Why not?" Evie concluded she wasn't being told something.

"Ambition," Queenie told her. "They stole from Silence and Night. There's Max." She nodded to a tanned boy with tousled blond curls and a golden mask.

"I'm going to nick over there and have a word. Max always has intel." Ciaran strode toward the boy.

"Tsar crew," Dev informed Evie. "Max is the leader of the hackers. Tech robbers."

"I'm gonna get the goss from Embry." Queenie strode toward the enormous fireplace and the collection of people in metal spider masks.

Mad and Dev remained with Evie, leading her through the party. Evie asked, "Do the other crews know? What LFS can do?"

Mad shrugged. "They suspect."

"Mad." A girl in a pale hijab and a dress that glittered like crushed diamonds against her brown skin strolled toward them. She was accompanied by two young men who wore masks with rays forming ankhs or stars.

"Sairish." Mad and the girl swiftly embraced, drew back. "It's been a while. This is Evie. She's new."

The girl's half mask swept up in rays of silver hearts.

"Welcome to my country." She looked Evie up and down before sauntering onward with her companions. "And welcome to the Kingdom."

"She's Oracle's leader." Mad smiled. "We're friends. They're the antiquarians."

Evie spotted a young man with spiky blue hair prowling amidst Nara crew and froze. When his powder-blue blazer fell open, several small daggers glistened in a holster.

"Nara have a new recruit." Mad turned to Evie. "So . . . about Nara and Fenrir . . . Silence and Night like us to be competitive, but, sometimes, the other crews are our backup. You want to know a dark secret? We use them as a distraction."

Dev sighed. "Although we did steal Nara's thunder when we went to LA after the Cobra and took that Hollywood job away from them. I expect we'll get a stern talking-to."

"Sadie is Nara's leader." Mad lowered her voice. "Her only loyalty is to Father and Mother."

"She may have gotten the Sirens in trouble," Dev clarified. "And then we nicked that casino heist from under Fenrir's noses because Reynard insulted Ciar. We're expecting Fenrir to retaliate. Any time now."

Evie's mind was spinning with the details of each crew's connection to the Dark Fable. She had not expected these complications. "That guy." Evie indicated the blue-haired young man. "He was at the Plaza La Mer. He sensed me when I was . . ." She couldn't say the ridiculous word "invisible." ". . . when I did the trick."

Mad glanced sharply at her. "He sensed you when you were *invisible*?"

Dev *tsk*ed. "Well, *that's* troubling."

It was more than troubling, Evie thought as she scanned the other crews. Even without the supernatural gifts La Fable Sombre shared, these other thieves were a hurdle she hadn't anticipated.

Evie and La Fable Sombre stood on a mezzanine overlooking a cavernous chamber of iron girders and stone, scattered with giant potted ferns and statues of wild-looking people. All the crews were assembled below. Evie saw the two girls in deer masks, whispering to the blue-haired guy, who was staring up at La Fable Sombre in their elevated position. Near them were three boys in Prada—more Nara crew.

From beneath an arch painted with a mural of sinister, black-winged angels, a couple emerged. He was classically handsome, bronze-skinned, a figure of cold, dark blue elegance with cropped brown hair. She was a goddess, her raven hair in twisty plaits, her gown white as death, her skin a creamy hue.

Evie whispered, "Are they—"

"Father and Mother." Mad spoke with reverence.

Mother Night raised a glass and tapped it with a little spoon. The sound reverberated through the room, and everyone hushed.

Father Silence spoke in an Irish brogue, his gaze skimming the assembly. "Tonight, we honor our achievements. We honor our dead. Three of us have died this year. Though all here know how life is rife with violence, it doesn't make those losses any easier."

Mother Night walked to the center of the gathering, the

train of her Versace gown gliding against the checkerboard floor. She recited names in a French accent: "Shoji Amano. Gladys Holt. Brendan Maguire."

Black banners were draped over the railings, each one bearing a symbol of whatever crew had lost a member. Evie wondered how they had died. Last year, one of those banners would have belonged to La Fable Sombre's lost girl, Vero Jordan.

"And, now," Mother Night bowed her head, lifting one hand. "We had hoped this would not happen. An entire crew has mutinied and they must face judgment."

Mutinied? Evie remembered the missing Siren crew.

No one said a word. Father Silence had drawn back into the shadows so that only his eyes glittered.

A pair of doors opened, and two Batavi in black suits hauled, between them, a battered boy with brown curls. They shoved him to his knees in front of Mother Night.

"Now then." The disdain in Father Silence's voice was like a double-edged ax. "We've had quite a rebellion. The Sirens have been exiled because they ran off with an object they were supposed to bring to us. A very valuable artifact. And you, Matthew Orion, are a Siren."

Evie gripped the railing.

"I'm sorry." The boy bowed his head. "It was Circe's idea to take the stuff—"

"Hush." Mother Night knelt before the boy, her gown blooming around her like a funeral lily. She exchanged a look with Father Silence. He snapped his fingers. A Batavi strode toward them, face grim. He handed Mother Night a wand-like object with a glowing orange insignia at the end. Dev hissed, "Is that a *brand*—"

Mother Night spoke. "You've broken our rules. Here is the consequence."

Evie didn't flinch—beside her, Queenie did—as Mother Night lifted the boy's cuffed wrists and pressed the brand against the back of his left hand. Flesh sizzled. The boy howled and curled over. Mother Night rose. She handed the brand back to the guard.

Father Silence's voice broke the quiet. "Now, it isn't as bad as it could have been. We'll catch the rest of your crew, Matthew, and they'll bear the same mark. From now on, you will be known as a traitor to the Kingdom."

The boy, who had half fainted, was dragged away amidst raucous shouts of "Traitor!" and "Bastard!" and profanities, a mob of contempt. Evie glimpsed the expression of terror and anguish on the exile's face, the look of someone suddenly bereft of family and society.

Father Silence raised a hand. The thieves fell quiet. Silence's pale gaze fell upon Ciaran and he said, "Let this be a lesson for you all, children."

Evie glanced at Ciaran, who seemed completely at ease.

Mother Night continued, her voice carrying, "Now the unpleasantness is concluded, we'll commence with the tributes."

One member from each crew approached Silence and Night, each setting an item in the center of the chamber: a diamond necklace in a white velvet box, the stone head of some strange god, a painting Evie was sure was a Magritte. Nara crew's leader, a black-haired girl in a metal deer mask, glided forward, cast a vicious glance at La Fable Sombre, then set down a flat box of engraved copper. She opened it to reveal sparkling sapphire jewelry.

"Evie." Mad set the velvet box containing the Queen Cobra into Evie's hands. "Don't be afraid."

"After that?" Evie glared at her. "You expect me to be okay?"

But she moved down the stairs to join the queue. A red-haired young man in a wolfish metal mask and a tweed suit appeared at her side. He carried a briefcase and spoke in a southern drawl. "So, you're Lost Forever Souls' new recruit. I'm Reynard."

"I don't care," Evie replied, using ice as a shield. Just like Jason Ra.

They approached the Mother and Father.

"Reynard. Fenrir never disappoint." Father Silence accepted the briefcase from the red-haired young man, opened it to reveal rows of crisp hundred-dollar bills. Reynard bowed and backed away to rejoin his crew.

Father's attention homed in on Evie. The moment Evie met his burning blue eyes, darkness seemed to close around her. Fear twined through her bones. When he spoke, amusement gentled his voice. "Evie Wilder."

She held out the box containing the Queen Cobra. Her hands trembled as she opened the lid to reveal the necklace of gleaming gold and lapis lazuli, the sapphires rivaling Nara's offering. Father Silence smiled and said, "Welcome to the Kingdom, Evie Wilder."

Mother Night stepped forward and kissed Evie on both cheeks, set hands on her shoulders, and studied her as if she could spot a fake when she saw one. Evie stood very still. Mother Night's perfume evoked the origins of the Queen Cobra, a fragrance of cardamom, myrrh, and henna. There was a bead of blood on her immaculate gown, from when the brand had torn from Matthew Orion's skin.

As the other crews dispersed noisily, Night asked Evie, "What do you think of our La Fable Sombre?" She slid her gaze upward to where Ciaran stood like a king, Mad a glamorous trickster in Nikes beside him; Dev, dangerous and enchanting, leaning against the railing; and Queenie, a Poison Ivy with one arm draped around Dev's neck. They stole Evie's breath away.

Evie lowered her eyelashes and told Silence and Night what they wanted to hear: "They're family."

Father Silence and Mother Night graced her with smiles before turning and departing. The center table stood unguarded as the other crews returned to their revelry, tithe offerings on display for all to see. No one would dare to steal, not here.

CHAPTER EIGHT

Spirited Away

That evening, Evie dined with La Fable Sombre on a pillared terrace. The intoxicating night air made her feel edgy and villainous. She should not enjoy that feeling. She sat at a table scattered with a feast of sausages, goat cheese, fig pastries, chickpeas, and saffron rice. Mad was balanced on the low wall, pink tulle swirling around her. Dev was speaking with Queenie.

"Are they late?" Evie nervously asked Ciaran as he stirred too much sugar into his coffee. No one was discussing the branding they had witnessed earlier.

"Could you eat with them here?" Ciaran's eyes were warm with mischief.

"I suppose not." She drank from a bottle of sparkling water and gazed out over Marrakesh. The night view was a wonderland of candy-colored lights.

"Good evening, children." Father Silence, a formidable presence in a tailored suit, moved onto the terrace. He sat at the head of the table. As his gaze tracked over them, Evie repressed a shiver. Silence gave her the feeling of *something* hidden in human skin. When his attention settled on her, she didn't dare meet his gaze directly, but only in glancing bits as he spoke to her. "Evie. You've a talent that's a jewel in our crown. Tell me, can you make others invisible?"

She thought of how she'd hidden in the cabinet with Tyrone during her first encounter with La Fable Sombre, how Dev in his tiger mask hadn't seen them. "I don't know."

"You'll practice." He smiled, and it was both a threat and a blessing. "You are La Fable Sombre's tithe offering, Evie. Not the Queen Cobra."

Around Evie, the others were quiet. She resisted an impulse to snarl at them and flicked a furious look at Ciaran, who seated himself in the chair beside her. He said, "Don't worry, black-bird. They're happy with you. I can tell."

"Ciaran." Father Silence kept his attention on Evie. "Let me remind you of all the times you made Night and me *unhappy*: Recruiting Jason Ra without our permission. That fiasco in Buenos Aires. Snatching the casino job that Fenrir had planned. Commandeering Nara crew's Hollywood crime spree after obtaining the Cobra—Nara were very upset by that." His mouth twisted wryly. He continued, "Making an enemy of the Basilisk in Jaipur and losing the Tiger's Heart. Causing a mansion to burn down in Edinburgh. Madrigal"—he cast an icy look toward Mad—"drag racing a royal son in Dubai."

Ciaran nodded and settled forward, hands loose between his knees. "And yet we always brought you the goods, Father. Well, except for the Tiger's Heart."

"Veronica's tragic death."

"Murder," Ciaran corrected. Shadows draped him as if drawn to him.

"You killed one of our Collectors, Ciaran."

Evie flinched. She hadn't known Lila Pearce had been one of Silence and Night's Collectors.

"No one here knew about it." Ciaran displayed an admirable lack of fear. "I take absolute responsibility."

"Of course, you do." Silence regarded him with a gentle smile and cold eyes.

"I made the poison," Queenie said quickly. "And we were all at the Plaza La Mer when it happened."

"It's no use scolding them." Mother Night appeared, her white sheath dress glistening with silver bees, her strappy pumps works of art. She walked to a chair and sat. "Your next job is in Marseille, children. Your strike is *L'église de Saint Saignant,* the Church of the Bleeding Saint. Before their mutiny, Siren crew managed to charm their way onto a vessel that discovered a sixteenth-century shipwreck. I've word they've hidden the treasures they stole in the church's crypt. What we want is a book—*The Bestiarum Vocabulum,* written by John Dee, Queen Elizabeth's court magician. Here is a drawing of that book."

Mother Night handed Ciaran a plastic envelope. Ciaran withdrew an illustration and lifted it for everyone to see: a black book, its cover stamped with the image of a golden gryphon and a silver harpy twined around one another. He said, "Consider it done."

"It's not bound in human skin, is it?" Dev asked warily. "I

told you, Mother of darkness, I am not touching anything made of human remains."

Mother Night smiled fondly, as if used to Dev's—Evie thought, reasonable—demands. "It was not made from people. It is a book of spirits and spirit names."

"So, it's made of magic and peril." Mad spoke lightly.

"It will only be considered magic by those who know how to use it and perilous to those who attempt to use it without knowing how." Mother Night cast a warning glance over all of them. "It is the most important item to Father and me, more than the gold or the jewels you'll find in that crypt. Evie, you are going to be crucial in getting Devon to that crypt, unseen."

Evie felt as if fire rushed through her. Doubt and terror vanished, soaring into euphoria at the idea of the impossible. Some dark other had taken over, something that loved risk and danger. The fear she experienced when she thought about what she could do . . . it was as if she were standing on a cliff, knowing she could fly if she fell. Carefully, she asked, "Why do you want this book? I mean, what can people do if they have it?"

"It's extremely valuable to certain Collectors," Mother Night explained.

"But how does the stuff in it really work?" Evie was fascinated. "Because of what we can do . . . are magic spells actually real?"

"We haven't tried any." Father Silence filled his wineglass. "And we've acquired many magic books. They end up in the hidden rooms of our Collectors."

Evie thought that was a shame. She studied the illustration of the *Bestiarum Vocabulum*, intrigued by the mystique of it.

She looked up at Silence and Night. "You don't bring any of these things home?"

"Evie." Dev nudged her.

Father Silence laughed. "Are you asking if we have a stash of occult items?"

"They do," Ciaran answered, buttering a roll.

There was a moment of quiet at the table. Evie shrugged and slid the illustration of the *Bestiarum Vocabulum* back to Ciaran, who cast her an admonishing look that said, *Careful with the questions.*

"We haven't practiced." Evie made her eyes big and innocent. "I can't will the invisibility so easily . . . the Plaza La Mer gala was the first time I went that deep. Before, it was just a fading feeling. Now . . ."

". . . it's like you disappear into a world of shadows." Mother Night spoke gently. "There'll be practice beforehand. You need to be in synch with your crew. To know what each one will be doing and where they are. There is no room for a mistake in Marseille. We aren't the only ones who know about the *Bestiarum.*"

"So, it *is* dangerous," Queenie the alchemist observed. Evie felt nothing but admiration for the other girl in that moment. "This book."

"Victoria." Mother Night spoke to Queenie as if she were an eldest daughter. "Of course, it's dangerous. Which is why we want it. Evie." She smiled graciously. "Would you like to ask us anything else?"

"Anything at all." Father Silence was all handsome benevolence. Evie could understand why La Fable Sombre considered them surrogate parents.

Until she remembered the branding. She looked down at her black-painted nails. "What are *your* powers?"

"Evie." Ciaran's tone was sharp.

Mother Night extended a hand to her. "I will show you."

It was an ominous statement. What was Evie to be shown? She faced away from the others and couldn't see their expressions. She knew that to refuse would be a misstep, an act of distrust.

Evie took Mother Night's hand. The world went dark. There was a horrifying, tipping sensation, as if she were falling—

Then she was flying through the night, through astral cold. She saw the lights of cities below, felt starlight glaze her skin—

Then she was lying, confused and terrified, on the floor of a place that resembled a basilica of black marble. Statues gazed down at her from niches in the walls. She scrambled up, caught herself against a pillar. Bile rushed up into her mouth.

Mother Night emerged from the shadows. "Forgive me, *chérie*, but it was necessary."

Evie shivered convulsively. "What did you do?"

Mother Night melted away into Father Silence, who said, "*This* is my power, Evie."

Evie realized Father Silence could *make himself look like other people.* She was stunned.

"Must you be so dramatic, Silence?" The real Mother Night appeared from the darkness.

"*Her* talent," Silence inclined his head toward Night, "is what brought you here."

Silence could shapeshift. Night could spirit others away to another location in a heartbeat. Those two immense powers . . . Evie hoped she didn't look as scared as she felt.

Mother Night said, "I apologize for the suddenness, Evie. As Silence said, this is a necessary evil."

To keep you in your place. Night didn't say those words, but Evie knew that's what she meant.

Mother Night beckoned. "There's nothing to fear when you are among us. Come."

Father Silence turned and began walking. Evie followed with Night beside her. They moved farther into the basilica, where Gothic architecture soared. The floor was like a dark mirror, swimming with light from lamps shaped like phantasmal insects. There were no windows. Evie noticed swirling friezes on the pillars, malevolent half-animal, half-human creatures. The statues in the niches had the same alien beauty. She sensed the *oldness* of this place. "Where are we?"

"Somewhere only Night can bring us." Silence turned to regard her. "In the catacombs beneath Paris."

Evie halted to stare at a wall hung with hundreds of miniature oval portraits and photographs.

"A family tree." Mother Night told her, gazing at it. "Our predecessors. We're an old order. Begun in medieval Paris. Our founders were Ismail Ameziana, son of a Moorish ambassador and a student of medicine. He had an extraordinary ability to heal; Bruno Zincalos, a supernaturally gifted tracker and marksman—and a highwayman; and Mariette Chevalier, a courtesan and disgraced aristocrat's daughter who could convince people to do almost anything she wanted. The three met when Bruno was wounded and sought sanctuary where Ismail was practicing, as did Mariette, after having stolen a valuable ring. Ismail was visiting from the city of Córdoba, where universities and libraries thrived. Bruno and Ismail protected Mariette. Mariette's theft spiraled into a movement to assist outcasts and runaways in Paris. After three others with strange powers joined, they became La Fable Sombre."

Father Silence continued, "'We are La Fable Sombre. We are the bitter in your cup. The thorn in your side. We are the spirit of revolution and revenge, the ink spilled over the stories of tyrants.' Throughout the centuries, we have stolen for wealth, knowledge, security, revenge. Power."

Evie silently repeated La Fable Sombre's motto, memorizing it. "So . . . you deal with powerful people."

"No, Evie." Father Silence's smile shot a chill through her. "They deal with us."

Evie realized she hadn't just joined a secret society of thieves . . . these people *wielded* whatever they stole.

She scrutinized the paintings and photographs. One painting, faded and burned at the top, depicted a courtyard where three people posed in fur, velvet, and leather: an ebony-skinned boy with a hawkish face, wearing a wealth of rings; a tanned young man with long dark curls and a clever look; and a girl, her auburn hair elaborately coiled, her coat lined with raven feathers like midnight against her pale skin. Further on was a photograph of two chic young women, leaning against each other and gazing into the camera with predatory glee. One of them wore a necklace of amber gems. *The Dolls,* she guessed, Silence and Night's former bosses.

"This way, Evie." Father Silence moved onward. Evie and Night trailed after.

They reached a set of dark metal doors engraved with more

strange figures. She didn't see any handles or locking devices and wondered how the doors opened.

Father Silence was watching Evie. "Beyond these doors are La Fable Sombre's greatest achievements. Every secret, every strange thing ever stolen and not sought by Collectors. Objects both mystical and magical. And we are the guardians."

Mother Night gently touched Evie's wrist. "Anything is possible with us. What more could you want?"

Did they expect her to be greedy? Ambitious? Evie was none of those. She was adventurous. She liked being part of something. She was terrified and galvanized by her powers. She knew these two were ruthless criminals, but she was flattered by their interest and confidence in her abilities.

"I was like you, Evie." Mother Night's voice was velvety with empathy. "I had no one. Passed from one family to another. I discovered who I was with La Fable Sombre."

Evie gazed at the immense doors decorated with friezes of animal-headed deities dancing, farming, hunting. She knew she might not have another chance to ask what she wanted. She turned away from the doors and the overwhelming mystery beyond them and asked, "So, are we kind of your children?"

Father Silence became very still, emanating that unsettling combination of saintliness and menace. Mother Night moved forward to clasp Evie's hands. "Of course you are."

The world blacked out again. Evie's gasp ended on the terrace of the Palm and the Lotus, where Mad caught her as she stumbled. For a moment, Evie couldn't hear because of the buzzing in her eardrums.

"—Evie? . . . you okay?"

"She's all right." Dev was at Evie's other side. "She just needs to walk it off, don't you, luv?"

Ciaran stood where he'd been before Mother Night had spirited her away. He met her gaze, his own darker than obsidian. "They're gone, blackbird."

"You *knew*," she snarled, pushing away from Mad. "You all knew what their powers were and didn't tell me!"

"That's right." Ciaran was calm in the face of her fury. "You needed to know how dangerous they are. You needed to be afraid in order to stay alive. Because if we fuck this up, Evie, they'll blame you. The new girl."

Evie stood very still as they all became very somber. Terror slithered through her as she recalled the sizzling sound the brand had made on the traitor's skin.

"If we fail, it won't be because of me." She stormed out, regretting that one moment of tenderness she had felt for all of them.

They weren't her family. She had let herself forget they were a gang of criminals.

She returned to her assigned room. She sat on the bed, in the dark, gazing sullenly at the balcony doors, which she'd opened, letting the scents of orange blossom and cardamom drift over her. The music of crickets soothed her, inspiring a memory of Summer, her mother, with her raven hair and freckles and dashing smile. Evie would listen, enchanted, to Summer's stories as Ezra and Juliet slept in bassinets, the cottage's patio doors opened to invite the ocean hush and the cricket symphony. Evie learned how her mom and dad had danced with a rock star in Prague. Driven motorcycles down tricky roads in Mozambique. Hiked up a mountain in South America to explore a Mayan ruin. Rudy and Summer Luna had been adventurers. Her eyes brimmed with tears.

Evie had a chance at such adventure now. For a life in which she *belonged* somewhere. She couldn't lose sight of why she'd done this, because there were so many distractions. La Fable Sombre had sought her out because they needed her supernatural ability. But she worried she could only summon it when she was in danger, not on a whim. She'd attempted it on the roof of the Silver Cove lair while eavesdropping on Ciaran and Mad and failed.

She breathed in, out. A true-'til-death. She moved to a mirror and willed the cold and the dark around her. A chill swept across her, and, for a horrifying second, she saw part of her reflection erased.

She let go of that thread of the supernatural and her entire reflection returned.

She stepped onto the balcony for air, gripped the railing. The garden, with its hedge sculptures, was harshly lit and surreal in the moonlight.

A shout made her heart jump. Three Batavi ran across the lawn, following a fleeing figure. She heard someone shout, "Shoot him, goddamn it!"

The figure paused beneath her window—a young man, profile proud and hawkish.

It was Jason Ra.

They'd kill him.

He didn't see her. He continued running.

She clambered over the balustrade and jumped down,

dashed through the hedges, cut diagonally to head him off. As he vaulted onto a low wall, she lunged and grabbed his hand.

He looked at her, startled and stern. She heard running steps and shouts behind her. She thought, *Don't see us.* She willed it. This time, the shadows twined around her and Jason. The cold bit at her as the outside world became a silent film and she heard the whispering of whatever entities existed in that shadow land. It was only the second time she'd drawn the darkness around herself and another—she'd done it, unknowingly, with Tyrone, back at the museum gala.

Jason swore. Even profanity sounded pretty with his London accent.

He dropped from the wall and Evie fell with him. They tumbled until she was on top. As the Batavi broke through the hedges, she continued to will the invisibility over them. Jason was silent, his gaze locked on hers.

"Where'd he go?"

"He was *right there!*"

"Did he get into the house? Shit, check with the boss." The three guards walked past Evie and Jason lying in the grass.

When they were gone, Evie, burningly aware of her slight curves fitting against Jason's sinewy angles, rolled off him. She hissed as she let the veil fall away, "What are you doing here?"

He stood. He wore a black suit and tie, a metal mask shoved up into his hair. She noticed a device in his left ear and a small pair of binoculars peeking from one pocket. He was doing some sort of goddamn *surveillance.* He glanced around. His hair wasn't even mussed. "You can be invisible? Well, isn't that something? Come with me. I need to show you—"

"Look." She ignored his offered hand and rose, stumbling a little, exhausted. "I should just leave you to try and climb over that wall—" Then she remembered him vanishing into a silver pentacle. "Oh. Right. Your goddamn pentacle magic act."

"I did have to climb over that wall—I did the trick farther away, just in case they could sense it somehow." He leaned to whisper in her ear. "I need you to come with me."

How did he make that sound . . . carnal? She grabbed his hand. "Come on."

"Wrong direction," he told her as she led him back toward the castle. The garden around them rustled as if sensing her fear. Palm fronds swayed. All the vegetation seemed spiky but smelled heavenly. They slinked through columns of tamarisk and cypress.

"I'm getting you through the front door and out. You're leaving." She gripped his hand and felt the shadows return, writhing around them with the whispering. Jason, unfazed, looked at her as the world around them became black and white.

"Our tricks don't work inside the castle," he warned her.

"We'll see." She was stressed and angry as they strode quickly through the quiet garden. "Is this Silence and Night's home?"

"No. It's their showpiece. Their lair. The place where they can be Father and Mother. They have separate homes elsewhere."

"Where?" She turned on him.

"I'd like to find out."

"What are their real names?" She glanced over one shoulder to make sure the guards weren't around.

"Let me show you what they really are, and I'll tell you."

She almost fell for it. She laughed sharply. "I've already seen what they are."

"This evening." He spoke in a low voice. "Was someone exiled? The poor bastard won't even make it past the gates. Let me show you where he ended up."

A cold sensation eeled through Evie's belly. "No. You know, if I let go of your hand, you're screwed, right? They'll see you. Don't annoy me." Her heart was galloping as they breezed past security at the door. She was freezing and the veil was beginning to feel gelid. She caught an elongated shadow out of the corner of her eye, writhing around Jason's torso.

They stepped into a hall that seemed to have become a thoroughfare for the slinky and feral denizens of the Palm and the Lotus. *Don't see us. Don't see us.* Evie kept the veil around herself and Jason. He said, with wonder in his voice, "How the hell are you doing it in here?"

"*Shh.*"

Unseen, Evie and Jason wove toward the stair leading toward the main foyer and the doors to the outside. Her hand was sweaty in his grip. She kept her attention on their destination. She needed to get him to the door. When they were alone between a pair of pillars, she whispered, "What did you want to show me?"

"Where the bodies are buried."

"Stop it." She turned, squinting at him as if trying to draw the information out of his skull. "Nothing you show me will convince me to leave them."

"Evie. They might promise you a season in the sunlight, but you'll always belong to the dark."

"How poetic." She tightened her hand around his. But his fingers, laced with hers, prevented her grip from becoming too painful. She continued, "I don't want to have this conversation with you again."

"I know all their stories, Evie. Those broken pasts are what make them so dangerous." The warning in his voice was beginning to make her afraid. And that made her angry.

"You know who's dangerous, Jason? *You.* You have a vendetta against them, and it isn't going to end well. I know you left after Vero was killed."

"Vero and I were friends. Before we joined La Fable Sombre." He was studying her carefully.

"Oh, I think you were more than friends."

"We attended the same schools. We were neighbors sometimes. We practically grew up together. Then we met Mad and—"

"And Ciaran." Evie understood what had drawn them to Ciaran, that mutual love of the thrill, the glamour, the peril.

"Mad wasn't with him then. She was living out of her car in LA. She and Vero became friends. Then *I* met Mad." His mouth curved a little.

Mad and Jason. Evie sighed. She hadn't seen *that* one coming.

Jason continued, "Mad became Ciaran's right-hand woman. And Vero's talent—she could locate objects—was valuable. I knew I lost her the moment she and Ciaran met. She was my first love, Evie. And she died in my arms with every bone in her body broken."

Evie felt cold against the back of her neck, as if a specter had breathed on her. "Is that what this is? You couldn't save Vero or Mad from a life of crime, so you're trying to save me?"

He stepped back, that brief bleed of passion gone. "The price for being one of them isn't worth it. Vero didn't have a chance to realize that. You do."

He was warning her to get out before it was too late, before she learned where the bodies were buried and became complicit in more than theft. He thought she still had a choice.

"You don't get to lecture me, Ra. You had a mom and dad? A family legacy? An education that I'm guessing you just blew off when La Fable Sombre recruited you. You don't know me."

He gently asked, "Is this enough, Evie?"

"This? This is one of the few highlights in a life where I've been trying not to *drown*." She was shocked at the bitter fury that made her words taste like poison.

He watched her. Then he said something that took all the light from her world: "What happened to you?"

She almost let go of his hand.

"Evie," he continued. "Whatever happened . . . that's *how it got into you*. Let me help you. This isn't the way . . ."

She turned from him. Her own shadow curved on the floor, her hair writhing in a breeze from the doors that had opened— she hoped no one noticed the shadow. Then his words sank in. "What do you mean?"

Queenie and Dev appeared. Jason's fingers clenched tightly around Evie's. She kept the veil close around them. As the pair strode past, Queenie's gown drifting over Evie's leg, Evie breathed out. Neither Queenie nor Dev turned. Evie and Jason continued swiftly toward the doors—

A pair of guys in snakeskin suits strode in and barreled right into Evie and Jason, breaking their grip. Breaking Evie's willpower. The veil of unseen parted in tatters from Evie and Jason.

"Hey, lookit where you're going," one of the guys snarled at Jason.

Heads turned.

Evie spun, curving one arm around Jason's neck, shoving him back toward the doors. She tugged his head down, whispered, "Play drunk."

He staggered in a perfect imitation of being wasted. They stumbled out the doors, clinging. His lips settled against her throat. She kept her arms looped around his neck, one hand in his hair. He was so warm . . .

Outside, they fell apart, both breathing quickly, their gazes clashing.

She dangled a set of car keys she'd lifted from the jerk who'd bumped into them. She smacked them against Jason's chest. He caught them. She said, "There can't be that many Porsches out there. Good luck. Get lost." She whirled away.

"Evie . . ." He palmed the keys and said, "I'm going to end Silence and Night."

"Don't get in my way, Ra." She stalked back toward the entrance, felt his gaze burning the back of her neck.

Inside, she tried to make herself invisible again, which, according to Ciaran and Jason Ra, she shouldn't be able to do within these warded walls.

And she couldn't. This time, the power, when she attempted to draw it around herself, waxed and waned. All she summoned was a ribbon of darkness that curled around one wrist and faded. Shaken, she hurried back through the castle.

In the upstairs hall, she flinched when a window opened and Mad slid through, lithe as a supernatural ballerina in her pink tulle gown.

"Hey." Mad tugged the tulle as it caught on a nail.

"I thought we couldn't use our magic tricks here?" Evie demanded.

"I *climbed* down to this balcony to *find* you." Mad fixed Evie with a severe look. Her lupine gaze, which sometimes reminded Evie of those paintings of fierce madwomen from the turn of the century, was relentless. "I was on the roof. I *saw* you with the Boy Detective."

"Security was going to shoot him." Evie was so tired. But Mad coming to find her made her feel LFS wanted her as much as she wanted them. The fatigue faded.

Mad looked solemn. "You can't let Jason Ra sweep you off your feet. Don't trust him."

"Of course not. Why would I? Don't tell the others. Are you going to tell the others?"

Mad looked as if she were seriously debating it. She shook her head. "No. He's prowling around you because you're the new girl, the ingenue gone femme fatale."

"Mad. I'm not a sap." Evie began walking. Her nerves were shot. She wanted to soak in a hot bath to get the shadow chill from her skin. "And when are you guys going to teach me how to do a heist?"

"Oh, Evie, I thought you'd never ask."

CHAPTER NINE

The Nightclub

This is going to be a practice run," Mad told Evie as they strolled down a Los Angeles street spattered with neon and pulsing with music. A group of glitterati spilled out of a night-club, calling out. One of them made a suggestive gesture to Mad, who flipped him the bird.

"And it's not dangerous?" Evie was wary.

"No. The club's owned by one of Ciaran's acquaintances."

Acquaintances. Evie noted the word choice.

With the swagger of a street criminal, a gang leader, a demon-souled charmer, Mad led Evie toward the nightclub. The big woman in a tracksuit guarding the door didn't even ask questions. She let them enter a swanky blue and black interior crowded with people who looked as if daylight would char them.

"What is this place?" Evie yelled above the pulsing Goth music as they approached the bar.

"It's a thieves' den, can't you tell?" Ciaran leaned against the mahogany bar. Red light edged his cheekbones, his dark sweep of hair, made his eyes black.

"Are we starting yet?" Queenie appeared in a silver cocktail dress, a necklace of tiny vials in whorls of silver around her throat.

Dev moved to her side and handed Ciaran a shot of vodka. He clinked his glass against Ciaran's. Ciaran lifted a forefinger and three more shots appeared on the bar.

"Pretend to drink up, Queens." Dev nudged Queenie. He eyed Evie. A diamond stud glittered in the left side of his nose. "You too, rogue element. Keep up appearances."

Evie raised her glass to her lips and faked a sip.

Ciaran tapped his ear, then his tie pin, where he had the earpiece and the mic—they each had communication devices fashioned into jewelry. Evie's was a small diamond snake that curved around her right ear, the mic in a matching bracelet. "Remember what we discussed. You saw the club's layout. You know the exits. Now we separate."

"Wait." Evie impulsively asked, "What's the best thing each of you has ever stolen?"

Ciaran tilted his head and decided to play along. "A girl's heart."

"And when was this?" Dev was fascinated. Ciaran just winked at him. Evie, also intrigued, wondered again who Ciaran had been before La Fable Sombre.

"My best purloined object . . ." Queenie considered her felonies. "A codex that belonged to Cleopatra the alchemist."

"Oh." Evie looked at her, impressed.

"Mine was a collection of Golliwog dolls from some rich wanker's house." Dev smiled dreamily. "They made such a lovely bonfire."

"I like that. And you?" Evie turned to Mad.

Mad answered softly, "Someone else's life."

Evie stared at her as Queenie said, "You're really going to have to explain that."

Mad shrugged, lowering her eyelashes. "I'd rather not."

Evie caught Ciaran's warning side-eye in Mad's direction.

"On that note," Dev indicated a jukebox in the corner. "Shall we begin?"

He and Evie drifted to stand beside the jukebox. The goal was simple—get money out of the club's safe. Evie was electric with nervous energy. And this was just a practice, wasn't it?

Mad threaded through the shady patrons, drawing gazes in her rose satin slip-dress. Her pink-dyed hair was twisted up with little diamond owls that also graced her collarbones. *Mad will be the Eye,* Ciaran's voice returned to Evie from earlier in the day. *The Eye watches for complications and trouble.*

Evie glanced toward Ciaran and Queenie, who remained at the bar. They began a sexy little argument.

Then there's the Flaunt, the decoy, the distraction. That'll be me and Queenie.

Dev asked, "You all right?"

No one had asked Evie that since she'd joined LFS. She blinked, glad she was wearing waterproof mascara. "Why do you ask?"

"It can be a bit overwhelming. Before I joined LFS, my biggest concern was that I'd fallen in love with a purple-haired cocktail waitress at a nightclub."

"What was her name?"

"Roxy. When that guy"—he jerked his chin at Ciaran—"convinced me to join LFS, I gave her a sapphire bracelet that had belonged to Lana Turner. She pawned it."

"Were you heartbroken?" Evie leaned against the jukebox.

Dev tapped a tigereye gem pinned to his tie. "Fell in love with another girl, who gave me this. Then stole all my cash. She said the pin belonged to a Roman soldier who used to take the tigereye into battle. It's probably worth all the cash she took."

"Who was the girl?" Evie asked, amused. She surveyed the club, remembering the first LFS rule: *Always be aware of your surroundings, the people near you.*

Dev sobered. "Vero."

"Oh." Evie's heart twisted. "Dev."

"She was a femme fatale disguised as the girl next door." He cast her a sidelong look. "You remind me of her."

Ciaran and Queenie had attracted a knot of menacing young sophisticates—Evie suspected revolvers in holsters beneath the boys' blazers and knives in the girls' garters.

Second rule: *Always know your opponents—these will be security guards. The mark. Sometimes, other thieves.*

Queenie struck Ciaran in the chest. He grabbed her wrist and yanked her to him. She twisted free and punched him in the jaw. There were whoops of approval.

Dev reached for Evie's hand. They moved into a gloomy hall. Dev said, "Do it now, Eves. You've got to be able to call it to you."

You and Dev will be the Strikers. It's up to you, blackbird, to make you and our lock charmer invisible.

She'd done it with Tyrone. With Jason. When they'd been in danger. Now, in this dingy hall reeking of spilled alcohol, with Dev's warm hand in hers . . . she didn't feel that spark of fear and panic that had changed her when LFS had come into her life, only a vague, fading sensation—

She heard a hissing sound, an eerie rustling, the drip of water. She pictured the darkness oozing from her fingertips, her lips, her pores, becoming a cold veil. Dev's grip around her hand tightened. She heard him swear.

Her eyes flew open.

She and Dev were swathed in shadows, the world mute, black and white beyond them. The eerie voices swooped closer.

"Oh, Eves," Dev whispered. "We're invisible."

"Hurry." Evie pulled him down the hall, toward the office and its locked metal door.

Dev set one hand on the pin-code lock, still clasping Evie's hand with the other. He bent his head and whispered to it in a tone that would've made Evie blush if she weren't on the verge of laughter.

The lock clicked. Dev smiled wickedly and pushed open the door. They slid in—

Third LFS rule: *Always expect the unexpected.*

The big striped cat leashed on a chain near the desk was something Evie didn't believe in, at first. Until the tiger moved from its supine position, its growling purr making the air vibrate. Evie, meeting its ruthless, golden gaze, was paralyzed. Its feral odor made her dizzy, even as she noticed its patchy orange fur and loose skin. She was very aware of teeth and claws.

"Hey." Dev's voice made Evie flinch. Not letting go of her hand, he took a step forward. He faced the tiger, safely out of range. "Hey, bruv, we're here to help. Evie, can you reach the safe? Behind that lovely painting of the naked girl?"

"Yes," Evie breathed, realizing the tiger couldn't see them, only scent them. Still gripping Dev's hand, she leaned on her toes toward the painting of some reclining goddess and lifted it. "Got it."

"We're gonna have to do this the old-fashioned way. Do as I say—turn the combo lock counterclockwise. Listen for a click. Good. Now, the other way."

Evie did as instructed. The safe finally opened. She stared at piles of gold jewelry. "It's not money. This isn't one of Ciaran's acquaintances, is it?"

"Just toss it into the satchel and let's go."

The tiger growled again as they backed out. Evie glimpsed a desperation in the animal's eyes that made her want to free it. She had once felt that way.

As they returned to the club, she let the veil fall from her and Dev. The loud, neon-splashed world returned. Evie reported into her mic. "Done."

Fourth LFS rule: *Always know where the other members of your crew are.*

"The Eye is shut." Mad.

"The Flaunt is finished." Ciaran's voice. "One more thing—go to the roof, blackbird. Stairs are to your left."

Evie exchanged a concerned look with Dev, who raised his eyebrows. He said, "Go on. I'm making a call to animal control and then a healthy donation to the local exotic animal shelter."

Evie wove through the club, toward the stairs. She ran up, past graffiti-scrawled walls. She pushed open a door and stepped into a room, where several men in suits stood around a table stacked with money and suspicious-looking plastic-wrapped blocks. They all looked at her.

Fifth LFS rule: *Don't trust anyone.*

"Hey!" one of them barked.

Evie backed away, feeling the darkness begin to swirl around her.

Then Mad descended from the shadowy ceiling. As two of the gangsters moved toward Evie, Mad kicked one of them in the head. He went down.

Dev and Ciaran surged past Evie, toward the men approaching. Mad landed, grabbed a tray of drinks on the table, and smashed it into another man's face. She said into her mic, "We're not going to teach you martial arts, Eves."

Then there's Tooth and Claw. If things get dicey, they're the muscle.

Ciaran dodged a fist. Dev spun with a laugh and kicked another man in the stomach. Mad somersaulted in the air and struck another man in the chest with one foot, told Evie, "We're going to teach you how to fight dirty."

As one of the thugs ran at Evie, she drew the invisibility around herself. He yelled in surprise, looking around. Evie circled him, found herself at the glass doors. She shoved them open to reveal a balcony overlooking the street three stories below. She glanced back in time to see Queenie step into the room from the hallway. Queenie unhooked the necklace of tiny vials from around her throat, yelled, "Get out!"

Dev and Ciaran backed toward Queenie as Mad glided in Evie's direction.

Queenie flung the necklace. The vials broke as they struck

the floor. The gangsters shouted as pink mist curdled. Queenie, Dev, and Ciaran dashed into the hall, slamming the door behind them.

On the opposite side of the room chaotic with swearing and clouds of rosy smoke, Mad alighted on the balcony railing. She grinned at Evie with the night sky behind her. She held out a hand, the knuckles bleeding. "Don't worry. I've practiced. I can levitate someone else."

"I can't." Evie shook her head.

"Eves. Come on."

Sixth LFS rule: *Always have an escape route.*

Evie drew in a breath, gripped Mad's hand, and clambered up to stand on the balcony railing beside her. Mad grinned. She began to rise from the balcony. Looking down, Evie saw the railing beneath her feet receding. She tilted in the air, almost screamed, straightened.

"Toes pointed downward, Evie," Mad instructed. "It's easier to balance that way.

Evie, expecting to plummet to her death at any moment, clenched her teeth and pointed her toes. It did settle her balance. She dared to look down again, glimpsed Ciaran, Queenie, and Dev running from the club, Dev pausing to kiss the hand of a purple-haired girl.

Evie laughed in delighted awe as, unfettered by gravity, she rose with Mad into the air, Los Angeles glowing below. Mad said, "Now, you're ready."

Seventh LFS rule: *Always trust your crew.*

PART II

La Vie de Voleur

CHAPTER TEN

Black Fox House

Evie stepped with La Fable Sombre through a Door, shuddered as that jellyfish darkness drifted over her, the crossing similar to being submerged in an ocean of shadows, a small terror. Her breath misted. Then . . .

The city of Marseille appeared in a rectangle. She saw the sunlit, yet dingy, primary colors, the glisten of a jade ocean. She stumbled a little on the cobblestones. As a blue door shut behind her, air scented with the tang of brine and gasoline swept over her. She sighed in wonder.

They stood on a steep street with a view of the port below. Everything seemed at once dream-hazy and sharp as razors. She began to feel a buzzy disorientation. Perhaps the more one moved through Ciaran's Doors, the more adverse the effects became. Did their bodies dematerialize when they traveled? Did their atomic structure come apart? Or were they just spirited through some supernatural shortcut? She thought of the brutal cold and the darkness that surrounded her when she became invisible, that black grassland she sometimes glimpsed.

"This." Dev gripped the railing and surveyed the tarnished beauty of their surroundings, genuinely enchanted. "I'm never leaving. My gran taught me Senegalese French. I could live here."

"Without us?" Mad laid an arm on one of his shoulders. "You'd languish."

Ciaran led them down a series of winding streets, past cafés, parked bicycles, florists, thrift shops. Evie loved the names of the streets and the shops: Rue d'Aubagne, Maison Empereur. Most of the graffiti was primal and gorgeous. On one cracked wall, a girl embraced an old-fashioned scuba diver. A three-eyed crimson goddess danced on the side of a discotheque.

They reached a street of stone houses. Ciaran set a hand on the gate of a courtyard clustered with flowers. A pewter plaque read Maison de Renard Noir. "Black Fox House. Our temporary headquarters."

As they stepped in, Queenie batted at shrubbery; Dev plucked a rose and tucked it behind one ear. Evie studied the ancient house. Its roofs were terra-cotta, its windows Romanesque, its pale stone walls tinted green with age and moss. A stone arch hewn into the forms of two foxes surrounded the crimson door.

"It looks as though it'll fall on our heads," Dev commented.

"Stop your bitching. It's lovely." Mad gazed at Black Fox House with adoration.

The interior was dusty, cluttered with antiques and old paintings. As they followed Ciaran down a gloomy hall, Queenie asked, "Were all the nice hotels booked? This place looks like it belonged to Dracula's grandmother."

"This isn't our floor." Ciaran led them up a grand staircase, a window of topaz glass casting his shadow into a writhing shape.

"I think it's haunted," Queenie declared.

"You think every place is haunted," Dev said fondly.

"Damn." Mad halted at the top of the stair. Evie moved past her, breathed out.

Before them was a lavish apartment, all silver wallpaper and stylish furniture, a kitchenette red as apples. Black marble ladies curved around doorways. The tall windows revealed a sweeping view of the city and the sea. There was an upper terrace with a pool.

"That"—Ciaran shed his coat, walking toward the glass doors—"is a right proper glory."

"We score the awesome accommodations," Mad told Evie. "Other crews get chain hotels. And we always take a little vacation on our second job."

"It's unfair." Queenie wandered. "The other crews have skills . . . scuba, tech, swindling . . . we're cheating. Not that I feel bad about it, because I don't."

"Does a witch own this house?" Dev poked at a skull on the fireplace. It was a real skull, painted with roses.

"Perhaps. The bedrooms are on the third floor." Ciaran sauntered toward a pair of ebony doors, opened them. "The master suite is mine." He grinned as he stepped in, closing the doors behind him. Mad threw a cushion at them.

Evie wandered up the stairs. She peered into bedrooms

decorated in different colors: mustard, forest green, robin's egg blue. She stepped into a pink room, heard a sound, almost like the flutter of wings. She turned, startled, and stared at a painting of a half owl, half girl.

Mad leaned in the doorframe. "Tonight, I'm going skylarking. I need to get a gift for a friend. Don't worry."

"See. When you tell me not to worry, I worry."

Mad grinned. "You want this room?"

"No. You take it." Evie hesitated. "Can I go with you?"

"If you want. Now, shoo, I need to nap."

Evie walked to a purple room and tossed her backpack onto the bed. She went downstairs, pushed open the doors to the courtyard, which looked so pretty in the rose-gold glow of sunset. A wild garden trailed down to a pebbly beach shrouded by willow trees. The water glistened and hissed against the shore.

She walked down the path to where Dev sat at a little table with a pot of tea and a game of chess on a portable board. "Evie." He gestured to the other chair. "Like a cuppa? Queenie makes great tea, black licorice and Sambuca. She's not just a chemist of distraction and death."

Evie sat and poured herself a cup. "What's with the chessboard?"

"Queenie usually plays with me, but sometimes I'm solitary. Don't make the obvious naughty joke."

"I know how to play chess."

"Want to wager some cash?" He wiggled his eyebrows.

"No." She studied the board. Her foster mom, the Roller Derby queen, had taught her chess, how to decoy, deflect, and desperado. She lifted her teacup and sipped. She moved her knight as a wind tore through the courtyard, whipping pieces of foliage and flower petals around them, stinging Evie's skin. "How long have you known Ciaran, Dev?"

"If you're fishing for info, luv, you'll need to pour me more tea." He tilted his head. Behind him, the sunset rivaled his ruby buzz cut.

"Can't you pour it yourself?" She lifted the teapot, tipping the tea into his cup.

"It's the symbolism of the thing. Also, if anyone asks, I can say you sweetened me up and took advantage. Ciar found me as I was about to get stomped for breaking into a shop—well, for charming the lock off a shop door and entering to borrow a few things."

"So, you've been with him the longest?"

"Not me. There was someone else . . ." His face shadowed. "I'm his second lieutenant. Queenie's his advisor. Mad's his right-hand woman. Vero was with them when I joined. Queenie came after. Ciar and I bonded over Manchester United. Mad and I clicked over silent films and cocktails. Queens and I love fashion and being clever." He watched her over his teacup. "You still rattled about Pearce's poisoning?"

"A vendetta. It's just . . . vigilantism. It's a slippery slope. But I get it."

"Now, see, you're rationalizing the murder." He paused and pain flickered across his face. "But Vero's death . . . we were devastated. We've been a bit harum-scarum lately. Reckless, you know. You strike me, Evie, as the type who doesn't want to live fast and die young."

"I don't plan on dying." She moved her knight.

"I don't plan on dying either. I want to live here on a vineyard with a sassy French girl or boy who likes to read and get fat on wine and pastries."

Evie set her chin on her upraised palms and studied Dev. She was suddenly scared for him, for all of them, because of what they were and how impossible all this seemed, as if they were breaking some divine rule and would be punished for it. She asked the question that had been on her mind since they'd left Marrakesh: "What's in that vault Silence and Night showed me?"

"Can't tell you because Silence and Night can't get in the vault. Yeah. They had me attempt it, and I couldn't. The thing must be made of a dead metal. I got no sense from it, like I do with other stones or metals. They even tried explosives. Nothing."

They can't get in the vault. "Okay. So, if they're the Mother and the Father, didn't the previous bosses give them a key? The Dolls?"

"Those two ladies committed murder-suicide. No one knows where they put the key."

Evie set down her tea. The coincidence was disturbing. Her parents. Jason's dad . . . all deaths involving suicides . . .

"The Dolls had a tempestuous relationship, apparently." Dev sipped his tea. "Silence and Night get on well enough. I don't see domestic bliss between them—doing laundry, going to the grocer's—imagine someone cutting them off in the supermarket parking lot? Can you picture them sneaking away from the kids for a sexy night out together—"

"Kids?" The world tilted a little. She forgot to strategize her game.

"Rumor has it. *Now* visualize having Silence and Night as your mummy and daddy. Tucking you into bed. Scolding you about exams—"

"Stop," Evie whispered. "I can't believe they have children."

"Why not?" Dev watched her. "They're not going to tell us, a gang of supernatural misfits with sociopathic tendencies, about their private lives."

That sparked a smile from her. "I think of us as supernaturally blessed adrenaline junkies."

"That's more like it." He grinned.

She asked, "Are you scared of Silence and Night?"

He leaned slightly forward, slid his bishop into a square. "Silence and Night? They fucking terrify me. But they don't scare our Ciaran."

Evie understood the warning—Ciaran Argent was dangerous.

It reassured her. Because Night and Silence, especially Silence, terrified *her*. She said, "What they can do . . . his shape-shifting or whatever . . . her flying through the air."

"Yeah. Like the witches and warlocks of yore."

Despite the topic, Evie smiled. She had never heard anyone use the word "yore." "So they scare you. But . . ."

Dev sighed through his nose. "Look, they've never threatened us. Scolded us, yeah. They taught us how to survive, had us learn from each other. We didn't figure out how to use our abilities by *them* teaching *us*. They trusted us to learn ourselves. They have faith in us." He paused for a moment. "They don't see us as any race, creed, color, or gender. They had all of us, all the other crews, take classes and get our education. So they brand a traitor or two." His brows knit. "And it's the little bits—Father taking me to my first fancy nightclub. Mother, me, and Queens making midnight omelets. So many little bits, Evie, you haven't seen. But you will. They're completely bewitched by *you*."

Evie thought divine beings or demons wouldn't see any race, creed, color, or gender either—just mortals, ready to be used. "Do *you* trust *them*?"

He was slow to answer, rolling a pawn between his fingers. His eyes beneath the veil of his lashes, appeared to flare gold. He set down the pawn. "I have to."

Evie thought she heard a girl's voice from where the willows and the shale path met the water. The water sound was mysterious. The violet evening dusted with gold made the world ethereal.

Someone was standing in the water beneath the willow's swaying branches. A wind swept the figure's hair into a writhing halo—

"Evie." Dev's voice drew her attention from the shadowy patch of water. "Your move."

She lifted a pawn, the hair on the back of her neck prickling. Out of the corner of her eye, she caught a movement near the willow. The wind that swept over them carried the musky fragrance of mud and wet stone.

—∿—

That evening, Evie went skylarking with Mad.

"There's a fire escape. We're taking the rooftops." Mad disappeared through the window and Evie carefully followed. As she stepped onto creaking metal, she saw Mad clambering upward. Evie climbed after. At the top, Mad held out a hand. Evie gripped it and was pulled up. She turned to admire the night view of terra-cotta roofs and the sea beyond.

"Why not just levitate?" Evie asked.

"Don't be lazy," Mad scolded. "This is practice too."

They had to jump a short distance to the next building. Mad clasped Evie's hand. They leaped. It was terrifying, but, by the third time, Evie was high on adrenaline. They threaded through a rooftop rave, where people danced to witch house music.

The next jump looked to be at least eight feet across. Evie balked. "No."

"Back up. We'll need a running start. Don't let go of my hand."

They ran. As they jumped, Evie, for a giddy moment, again felt suspended in air.

They landed on the terra-cotta tiles, Evie stumbling, Mad graceful as an acrobat.

Mad led her to another fire escape and began climbing down. "We're doing some shopping." She pried open a window, slid in.

Evie jumped down into a bathroom. A pink night-light lit their way into a boutique, where streetlamps cast long shadows across the carpet. Mad began selecting items. She glanced at Evie. "We need to look like we belong at a fancy party."

"You always steal your designer clothes?"

"Not always. Just when it's fun. Do you know how much this one is? Two thousand dollars."

Evie plucked a ball gown of smoky black gossamer from a rack. Mad slinked into a Cinderella gown of white tulle. She shrugged on a pink-and-silver bomber jacket, tossed a similar jacket of black and flame red to Evie.

They returned to the roofs, Mad swift in her ballet flats, Evie in sneakers. Mad caught Evie's hand and led her across an arch of wrought iron connecting an old building to a Gothic mansion. Evie could hear the sounds of a party inside. Light winked off the Ferraris and Cadillacs in the driveway.

"Is this what it'll be like, Mad, when we get to the Church of the Bleeding Saint?"

"Oh no. That's going to be a strategy." Mad moved to a skylight, flipped it open.

Evie crouched on the edge and said, "Look, I understand the money needed for this lavish lifestyle, but do you really need a side hustle? I know that nightclub in LA didn't belong to Ciaran's friend. Why the petty crimes?"

"Eves." Mad looked at her, serious. "We are criminals. It's like that story about the crab and the lizard."

"I'm sorry, what?"

"You know . . . the lizard says he'll carry the crab across the sea and the crab pinches the lizard, and, as they're drowning, the crab says, 'It's just in my nature.'"

"I think that was a scorpion and a frog. So, stealing is just in your nature?"

"I can't help it." Mad slid into the room below. She called up, "Come on."

Evie peered in, saw Mad hanging upside-down from a beam just below the skylight. Evie lowered herself, toes first, onto the beam. She didn't look at the drop to the floor far below.

"Trust me." Mad smiled, radiant. "Take my hands."

Evie crouched, reached for Mad's hands, clasped them. She took a breath and slid from the beam, let herself be lowered until she could jump to the floor. Mad astronaut-somersaulted and landed on her feet.

The room was enormous, with walls of bookshelves at least twelve feet high. Mad walked to a cabinet of drawers and opened several, found what she'd been searching for—a package of white gloves. She tossed a pair to Evie.

"We're looking for a safe. I suspect it's behind some books." Mad switched on a flashlight she took from her backpack. She flung another flashlight to Evie. "The gift I want will be in that safe."

Evie tugged the gloves on and aimed the flashlight at a row of books. As they began to rummage, Evie asked, "When did you know? That you could do the levitating all the time?"

Mad was turned away, tracking her flashlight beam over the shelves. "I didn't do it again until I was in high school. I'd start levitating a few inches whenever. No one noticed. I was with my friends in a band. One night, I was singing, and I began to rise. Like, a *lot*. People noticed. Lost my friends that day. They thought I was a freak."

"We *are* freaks." Evie shrugged.

"No, Evie. We're glorious specimens of evolution."

They spent a few precious moments white-gloving through vintage children's books with quaint titles like *Queen Summer and the Golden Frog* or *Cyrus Rabbit's Carousel*. Evie found herself calmed and delighted by this whimsical theft.

"Found it." Mad aimed her light upward to reveal a small metal door in the wall behind a shelf of children's books. She began to rise in the air. The sight still unnerved Evie, who waited tensely while Mad, leaning close to the safe, turned the combo lock and listened for clicks.

Voices came from beyond the doors, a thread of music. Evie asked, "Mad . . . who are we stealing from?"

"A famous magician who has a lot of magic books. Priest, the man we're getting this for, has the info we need for weird artifacts. He knows stuff." She sighed. "I really want one of those on our team, a book person with arcane knowledge—"

"This Priest knows about the *Bestiarum Vocabulum?*"

"He's gonna tell us what that book is all about. What it can do. Why Mother and Father want it."

Mad opened the safe and sorted through the books inside. She finally withdrew a small crimson volume in a clear plastic envelope and tucked it into her jacket. She hesitated, then grabbed another book, slid that into the other pocket. She descended, toes pointed downward, arms outstretched. Her feet touched the floor.

The door opened and a silver-haired couple stumbled in, arms around one another. Evie began to wish herself invisible, reached for Mad's hand—

Mad stepped to Evie, swept an arm around her, and waltzed with her out of the shadows.

"Oh." The silver-haired woman pulled away from the man, who straightened his suit. "We didn't know anyone—"

"Don't worry about it." Mad dipped Evie, who looked, upside-down, at the couple. She winked.

The couple hustled out, the woman whispering, "Adorable. Kids these days . . . so free . . ."

Laughing, Evie and Mad dashed back to the area beneath the skylight. Mad clasped Evie's hands. Evie closed her eyes and felt the air shift around her, the absence of gravity as her feet left the floor . . .

She opened her eyes in a panic, on the roof beneath the stars.

"Where are we going now?" Evie laughed, breathless. She didn't want this night to end.

"To deliver the book we just stole."

They jumped. They wove through the rooftop rave. When they exited the building, Mad walked over to a pink moped. She swung onto it, scooping up the helmet. Evie accepted a second helmet and got on behind her. "How did you—"

Mad dangled a set of keys. "The girl at the rave in the pink coveralls."

As the moped sped through twisty streets, Mad somehow avoiding vehicular homicide, Evie tilted her head back to gaze at the sky.

They swerved to a stop in front of a stone house on a street called Rue de Verdun. The house's twisty grille of a fence revealed a courtyard with plants in giant urns. As Mad and Evie swung off the bike, the gates opened to reveal a beautiful ebony-skinned man in a dark suit and velvet greatcoat. "Madrigal, *darling*." He strode out and caught her hands in his. "How *are* you? And who is this?"

"I'm dazzling. This is Evie. She's new."

The man extended a hand to Evie. "I'm Priest. It's a pleasure to meet you, Evie."

Evie didn't know whether to shake his hand or kiss it. She

settled for shaking it. His eyes were hazel warm. She said, "You're American."

"Ex-pat. Marseille, this dirty, glorious beauty, is my soul's home. Well, one of many places my soul feels at home. Come in. Come in. I've espresso and pastry."

Evie and Mad followed Priest into a courtyard where urns frothing lavender sent a heady fragrance into the air. Beneath a lemon tree were a café table and chairs. On the table was a tray of pastries, three little espresso cups, and a porcelain carafe.

"How is Ciaran, that wicked boy? Queenie? Dev?" Priest poured espresso into the cups. "All well? All alive?"

Mad bit into a chocolate-filled croissant. "We're invincible."

"You're young. Young people believe such nonsense. You be careful, Madrigal. And Evie, don't let them drag you into anything you don't want to do. Now, did you find my book?"

Mad pushed the crimson book across the table. Priest carefully drew it from the plastic, caressed its discolored red binding, the curving gold sigil on the cover. He opened it, revealing pages inked with symbols and script. He took a jeweler's monocle from his coat and examined the pages.

"What is it?" Mad asked airily.

"A journal of astrological charts and notes by Carl Jung. Not many know the father of psychology was quite the mystic." His cynical expression became one of dreamy satisfaction.

Mad rolled her eyes. She ate another pastry. Evie finished off a small cake of strawberry and marshmallow. The mocha espresso, rich and chocolatey, was perfect.

"That's authentic." Priest repackaged the book, smoothed the envelope as if he wanted to keep touching the book.

Evie boldly asked, "You know what we're here for. Don't you want any of the shipwreck treasure? Are you like Mother Night and Father Silence?"

"Darling, I'm *nothing* like them. I love books. That's what I collect. Not gold ingots and such." He flicked his fingers. "All that gold. You can't sell that nowadays unless you melt it down, and do I look like a blacksmith?" He smiled. "So. John Dee's *Bestiarum Vocabulum*."

Mad took a plastic envelope from her jacket and slid it to Priest. "Here's a picture of the desired object."

"Ah." He withdrew the illustration. "The *Bestiarum Vocabulum*. John Dee's compendium of animals with supernatural connotations. The animals are symbols of spirits that ancient societies worshipped as creator deities. Fascinating stuff. John Dee was Elizabeth the First's astrologer, astronomer, occultist, and alchemist. He had one of the largest libraries in England. A man after my own heart."

"So, he was basically a sorcerer." Evie rested her arms on the table.

"A Collector, as well."

"What can the book do?" Mad demanded.

"It was allegedly written by demons, to call them, to amplify their power. It is listed by Collectors, such as myself, as one of the most dangerous magic books in existence."

Mad tapped a finger against the table. "How does it work?"

"A magic book written by anything otherworldly can be opened by blood. Even a drop. Most books have a lock, but the key can often be an everyday item transformed by proximity to the book, such as a needle or a nail. If the magic book wants to be opened, it can be coaxed to do so. But, as I said, sometimes merely being close to it can have effects."

"Why don't you want it?" Evie was watching Priest and Mad; the man's attitude toward Mad was one of careless affection.

"Oh, I've plenty of books and, honestly, I wouldn't go near this one. I am not fond of magic books—it's like having spiritual plutonium in your possession. Speaking of spirits, Madrigal, did I ever thank you for Houdini's Ouija board?"

"A present from one diva to another. Thank you for the *Metropolis* reel."

"Robot Maria." Priest grinned.

And it dawned on Evie that *Priest* was the man who had taken Mad in as a runaway. He was her former guardian.

"Madrigal. May I advise that you not give that book to Silence and Night?" Priest slipped the envelope back to her.

Mad tilted her head. "You really think we have a choice."

"I understand giving that pair anything they ask for"—Priest shook his head—"is *not* a choice."

Just then, another wind swept through the courtyard, causing orange blossoms to skate across the table. Evie shivered. She felt as if the wind were bringing something with it, a warning breathed upon her skin by some elemental divinity.

"The mistral," Priest told her knowingly. "The wind of misfortune and madness."

"I know," Evie said. "Van Gogh hated it. He called it the devil."

—◈—

When Evie and Mad returned to Black Fox House, they entered the main room to find Ciaran brooding in a wingback chair. He said, "We've a guest."

"Oh, he's unhappy, the prince." Mad strode toward him as Evie lingered near the entrance.

"You weren't supposed to take Evie." Ciaran rose.

"She's one of us," Mad challenged.

"I didn't want him to know about her." Ciaran looked furious for an instant. Mad levitated an inch, toes down like a ballerina. All the doors around them slammed shut. Cold crept through the room.

"It's okay." Evie moved swiftly, placing herself between them, facing Ciaran. "We got the information we needed. Who's the guest?"

Ciaran eased back into his chair. "Mother Night."

Mad shot an alarmed glance over one shoulder at Evie.

"She wants us well-fed for tomorrow evening. She's in there." Ciaran jerked his chin toward the closed doors to the kitchen. "Cooking. With Queenie."

Mad walked to the dining room and flicked on the lights. "The table isn't even set."

Evie flinched as the kitchen door opened and Mother Night, her black hair in plaits and her white Isabel Marant dress protected by an apron, emerged. She swept a cool gaze over Mad and Evie.

"There you are. Set the table *s'il vous plaît*. Ciaran refused to do so." She returned to the kitchen, her stiletto heels clicking. "*Dépêchez-vous!* The bouillabaisse is almost ready."

Mad opened a cabinet and began taking out plates. Evie

moved to help her because disobeying Mother Night seemed something only Ciaran dared. After a moment, Ciaran rose to assist. Meeting Evie's gaze over the crystal, he smiled crookedly. Dev arrived, immaculate in dove gray Valentino, with a massive bouquet of flowers.

La Fable Sombre dined on grilled sardines, oysters, tender squid, and fish smothered in olive oil and garlic. Everyone behaved, with Mother Night at one end of the table and Ciaran at the other. Queenie could have been Mother Night's daughter, she was so poised in the woman's presence. Dev watched Night as if she were a goddess. As Mother Night spoke with Ciaran, Mad sat at Ciaran's right hand, reading the vintage children's book she'd stolen from the collection.

Evie wondered what Mother Night would have done if she knew about Mad visiting Priest. She concentrated on making it through dinner and keeping her wits about her.

Afterward, Mother Night moved to Dev and slid a silver and diamond pin into his tie. "It belonged to Steve McQueen." She gave Queenie a pair of vintage boots that laced to the knee. "They were Amelia Earhart's." She placed a ring of ruby and gold onto one of Ciaran's fingers. "Worn by Lorenzo de' Medici." Mad unwrapped a first edition *Alice's Adventures in Wonderland* and held it, staring at it, her hands trembling slightly.

Mother Night walked to Evie, who didn't move as the woman reached out and gently tucked Evie's hair behind her ears. "I've nothing for you, Evie. I don't know what you want."

"I don't want anything," Evie whispered.

Night stepped back. "Everyone wants something. I *will* find out. *Au revoir,* children. I'll see you at the next Thieves' Night."

After Mother Night had gone, La Fable Sombre rambled into the main room, where they sat on the floor to plot their second heist of the year. Ciaran had spread out the blueprints to the Church of the Bleeding Saint. He moved pieces from Dev's chessboard across the map. He looked at Mad. "Apple of my eye. Comrade in arms. My BFF. Would you explain the semantics to our newcomer Evie?"

"I sure will, you dashing devil."

Dev sighed. "You only called me apple of your eye once."

"Was I drunk at the time?" Ciaran inquired.

"I believe you were."

"Enough flirting. Someone explain it to me." Evie was fed up with their Mad Hatter repartee.

Mad threw back her shoulders. She sat on the floor, hands in her lap. She moved the chess pieces, the black queen and the black knight. "Ciar and Queenie will be the Flaunt, posing as a passionate couple—they fake it so well—who want to be married at the church. I'm gonna be the Eye again, to make sure no one else shows up. You and Dev will be the Strikers. While everyone in the church is distracted by Ciaran and Queenie's drama, you and Dev will be on the move."

"Who's Tooth and Claw?" The brawl at the LA nightclub had been a lesson in fighting, but Ciaran and Mad had also recently shown Evie some self-defense techniques.

Mad exchanged a look with Ciaran. "We shouldn't need Tooth and Claw."

Evie doubted it would be so easy. She stared at the map to the church crypt. "I can only invisible one person at a time. So *only* Dev."

"It's uncanny. What Evie does." Dev stretched his arms over his head.

Ciaran watched Evie. "We need to get in and out, fast and quiet. No mayhem. Like Mad said, there shouldn't be any need for Tooth and Claw, but . . ."

"Always expected the unexpected," Evie finished.

"Always know your opponents." Queenie tapped the blueprints. "Some church staff. No problem. But what if the Sirens are guarding it?"

"We can fight the Sirens." Dev looked regretful.

"I don't want to fight Circe," Mad said fiercely. "So we've got to stick to the invisible plan. You are the star of the show, Eves."

That statement should have made Evie nervous, but warmth blossomed through her, softening her heart. "Why can't we just Door into the church? We have photos for Ciaran to visualize with."

"I try not to use the magic doors with places I haven't been," Ciaran explained. "Photos aren't always accurate."

"The skyscraper incident," Dev recollected.

"You're telling me about that later," Evie demanded. She looked at Mad. "So, how do we get in?"

"We arrive in three separate cars. Queenie and Ciar will get there first, as the bride- and groom-to-be. I'll be a tourist, but I'll get to the roof my way, maybe even be mistaken for an angel. That leaves you, Evie, and Dev to enter through the cemetery as the sun is setting. There's a back door." Mad set a finger on the church blueprint. "That hall leads to the crypt." She drew from beneath the map a brochure for the church. "See? They even have pictures because they give tours. You see that symbol?"

Queenie said, "That's where the crypt will be. It supposedly holds a dead saint or whatever who turned part of a sea into blood. I get now why the Sirens chose the place."

"I can get us in. Stone loves me." Dev's relationship with the world of inanimate objects was a source of fascination for Evie.

Ciaran continued, "We all meet in the church, abandon our rental cars. I open a Door back to the place we'll be staying in Marseille. We never Door directly back to our lair. Just in case."

"And all this time, me and Dev stay invisible?" Evie didn't know if she could hold the veil over herself and another for more than a few minutes.

"Only until you get into the crypt," Ciaran told her. "Now, in the event the Sirens do have sentinels . . . Queenie's got a distraction for that." He grinned. "Don't you, wifey?"

"So, why don't we sneak into the church at night?" Evie asked.

Dev replied, "At night, it might be more heavily guarded. Daytime, all we've got to worry about are a few priests and the church staff."

Queenie flexed her hands. "I've got something I've been working on." She drew a perfume vial from one pocket. "It's a subtle version of the idioblast—that's when a plant fires barbed calcium oxalate crystals into the mouths of predators. This stuff will work on people. It'll stun them for quite a while. I made it with plant phenolics and a Wish of subjugation."

"Queens." Dev's smile was fragile. "Who was the guinea pig for that nightmare concoction you just described?"

Queenie smiled sweetly back. "A pair of assholes at a bar."

"Ohh." Mad nodded. "I remember those guys. I was

wondering why they just stood there, drooling, for, like, ten minutes."

"What was the one you used at the LA heist?" Evie asked, intrigued by Queenie's Poison Ivy chemistry.

"A hallucinogen. That was called White Rabbit."

"You're a marvel," Dev said dreamily.

"I still have that tie you gave me, the one made of spider silk." Ciaran lounged against the sofa. "Remember Monte Carlo, when we had to make a hasty exit out a window? A handy piece of rope that tie was."

"Was that just practice for the craziness in Dubai?" Queenie stretched her legs. "That princess wanted us dead. You're lucky my grandparents let us hide out with them for a while afterward."

Mad laughed. "Your grandfolks were fabulous. It was like staying in a log cabin with Patti Smith and Iggy Pop."

"They *were* in a punk rock band when they were teens," Queenie admitted.

Dev grinned. "That Dubai princess wasn't nearly as wicked as that freaky family in Scotland. They were so *pale*. Red lips and black clothes, nesting in that decaying mansion. What was the thing with that tear-catcher bottle Silence and Night wanted?"

"Priest told me it was a haunted bottle." Mad stretched her arms over her head. "I'm really surprised that mansion burned so quick."

Evie listened, wide-eyed, to this history.

Dev folded his arms on his updrawn knees. "My favorite stunt was when you and Vero roller-skated through that auction in Crete and grabbed that statue."

"Remember when Vero and Jase pretended to be royalty in

Monte Carlo?" Mad laughed. "While me and Ciar searched all those rooms looking for that magic zodiac device?"

"You robbed those guests, I recollect." Ciaran looked at her fondly.

"We deserved a tip for all the trouble we went through. And they were *awful*."

Queenie looked at Evie. "The tail end of their first year was when Ciaran found me. Can you believe they've been together for nine jobs?"

Yes. Evie thought, glancing around at each of them. She could believe it. She settled back, listening to La Fable Sombre laugh and swear as they reminisced. As they talked deep into the night, she fought to remain awake, not wanting to miss one bit of information.

———∿∿∿———

She opened her eyes and sucked in a breath as if emerging from the depths. She lay on the red velvet loveseat with a ceiling of swirling plaster above. Dazzling sunlight made her raise an arm over her eyes.

"Evie." The voice was like a riptide, dragging her head around. Ciaran sat in a chair nearby. He looked amused and relaxed. His feet were bare. His shirt was unbuttoned, and the glimpse of his skin made the moment awkwardly intimate.

"What're you doing?" she asked drowsily. "Watching me sleep?"

"Mad's in the kitchen making you breakfast, and she'd hit me with a frying pan if she thought I was watching you sleep. You're a very boring sleeper. Although your snoring was more melodic than Dev's singing last night. Sinatra was probably turning in his grave."

Evie squirmed up beneath a lovely cashmere blanket. Ciaran leaned over and handed her a glass of something that tasted like a blast of pure citrus, that instantly quenched her dry mouth. She figured she must look like a trashed doll, with her eyeliner smeared and her hair in sleep snarls. "What time is it?"

He checked his watch. "Almost two o'clock." He smiled at her. "Time to go to church."

CHAPTER ELEVEN

Hallowed Ground

Evie, seated next to Dev as he drove, decided to pretend she was in an Audrey Hepburn film that happened to involve a risky heist. He glanced at her—she wondered if he was worried because she was the linchpin of this strike. In a black turtleneck, denim capris, and sneakers, she felt like a teenager on a French vacation, not a girl who could become very dangerous because she could convince people she wasn't there. Queenie's gifted gloves were tucked into a pocket.

The road curved into a not-so-nice part of Marseille, where graffiti daubed decrepit buildings. Dev parked in a weedy lot and leaned a tattooed arm on the windowsill. "I looked up the history of this church. *L'eglise de Saint Saignant.* It's not pretty."

"Do tell." Evie was frowning down at Dev's burner phone, waiting for the text that would alert them it was safe to approach the church. Ciaran, Queenie, and Mad had already arrived.

"Guillotine executions during the French Revolution.

A sorceress's curse. A kid murdered in medieval times and buried underneath to be a guardian spirit." He tapped his laptop, the battered device from which he could ghost security cameras by proximity alone. "I can trick cameras, but not guardian spirits."

Evie wondered what was waiting for them at the end of this road, in that church.

A text pinged on Dev's phone. She peered at it, read, "*'Ready to charm some locks, scouser?'*"

Dev laughed. "Text Ciar back: 'Deffo, rude boy.'"

"Okay." Evie lifted the phone. "He texted a middle finger emoji."

They got out of the car. Evie tucked the phone into Dev's pocket and told him, "When we get there, you can't let go of my hand. And ignore the weird voices."

Dev handed her an earpiece and a mic. He wore a black sweater, jeans, and Converse. His earpiece was a bronze cuff shaped like a tiger. He grinned. "Except those of our beloved crew, yeah?"

The Church of the Bleeding Saint rose in a forgotten wilderness amidst granite blocks of eighteenth-century apartment buildings. The church, seeming resentful of the rundown neighborhood in which it existed, was a grim structure with Romanesque and Gothic elements, thorny spires and glowering angel statues. The stained stones were furred with bright green moss. Beyond was a graveyard of crumbling mausoleums and statues missing limbs and faces. The pitted parking lot had only three vehicles in it—Ciaran's white roadster, a battered motorcycle, and a tangerine car that probably belonged to a priest or a caretaker.

Evie and Dev slinked through the wooded lot scattered with bottles and fast-food wrappers. As they made their way toward the stone wall around the collection of tombstones, Evie breathed in the scent of clover, and it calmed her nervous euphoria.

Dev halted at the wall. "Wait here," he told her. "I'm scoping it out, making sure Ciar and Queenie's tempestuous wedding is distracting the proper folk. Don't take your eyes off me. As if you could."

"Don't mess up your fancy heist gear."

He flashed a smile and vaulted over the low wall.

She leaned against a tree to watch as he moved through the graveyard, toward the back of the church.

She thought she glimpsed a pale figure amidst the trees. She squinted and peered harder. It couldn't be a child in a nightgown—

She heard Queenie's voice in her earpiece. "Something's wrong. Ciaran's down. Like, he just spit blood. I'm dizzy. The priest, here, looks real confused."

Ciaran's voice was gravelly with pain. "Get it done. Now."

Panic savaged Evie. She raced through the weedy cemetery. Zigzagging through the statues and headstones, she saw that the rear door of the church was open. Glimpsing Dev in a beam of light, she dashed inside—

—and ran into him because he was hunched over, gagging. Vertigo overwhelmed her, followed by a gut-wrenching nausea. She clutched at the wall, the stone cold and unforgiving beneath her fingers.

"Some kind of gas?" Dev straightened, his pupils so dilated his eyes looked black.

Evie clutched his shoulder. "Ciar and Queenie—"

"Can handle themselves. Mad will be there. We need to get moving."

She grabbed his hand and wished *unseen*. Darkness curled around them as the true world withdrew into black and white. Dev's hand tightened painfully in hers. The whispers began.

"Evie." Dev's voice was distorted. "It's cold as *death*. And *what* is that whispering? I didn't hear it before—"

"Don't worry about it," Evie ordered. "Which way?"

Dev unfolded the map to the crypt. His hands shook a little. "This way."

She felt a flash of dizzying heat. The obscuration veil wavered. Dev frowned. "You okay?"

"I . . ." The cold bit into her again as the dark swept back around them. "Yeah."

They descended a stair lit by humming fluorescents, followed the route to the crypt—

Two young men dressed as priests rounded the corner. One had braided hair; the other, tattooed hands. They weren't priests. Evie slammed back against a wall. Dev followed suit.

Don't see me, Evie thought desperately. *Don't see us.*

The two young men passed without a glance at either of them.

"They were Fenrir," Dev whispered to her.

"What are they *doing* here?" She felt the cold and misty darkness fall away and the bright world return. "Dev . . ."

"We're not invisible anymore, are we?"

"Something's *interfering* with us."

They reached the metal door to the crypt, where Dev crouched to examine the lock. As Evie worriedly studied the ghoulish images of dancing skeletons engraved on the door, Dev pressed one palm against the metal. Nothing happened. He tried again, murmuring, coaxing.

"What are you doing?" Evie hissed. "Stop messing around."

"It isn't working." Panic frayed his voice. "This has never happened to me before. It's a basic combo lock."

He sat back on his heels. He set both hands on the lock, bowed his head. Sweat broke out on his face. A smell like molten metal bit the air.

Evie ripped off one of Queenie's gloves, stood on tiptoe to hold the material near a lamp. The glove became rubbery goo. She crammed the goo into the lock. She pulled Dev back from the door.

The green glob expanded, hardened. There was a creaking sound, followed by a loud *crack*.

The metal door swung open, revealing another set of stairs curving downward. Flickering light bulbs mimicked torches. The fragrance of earth and rot drifted up to them. The sight muted Evie's triumph.

"Queens." Dev grinned. "I have *got* to propose to that woman."

Holding hands, they hurried down the stairs. At the bottom, another door waited. Dev had the same problem convincing this lock to click in the right places. As he whispered adoringly, frantically, to it, Evie glanced over one shoulder. Her skin crawled. Her ears were buzzing. "We have got to hurry—something's making me dizzy."

"I don't feel so fine myself."

Evie used the second glove in the same fashion.

The lock burst. The door fell open.

She and Dev stared at the crates of objects piled within—a dragon's hoard of gold and spilled jewels. She felt something primal uncoil within her at the sight of all those gems and precious metals.

"Wait." Dev barred her entry with one arm. "Look at the pattern in the floor."

Evie studied the different-colored stones set into the stone floor, forming a crescent. Dev put one foot on the inset stone. Nothing happened. "Okay." He nodded. "Stick to the yellow stones. Don't step off them."

Mad's voice crackled in Evie's ear. "We've got company."

Dev swore and Evie fought panic. Then, Ciaran's voice came through, hoarse but still commanding: "Find it, blackbird."

They unslung their backpacks and began clawing frenziedly through items. A crown. Necklaces. A dagger. Tiny statues. So many coins . . .

"Ingot?" Dev slid a gold bar into his backpack. He set a silver tiara on Evie's head. She picked up a crucifix blooded with rubies—

And dropped it with a gasp. She stared down at her hand, which felt as if she'd grabbed a metal tray from a hot oven. Dev looked at her. He touched the crucifix. And snatched back his hand. Evie, staring at the burn forming on her skin, whispered, "*What?*"

"Chemicals. Some of the jewels must be doused with chemicals." He took two pairs of leather gloves from one pocket and handed a pair to Evie.

Dev began opening trunks and fancy boxes, using a gold

ingot to break some locks because his charm wasn't working. Evie stood in a stillness of panic. She was the newest. If this strike failed, Silence and Night would blame her, as the weakest metal in the chain.

"What would you do with a magic book?" She spoke as much to herself as to Dev. "If you didn't want anyone to find it?"

Dev ceased his frantic search through the ridiculous hoard. He smiled slowly. "I'd make it so no one would notice it."

"Camouflage." Evie and Dev scrutinized the trunks, the jewelry, the gleaming artifacts. "So look for something roughly the size of that book—"

Mad's voice cut through their earpieces: "It's Fenrir."

"Are they supposed to help us?" Evie asked, and everyone replied, "No."

"Bastards." Dev began flinging jewelry and idols aside. Evie studied the pile, calculating.

"A book. A book shape. Not to be noticed. Something an Elizabethan gentleman would carry with him on a trip. Something that would be considered lavish, but practical."

"Ah, hell, Evie—"

He spied it the same time she did.

They both lunged for the gold and onyx chess set, a box that could unfold to reveal the pieces. It was locked.

"Open it, Dev. Whatever's messing with our abilities here . . . you've got to get past it."

She held the chess case as he gazed at the lock. Then he closed his eyes. He pressed two fingers to his lips, opened his eyes, and placed those fingers on the lock, his brows drawing together. His eyes became golden.

The lock clicked. Evie unfolded the case that was also a board, revealing golden chess figures in a drawer, and beneath . . . Dev lifted out the *Bestiarum Vocabulum*. The book was the size of a journal, sealed with bands of black lead. Evie could see that it was packed full of parchment paper. He shoved it into his backpack, muttering. "Doesn't seem like much."

Evie was fighting waves of dizziness and nausea. "Let's get out of here."

"Right. Just be careful not to—"

Evie, forgetting, had backed up, setting one foot on the gray stone, off the pattern of yellow.

There was a click from behind one of the walls. Something rumbled like a dragon waking. Evie's hypervigilance kicked in as Dev yelled, *"Run!"*

The floor cracked up the middle as they raced for the exit.

"Evie!" Dev reached for her. The wall behind him crumbled, revealing a horrifying mosaic of bones and skulls set into small nooks.

The floor gave way. Evie was sucked into darkness.

She hit a surface in a rain of dirt, stone, and other debris. Coughing, she scrambled up, wincing at the abrasions on her knees and the heels of her hands. She fumbled for her cell phone.

"Evie?" Dev's silhouette appeared, kneeling opposite. He lifted his phone on its flashlight setting. They were in a pit, walled in by more bones and skulls, a distant glow above. Dev sat back, his eyes wide. "I can't be in here." He kicked away a skull that had landed near him.

"Dev." Evie could see the panic manifesting in his darting eyes. "It's *okay*."

"No, it's not. We're going to die here . . ." He folded his arms over his head.

"Dev." She was fighting her own terror.

He shuddered. "I was just a kid . . . my widowed mum fell in love with a bastard. When she was on a visit to my gran, he locked me in a closet for three days . . ."

She hunkered before him, gripped his shoulders. "You got free, didn't you? Is that how you found out what you could do?"

He lifted his head. He was breathing too fast, sweat beading his brow. But he flashed a smile. "That's when my imaginary tiger friend showed up. That's when I began charming things." He lifted his phone. "My mobile's got no reception, and I think my mic's broken."

"Same." She examined the gruesome walls of the crypt as uneasiness crept over her. She studied some of the nooks, thought of handholds. "We're going to have to climb." She turned to him. "Didn't you and Ciaran scale a very tall building in Dubai?"

"That was Ciar and Mad." But Dev pushed to his feet, small bones crunching beneath his boots.

Their first attempts to climb resulted in scrapes and bruises from falling—the ancient bones weren't stable; they broke off or splintered.

Dev turned in place. "This is an oubliette. Where they throw people to *die*—"

"We're not dying." She really needed him to calm down. "When you were trapped in that closet as a kid . . . How did you get out?"

"I coaxed the lock open." He slumped against the wall, his head tilted back, eyes shut. "This is a bit different, luv. It's not a closet. I'm a man for locks and tricks. And, as you've noticed, our tricks aren't working."

Evie turned, staring fiercely at the walls of bones and skulls surrounding them. "You hear that?" It was a whispering, rustling sound, as if a host of phantom dancers were whirling around them.

"Yeah." Dev slid back to his feet, darting his phone's flashlight over the floor, the niches of bones. One of the skulls fell, tumbling across the stone. Evie moved to the skull, saw, beneath the dirt and debris, a pattern on the floor, a mosaic. She brushed dirt away with one foot.

"A pentagram." Dev stared down at it. At least he was engaging and not a nervous wreck.

Evie felt all tingly standing in that pentagram. "You *charmed* that lock to open, right? You used the trick to escape that closet. That's what you do. You persuade objects to help you."

He closed his eyes, breathing slowly. "So I'll just ask these nice bones to help us out?"

"Yes," Evie whispered. "Come stand with me in this symbol."

Dev joined her in the pentagram and began to speak to the dead. "C'mon, luvs. Let's Mickey Mouse this shit." The bones around them rattled. A femur clattered to the floor. A skeletal foot followed. Evie watched in alarm as words inked across Dev's skin, accompanied by gaudy illustrations similar to those in medieval manuscripts. "Uh, Dev . . ."

"Have you seen *Fantasia*? *The Sorcerer's Apprentice* with Mickey Mouse?" He closed his eyes. He looked as if he were standing before a stained-glass window, his skin glowing with illuminated illustrations and dark script. She watched as bones flew outward, reassembling themselves in an uncanny anatomical feat against the wall. Dev's eyes remained closed as he continued to charm the dead. Spines and tibia, femurs and skulls, all knit together with an eerie, clacking sound that made her want to curl into the stone at her back.

Dev opened his eyes and stared with her at the grisly ladder of bones twisting up toward freedom. The illuminated manuscript images faded from his skin. He said in a hushed voice, "I think there's something wrong with me."

"No. You're carrying the *Bestiarum Vocabulum*. I think it likes you." She set one hand on a cold femur—*don't think of it as being human, don't think of it*—set her foot on another. She began to climb, telling herself that the ladder wouldn't fall apart, no matter how much it creaked, that she wouldn't tumble back down. "Come on."

As Dev followed, the bones swayed to one side. Dev cursed. Evie, her hand on a skull, found herself staring into the sockets at a darkness that stared back at her. Something chanted in a language she didn't understand. The skull's jaw fell open.

She clambered quickly up, one bone after another.

Then she was heaving herself over the lip of the oubliette, with Dev following. They collapsed on the floor.

"I made human bones dance." He sat up.

"I don't think it was just you." She considered the pentacle, remembered the ghostly figure she'd seen outside. "I think there *was* a guardian down there, someone who got sacrificed for that purpose long ago. Like you told me when you were reading me this place's history."

He cast a horrified glance at the pit, whispered, "You don't think it'll follow, do you?"

"No." She stood up, disturbed by how calm she felt. "Let's go."

"Whatever you say, boss." He shifted his backpack, handed it to her. "You hold that thing now. I felt like I had snakes crawling beneath my skin."

Evie reluctantly accepted the backpack containing the *Bestiarum* and gave him hers.

Skirting the pit, they returned to the metal door, slipped through it.

When the two young men dressed as priests appeared, she and Dev fled.

They burst through a door into the church nave, where Queenie stood holding Ciaran upright before a startled-looking old man in a priest's cassock. Ciaran was bent double. Queenie, her hair in her face, looked sick. Three hard-faced young men were stalking toward them down the aisle. The bigger two headed for Ciaran. She recognized the third one in the three-piece suit and red mane—Fenrir's leader, Reynard. He called out, "This is payback, Slick. For that casino job."

Ciaran laughed, in obvious pain, winced, and attempted to straighten. Blood trickled from the corner of his mouth. What was wrong with him? Panic edged Evie's vision with black. Ciaran said, "Daddy isn't going to be happy with you."

"You think he'll care how he gets this prize? As long as I give him that devil book, he'll be fine."

"Then maybe . . ." Ciaran drew himself up. His smile was vicious. ". . . you'll get a kiss from Mother Night?"

Reynard pointed at him. "Watch your mouth."

"We need to get to Ciar before the big guys do." Dev strode forward.

Evie ran toward Ciaran. He grabbed her and yanked her to

him. She made herself, and him, invisible. As the gossamer darkness folded around them, he gazed down at her and smiled. "Why, Evie, you've got words on your skin. And pictures."

She felt them, cold and slithery against her flesh. The *Bestiarum* was affecting her, *enabling* her to use her abilities. She yelled, "Queenie!"

A perfume bottle slid into Queenie's right hand. She sprayed her idioblast at the two Fenrir, one of whom inhaled and reeled. The other dodged, only to be met with Dev's fist.

The fatigue hit Evie. She staggered, felt the *Bestiarum's* reptilian magic fall from her, along with the veil of invisibility.

Two more Fenrir appeared. Ciaran turned, his eyes dark. He said to Evie, "Get that book out of here."

Queenie spun and sprayed more mist into another Fenrir's face. He fell, braids haloing outward. His comrade slammed Queenie against a pillar with one tattooed arm. Ciaran hit him, hard. They grappled. Dev and the big Fenrir were still fighting, both bleeding.

Evie slid to one knee, battling that weird exhaustion. She desperately wished herself unseen, but could feel it—the power, the *will*—ebbing, fraying. She saw illuminated manuscripts scroll up her arms as the *Bestiarum* hummed in the backpack. It wanted to help her. It wanted—

A small crucifix flew off the wall, hurtling toward her. She ducked. The crucifix struck an angel statue and red trickled from beneath the pale orbs of the angel's eyes.

Rising with an effort, Evie stared at the bleeding statue as the Fenrir leader stalked toward her. She thought, *Don't see me. Don't—*

The power, the words on her skin, vanished.

Reynard drawled, "There you are. What've you got there, in that pack, honey?"

She backed away from him. "You think Silence and Night will love that you messed up this job?"

"I think they'll just love that they got that fucking book, and I'm going to give it to them." He curled the fingers of one hand in a "gimme" gesture. "Hand it over, there's a good girl."

As she struggled to draw the ribbons of invisibility around her, a stained-glass window depicting a female saint cracked up the middle. Reynard turned his head toward it. He looked back at Evie.

He lunged and shoved her against a pillar, attempted to yank the backpack from her. She clawed at him, hating that he was stronger. And vicious—he smacked her across the face. Blood burst into her mouth as her teeth cut into her bottom lip.

I'm going to kill him.

Reynard laughed, breathless, as he pressed an arm against her throat. "Did you just growl at me, honey?"

"Evie!" She heard Ciaran roar her name. The fighting continued between him, Queenie, Dev, and the other Fenrir. She glimpsed a knife in the hand of a big Fenrir with a red mohawk.

Reynard glanced back, returned his attention to Evie, and grinned. "That's Lycan. He's new."

Evie kneed Reynard in a classic move. He stumbled back, swearing. He snarled, "You bi—"

Mad glided down before Evie, to face him. "Hey, Reynard. Nice threads. The Dickensian-gent-meets-thug look really works for you."

Reynard sneered. "And here's the crazy blonde—"

Mad swept up and slammed a pink Nike into Reynard's face, breaking his nose. He howled. Mad said, her back to Evie, "Roof. Get that book outta here."

Evie ran for the stairs.

At the top, another Fenrir appeared. Evie whirled to run back down, but he caught her in a bear hug. She kicked a wall, trying to topple them both. He teetered. She slid free. He grabbed the backpack and dragged her. She twisted around, clawing for his face. A fist in her stomach bent her double with agony. Despairing, she felt the backpack torn from her shoulder, saw the Fenrir's grin.

An arm slid around his neck and yanked him back.

Jason Ra slammed the Fenrir against a wall.

The Fenrir spun. Jason stepped back, avoiding a fist. With swift grace, he caught the Fenrir's wrist, bent it back. The guy yelled. Jason kicked him in the knee. The Fenrir crumpled, groaning.

Jason turned to Evie. "Follow me."

She wanted to fling her arms around him. She wanted to yell at him.

They ran through a door, which he kicked shut. When someone began banging on the door, Evie locked it. They looked around, but there was only one window. Jason told her, voice level, "You're the Flaunt." He stepped behind the door.

The door crashed open and a narrow-faced Fenrir strode in, wielding a baseball bat. Evie backed away, bent down to clutch her ankle. "Ow," she said, and it wasn't completely acting—she hurt in so many different places.

"Aw," the Fenrir said, grinning, "poor little lady—"

Jason slammed the door against him. The Fenrir whirled—into a fistful of the brass knuckles Jason wore on his right hand. The Fenrir fell back, stunned, dropping the baseball bat. Jason punched him again. The Fenrir stumbled, regained his balance, and hit Jason back. As Jason struck the wall, Evie went for the bat, grabbed it.

Jason surged forward. He bashed the Fenrir in the temple. This time, the Fenrir went down.

"Those." Evie pointed at the brass knuckles as Jason took the baseball bat from her, twirling it. She hated the admiration in her voice. "What *were* you, Ra, when you were with them?"

He didn't answer, peering into the hall. He motioned to her. He loped up a staircase. She raced after.

Two more Fenrir in priests' cassocks appeared at the top of the stairs. When they saw Evie and Jason, they began descending.

Jason smiled with startling charm. He held up his hands, the baseball bat still gripped in one, and spoke in his proper British: "Gentlemen. We're on our way out. No trouble. We're just tourists."

The two Fenrir laughed.

Jason lunged up the stairs, struck one Fenrir with the bat. The guy went down, swearing, his face dark with blood. Ducking a punch from the second Fenrir, Jason swung the bat at the boy's legs. The Fenrir tumbled past.

Evie raced up the stairs after Jason. At the top, she looked over the railings, into the nave below, where Ciaran stood over the big Fenrir with the red mohawk. There was blood on Ciaran's shirt. Queenie and Dev were still fighting two others. Ciaran whirled to help them, moving with vicious efficiency.

"Evie." Jason's voice was low. "Do you know why your tricks are glitching here?"

She stared at him. She suspected what the answer was. "You don't get to ask questions. I take it you were mostly Tooth and Claw when you were one of them? You fight like it."

In two strides, he was close. He whispered, "They are going to get you killed." He drew back. "Ciaran taught me how to fight." He headed for a window, flung it open to reveal a tricky slant of roof with an angel statue facing away from them. He climbed out. She slid after.

Outside, she felt the oppression that had muted her power vanish. She followed Jason across the tiles, saw a ladder that led onto a rooftop further up. "Jase—"

A hush of sound from behind her made her glance back, apprehensive.

The angel statue had turned its head. Shocked, Evie watched as the stone feathers on one of its wings seemed to ripple.

"Evie," Jason called sharply.

Beside her, a stained-glass window webbed with a crack. A piece of red glass depicting a crimson snake fell and shattered. She recoiled.

"Evie. *Come on*." Jason held out a hand. "I know the way down. Give me your backpack."

She clutched the straps of the backpack containing the *Bestiarum*. "No."

"*Evie.*" His voice dropped an octave and danger radiated from him as if an electrical storm were crackling beneath his skin. "Give me the backpack."

She took a step away on the slanted roof. "Who are you even helping here, White Hat?" She realized it suddenly. "Proof.

You want the *Bestiarum* because it's *proof.* You're collecting *evidence.*"

He stepped forward. She saw, then, what he'd been to Ciaran and La Fable Sombre. He said, "Silence and Night cannot get that book."

She backed up, her breathing shallow. "Stay away."

Her foot skated across a mossy patch.

Then she was tumbling down the roof, clutching at tiles that lacerated her skin like monstrous scales. Jason dropped, sliding after her, reaching desperately for her hand—

She was falling—

A hand caught hers in midair. For a quick moment, hanging suspended, Evie thought the stone angel had come to life and saved her.

She looked up at Mad, who smiled down at her, levitating, her golden hair swirling. "Gotcha, Eves."

Evie glanced back at the roof, at Jason, crouched there.

Mad glided Evie through the air, away from the church, the wind sweeping through their hair and clothing. When they touched ground—Mad, with grace; Evie, falling to her knees—Evie realized they'd landed in the wooded lot beyond the graveyard.

"Jason." She turned toward the church. She could see him on the roof like a wingless angel.

"This was a trap." Mad reached for her hand. "Forget him."

The Renault Dev had driven burst through the weeds, spun to a halt a few feet away from them.

Ciaran opened the driver's side door and got out. Queenie and Dev were in the back, Dev grinning, Queenie coiling up her hair. "You drive, Mad." Ciaran strode around to the passenger side. Evie squeezed in next to Dev while Mad slid behind the wheel.

As Mad spun the car in a spray of dirt and shredded grass, Evie leaned forward to tell Ciaran, "Nothing was working in there for us."

"Hallowed ground," he told her, one arm on the seat back as he turned to her.

"What does that mean—"

"It means I couldn't open a goddamn Door."

Mad swung the car onto the road, skirted around another vehicle. Everyone clutched at something as the car, speeding down a narrow street, barely avoided another collision. As the car drifted around a corner, Evie's stomach lurched into her mouth. Dev swore. Queenie looked bored. Mad laughed as if she were having the time of her life.

Ciaran continued, "Silence told me about a strike he and his LFS attempted in a church in Madrid. Their abilities glitched." He braced one hand against the ceiling as the car spun with a squeal.

"Did he warn you that might happen?" Evie glared.

"No, blackbird. It was a onetime thing. But now . . ."

"Replication," Queenie said darkly. "Two experiments—experiences, for us—same result. Holy ground affects us in a bad way."

"Who else is getting a terrible feeling right now?" Dev met Evie's gaze.

Expect the unexpected, Evie thought. *But who expected our powers to fail?*

The car dodged a boy on a motor scooter, squealed around a corner. Queenie yelled, "We're being followed!"

Evie looked back—a silver car was weaving after them.

Mad spun the car in a screeching figure eight. Evie shut her eyes as the Renault shot into a narrow alley, scraped a dumpster, and slid onto a main road. Looking back, Evie saw the silver car dodging through the traffic in close pursuit. She saw the driver's red hair. "Reynard."

"Hold on," Mad warned unnecessarily, punching a button on the car's stereo. A song about a fortunate son blasted out. Dev moaned, "Not this one."

Evie, as they glided into a roundabout, gripped the grab handle above, and said, "I like it."

Queenie told her, "You won't after this."

"It's Mad's getaway driver music." Ciaran grinned with unconcerned delight. "We'll be out of this by the end of the song."

Evie didn't see how that was possible.

Mad sped the car down a winding road. Evie heard sirens. Her eyes widened when she saw a police car swerve to block them. Mad hit the brakes. Tires squealed. She slammed the Renault into reverse, backed down the winding road, head turned, one arm over the seat's back, one hand deftly spinning the steering wheel—

They entered the roundabout in reverse. Ciaran laughed. Evie, gripping the grab handle, turned to watch the receding view as Mad sped backward through the roundabout. Horns blared and tires screeched as other vehicles got out of their way. Mad ribboned effortlessly past them.

The car rocked to a screeching halt. Mad swore. Evie looked back. Police cars were blocking the four exits to the round-about. Mad's gaze slid to the left, to a stone pedestrian bridge over a large pond. Dev warned, "No. *No.*"

"Go for it," Ciaran encouraged.

Mad twisted the steering wheel one-handed. The car sped toward the bridge, which was half the car's width. She jerked the car so that the tires on the right side slid up a low concrete wall sloping into the road. The car tilted onto its two left wheels as it glided sideways over the narrow stone bridge, the terrible sound of the car's metal undercarriage scraping against the bridge's low wall causing Evie's teeth to clench. Ciaran turned his head and flashed a smile.

As the car righted itself with a bone-jarring crunch, Mad laughed and spun the wheel. An insane screeching noise pierced Evie's ears. The car veered onto a curving road, onto the freeway, and traffic swept around them.

"I felt it." Queenie continued. "When I stepped into that church. Something was wrong. Something was . . . off. My perfume didn't stun them like it was supposed to. I might as well have used pepper spray."

Ciaran said, "Someone knows what we can do. If the Sirens hid their treasure in that church . . . someone told them how holy ground affects our tricks."

Dev asked uneasily, "Why is that, exactly?"

"I don't know." Ciaran narrowed his eyes. "I'm going to find out."

Evie wondered why Mad hadn't mentioned Jason Ra. She couldn't get the image of him crouched on that church roof out of her head. She recalled the stained-glass windows cracking, the crucifix flying off the wall. A chill settled in her stomach.

"Who knows what we can do?" One side of Dev's face was darkening with bruises. "The other crews don't. We're a secret —well, we were. We're not anymore. Fenrir will blab about our specialness. But, outside of the Kingdom, no one really believes LFS exists."

"Someone believes," Evie said, faking calm. "And someone knows what makes us weak."

Mad didn't drive them back to Black Fox House, but to a hotel. Ciaran led them through the hotel's moss-green corridors to room 707, where Evie discarded her backpack alongside Dev's. Queenie huddled on the sofa, arms wrapped around her knees. Dev paced, his eyes tawny gold.

Ciaran unzipped the backpack and drew out the *Bestiarum Vocabulum*. Mad crouched beside him and brushed her fingertips across the cover.

"That book worked," Evie told them. "For me and Dev. But it's unpleasant. It needs a key to open it, Priest said. Any pointy object will do."

Ciaran held out a hand, his gaze never leaving the book. "Mad?"

Mad slid a wicked-looking silver pin from her coiled hair and set it on his palm. Ciaran inserted the hair pin into the lock of the lead clasp. It clicked. He opened the book to pages of gorgeous, jewel-like illustrations—strange creatures—and inky script, charts, and sigils. Gilt decorated some of the pages. Evie laid one hand against a picture of an entity with a face of butterfly wings. The book hummed like an energy source.

"Evie said it liked me." Dev kept his distance. "I think it likes all of us."

"We won't share that info with Mother and Father." Ciaran looked up at them.

"So, what do we do with it?" Evie recalled Jason's warning about the *Bestiarum*.

"We give it to them." Ciaran shut the book.

"Not so fast." Mad opened it again, leaning over it. "Let's look at it more."

Evie, who was afraid of the book and its menagerie of nightmare creatures, nevertheless was also drawn to it. She knew, she *knew*, this book was somehow connected to their abilities.

That's why Silence and Night want it.

———❧———

They returned to the lair, using one of Ciaran's Doors. No one wanted to leave the main room that night for their own apartments. Scraped, bruised, and disheartened, everyone remained, playing games or pretending to read, occasionally glancing at the treasure scattered on the pool table. Mad had a bad nosebleed.

Evie had so many questions. She felt boneless and bloodless. It had taken Ciaran a good two hours to recover from whatever had afflicted him in the Church of the Bleeding Saint. He stood at the window, gazing out at the evening-drowned courtyard. A bruise darkened his jawline. He said, "I don't know if our tricks failed because it was a church or because sacred places have certain protections."

"Against *bad* things," Evie reminded him.

"Against *magic* things," he challenged.

Queenie lay on the sofa. "Stuff was happening. Weird stuff. A window cracked. A crucifix flew at Evie."

Mad shook her head. "We're thieves. We're not evil."

"But remember when we all felt *off* in the Saint Street Café, which used to be a *church*?" Evie waited. Into a silence thick as blood, she inserted a dagger of a question: "Why didn't Father Silence and Mother Night warn us about the church's effects? It *had* to be that."

Ciaran gave her a measuring look. Mad stood still. But Evie noticed her toes were an inch above the floor. Ciaran said, "They couldn't prove it. It was one time for them, years ago."

"So, holy places are like our kryptonite?" Dev gazed into his teacup. He continued grimly, "I thought it was just malachite."

"Malachite?" Evie pounced on that. "What the hell happens with malachite?"

"Malachite," Ciaran told her, "dulls our abilities. We don't know why."

"In the Middle Ages, people wore malachite amulets to protect them against evil," Queenie whispered.

Ciaran turned from the window. "The Boy Detective. He knows what we can do." His face shadowed. "Jason was there, wasn't he? It was a trap."

Mad spoke fiercely, "No, Ciaran. Jase wouldn't do that to us."

"Then you don't know him as well as you think." Ciaran's eyes went black, and Evie was suddenly terrified for Jason.

She needed to navigate this catastrophe. "Why did the Sirens betray Silence and Night?"

Dev drank his tea, rings flashing on his fingers. "No one really knows. It wasn't a lucrative betrayal, was it?"

Evie nodded. "Would the Sirens really have gotten so much money for what they stole that it would be worth crossing Silence and Night? And why hide it in the crypt of that church? You said the other crews don't know what we can do. What weakens us."

Mad affirmed, "We *were* a secret."

"But you said some of them *suspect* we're different. *Someone* told the Sirens the secret." Evie watched Ciaran as she went on. "Does Reynard from Fenrir know what we are?"

Ciaran looked merciless. "He does now. That new Fenrir with the red mohawk . . ."

"Reynard called him Lycan," Evie recalled.

"He was here to provide more than muscle." Ciaran leaned against a pillar, arms folded. "His eyes glowed like a jack-o'-lantern's. He had the same electric snap I sense in all of you. Then it sputtered. But the bastard had a knife."

"Fucking Fenrir," Dev muttered.

"You think he was like us." Evie didn't like that at all.

"He was like us." Ciaran let that statement scar the air. "Only whatever his power was, it glitched as well. Hence, the knife."

"An assassination attempt by Fenrir?" Queenie was doubtful. "We need to tell Silence and Night—"

"No." Ciaran shook his head. "Not yet. Not until I've spoken to Reynard."

Evie repeated her question. "Why would Siren crew mutiny? Mutiny would be an act of desperation. Of fear."

"So what were the Sirens afraid of?" Mad sat on a windowsill.

Ciaran watched Evie. "We've several intriguing questions: Who knew the church would fuck us up? Are Fenrir aware of their newest recruit's—Lycan's—abilities? Why did the Sirens mutiny?"

Evie thought each question led to the same conclusion, one everyone had reached, judging by the sudden silence.

Whoever had told the Sirens about La Fable Sombre's powers had suspected holy places would affect their special abilities. They had an unknown enemy who knew more about their powers than Silence, Night, and Ciaran.

Who knew more about their powers than *they* did.

—⁓—

After making her way down the hall with its peeling wallpaper and flickering antique lamps, Evie stepped into her apartment and leaned against the door, breathing in, out. *A deep true-'til-death.* She reached for the light.

Something moved in the shadows. She froze, fear a copper taste on her tongue. She glimpsed something, its limbs black, its head a mass of shadows.

She flipped the lights on and met her reflection's gaze in the big mirror she'd hung on the door. She cursed her tricky imagination. She walked to her bed and curled there, all her bruises and scrapes hurting. She listened to the silence around her. She knew why everyone was quiet.

La Fable Sombre were beginning to realize they weren't invincible.

—⁓—

Evie woke in the dead of night. She turned over and stared at the ceiling. How had Jason known they were going to be in Marseille and at that church?

She sat up in bed, switched on the light. She lifted the maiden death medallion and studied it. She used her thumbnail to open it—the two photos in the locket were still there. She ran one finger over the lacquered maiden death.

She retrieved a screwdriver from her art toolbox and pried carefully at the bubble of the maiden death image. It popped off. A device like a tiny black seashell fell into her palm, its minuscule light blinking. She'd never seen a listening device before, but she knew it was a bug.

Jason Ra. You bastard.

She set the bug on the floor and raised a hammer from the toolbox to smash it. She hesitated. She picked up the bug, placed it in the medallion, and glued the lacquered maiden death back over it. For now, she would leave the bug alone, let him believe he was looking after her. She tucked the medallion into her T-shirt and curled up in the dark.

Knowing Jason was out there somehow made her feel safer.

Chapter Twelve

The Darkness

Silence and Night's second tithe was held in the Marrakesh courtyard of the Palm and the Lotus. There was no ritzy cocktail gathering this time.

Meeting La Fable Sombre in the hall, Evie surveyed her crew. Dev and Ciaran proudly displayed their bruises from the Marseille Strike. So did Mad, sporting a fading shiner around her left eye. Queenie and Evie had spent nearly a half hour in front of the mirror with concealer and strategic eyeliner to cover their welts. The things Queenie vowed to do to Fenrir were imaginative and sadistic.

Comfortable in tartan capris, a black turtleneck, and battered black Converse, Evie asked warily, "If Fenrir are there . . ."

"I want to see the expression on Reynard's face"—Mad stuck her thumbs through the straps of the small backpack that held the *Bestiarum Vocabulum*—"when we give this to Silence and Night."

"Come on then." Dev walked gracefully, resembling a college aristocrat in a cable-knit sweater and houndstooth trousers. The lamplight gilded his profile. "You ever wonder why these events are always held at night?"

"Silence and Night are not vampires, Dev." Queenie seemed to be continuing an old argument.

"We've never seen them in daylight," Dev slyly reminded her.

As Evie listened to them, the tension slid from her shoulders. Ciaran's fingers brushed hers, and he cast her an encouraging look. She smiled fiercely.

They passed beneath an arch of stylized lions to ascend an outside stair. The courtyard of spiky plants was a lamplit space where the crews, unmasked, sat on walls, stairs, or crouched near pillars. Torches flashed elemental swathes of orange over solemn and grim faces.

Silence and Night moved from the shadows, both in white linen that rippled in the arid wind.

There were no deaths to honor or traitors to brand, which relieved Evie. She leaned on the railing as the crews presented their best. Last were Reynard and another Fenrir, who set a fancy railroad trunk next to the offerings. Reynard flung the lid up to reveal a wealth of flash: watches, jewelry, and other small, expensive items.

"Bank heist in Austria." Mad's mouth curled in scorn. "We should've snatched *that* job." She began to amble down the stairs, unslinging the backpack. Evie saw Mother Night turn and raise a hand. Father Silence said, without looking at them, "La Fable Sombre may present their tithe at dinner."

Silence and Night withdrew. The other thieves began to

mingle. Ciaran descended into the courtyard and walked straight toward Reynard. To his credit, the leader of Fenrir didn't move. Evie forgot to breathe as Ciaran laid one hand on Reynard's left shoulder. The poison ring gleamed. Ciaran said, "We'll keep Marseille between us, Reynard."

Reynard quickly stepped back. His crew surrounded him in a crescent formation. Evie, Dev, Queenie, and Mad moved to stand near Ciaran.

"No hard feelings?" Reynard's smile was vicious.

"None at all." Ciaran's languor reminded Evie of a predator sizing up his next meal. "How's Lycan?"

"Who?" Reynard asked innocently.

"*Lycan*. The big guy with the mohawk and the glowing eyes." Ciaran's smile was beautiful. "The one who tried to stick a knife in me. Your newest recruit."

Reynard shrugged and slid out of Ciaran's grasp. "Yeah. Lycan. He quit. Father isn't happy he's gone."

The threat of violence smoldered in the night air. Ciaran turned the skull ring on his forefinger. "Well, whoever he was, he pricked himself on something fierce."

Reynard stared at the ring. Then, at Ciaran. His lips peeled back from his teeth. "You mother—"

Ciaran turned and walked away, back across the courtyard. As Dev, Queenie, and Mad formed a little battalion behind them, Evie strode beside him.

"Ciaran." Her voice was taut. "You didn't . . . that big guy back at the church . . . Lycan . . ." She had seen them fighting. Not how it had ended.

"He intended to kill me, Evie."

Evie didn't look at his poison ring. *It was self-defense,* she told herself.

The fear that had flickered across Reynard's face told her he wouldn't be interfering with any more of La Fable Sombre's jobs.

------∿------

Mother Night and Father Silence waited for La Fable Sombre in a splendid pavilion of gold and scarlet lit by hanging lamps of azure and topaz glass. Mother Night, in a sleeveless white gown, poured mint tea, while Father Silence studied each of them. Outside, the desert was a realm of midnight blue and star-strewn sable. In the distance, Evie could see bonfires and hear bass music as the other crews celebrated.

Ciaran had killed Lycan. It was the second time he'd killed. The thought haunted her.

Evie presented Mother Night with the *Bestiarum Vocabulum* as they sat on embroidered cushions around a Moroccan feast. The book hummed in Evie's hands, as if alive, causing her unease. What had made it? It had belonged to an Elizabethan wizard, but Evie could sense it wasn't from this world. Mother Night accepted the book as if it were a newborn, her perfectly manicured nails tracing the images on the embossed cover.

"Was there any opposition?" Father Silence asked with a hint of humor.

"Our tricks didn't work very well," Ciaran spoke amiably, before anyone could say anything. "But we managed the few thugs the Sirens hired. Jason Ra showed up." He didn't mention Fenrir.

Father Silence's humor vanished. His pale eyes met Ciaran's. Clearly, neither was afraid of the other. She wondered if Silence knew about Fenrir, if he suspected there was more to Lycan's "disappearance." Reynard wouldn't be able to tell him, because Fenrir had come to Marseille without Silence and Night's blessing.

A chill shot through her—how had Fenrir learned about their mission?

"Jason Ra." Father Silence said, and it was a death sentence. Evie felt it in her bones, in the splintered way Silence spoke Jason's name.

Silence flashed a smile and turned his formidable attention on Evie. "You brought the *Bestiarum Vocabulum* out of its hiding place. You've done extremely well, Evie. This lot"—he flicked a fond look at Ciaran, Dev, Mad, and Queenie, who were gently arguing over the spectacular food laid out before them—"they're easy to please. But we don't quite know you yet." Father Silence sat with an arm on one bent knee. His white linen clothing gave him a deceptively saintly air.

He suddenly looked up. "Pardon me." He rose and walked out to speak with one of the young guards.

"You want knowledge." Mother Night spoke to Evie. She absently stroked Mad's hair as Mad laid her head on one of her shoulders and bit into a pastry. A bracelet of obsidian beads glistened around Mother Night's wrist.

"Yes," Evie admitted. "I want to know about things more than I want to own them."

Ciaran glanced at her, approving.

"Go to Father. He'll answer any questions you may have."

Mother Night nodded to the desert outside of the tent, where Silence stood alone now, smoking a cigarette and gazing outward. "That is your reward for *un travail bien fait*. A job well done."

Evie reluctantly separated herself from the others. As Queenie leaned toward Mother Night to say something, Ciaran reached out and clasped Evie by one wrist, whispered, "No personal questions."

Evie nodded and walked to Father Silence. In a tense situation, her instinct was to become invisible. She had to fight that urge. She asked Silence, "What is La Fable Sombre? You told me some history before."

He dropped his cigarette into the sand. He was barefoot. He gazed up at the dazzling display of stars. "Walk with me, Evie."

They moved across the sand, Evie aware of the desert stretching endlessly to either side. In the distance, she saw the Thieves' Night celebration continuing amidst the blossom of bonfires.

Father Silence spoke like a storyteller. "The Dark Fable was created long ago to collapse kingdoms, to destroy monarchies, to give power to the powerless. Every assignment is part of a plan that goes back centuries—destroy the status quo, the machine of order, the establishment. We are a secret. Rebels and revolutionaries. Everything in that vault beneath Paris was collected to keep the world from harm. We were never shown what was in it before our predecessors met their end."

Evie chose her words carefully. "What were *your* Mother Night and Father Silence like?"

"They were Mother Night and *Mother* Silence." He spoke tenderly. "When Ruby and Annabelle found me, I was fifteen and living on the streets of Belfast. Night was fourteen when she ran away from an orphange in France. And the others in our group . . ." His mouth hardened. Evie watched him, fascinated—he radiated power and myth like some ancient emperor. "All of us, taken in like stray cats."

He turned to her, his eyes pale in the starlight. "That is not how Night and I see any of you. Nor the other crews. Ruby and Annabelle collected us as if we were pretty pebbles. We see you as our children. The Sirens' betrayal was all the more wrenching to us because of this."

Evie continued to walk with him. "What will you do with the *Bestiarum Vocabulum* if you can't put it in the vault?"

"I'll transport it to my home and keep it safe."

She glanced at the bracelet of obsidian beads on his left wrist, identical to the one Mother Night wore. "So, you only keep the artifacts? Not the jewelry, the paintings, the cash?"

"Some of the cash. Most of the items are sold. The artifacts, the rare ones, those we keep." He looked at her, and it was as if some fallen angel were making its way into her soul with a razor blade. "Are you asking the right questions, Evie?"

She couldn't ask the questions she wanted to: *Do you have families? Where do you really live? Why is everyone so afraid of both of you?*

"I think so." She made a little dune of sand with one foot. "I think I'm done with the questions for now."

They returned to the pavilion, where Mother Night was laughing beautifully at some story Mad and Queenie were telling her. Night glanced at Silence, who lifted a black envelope and handed it to Ciaran. Ciaran slid out a detailed illustration of a black jar in the shape of an unidentifiable curled beast. Little figures of other beasts paraded around the handle, the jar's middle.

"The Anesidora Pithos," Night told them. "Pandora's jar."

"*No. The* Pandora?" Mad plucked the illustration from Ciaran and laughed in delight.

"Yes. *The* Pandora." Father Silence laid a hand over Mother Night's, both of which rested on the *Bestiarum Vocabulum* in her lap. "It is going to be offered at an auction of rogue thieves and unsanctioned Collectors in St. Petersburg, Russia."

"This is going to be a dodgy one." Dev ran a hand over his buzz cut.

"This is a powerful object. Like the *Bestiarum,* you will not be able to open it." Mother Night didn't know that they *had* opened the *Bestiarum.*

"Is this jar the one that all the monsters came out of?" Mad handed the illustration back to Ciaran.

"Yes, this is the one all the monsters came out of. The thief selling it doesn't even know what it is." Father Silence's gaze fell upon Evie. "Be very careful with this one."

Evie told herself she was being paranoid, that Silence wasn't warning her and her alone.

———✺———

Evie stood in the night-drenched desert as a twisty zephyr played with sand, bonfires, hair, and clothing. The thumping bass of the music was almost ghostly, echoing in the canyon strewn with the cars everyone had driven here. La Fable Sombre were clustered around a silver roadster. Mad, barefoot, walked on the car's roof, holding a glass of champagne. Her gold-streaked hair was in two braids, her wolf eyes lined with rosy kohl. She wore a black bomber jacket and a pink camisole dress. Queenie leaned against the roadster, talking to Dev, who was idly dancing to the music pulsing from the car. Mad, Queenie, and Dev wore crowns of pink damask roses.

"My, aren't we a sight." Ciaran eyed them. He was sleek in a black Henley shirt and jeans. "Proper delinquents, we are. Why don't you lot mingle?"

Mad twirled on the roadster's hood. She stepped off. Ciaran took her hand as she seemed to float for a moment. "Watch that," he warned as her feet settled on the sand. "You don't want the others to see. Fenrir are holding our secret close to their little black hearts."

Evie looked around at the other crews, some of whom had glammed up, but most were in jeans and hoodies. Someone had tossed sparklers into one of the bonfires and pinwheels of light stung the air, left a snaking glow on Evie's retinas when she blinked.

Fenrir were keeping their distance, drinking and smoking near one of the fires.

Evie set her focus on Ciaran, who had taken a bottle of beer from a cooler and was popping the cap off. Watching her, he drank from the bottle. His silver skull ring gleamed.

Mad handed Evie a bottle of something fizzy and pink. Evie idly asked, "Silence and Night seem rich as lords, so why can't they just buy the mysterious objects they have us steal?"

Ciaran looked devilish in the flamelight cutting across his cheekbones. "Some things aren't for sale."

Evie met Ciaran's gaze and thought, *He's more dangerous than Silence and Night. He's hungry.* "Who's going to be the new Silence and Night when they retire?"

"Why Queenie and Ciar, of course." Dev draped an arm around Mad and Queenie's shoulders. "Mad and I are too harum-scarum. Let's get some s'mores."

Queenie spoke as they sauntered away. "I get the best s'more, for I am the future queen . . ."

Evie, worried about their refusal to talk about Lycan, shoved her hands in the pockets of her hoodie. She looked at Ciaran. He shook his head.

"It's not the first time, Evie, we've had collateral damage. Ask Mad. Ask Jase." He surveyed the other crews.

"I know Lycan tried to kill you—"

Those gray eyes flashed to her. "He was like us."

"Tell me what you know. Tell *us.*"

"When there's something to tell, I will." Ciaran slid onto the hood of the silver roadster, all of him in darkness but for the glint of the skull ring and his eyes. He cradled the beer in both hands as his shadow twisted across the sand. It was as if night had come out of the sky in male form. There weren't enough stars in the universe to make Ciaran Argent anything but darkness.

"Being invisible. It's a power we all share, isn't it?" He spoke softly. "No one notices any of us. We're the lost causes and the never-will-bes." There was no anger in his voice, no bitterness, only pride.

"The world doesn't see us." Evie drew herself up beside him. She watched the other crews.

"But someone does. Someone has it in for us. And I'm still figuring it out. I'll tell all of you when I do."

They were quiet a moment. Evie continued, "Tell me how you found out about the Doors."

"I found the first Door when I was eight, before I learned fictional worlds are a bad idea." He absently stroked the scars on one arm. "So, I stole a book about great cities and began visiting them. Also"—his smile was crooked—"I learned I can't time travel."

"You brought us to a fictional world on Valentine's Day."

"The 'Great Gatsby' is what I call that one. It was my favorite book. The fictional worlds are dangerous, Evie, because you never know what you're going to get. You can't stay in them for very long, because they start to unravel, smear, or decay. Like a theater set aging in time-lapse photography. It's terrifying."

"What was your first fictional world?" She leaned back on her arms.

"Well, I was eight. It was Winnie-the-Pooh. The Hundred Acre Wood."

She cast him a look of shock and delight. *"No."*

He shuddered delicately. "Let me tell you, a real-life Eeyore isn't nearly so charming as the one in the story. And Dev insisted on Narnia for his first trip. He'll never see Mr. Tumnus the same way again, I'm afraid. Queenie's practically written an entire thesis on how those worlds exist."

Evie laughed, awed. "Can you take me to Middle Earth—"

"Absolutely not. No. It'll never happen. Don't ask again. Those worlds are like spray paint on mist or pretty paper that rots. I *did* learn a neat trick. If I left an object with a drop of my blood on it, I could track my DNA anywhere in the world." He glanced at her, studying her in that way of his that made her feel they had known one another in a different life. "That trick may come in handy sometime."

A wind swept around them, tousling Evie's hair into her eyes. As she lifted a hand to push the tendrils back, Ciaran's fingers brushed her brow, sweeping the hair away. He said, "Like little black snakes, that hair. It's called Chergui, this wind. It travels and becomes other winds, in other places. Other names. Always causes erratic behavior. Some unlucky souls can hear the voices of the dead in the wind." His gaze tracked to Dev, Queenie, and Mad dancing near a bonfire. "I would die for those three, blackbird."

Evie believed him.

He set his hand on the car between them. The skull ring grinned at her. "And I would die for you as well, Evie Wilder."

She breathed out, a deep true-'til-death. She carefully placed her hand over his.

"Ciar!" Mad called. "Get over here and show us some moves!"

He slid down from the roadster. "Mad calls, I answer." He strode toward the dancing. He moved among the other crews like a king. He slid an arm around a golden-haired boy and twirled him in a brief waltz, spun and dipped a girl in emerald silk.

Evie remained, her smile fading.

She found herself drinking more than she'd planned. They weren't on a job, and the buzz made her feel fearless. With liquor, the flame-gilded and rowdy camaraderie of the thieves around her was seductive. One of the Tsars was DJing out of a van painted with images of the Russian witch Baba Yaga. As music crashed out over the desert, a rainbow of colors ghosted from glow necklaces and bracelets, lighting up the darkness. Nearly everyone was dancing.

Drinking from a plastic cup, Evie threaded among the fires, curious about these people chosen by a secret society. They were a single force now, had set aside all their petty allegiances and grudges, mischief and mayhem, to reveal a softer side. Mad was dancing with Arachnae crew near the DJ's van. Dev sat in a folding chair near a fire, strumming a guitar. Queenie was moving among the crews, a queen bee in her element. The Nara guy with the spiky blue hair was stalking the fringes, ignoring the come-hither gazes cast his way, his attention hooked on Queenie as she mingled, regal even in a flannel shirt and ripped jeans, laughing at something a Tsar said, accepting a bottle of beer from a lanky Fenrir. The Nara guy—Knife, that was his name—turned when his leader, the girl in cat-eye glasses and Prada, moved to his side and spoke to him.

Evie tilted her head back to watch the stars.

Darkness swept down around her. She stood, terrified and numb, listening to the drip of water as something vaguely human-shaped glided toward her from the dark—

The desert and the stars returned. She shivered away the heart-staggering dread. The dancing, glow-striped bodies around her were giving off an invisible energy she could almost feel, like static electricity humming through her.

"It's all so beautiful, isn't it?"

Evie turned her head to find a girl with a glorious brunette mane standing beside her. The girl's smile was a rueful curve as she surveyed the thieves. Hearts and roses resembled splashes of blood on her jeans and denim jacket. She looked familiar.

"I remember this used to be everything to me." The girl had her hands in her back pockets. "Parties. Adventure. Money. I wish I'd enjoyed it more."

Evie found herself wishing the same.

"I wish I'd gotten away from them before the ground hit me."

Evie, who had let her attention drift, snapped her gaze back to the girl.

The girl was gone. As the wind swept Evie's hair into her eyes, she realized who had been speaking to her.

Vero Jordan.

She frantically scanned the desert for any other dead people. She dumped her cup into a garbage bag and leaned against a yellow jeep. She sank into a crouch, her arms over her head. *I'm hallucinating now?*

"Evie." Jason Ra, in a black hoodie and jeans, emerged from the dark. The upper half of his face was shadowed by the hood, but she recognized him. She'd been expecting him, had been the one to initiate their rendezvous through the little bug he'd planted in her medallion. But now, still shaken by her brush with the supernatural, she wasn't prepared.

He turned and walked toward the indigo shadows beyond the bonfires. She rose to wordlessly follow. He halted, extending a hand. "What I have to show you is near the Palm and the Lotus, but not on the warded grounds. I'll be able to spirit you back."

She twined her fingers around his. Ciaran's nomad Doors were nothing compared to what Mother Night had done with her witchy, howling-darkness transport. Evie once again wondered what all this traveling through the borders was doing to her molecular structure and expected she might one day fade away for real.

"Close your eyes." Jason held her hands. As the silver pentacle tinsel-glimmered around them, Evie breathed out in awe. She heard a sound like galloping hooves, bit her bottom lip as the desert spun around them. She didn't close her eyes. She saw that other place—the black grasslands—swirl violently around them, glimpsed something massive and equine running in circles.

When the pentacle faded, they were still in the Agafay Desert, in a secluded spot, with a slope looming to one side. Jason walked to a patch of sandy, rocky ground. The moonlight was as bright as a lamp. He told her, "The last time I was here, a Tsar was exiled after hacking into one of the Collectors' accounts."

Evie watched as he began kicking at sand and pebbles. He swept one sneakered foot across a stone surface. He crouched down and gazed at the stone. "Silence's guards brought him out here."

Apprehensive, Evie backed away. He continued, "The bodies don't get tossed into unmarked graves. Silence and Night are superstitious. They leave a marker to prevent the dead from roaming."

The dead *did* roam. Evie had learned that.

She watched as he rose and nudged sand away from a second square stone. He revealed a third. He looked at her. "A secret society of thieves wouldn't exile members, let a witness slip into the world. For people like Silence and Night, this is the only option. After the exiles are branded, for show, they're secretly brought here and shot in the head."

Her stomach heaved. "Ciaran knows about this?"

"Ciaran showed me where it was. He wanted someone else to know. He didn't want to scare his crew, lets them believe Silence and Night are benevolent, that they're safe as long as they don't cross Mother and Father." Jason was grim. "He thought Mad, Dev, Queenie, and Vero would run if they knew."

"Jase." Evie reached out to touch his wrist. "That's when you and Vero . . ."

"Decided to leave." Jason drew back and Evie's guts twisted when she saw at least a dozen stones in the sand. This was a graveyard. Bile rushed up in her throat. Jason tapped one of the stones with his foot. Evie walked to it, stared down at the name chiseled into it. *Matthew Orion.* She was almost sick. In a flash, the desert night became a liminal hellscape, with Jason anchoring her to reality.

Jason continued, "Silence and Night found out about my dad being Interpol, that Vero and I were planning to leave . . . they decided to kill us on that strike."

"It wasn't Ciaran who told them. What reason would he have?"

"I don't know." Jason shook his head. "When he's ready to mutiny against those two dragons, he'll turn all of you against them. By poisoning Lila Pearce, he declared war on Silence and Night."

Evie regained her composure. "Why would Ciaran mutiny against Silence and Night *now*?" She turned, desperate. "Silence and Night could have learned who your dad was on their own.

They might have suspected you and Vero would run because you were the two who had something to lose. It was *Vero's murder* that triggered Ciaran to finally turn against them, if he's planning on doing so." Would it take more than this graveyard of traitors to convince LFS to mutiny against the pretend mom and dad they idolized?

Jason gazed out over the desert. "You don't believe me."

Her throat tightened in sympathy. "It's all circumstantial, except for this. This, I believe. Silence and Night killed your dad. And, maybe, caused Vero's death. But I can't believe what you say about Ciaran." Because that would destroy everything she'd worked for.

He took a step toward her. "Meet me at the Silver Cove Bowling Alley Saturday night at seven. I'll bring you to the leader of the Sirens. And she'll tell you why her crew mutinied."

"Take me back." She shoved her hands through her hair, fraught with fear. "Take me back to the party. I'll meet you Saturday."

Because she had another question for Circe the Siren: who had told Circe holy ground affected LFS's powers?

"Evie." Jason clasped one of her hands. "Tell me your real name."

She looked straight at him. "Evie Wilder."

His gaze went cold. Then the darkness came to sweep them away.

—⁓—

Set on edge by a night full of supernatural threat, Evie stood alone near a bonfire, gazing into the flames. She lifted her head as Mad flung an arm around her shoulders. "I've been looking all over for you."

Still stunned by Jason's revelations, by that graveyard of Silence and Night's victims, Evie wanted to tell Mad everything, including how she'd seen Vero's ghost. While levitation and Doors that instantaneously transported one to other countries almost had a wild science to it, ghosts were dead people who wouldn't stay dead—they were horrifying.

But if she revealed Silence and Night's treachery, she'd be ending La Fable Sombre. She whispered, "Tell me about Vero, Mad."

Mad eyed her. "Are you having some type of crisis? Because, if you are, you need to deal with it and contain." Genuine concern laced her voice.

"Tell me about *Vero*."

Mad sighed. "In LA, I was working at a diner. Vero caught me levitating in my roller skates in the parking lot. She showed me what *she* could do—she could *find* things." Grief cracked the carefree code in Mad's voice. She looked around at the gangs of kids in the fire-spotted desert. "I met Jason when Vero and I were racing some jerks in her Corvette, and they sideswiped us into a ditch. Jason arrived, the white knight. He and Vero were friends." Her voice drifted. "We started hanging out together—Vero, Jase, and me. Then we met Ciaran."

The damn wind circled them again, causing one of the bonfires to roar upward. Evie glanced into the night surrounding the party, wondering apprehensively if other spirits related to La Fable Sombre were waiting. "Do you know why Vero and Jason were going to leave La Fable Sombre?"

"I don't know." Mad slid her gaze away. "Let's go eat toasted marshmallows with Oracle crew. They've got the best booze and we're just having fun tonight. Okay?"

Evie, troubled, followed Mad, hoping no other spirits would make an appearance.

CHAPTER THIRTEEN

The Blue Moon Motel

Curled in the center of her bed in the Silver Cove lair with her laptop, Evie scanned articles about Vero Jordan. About Lila Pearce. About Samuel Ra, the Interpol agent who had been Jason's father. Vero had been attempting to steal a painting from Pearce's penthouse in New York City when she'd "fallen" out of a window, trying to escape. Vero Jordan's unknown partner—Jason—had broken in and assaulted two security guards, shoved a third out of the same window. Samuel Ra had been investigating the attempted theft, claiming it was the urban legend La Fable Sombre.

Evie tapped her teeth with a fingernail, focusing on an article with a photograph of Lila Pearce, standing with her assistant, a girl with long black hair and cat-eye glasses.

The girl was Sadie Sakamura, the leader of Nara crew.

The game pieces had been set before Evie, and she'd been playing blind. Until Jason's revelations had steered her across the board. Silence and Night had engineered Vero's death, manipulating Lila Pearce through Nara crew. All because Jason and Vero had planned to leave LFS.

But how had Silence and Night found out?

Unsettled, restless, anxious, Evie wandered down to the main lair. Her gaze fell upon Dev's tangerine laptop Sharpied with doodles of one-eyed hearts and a Kawaii mongoose. A pair of Queenie's red stiletto heels were discarded near a chair. Mad's Vonnegut novel was set on top of a tin of Dev's British tea. Ciaran was the only one who hadn't left any spoor in the room.

She walked toward the room Ciaran used as his study. When she switched on the lamp, the first thing she saw was an eerie painting of a white-cloaked girl gazing upon a congregation of small people lifting their arms to her in worship. Behind the girl were shadowy titans. Evie tore her gaze from the weird painting and moved to the desk. Beside Ciaran's silvery laptop was a revolver. She glanced around, rummaged through some desk drawers. Nothing interesting. Why had she thought she'd find anything personal? Ciaran was a tabula rasa, a blank page. Every member of La Fable Sombre had a theory about him, but not one had heard his story.

She returned to the lair, scooped an orange from a bowl, and dropped onto the sofa. As she peeled the orange, she recalled the way Mad ripped the rinds off oranges and went at them like a vampire; how Dev preferred lounging anywhere but a chair whenever he schemed; the way Queenie always stood still, observing, or calculating chemical elixirs on her phone; how Ciaran, whatever he was doing, seemed too mature for nineteen, a warrior king. She was comforted by their clutter, but . . .

If, because of Vero's murder, Ciaran was planning a mutiny against Silence and Night . . . *It can't happen,* she thought, desperate. *Not now. It can't.*

Ciaran had invited her to join a society of thieves and ended her life of indentured servitude. Ciaran, whose cavalier mask seemed to fall away whenever he looked at her, the calculation in his eyes replaced by genuine admiration. Had he felt betrayed by Jason and Vero? For plotting to desert the family he had created? She didn't believe he'd betrayed Jason and Vero to Silence and Night.

But she had to find out.

———※———

Evie had never been to Ciaran's apartment. As he ushered her in, she received a swift impression of black polished wood and high ceilings. The furniture was stark. The light fixture was a B-52 airplane model with a Forties pinup girl painted on it. Beyond was a bedroom of mist- and steel-gray tones. A buffalo skull brooded over a fireplace of black marble. It was all very cliché alpha male—intentionally so, Evie suspected—and there wasn't a hint of who Ciaran Argent might once have been. *Well played,* Evie thought with grudging respect as she scanned for personal details, which were nowhere to be found.

She sat in a wingback chair. Ciaran dropped into the chair opposite.

"I'm going on a date with Jason Ra this Saturday." She watched his face for any tics, a flickering in his gray eyes.

"Of course you are." Legs apart, he leaned forward, causing the conversation to suddenly become intimate. The good humor in his voice made her wary.

"I'm going to find out what he knows," she promised. "He's getting really zealous about taking us down." She phrased her next question delicately. "How did Silence and Night find out Jason and Vero were leaving?"

"I don't know." Ciaran watched her. "They want Jase back. That talent of his is extra special."

"There's no way. And Silence looked ready to end him."

"Silence changed his mind. Evie." Ciaran's expression was serious. "Jason's going to tell you things you might not want to hear about us. About me."

He already has. "He thinks Silence and Night are responsible for Vero's fate—did you know the leader of Nara crew was Lila Pearce's assistant?"

"I knew. As for Vero . . . I blame myself for that." He shook his head, hands loosely clasped, several rings gleaming on his fingers. She didn't see the skull ring.

She hunched forward. "Silence and Night sent Jason and Vero to steal from one of their own Collectors? Why?"

"They had already set Sadie, the leader of Nara crew, in place with Lila Pearce. As a spy. Pearce had a painting Silence wanted, something to do with La Fable Sombre's past . . ."

"They never steal from their sanctioned Collectors. You didn't find that odd?"

Ciaran regarded her. "What are you trying to ask me, blackbird? If Silence and Night sent Vero and Jason to their deaths—"

"I saw the graveyard in the desert."

He sat back, anger flashing in his eyes. "The people in those graves were traitors, Evie. They endangered the Kingdom and all of us."

"Then so did Vero and Jason," she quietly reminded him.

He met her gaze and said, with terrifying calm, "Vero was murdered by Pearce's thugs."

"When will you tell the others about that graveyard?" she challenged.

"Blackbird. Trust me, will you? This is very fragile." His voice became intense. "Do you want everything to fall apart right now? Because I think you really, really don't. Go with Jason. Find out how bitter and disillusioned he is. I'm sending Dev and Queenie with you as temporary chaperones until he spirits you away. I want them to make sure none of Silence and Night's people follow you."

Evie couldn't protest. Ciaran was being reasonable. Would a guilty person be that amenable to her speaking with his nemesis?

A clever one would, that serpentine girl-voice whispered in her head. *And he is lying to you.*

Jason sat on a bench in the Silver Cove Bowling Alley. As Evie stepped in from the rain-slicked street, the aromas of popcorn and burned sugar wafted to her. She watched groups of people who were not like her drift past.

"Look at him." Dev spoke from Evie's left, while Queenie remained silent and disapproving on her right. "Straight out of a noir *GQ*. How *does* he get his hair to do that little swoop?"

"He's pretty, but sharp." Queenie looked at Evie. "Touch him and he might cut you."

"I don't need the metaphor, Queenie." Evie wanted them to leave. Instead, they strode toward Jason before Evie could say anything. They sat on either side of him.

With zero fear, Jason said, "Victoria. Devon. How are you this evening?"

"It's bloody impolite to use our real names." Dev studied Jason with sober intensity. "What are you doing, mate? Is this some kind of suicide dive of yours? Messing about with one of ours."

"A girl with big, smoky eyes and an ungrateful demeanor." Queenie laid one arm on the back of the bench as Evie approached.

"What *happened* to you, Jase?" Dev spoke wistfully. "Remember Berlin? You should've seen him, Queens. We had to fetch an ancient coin worth more than England at an industrialist's birthday. Mad was an acrobat. Ciar was the magician. I was the DJ. Jason was the scariest security detail ever, shades and a suit as sharp as shark teeth. The way you spoke to that rich bastard, Jase—you wouldn't think to look at him, Queens, that he could threaten enough to set a chill in the bones. Mr. Industrialist gave the info up, right quick."

Jason's expression told Evie that those memories were false notes in a symphony of bad blood and betrayal.

"Dev. Queenie." Evie folded her arms.

"Ciaran doesn't mind, mate. G'wed and speak to our Evie." Dev spoke affably, rising. "We're just here to make sure no one follows you two."

Jason kept his gaze on the entrance, all his muscles tensed.

"Unless." Dev cast him a dazzling smile. "You want all three of us on your date?"

Jason's teeth clicked together.

"Let's give them space, Dev." Queenie rose, pulling Dev with her. The pair of them slid into the crowd.

Evie, in a black turtleneck, jeans, and chunky loafers, shoved her hands in the pockets of her bomber jacket. "Where are we going on our date? Some place fun, I hope."

"You're even beginning to talk like them." He stood.

"Am I?" She reached out. Wordlessly, he closed his fingers over hers. She drew the shroud of invisibility over them. As she led him through the crowds, no one saw them, no one made eye contact. People jostled against them but didn't seem to notice them. Evie led him outside, into a night sparkling with rain. "You're going to spirit me away." She didn't look at him as they stepped into an alley. "Where?"

"To Madrid. To meet Circe." He gently clasped her other hand. "Close your eyes. Seriously, you didn't last time and that's dangerous."

"It's like the scariest amusement park ride ever." She closed her eyes, experiencing a little thrill. She heard the sizzle of the silver pentacle manifesting, heard that sound again like galloping hooves. The otherworld ribboned around her, an indigo darkness she could *see* beyond her eyelids, it was so complete.

She opened her eyes in a different alley. Jason led her out of it, through the parking lot of a drive-in movie theater surrounded by buildings glowing with violet and topaz lights. She sighed in wonder, recognizing the ornate, elemental architecture of

Madrid. A black-and-white movie was being projected on a giant screen.

"So, how'd you find Circe?" Evie asked, curious. "She and her crew must be in hiding."

He answered carefully. "I've cultivated a network of ex-cons and thieves—yes, it's very Sherlockian. I asked in the right places if anyone was interested in a miniature statue from the temple of Diana in Rome. Circe just lost her shipwreck loot—I knew that object would be irresistible to her."

"And why are we meeting her?"

"To hear the truth." He led her to a sea-blue Tauro among the other parked cars.

The girl seated on the car's hood didn't look away from the film. She said, a Zimbabwean accent softening her words, "I know you're supposedly a White Hat now. But I'm still going to have to feel you up for sharps or shooties, yeah? And your girl, there."

Jason let the girl pat him down. She wore a yellow hoodie over a blue plaid dress, her boots glinting with zippers. She gracefully turned to Evie, who lifted her arms and allowed it. The girl told her, "I'm Circe. Who are you?"

"Evie. I'm nobody."

Circe sighed and set a sea-horse shaped purse down beside her. Evie saw the glint of a gun inside. Circe saw her looking and shrugged. She drew herself up onto the Tauro's hood again. Jason sat beside her. Evie leaned against the car, watching them. Circe said, "You can ask the questions, Jase. But *she* stays quiet. I don't know her."

Evie couldn't argue with that logic.

Jason asked, "Why did you mutiny, Circe?"

She hunched up, her cloudy hair glittering from beneath the hood. A silvery octopus laced the ebony skin of her right wrist and hand. "Because we stopped trusting Silence and Night. It's why *you* left Lost Forever Souls, isn't it?"

"Is that how they are thought of by the other crews?"

"Oh, yeah. Something *off* about LFS." She jerked her chin at Evie. "She's one of them, isn't she?"

"You can trust her. Why did *you* stop trusting Silence and Night?"

"Our new recruit—Morgan. There was something not right about her, something . . ." Circe looked directly at Jason, her eyes a startling jade green. "Like you lot. Like La Fable Sombre. An energy that vibed wrong. Then I began my own prying about, found out some things."

"What things?"

"That maybe the five other members of Silence and Night's original crew never made it to retirement. That the remaining members were out there, hiding from them. Oh, you want my source? My mother. Who had been seeing a member of LFS when she was young, when Silence and Night were our ages— hard to imagine, that. So, my mom's boyfriend . . . he was murdered. I remember my mom being all upset about it when she *reminisced*. So why would Silence and Night's former cohorts be on the run? Then there were those 'traitors' they branded in front of us, who were never seen again. I heard about Matthew Orion. And your Vero was murdered . . ."

"Do the other crews have their suspicions?"

"The other crews are a little less curious and a whole lot

greedier than me and mine were. When we found out what we'd gotten from that shipwreck, that magic book from Hell . . . our newest recruit tried to steal it. She nearly killed me when she touched me . . . my heart *hurt*. My crew chased her away. So, we took the shipwreck loot and disappeared. That's when I came to you for help. Hiding the loot in that church didn't work like you said it would." She glanced at Evie, who cast a shocked look at Jason—*that* answered one of the questions she'd had. Circe continued, "Tell me something, Jase—why do you care about La Fable Sombre? Let them learn the hard way."

"How do you feel about *your* crew, Circe? Would you let them fall to Silence and Night's treachery?"

"Bloody White Hat." She smiled. "LFS have Ciaran Argent. He's a right bastard. I wouldn't cross him. When he got that magic book, did he keep it or give it to Mother Nightmare and Father Slit-Throat?"

"You're out of it, Circe." Jason's eyes were on the film. "What does it matter?"

"I really didn't want them to get that book. I should have tossed it back into the ocean. So what's your deal?" Circe turned to Evie. "Jase's instincts are usually good, so you planning on leaving?"

"No. I'm not."

Circe looked almost pitying. Then she shrugged and glanced at Jason. "Where's Diana? You promised me."

Jason reached into his coat, drew out a small bronze box. Circe opened it to reveal a stone statue of the huntress goddess Diana. She grinned. "Jase. She's perfect."

"Circe." Evie spoke quietly. "All my respect to you for your decision. Do you believe Silence and Night murder people?"

"Haven't you seen the graveyard?" Circe touched two fingers to her brow in a salute. "All my respect to you, girl, if you're planning something that's gonna put you on their bad side."

⎯⎯∿⎯⎯

Jason returned them, by spirit pentacle, to Silver Cove. They strolled through an older part of downtown, into a courtyard dominated by a Spanish mission church that was now an art gallery, closed for the night. Beyond a banyan tree glowing with lights, swoony music echoed through the courtyard from the nightclub beyond. Evie asked, "Why did you tell the Sirens to hide the *Bestiarum Vocabulum* in a church?"

"Silence and Night shouldn't have gotten that book, Evie."

"Why a *church*, Jason?"

Jason sat with her on the steps of the Spanish mission. The lights strung from the banyan tree cast a mosaic upon their skin. "Because what we can do is muted on sacred ground. *Any* sacred ground. I found that out when I was in Edinburgh with LFS and attempted to spirit myself into a church—I nearly ended up splattered against an outside wall."

"And you didn't tell the others?"

"I was new to it, Evie. Then there was that time in Barcelona . . . But the Marseille church was a test."

"Thanks." She tossed a question with a shrewd look that scrapped his careful approach. "What do you think we are?"

"I don't know. Sometimes, I see it. I hear it, when I'm alone. The thing that gave me power."

"What do you see?" she whispered.

He shook his head. "When I was thirteen, I ran onto a Los Angeles highway to save a dog—I saw a semitruck heading for me. I vanished into a spinning darkness scattered with silver symbols."

Evie shivered. Jason nodded. "It gets worse. As I held the dog, I saw something in that darkness —an equine shape with a black horn spiraling from its head. I fell out of that insane night, onto my knees, in front of my dad's house, the dog dead in my arms, twisted up, as if it had broken its bones trying to escape. A week later, I was sitting alone in the diner near my school when Ciaran Argent took a seat next to me." He continued wistfully, reminiscing, "Our first heist was in Barcelona. Ciaran, Mad, and I. We were sent to steal an ancient ring. After the strike, I remember walking down the aisle of the La Sagrada Familia church. Mad was wearing a champagne-pink gown. Ciaran slung an arm around my shoulders and slid that ring that had belonged to an emperor onto one of my fingers and said, '*You're one of us now, mate.*'" He smiled wryly. "Then we all began to feel sick and had to leave. We thought it was just the adrenaline fading, not that we were allergic to holy places." He lifted his gaze to hers. "But, in that moment, Evie, I had a family to replace the one that had fallen apart."

Evie understood. Jason had recognized in Ciaran his darkness, the desire to act as he wanted, to not be held back by laws and civility. It was as if he'd manifested a dangerous avatar as a brother.

If Silence and Night were king and queen, Ciaran Argent was their red-handed prince.

Jason clawed his fingers through his hair. He whispered, "Zeppelin. That's what I named my power."

Evie felt a prickling sensation on the back of her neck, as if someone were watching them from behind the mission door. She glanced over one shoulder at the door, sensed an unsettling presence behind it. She said, "I don't have a name for mine." Only an image of a serpentine girl with venom-green eyes and snakes for hair.

"It came to me at a bad time in my life, Evie. Before the dog incident."

"You make it sound like it's a curse."

"It's brought me nothing but blood and grief." The tautness in his voice made her throat tighten in sympathy.

"Jase. Is revenge worth all this? The surveillance, the evidence grabs . . . trying to prove to the world that LFS exists?"

"Proving *Silence and Night* exist. My life depends on it. I'm in hiding now. If they find me, they'll kill me. The only reason Ciaran hasn't thrown me to the wolves is because he's using me as a distraction."

She looked away, down at her hands, fingers twined. "Jason . . . Ciaran thinks they want you back. Yours is a rare talent. You're a Traveler—"

"They have Ciaran. For now." His mouth twisted. "They sent me to my death, Evie. Don't tell me they meant for only Vero to be killed."

Her throat ached in sympathy. "I know what it's like to lose people you love."

He narrowed a glance at her. "What happened to your parents?"

"They're gone." She hunched her shoulders, folding her arms. She remembered what Ciaran had said about Jason's mother. "What happened to you, Jason? To make your powers manifest?"

With difficulty, he said, "My mom died. My dad raised me after that." He paused. "I wasn't a good son. He named me Jason after the hero in the *Argonautica,* his favorite epic poem. I think he had high expectations." He looked at Evie and gently asked, "What was your mom like?"

Evie spoke dreamily: "My mom had green eyes and hair like mine and freckles. She told me fairy tales from all over the world. This horrible world," she whispered, fury in her voice. "I wish I could break it."

"Evie . . . that rage . . ." He looked out over the courtyard. "It's the brittle thread that connects La Fable Sombre. It's what cursed or gifted us with what we can do. You can let that fury carry you forward on a tide that will drown you and everyone around you, or you can leave them. I can help you."

She looked away. "No. You can't. Something is making my skin crawl here." She stood up. "Let's go get some drinks."

They strolled toward the nightclub, all sea-blue lighting streaked with goldfish neon. Inside, they wove toward the bar with its Art Nouveau theme. Evie flashed her fake ID. "What's your poison, PI?"

Jason leaned against the bar. "A whiskey sour." He took out his wallet. Evie slid a hundred-dollar bill to the bartender and ordered two bourbons. She had a plan. Jason smiled wryly and put away his wallet.

"Jase." Evie stepped closer to him. As the female singer began a Ragtime-y version of the White Stripes' "Seven Nation Army," Evie reached up, her fingers drifting across his neck, her dark lashes lowered. "Let's dance."

His hands slid to her hips. He bent his head, his lips a breath from hers. "Evie."

She draped her arms around his neck. She wore a gloss that made her lips glimmer like frost-glazed strawberries and smoky kohl around her eyes. As they danced, he whispered, "I'm holding a girl of smoke and mirrors. I don't know you at all, Evie Wilder."

She wanted to crack his perfect façade, wanted to know all his secrets. Problem was, he wanted to know all of *hers*. As they swayed to the music, his hand against her back, the other sliding to her waist, she studied the Cupid's bow curve of his lips. He held her as if afraid to break her.

She led him back to the bar, where she ordered a bottle of bourbon and pretended to drink more than she actually did, filling his glass every time it emptied. His eyelids were heavy, but this was going to be tough. Like chipping at a gorgeous glacier. "So, Jase, why'd you decide to be a private eye?"

He seemed to be considering how to answer her. He said, "When I left LFS," again, the wry curve of his mouth, "a three-month fall from grace began, a separation from anything resembling the order my dad taught me. Losing Vero and La Fable Sombre . . ."

She winced a little, guilty about plying him with booze. His past was bleeding from him like a wound she'd unstitched.

He continued, blurrily, "Then I met an OG private eye. Had a face like a battered lion's and a quicksilver intellect you wouldn't expect from his cheap suits and the way he talked. He'd tracked me down after I'd stolen from one of his clients. He gave me a business card and offered me a job." Jason downed his third bourbon. "I wound up in that cluttered closet of an office, listening to Johnny Cash and drinking tea, and I began to learn just what a private detective could be, what my dad had been. People call PIs when they're desperate, Evie, when their options have been exhausted. That PI told me, '*I am hope when everyone else lets them down*.'"

"But," she gestured, deliberately slurry. "You're plotting to bring down *my new family. Your* friends. I can't let you." She propped an elbow on one of his shoulders. "I think I drank too much . . . Do you live far?"

"Do you think it's a good idea to bring you to my hideout?" he gently asked.

"You won't try and take advantage of me."

"That's not what I meant—"

She began her third act, sliding toward the floor. He circled an arm around her, keeping her upright. He said, "All right then. Let's go."

"Why?" she whispered the word.

He looked at her. "Why?"

"Why are you trying to save me?"

"Because I was like you once. And I wish someone had saved me.'"

—◦◦◦—

They walked to where he was staying, and Evie kept up the act, laughing breathlessly, stumbling a little. When they reached the Blue Moon Motel, she halted, staring at the kitschy buildings, the doors painted bright blue. The motel's neon sign was a slinky coquette curved around a crescent moon. "*This* is where you live?"

"My parents were rich. My London gran is rich. My

grandmother in Cairo is rich. I'm not." They entered a room. She looked around, saw books and a laptop and a blank bulletin board scattered with red push pins. She frowned at the bulletin board. "That is not a good Sherlock board." She turned to see him shedding his coat to reveal a black sweater that had seen better days. He told her, "You can take the bed. The sheets were changed this morning. I'll sleep on the sofa."

She sat on the end of the bed and gazed out of a window with a view of the woods behind the motel. He told her, sounding wistful, "I can see the stars."

"You don't have a home to go back to?" This made her sad.

He moved into the bathroom, turned on the faucet. "This is just a war camp. My London grandmother wants to drag me to her terrifying yellow and black mansion—she's a former Bohemian and listens to Stevie Nicks, so she's cool—but I can't. I can't be anywhere Silence and Night might find me."

Evie turned her head, staring at the empty bulletin board. She got up and opened the fridge, sighed when she saw a bottle of Jack Daniel's. She grabbed it, found two coffee mugs—one had a smiley face and the other was painted with a unicorn reading a book.

After splashing his face, Jason stepped from the bathroom. Water glittered in his hair, on his eyelashes. He sprawled on the sofa, one arm over his eyes. "How many glasses of bourbon have I had?"

"Don't know." She dropped beside him and set both mugs on the coffee table scarred with old cigarette burns. "Did you know you have Jack Daniel's in your fridge?"

He lifted his arm over his head and regarded her with one eye. "You shouldn't be here."

She curled on the sofa, watching him. "Let's talk some more."

"I thought that's what I've been doing. Why don't *you* talk?"

"Here." She handed him the mug of Jack Daniel's. "You're going to need this, because I'm going to ask some brutal questions. You answer truthfully. And versa vice . . . I mean, vice versa."

His head drooped. He swiftly raised it. "Do go on."

She went for the throat. "Did you ever kill anyone?"

His eyes shuttered. He tossed down what was in the mug and set the mug back on the table. "Yeah."

That wasn't the answer she'd expected. She didn't like it. She wanted him to change it. But she continued relentlessly. "Did you and Ciaran ever suspect Silence and Night were a danger to La Fable Sombre?"

"Yes."

The last question was meant to accomplish something else, so Evie spoke carefully. "Do you really want to destroy La Fable Sombre? Or just Silence and Night?"

He didn't answer. She shot a look at him, only to find his eyes closed. She'd overdone it with the alcohol. He'd drowsed off.

She got up, moving silently. He'd set his phone beside his laptop. She picked up the phone. *Let's see who you are.* It wasn't locked. She was able to scroll to a pathetically sparse list of contacts. She tapped the gallery of pictures, found a photo of Jason, Mad, and Vero Jordan in front of an ice cream stand on the beach. The next photo was of Jason sitting with Ciaran in a nightclub, both in designer suits. She scrolled through other photos of his life with La Fable Sombre. He seemed different in those pictures—edgy, ready for violence.

Then, just for kicks, she looked at his playlist: Joy Division. Bauhaus. The Cult. Led Zeppelin. Guns N' Roses. Leonard Cohen. She put in his earbuds and listened to a song or two. Jason was now sprawled on the sofa and sleeping as seriously as he moved through life.

She picked up a few books on the table. Dostoevsky's *The Idiot*. A graphic novel—*Batman: The Court of Owls*—that brought a quick, sharp laugh from her. A small book with a worn red binding, the words "*Argonautica*" stamped in gold on the cover. She opened the book to find a black-and-white illustration of a boy in a fleece cloak, its hood adorned with ram horns. She leafed through the pages and found a scrawled message: You were a wild child. You have become a good man. I'm proud of you. Love, Dad.

She set the book down. She lifted his eyeglasses, examined the minuscule camera. She set the glasses down, touched the earpiece she'd seen him wear. It was made of a pearly black material like seashell, like the bugging device she'd found in her medallion.

She opened his laptop, was delighted by the screensaver: the Greek hero Jason on his ship with his Argonauts. It was a painting by William Russell Flint—one of her dad's favorite artists because of his Maxfield Parrish style. All Jason's files were neatly lined up, and all had mysterious names: *November Rain. Heart-Shaped Box. Kashmir. House of the Rising Sun . . .*

They were named after *songs*. Which one would hold information about the Dark Fable? She scoured the file names, tapping her teeth with one black-painted pinkie nail. She grinned.

She clicked *Paint It Black*.

Old-fashioned photographs appeared. Newspaper articles. Paintings. Words written in Latin. As she scrolled, illustrations of strange creatures appeared with descriptions beneath. A stag-headed man. A catlike creature wearing a crown of stars. A woman with talons for feet.

One painting was the portrait she'd seen in Silence and Night's basilica, of the founders of La Fable Sombre in their medieval gear. The caption beneath read: "Medieval Paris. First members of La Fable Sombre. A university student. A highwayman. A courtesan."

Next was a black-and-white photograph of a group of slinky young people. The couple in the center were straight out of a silent film—a girl with a cap of black hair and a devilish smile; a young man with a mesmerizing gaze and slicked-back hair. The caption beneath read: "Zoe Becker from Chicago and Kaden Idrissi from Morocco. The Stars. Joined in 1920. Became Mother and Father in 1930."

"The Gilded Age": A photograph of a young man in a tux, leaning against a column. Seated in a chair beside him was a girl with long pale hair, her gown dark and sweeping. "The Elegants. Oruko Musa from Nigeria and Astrid Ehrling from Denmark. Future Father and Mother."

Evie became lost in the La Fable Sombre history Jason had puzzled together. How had he tracked down all of this? She wanted to steal it. She skimmed bits and pieces, devouring the information. There had always been eight crews, since fifteenth-century France: La Fable Sombre, the flagship of the Kingdom, and seven others—the names of these crews varied throughout the centuries. Every ten years, the Father and Mother changed.

Two of the best in La Fable Sombre became the next Father and Mother. Ten years later, *that* Father and Mother retired and were replaced.

She scrolled to a photograph from 1950, of seven glamorous people who could have been extras in a movie she'd once see with Mad. This photo was tagged *The Hunters*. And the couple in the center—the clever-faced young man with hands in the pockets of his three-piece suit and the girl with the arch look and the flared dress . . .

"Ava?" Evie whispered, peering hard at the picture, thinking she must be mistaken. But the arch girl was definitely Ava Dubrowska, and the leonine boy, Ava's husband. She even wore the mermaid necklace.

Jason stirred. Evie threw a glance at him. She mournfully closed the laptop.

She moved from the room, closing the door gently behind her.

—⁓—

As soon as the door shut, Jason glided up from his false sleep. He hoped she'd found what he'd wanted her to.

—⁓—

A different Evie strode confidently up the steep stairway of the Pink Blight. She passed a group of guys without incident, the invisible veil cloaking her. The men shivered and looked around, one commenting, "What the fuck was that?"

She still had her keys, the ones Ava had given her. Because, of course, Evie realized with sudden clarity, Ava owned the Pink Blight, which had been something back in the day.

When Ava answered her door, sheathed in a purple wrap dress patterned with nightingales, she smiled. "Evie!"

"I'm La Fable Sombre." Evie watched Ava's honey-sweet gaze darken until it was as if something taloned and winged watched Evie.

Ava stepped back, ushering Evie in. "So you know."

As Evie sat on the turquoise sofa, surrounded by the butterfly-gaudy stained-glass lamps and tasteful tchotchkes that were probably the real deal and worth a mint, Ava moved into her kitchen, calling back, "They recruited you."

"Did you know?" Evie demanded.

Ava reappeared with a tray holding a teapot and cups decorated with blue shepherdesses. She made a performance with the tea, pouring it, adding a bit of cream and sugar to each cup. "We can sense each other, our kind. Although my power left me ten years ago. When I saw you disembark from that Greyhound bus as I sat in the diner . . . I knew. And I knew they would come looking for you. There is always someone who can travel the spirit roads, who will lead them to new recruits."

Ciaran and Mother Night. Jason. Evie frowned. "And you didn't feel it important to tell me this?"

"Oh, Evie, really." Ava cast her a knowing glance. "Would you have believed me?"

Of course Evie wouldn't have. She remembered stepping off that bus and seeing Ava crossing the street in the rain, holding a lavender umbrella. When Evie had come to Silver Cove from Los Angeles, Ava had been her first friend—because she'd recognized something in Evie.

"You own this building." Evie couldn't help the accusatory tone.

"With two others of my crew, when we retired. It was differ-ent then." Ava wistfully stirred her tea. "This place."

"You fixed up the attic."

"You didn't seem the type to accept charity."

"You were going to boot out the Brute."

"I was. I am not management, unfortunately, or he wouldn't have gotten in. His fall out of a window hastened his exit." She arched a knowing eyebrow, and Evie saw that girl from the photograph on Jason's laptop.

"You joined LFS in 1950," Evie noted.

"And how did you discover this?"

"I have my sources." *A gorgeous and difficult source with a shady past,* she thought.

"Hmm."

"How did you meet *your* La Fable Sombre?"

"My father and I fled to Romania when I was eight." Ava flicked her fingers against her teacup. "And that's where I met, ten years later, a young man like a beautiful lion. An Ameri-can." There was laughter in her eyes. "Then I met his friends. I was the new one. Our Silence and Night were the Rebels— they'd caused chaos during the war, in the countries that had fallen. Chaos for the Nazis. Our Night was a pilot, a girl from Idaho, freckles and all. And our Silence, an archaeology stu-dent from Cairo."

Evie whispered, "And then you figured out what you could do."

"Yes. When the power left me a few years ago—it didn't like that I was old and frail—it was an abandonment. But it was also as if a darkness had lifted from my spirit." Ava leveled a direct gaze upon Evie.

Evie stared at the woman who had never appeared more

than seventy and a youthful seventy at that. "Old and frail" is not how Evie would describe Ava Dubrowska. "You must have killer genes or miracle makeup, Ava. Or is that . . ." A shiver crept up from the tail of her spine to between her shoulder blades. "Is it because of the power?" She leaned forward. "What *is* our power? Do you know?"

The troubled look that flicked across Ava's face was not encouraging. Ava gently asked, "What can you do?"

"Be invisible. What could you do?"

"I could sing and lure people to become docile. It was very useful when we were stealing from vicious men who'd robbed the people they'd murdered." Evie saw the steel beneath Ava's gentility. "As for what it is . . . I could see it sometimes, my power. It looked like a little white-haired girl in a pinafore, only she had a bird's talons instead of legs. What shape is your power, Evie?"

That image swam up from the darkness in Evie's mind, a pale girl with slit-pupiled eyes and serpentine twists of hair. A girl who whispered to Evie in a language that sounded Greek. A girl who had visited her in a nightmare when she'd been thirteen, who had crouched over her, chanting, pressing her clawed hands into Evie's chest as her black gown slithered over Evie's legs. Evie would wake drenched in sweat, sick and pale and parched. The nightmare girl had gone away when Evie had begun to surf the red tide of puberty. "A girl. Like Medusa."

"The Greek gorgon who turned people into stone?"

"Everyone knows mythology these days." Behind Evie, something fell from a shelf and shattered. She jumped, twisted around to see a porcelain angel on the floor, its head and one wing spinning across the hardwood. Her stomach hurtled a little.

Ava ignored the fallen angel. "Holy places tame the power. You need to watch out for palo santo wood. Gabrielle, our maker of potions when we were La Fable Sombre, believed that malachite and holy wood had some sort of chemical properties that didn't agree with whatever caused our powers."

Evie was still staring at the broken angel. "What *are* our powers?"

"They are us, Evie." Ava smiled gently. "All that we are. All our fears and desires. Our way of keeping sane, of thriving in a darkness that seeks to crush us."

"You were a Mother Night. And your hubby was a Father Silence."

Ava inclined her head the slightest bit before pinning Evie with a shrewd look. "And have you met the current Father and Mother?"

"They are terrifying."

"Well, they need to be formidable, Evie."

"Do they, though?" Evie felt her voice dropping off. She was exhausted. "Did your crew ever kill anyone?"

"What a question. We were *thieves*, Evie. Not assassins. That blonde firecracker I saw you with—did *she* push Mr. Brute out of the window? He was still drunk when he told the authorities that an owl girl had lured him over the ledge." Ava narrowed her eyes. "Have they harmed people, your La Fable Sombre?"

Evie thought about Lila Pearce being poisoned by Ciaran. She remembered Lycan and the blood on Ciaran's shirt. And

Vero . . . She didn't want to lie to Ava. She stood and retrieved the broken angel. She replied, "I can't leave them."

"Oh, Evie."

Evie set the broken angel on the table. "I should go now. Thank you for the tea. I'll be seeing you."

"Evie . . ."

But Evie had already stepped out, letting the door shut behind her. She knew some things now.

—◆◆—

Queenie and Dev picked Evie up in front of the Pink Blight after she texted them. As Evie slid into the passenger seat of the Aston Martin, Dev met her gaze in the rearview.

"How was your date, young lady?"

"Informative."

"You are a reckless girl." Queenie eased the car into the usual Friday night traffic on the boulevard. As they passed the little abandoned courtyard where Evie used to sit during nice evenings, Evie experienced a nostalgic pang. Dev glanced back at her.

"Queens is wearing a Piguet watch. I've got a gold-and-diamond ring. And you, luv, are wearing a pair of shoes that probably cost more than me monthly paycheck when I was a bag boy at the supermarket. You think we'll get through this neighborhood alive?"

Evie glanced down at her loafers with their baroque shape. They *had* been expensive. But she deserved them, after that Marseille debacle. She shifted her backpack onto her lap, looked out the window. "I still have friends in this neighborhood, so don't badmouth it, Devilmaycare."

"I am sorry, Eves. Truly." He batted his eyelashes at her. "But I *am* a villain."

As they pulled up to the warehouse lair, Evie saw a big black Lincoln with mirrored windows parked at the curb. Her good mood was butchered by apprehension.

"I hate it when they show up out of the blue." Dev got out of the car and strode to the entrance. He glanced at Evie as she and Queenie moved to stand beside him. "Papa Silence must be here to tell us more about that nifty Pandora jar. Don't get nervous."

"Nervous?" Queenie smiled. "We just escorted Invisible Girl on a date with our mortal enemy."

"He's not," Evie whispered.

"He's Jase." Dev shrugged. "He's not going to screw us over. Oh. Wait. Yes, he is."

"He's going to nuke Silence and Night and take us with him." Queenie's whisper was furious.

Evie glared at them.

The doors opened and one of Silence and Night's hired muscle stood there, scowling, arms folded, his eyes narrowed in swirls of black kohl.

"'lo," Dev greeted with a swagger. "How's life in the Batavi guild?"

"He's waiting." The Batavi pointed to the warehouse mural, which had been opened to reveal the stairs up to the lair.

As they stepped into the main room, Evie drew her shoulders back. All the lamps were lit. A song about a black hole sun blasted from the speakers attached to the tricked-out Victrola turntable. She heard Mad's laugh, the clatter of pool balls. In the alcove where the moss-green walls were hung with antique sports memorabilia, Father Silence, having shed his blazer, leaned over the pool table, concentrating on the shiny targets, cue skillfully aimed. Ciaran stood nearby, twirling his stick. Mad, wearing a pink cotton prairie dress, sat in a chair. She held her stick like a spear.

"I didn't realize," Father Silence spoke idly, "Madrigal was a pool shark." He struck the cue ball and all the balls on the table bounced against each other, finally gliding into individual pockets.

"Did she hustle you out of cash?" Dev shed his blazer. "I can win it back for you."

"As if." Mad rose. "Papa's here to give us more info on our next job."

Ciaran led them to the main room, where crimson cartons from the Lotus Palace were waiting. Everyone sat, divvying up the cartons.

"The House of One Thousand Nights is in Russia." Father Silence tucked chopsticks neatly into his carton. "The auction itself is called Angel's Vault. It moves from location to location once a year. This year, it's being hosted by the Petrov family. Their matriarch is Nicola Petrov."

"Nikki Petrov? She mutinied from the Misfits in the 80s. Stole something and took off." Mad looked up sharply. "A *former member of La Fable Sombre* is hosting this year's Angel's Vault?"

"That's right." Silence watched Ciaran, for any fractures in his façade, Evie suspected.

Ciaran shrugged. "I always like a bit of a challenge. She'll be expecting us. She isn't as powerful as she used to be."

Evie scooped noodles from her carton. She watched Father Silence remove a black plastic folder from his blazer and toss it onto the table. "Here are your identities. No one asks questions at Angel's Vault. Unless, of course, you're suspected of being the law."

"We're playing *roles*?" Mad was breathless. "Oh, this is going to be even better than I thought."

Ciaran swept up the folder and removed its contents. He shoved aside cartons to lay out a map of a castle and the grounds surrounding it. He set down five cards with individual names and what appeared to be character descriptions. Evie was fascinated by these but refrained from grabbing one. There was a photograph of the House of One Thousand Nights and other pictures of what Evie assumed to be pertinent information.

"The third and final heist of the year." Father Silence's gaze swept over each of them, settled upon Evie. "And if you succeed . . . rewards."

Evie carefully lifted a new illustration of the Pandora jar and studied it. "Was she real? Pandora?"

"She was, according to that object. Whether the jar contains anything or not . . ." Silence moved to his feet. He idly perused the shelving unit of vinyl. Ciaran loved music, and his collection was eclectic and surprising. Evie wondered if he brought it to every lair. Then she wondered how many lairs La Fable Sombre had inhabited. She asked, "Where will you put the jar once you have it?"

Silence turned and gave her that saint-with-an-edge smile. "Mother Night will be responsible for that. Blend in. Case the grounds. Find out where the vault containing the item is. You'll be staying at the castle." He sat back down, reached for one of the red cookies scattered on the table. "Now, shall we read our fortunes?"

While the others cracked open their cookies, Evie got up and selected a vinyl from the collection. She replaced what was playing on the Victrola. As Prince's "When Doves Cry" pulsed through the space like an ancient hymn, Queenie began to sing along with Mad. Dev rose and drew Mad to her feet, twirling her. Ciaran joined in the singing, his voice resonant. Evie laughed, watching them.

Radiating innocence, she met Father Silence's burning blue gaze and pretended she hadn't just issued a challenge.

Chapter Fourteen

The Devil's Own Luck

Evie sat apprehensively in the back of a Rolls-Royce Phantom, opposite Ciaran, tugging at her blue silk cocktail dress. Beside her, Dev, a red lotus tucked behind one ear, was telling Queenie about his false persona's character arc. Mad was the driver, chic in a diamond collar and a pin-striped suit. She wore a pink wig, coiled up into two knots.

"So these Collectors...," Evie ventured. "If they're not Silence and Night's clients—who are they?"

"Mob bosses. Rich criminals. Oligarchs. Retired thieves." Ciaran's eyes were obsidian in a stripe of light. He never fussed with anything, had zero twitches, and could be as still as an assassin. Evie didn't think he was ever nervous—it was as if he *absorbed* chaos.

"*There's* our Door." Mad drove down a woodsy road, high beams on. Amid the trees, Evie saw a garage with an advertisement for cigarettes faded on its bricks. Ciaran raised a hand.

The air seemed to crackle. The garage door rolled up, revealing a night road lined by forest. Snow was falling. Mad drove toward that other night. Shadows folded around the vehicle as if they were in some supernatural car wash. Evie looked into the darkness outside the windows, thought she saw shapes, inhuman faces. She shivered.

As the Phantom slid out onto the road, Evie looked back—they had entered through a wooden barn. Then they were driving through a country of snow and forests, with mountains in the distance. She checked the time on her phone—it was still five thirty.

"Welcome to Mother Russia." Dev looked out the window. "And hope she doesn't know we're here."

Evie breathed out when she glimpsed, in the distance, the glowing constellation of a city with Byzantine onion roofs, a pinnacle-like tower of diamonds, and flood-lit eighteenth-century architecture. She had to refrain from wriggling in her seat because of the thrilling energy that sparked through her.

Mad swung the Rolls-Royce off the freeway. Everyone but Ciaran swayed to one side.

"Thanks, Mad." Dev had had Queenie practically flung in his lap. She straightened. Evie squinted when she thought she saw a rosy blush sweep across the other girl's cheekbones.

Mad turned onto a country road where mansions loomed behind imperious gates. Pale statues rose among evergreen topiaries. Evie's nerves were vibrating. None of her comrades seemed at all stressed or nervous, chatting and teasing one another.

After a while of bumping along, Mad stopped the car in a clearing. "Here we are."

Dev straightened his Gucci blazer. "I've come a long way from council housing." He glanced at Ciaran. "What about you?"

Ciaran laughed softly and didn't answer. Dev sighed. "Did you know, Evie, Ciar's dad was a notorious jewel thief who ended up in prison? Ciar lived on the London streets and learned to sneak into the houses of the rich to steal from them."

"That's not very imaginative." Ciaran's mouth twitched. "You'll have to do better than that."

"Coats." Mad dug furs from the back of the car and handed them out. Evie ran a hand along the blue fur of her coat before shrugging it on.

"Are we walking from here?" she asked.

"That we are." Mad slid out of the Rolls, her white fur coat billowing. Queenie unfolded from the car, her burgundy gown a carnage against the snow. A necklace of red beadwork splashed across her collarbones. Mad continued, "We aren't supposed to know each other, so we'll separate the closer we get."

In the dark, in the falling snow, they walked down the forest road, which became a paved lane leading to a stone wall with looming wooden gates carved into rearing horses.

Dev held out a hand to Evie, who clasped it. She wished the veil over the two of them. It came as shadows and cold. They walked to the gates, Dev reaching into his pocket and taking out his phone. "It's amazing how vulnerable security cameras are. I'll just freeze the images of a deserted road until we all get through."

Dev charmed the gates open. He and Evie stepped forward.

Ciaran, Mad, and Queenie followed. Evie let the veil fall from her and Dev as they all kept to the shadowy landscaping of trees and hedges. At the end of a curving drive loomed a castle, this one of pale stone, with blue roofs and half-animal statuary curving from the eaves. A massive stairway swept up from the glittering snow. Lamps like small moons glowed in the night. An army of luxury cars was being driven away by valets as people in evening wear ascended the stairs.

Ciaran and Dev slipped from the shadows, joining the guests moving up the walkway. A man in a suit and earpiece met them before the stairs. Ciaran presented a black card. He and Dev were waved through.

Evie, Mad, and Queenie approached the castle. Evie, dazzled by the winter evening and the sheer impossibility of being in Russia within minutes, moved dreamily. She thought over the plan they had argued and agonized over until three in the morning the night before. *Step one: Get through the gates and separate.*

Mad flashed a black card at the security guard. They were allowed to ascend the stairs. They entered an enormous hall, where two golden horses curved to either side of a grander staircase. People in flashy jewelry and expensive clothing wandered around. A banquet table displayed pretty appetizers and cakes so tiered and detailed, they were works of art.

Mad circled a giant taxidermy bear in the center of the room. Queenie eyed a pair of young men in tweed suits, their hair threaded with gold leaves.

"It's a hotel for criminals." Mad peeked from behind the bear.

Evie experienced a moment of disorientation, in this place, surrounded by what she could only imagine were very wicked people. Once again, she thought, *What am I doing?*

"Let's get some food. I'm ravenous," Queenie declared. She headed for the banquet table.

"Come on, Eves." Mad swaggered after Queenie, hands in her blazer pockets.

Just as she followed her two friends, Evie glimpsed a young man in a black suit, his profile almost pharaoh-like—but his hair was blond, not glossy raven. She stopped cold.

A group of young elegants in Armani sauntered past, conversing in another language, and she lost sight of Jason Ra. Mad winked at one young man with a diamond stud in his nose.

"Don't flirt," Queenie told her. "Please don't flirt."

Step two: Blend in.

Mad led them up the stairs and used the black card to unlock a pair of doors. They entered an enormous suite. Huge windows overlooked a wild park. Everything was patterned in silver and blue. A gigantic painting of black horses running beside the sea hung over the fireplace. Mad told them that the castle, with its odd statues and stained-glass windows depicting occult folklore, had been the secret vacation home of Peter the Great. The air in the castle was chilly, as if, somewhere within, something was sucking up the energy. Evie heard music thumping, drunken voices, shouts, and laughter. Occasionally, there was a crashing sound.

They were among thieves.

—◌◌◌—

An hour later, as Evie was brushing her teeth in the palatial bathroom, she began to shake as if a terrible chill had splintered into her bones. She spit out the toothpaste, shoved aside zit cream, deodorant, and lipsticks labeled Raven Blood and

Birthday Sugar, to brace herself against the sink. She shivered, splashed warm water over her face. But she couldn't stop shaking. She sank to the floor, her arms over her head. She breathed deep as darkness began to overwhelm her, the past few weeks collapsing inward. *What am I doing? I could die.*

"Evie?" Mad's concerned voice came as hands gripped her shoulders. "You're so *cold.* Queens, get a robe."

A robe was swept around Evie. Mad rubbed Evie's hands. Queenie was leaning in the door frame, holding a steaming mug. "I've got tea."

Evie told them, "Stop hovering."

Queenie crouched beside her, barefoot in a T-shirt and jeans, and handed her the tea.

As Evie sipped, panic sank its horned head back into the abyss. Mad draped an arm around her shoulders. "We're meeting the boys for a private dinner. No one'll notice—there are like over a hundred guests here."

"I need steak and seafood." Queenie stood. "So get it together, Invisible Girl."

Feeling as if she were surrounded by bossy older sisters, Evie pushed herself up. "I'd better get ready then."

Evie, Queenie, and Mad moved through the House of One Thousand Nights. The housekeeping staff hadn't yet come around. There was glitter on the floor. A feathered mask was flung on the statue of a naked woman. The carcass of a roast chicken sat on a pedestal—the small statue that had been there previously was gone. There were glasses of wine everywhere. Queenie grabbed an unopened bottle of Chardonnay on a table. Mad plucked a

240

fancy lollipop wrapped in cellophane from a bowl and handed one to Evie, who wondered if it was wise to be sampling food left around in a castle full of sketchy characters. But the lollipop tasted like champagne, and there was a sugar-mummified butterfly inside it. The treat was a perfect metaphor for everything around her: extravagant and ruthless. Mad continued, "We're meeting Priest here. He can tell us more about Pandora's jar. What it can do."

Evie halted at the foot of a staircase that led to a landing. At the top was an enormous painting in a frame of gold knots—a Pre-Raphaelite girl in a black gown, her face painted to resemble a skull, her hair a tangle. She held a symbolic heart. The painting was a maiden death, similar to the one on the medallion that had belonged to Evie's mother. Evie placed a hand over the medallion that rested against her collarbones.

"Eves, let's *go*," Mad called back to her.

Evie, Mad, and Queenie moved into a large room, where a table was scattered with plates containing steak, shrimp, and delicate savories. Little cakes sat beneath glass domes. Ciaran was sprawled in a chair, one booted foot on the table. Dev swung a chair around, and Queenie sat, twirling her crimson rabbit foot with its pewter hare face. Mad strode toward the table and leaned down to whisper in Ciaran's ear.

As Evie observed them, these glittering predators, Ciaran's gaze fell upon her. She stood there in her short fur coat, electric blue dress, and Prada loafers. She was one of them now. A radiant joy bloomed within her, and it took her a moment to realize what it was, what she felt whenever she remembered Juliet and Ezra. It was beyond affection.

It was love.

"Evie." Mad, draped against Ciaran's chair, beckoned to her. "Come on."

Evie smiled and moved toward her family, letting the door shut behind her.

—⁕—

Ciaran had meant them to be relaxed. In that suite he and Dev shared, he set the map of the House of One Thousand Nights and its grounds on the table amid the leftover feast and drops of spilled coffee.

"You don't think they have cameras and listening devices in these suites, do you?" Mad tossed her hair over one shoulder.

"No. Because the guests are crooks or the criminally wealthy—all ultraparanoid." Dev tapped the blueprint to the House of One Thousand Nights, traced the paths to the outbuildings. "These blueprints are new. There's nothing on this map about the stone structure Mad saw when she went to the roof."

"You"—Ciaran looked at Evie—"Dev, and Mad will be investigating this building."

"You think it's the vault," Evie guessed.

"I can hear something outside of these walls." Ciaran's eyes hooded. "A hum like an electric current. I felt the same when we were near the *Bestiarum Vocabulum*. It's the sound of something containing a whole lot of power."

"So, how do we do this?" Evie challenged.

Ciaran told her, "Mad's going to be the Eye. You and Dev, the Strikers. Queenie and I, the Flaunt, as well as Tooth and Claw—because I've only seen a Russian security company around and that's concerning."

"Will we need to fight?" Queenie looked at Evie. "If you can make us all invisible, there shouldn't be any violence."

Evie flashed a look around the table. "I can only invisible one person at a time, and that takes effort. I don't know if I can . . . cast it . . . over someone without contact."

"We're all going to practice. Here, in this room. To make sure everything works." Mad began to levitate. "To make sure there's no malachite or anything else that might mess us up."

"Because the person throwing this party was once LFS?" Evie stepped back from the table.

"Nikki Petrov has a rep for villainy." Dev sauntered to a cabinet, opened it to reveal a widescreen TV and a stereo. He tilted his head a little.

The TV flicked on to a movie channel. As a sultry song haunted the air, Dev smiled. Evie walked to him, saw that he wasn't holding a remote, stared at the TV. "You can do that?"

"Any bits of electricity. I can charm a device as easily as a lock."

"What about you, Queenie?" Evie wondered how the Alchemist was going to practice *her* ability.

"I'm already doing it." Queenie put her feet up on the chair Dev had vacated. "I added something to everyone's coffee."

"What?" Dev spun. Mad stopped levitating. Evie almost dropped the mug she held.

Ciaran laughed. Queenie smiled. "Relax. I'm joking." She pushed aside Dev's chair and stood. She dumped fruit from a crystal bowl, poured water into it from a pitcher. She drew two vials from a pocket and uncapped them. "Turn off the lights."

Evie flicked the switch. She watched Queenie pour whatever

was in the vials into the water. Incandescent bubbles began rising, pink, blue, purple, and emerald, drifting toward the ceiling. Dev reached out and popped one. Neon color burst outward. He flinched back, grinned as the color continued to mist, before fading.

"It's not radioactive, is it?" Mad poked a bubble. Pink radiance splashed around her, momentarily painting half of her face.

"It's just like the solution used for smoke bubbles in fancy cocktails. Only filled with a chemical I devised that echoes an extended version of sonoluminescence." Queenie popped a bubble and resembled a mermaid in the blue light that bathed her. "And a Wish."

"You would have been wasted at NASA." Mad rose to pop a purple bubble. The garish light made her look unearthly.

"Your Doors?" Evie turned to Ciaran. He got up, opened a closet door, revealing Times Square at night. He closed the Door.

Evie shrugged and silently called the veil around her. This time, it seemed to flutter like black butterflies, clinging to her, followed by those whispering voices.

"I know you can cover whoever you have contact with," Ciaran told her, his voice muffled by the veil, "but I need you to make Mad invisible when you *separate*."

Evie stood in the veil, staring up at Mad as the other girl rose toward the ceiling. Evie lifted one arm, felt the ribbons of darkness writhe from her. She willed the darkness as if it were a living creature. It swept from her in butterfly bits, toward Mad . . .

. . . and faded. The veil around Evie shredded, vanished. Fatigue pooled through her from just that simple effort.

"Evie. You can do it," Ciaran said calmly. "Close your eyes and concentrate."

She did so, keeping her arm raised. The cold darkness she summoned clung to her again, accompanied by a girl's eerie singing. Evie heard water dripping, saw a dark cavern, a female form rising against a glowing green light—

"Evie!" Ciaran's urgent voice snapped her eyes open.

The short distance between her and Mad, who still levitated, was scarred by a jagged rip in reality that revealed a violet sky and a landscape of black grass. Mad hovered in a flurry of black butterflies.

The gap vanished. Evie and Mad were wrapped in the veil, the room beyond them leeched of color. Ciaran's, Queenie's, and Dev's voices were muted. Mad spun with a laugh—

Evie let the veil vanish. Her eardrums popped as Mad fell. Ciaran lunged, caught Mad. Queenie and Dev were immediately on either side of Evie as she staggered.

"I'm okay. I'm okay." She shivered, lifted her head to see Mad with one arm looped around Ciaran's shoulders. She couldn't believe what she'd done, cast invisibility over someone from afar.

Mad was still laughing. "That was brilliant."

Ciaran met Evie's gaze. "There you are, blackbird."

CHAPTER FIFTEEN

The Knight

Evie woke before Queenie and Mad, as the sunlight was fading in their suite. They had been up with Dev and Ciaran until six in the morning, plotting. Evie had slept like a vampire.

She dressed quickly and left the suite to seek out Jason Ra—she had recognized him despite his disguise of blond hair and thick black glasses. It was curiosity that drove her and, also, an urgent desire to swear at him.

She spotted him crossing the foyer below. She made herself invisible and followed him through the House of One Thousand Nights. He moved among the Collectors and thieves in the halls and drawing rooms, avoiding the knife-throwing contests, the slinky girls.

He approached a familiar man speaking with a woman whose hair was spiked with diamond pins. When the man spotted Jason, his face immediately became a mask. He didn't run. He casually stepped back from the woman, turned, and walked down the hall, his tangerine suit glowing against the black and gold of the corridor. *Priest,* Evie thought, intrigued.

Jason followed the man who was LFS's consultant down a flight of stairs, through a pair of crimson doors, and into a bar with murals of Minoan bull dancers on the walls. Watching, Evie kept the shadows veiling her. It was as if the stone and wood, threaded with ancient secrets, nurtured what she was.

Jason leaned against the bar near Priest and ordered a ginger ale. The bartender eyed him with scorn, her silver nose ring glinting. Priest said to the bartender. "Bourbon, please."

The bourbon appeared. Priest eyed Jason over the rim of his glass as he drank, ice cubes clinking. He set down the glass. "I know who you are. You're the one who left."

Jason took a paper from his pocket, unfolded it, and slid it to Priest. "You're a Collector. What do you know about this object?" Jason tapped the paper sketched with the image of the amphora jar that was the Anesidora Pithos. "I know this is being offered in the secret auction. What is it?"

"What's in it for me?" Priest's voice trailed off when Jason lifted his phone and showed him a picture of an old book with a frayed pink cover scarred with gilt symbols. Priest whispered, "The *Cara Dora* . . . a book of the Order of the Golden Dawn. Do you have it?"

"I have it. I can get it to you by the usual means." Jason's incredible poise made Evie a little less afraid for him.

"Before I answer"—Priest eyed the illustration—"I want to make sure I'm not betraying my darling Mad. Or crossing Ciaran Argent." It was a warning.

"I just want to know what this object is."

Priest drew a pair of glasses from his blazer. He examined the sketch. "A vessel."

"Yes?" Jason prompted.

"Vessels *contain*. The Anesidora Pithos is from an ancient culture that believed in spirits or demons that take the shapes of animals—dangerous spirits capable of great harm. Silence and Night *cannot* get ahold of this object."

The shadows that wrapped around Evie began to stir like sentient creatures. She kept them close to her, urging them to stay twined around her.

"Do *you* want it?" Jason asked Priest.

"Hell, no." Priest ordered two more bourbons. His gaze pinned Jason. "Why did you leave LFS?"

"Someone died." Jason pocketed the paper with the sketch. "And you?"

Priest's niceness peeled away as if stripped by turpentine. He became all edges. "Same."

Evie almost let the invisibility unravel from her as shock blindsided her: Priest had been *one of Silence and Night's crew*? She should have known.

Priest knocked back his drink, set the glass down. "You'll be on the run forever, never knowing if they've found you."

"Why are you helping Ciaran Argent?" Desperation tangled in Jason's voice.

"I trade in knowledge." Priest shrugged. "They're La Fable Sombre."

A group of people in gold jewelry, eyes glittering, entered. They spoke Russian as they crowded the bar. Both Priest and Jason tensed. When no one made any attempts to come at them,

Priest asked Jason, "What are you up to, James Bond Junior? Striking out on your own? It isn't revenge, is it, for something they did? Oh, dear. How boring."

Jason said idly, "I'm ending Silence and Night."

"Yes. Revenge." Priest nodded sagely. "And what did they do to you?"

"They murdered two people I loved."

The light left Priest's eyes. "They do that." He checked his watch. "Time's almost up. I'm meeting with them soon, two of your former partners in crime."

"What are we?" Jason whispered the question Evie had never gotten a satisfying answer to. She listened, scarcely breathing. "If you were like us . . ."

"Hell if I know. Silence and Night made up their dark mythos when we were young and first recruited. Silence was raised Catholic. Night was brought up in an orphanage ruled by nuns. They have a macabre sort of piety, that pair. Can you believe they have a family? Conjured at least one human being into the world. I remember Night being round as a moon, years ago. And they've two hidden away in European boarding schools." Priest levered a look on Jason.

Evie almost forgot to keep the darkness of the veil close around her. She flickered into visibility, and a young couple nearby stared at her. She drew back into the shadows. The veil folded around her again. The couple hurried away.

Jason and Priest continued their conversation in a world leeched of color. Priest was saying, "Silence and Night believe our powers come from . . ." He pointed downward, indicating Hades, the Underworld, hell.

"What did your predecessors believe?" Jason demanded.

"The Dolls? Ruby was a Somali Goth goddess, and Annabelle was like David Bowie if he'd been born a girl in Jaipur. God, I was in love with them. They believed our powers were an evolutionary development, that we *manifested* them."

"What happened to the Dolls?"

"Oh, *you* know." Priest's look was dark.

"Silence and Night murdered them," Jason pronounced, and Evie wasn't shocked by that at all.

"Yes." Priest's mask cracked again, revealing the anguish beneath. "Silence and Night killed them. And made it look as if they'd killed one another. That's Silence and Night's modus operandi."

"I'm aware of it." Jason was grim. "Where are your fellow LFS members? I'm guessing they didn't retire."

"They are dead." Priest downed another bourbon. "Except for the Basilisk, the treacherous bastard. No more questions. Get that item to me." Priest handed Jason a pink business card with a name and address on it in gilded script.

"How do I find the Basilisk?" Jason asked as Priest winked at one of the bartenders while setting down a hundred-dollar bill.

"You won't. And you don't want him to find *you*. If you desire to end Silence and Night—get ahold of the Pandora jar, the Anesidora Pithos. Do *not* let La Fable Sombre take that jar back to them." He hesitated, seeming to debate whether to offer up another bit of information. "Don't seek me out again." He slipped away, the shadows submerging him as if he were a bright salamander disappearing into a murky pool.

Evie watched Jason set his elbows on the bar and push his hands through his dyed hair.

What are you doing? she thought imploringly. *Here among the serpents?*

She touched her maiden death medallion. She tapped it thoughtfully. She raised it before her eyes, squinting. As she strolled away, the ribbons of invisibility unraveling, she lifted the medallion and spoke to it. "I'm going for a walk in the statue garden."

She used the front entrance, flashing one of the black cards they'd each been given. The winter air made her feel isolated as she moved down the enormous stair. She followed a path into a barren garden, where the statue of a girl stood, arms outstretched. The statue had tiny horns. Evie moved down the path, to the next statue, a boy curved like a crescent moon, his feet talons.

When she heard the step behind her, she slyly said, "You always manage to find me."

Jason Ra moved to her side. She looked at him. Even wearing a stupid Laplander hat and black-rimmed glasses, he seemed remote and dangerous. Vengeful people were always dangerous, to themselves as well as to everyone around them. Evie had read that somewhere. "That's not a great look for you, Ra."

"How did you know?" He jerked his chin at the maiden death medallion.

"Why else would you give it back? It was a ruthless move, planting a bug inside." She twirled the medallion. "I respect that." She led him toward a wooded hill. They reached the summit, where a tower, a folly of white stone, rose. They trudged up the stairs to the roofed top. Evie almost tripped on the handle of a trap door set in the floor. As they sat on a bench and gazed out at the wintery landscape, she asked, "Are you going to try and sabotage this? *Don't.*"

He hunched forward. "They were my family too, for a while."

"Ciaran didn't kill your father, Jason."

"No. But he works for the man who did."

She couldn't argue with that. She hunched up.

"Interpol doesn't believe they exist, Evie. My father believed. He was killed because of it. That's what you've joined—an ancient guild that protects itself with murder. They all have their secrets, your new family, and bad pasts. Vero and I were accepted, but our inclusion went completely against La Fable Sombre's code of outcasts only. All our unnatural abilities manifested through a crisis. Every person in your new family, Evie, is damaged. La Fable Sombre is a beast that feeds on broken lives."

"What do you expect me to do, Ra? Leave them? I have nowhere else to go." Dealing with Jason Ra was like trying to outwit her own reflection. "I can't."

"I thought the same. Until I held a dying girl in my arms."

Her throat knotted up. She kept her gaze from him, focusing on the ground between her boots. He removed his glasses and watched the sky. "Look," he said softly.

She looked. A vast rainbow of incandescent colors began to ribbon across the sapphire blue. As the light show flowed behind pine trees on a ridge, simply breathing the air felt magical. They watched the aurora borealis continue to glow in the sky like a city of melting jewels. Turning, she caught its reflection in his eyes.

"Why did you join them?" Her question was a plea. *I need to know what you want, Jason Ra.*

He watched the sky radiate with neon pinks, greens, and purples. Softly, he said, "I was angry. I was grieving. I blamed my father for something that I shouldn't have."

His mother, Evie realized with a surge of concern.

"It's as if Ciaran sensed it, as if he could follow the scent of anger and loss. Mad and Vero were my calming muses. Ciaran was the tempest that drew us in. Before him, the world ruled us." Bitterness edged his voice. "He made us feel like *we* ruled the *world*. We were careless. Cruel. I did things I'm not proud of. And Mad changed too. And Dev. And Queenie." He looked at her.

Evie thought of Mad blithely luring the Brute out of the window. Queenie had created a poison because she could. Dev had no problem using his powers of persuasion on people as well as objects. Her mouth tightened. She decided to take control of the direction this conversation was taking. "I know you're here to sabotage this."

"What Silence and Night are asking you to steal . . . the Anesidora Pithos—you can't give it to them."

Evie watched the aurora borealis, awed by its spectrum of colors. "My mom used to read me fairy tales and myths. She always made the monsters sympathetic. The false mother in Rapunzel was just heartbroken and lonely. Medusa the Gorgon was protecting her sisters. Maybe Silence and Night . . ." She shook her head. "And Pandora might have unleashed nightmares, curious and reckless as she was . . . but she also let hope into the world." She sighed. "Hope is the worst monster of all. Hope is a fickle flirt. He promises you that everything will be okay. Then he just flicks his cigarette at you and grins and says, 'Fooled you.' The bastard."

He watched her. "You're a very cynical person."

"Yes, I am. Aren't you worried Ciaran's going to know you're here? Or are you unwisely taunting him?"

"Does that seem like something I'd do?" He pulled off the stupid hat, revealing that blond dye job that made her wince. "He *knows* I'm here, Evie. He uses me the way he uses Nara and Fenrir when they try to compete—as a distraction. Only he's using me to deflect Silence and Night's attention."

Evie wanted to clasp one of his hands but curled her own into her pockets. "Ciaran must have known you'd tell me about the gravesite in Morocco, about his plans."

"He's counting on it." Jason's eyes were all dark.

Evie didn't like that statement. "He wants me to hate Silence and Night. Because he does."

"And do you?"

"What reason would I have to?" She reached out and touched his hair. "That is awful."

He slid a hand through his hair. She watched, incredulous, as it darkened to its original color. "Neat trick," she whispered. "What *is* your trick, exactly? I thought it was . . ."

He swept a hand over his face, and she was gazing at a different person, could see Jason in only the eyes. She shivered.

The pieces fell into place. How he was never caught at LFS's locations, how he could spirit away, how he could change his appearance. She whispered, *"You can use other people's powers."*

"Whatever gives us our power can be learned like code." He carelessly swept a hand over his face, and she was relieved to see *him* again. "I can learn bits and pieces of others' and store it away. I've picked up a bit of Silence's. Night's, as in the spiriting away. Mad's. Never learned Ciaran's or Queenie's. I can do a bit of what Dev does."

"And mine? That's why my invisibility worked at the Palm and the Lotus when I was with you, when it wasn't supposed to. You *amplified* it." She let out a short laugh of amazement. "What you can do . . ." A grim realization struck her. "Ciaran needs you, Jason. He wants you back."

"I know." He met her gaze and her heart suddenly felt like it had flaming daggers in it. "I learned Vero's talent. I learned how to find valuables. Including people." He bent his head, slid his phone from a pocket. "Silence and Night have the two missing children Micki O'Malley had been searching for before he passed. The ones I promised him I'd find."

Evie felt the world tilt. She thought the glorious sky might come crashing down. She gripped the edges of the stone bench. "*Micki O'Malley* was the detective you were working for?"

Jason nodded. "The children were in boarding schools in Europe. But Silence and Night brought them back to their separate homes for winter break. I need to find those homes . . . but Silence and Night, being what they are, have wards against our tricks."

Evie opened the maiden death medallion and stared down with blurred vision at a tiny photo of her siblings. Her voice fragile, she asked, "Do you have a picture of the two teens Silence and Night are raising?"

Jason lifted his phone. The gentle concern radiating from him twisted the daggers in her heart. On his phone was an image of a teen boy in a NASA T-shirt, his hair a messy darkness. The girl beside him was statuesque in a tiger-lily orange dress, her hair a brunette tumble.

Evie raised the medallion so that he could see the photo of little Ezra and Juliet. "My brother and sister. Everyone thought they'd been killed."

The two teens in the image on his phone were older versions of the children whose crumpled photo nestled in Evie's medallion. Joy and shock soared through her.

They're alive. They're alive. They're alive . . .

"How long have you known, Jason?" Tears were the enemy. She blinked them back into her eyes. The daggers had left her heart and spiked her throat. All this time . . . he hadn't been merely trying to protect her like some hero knight in the shadows . . . he'd been searching for her brother and sister.

"Since I took your medallion and saw that photo." He remained still, as if afraid she might shatter. "You changed your name from Elizabeth Luna."

"I had to. All this time . . . ," she whispered, the daggers falling away. "*You were looking for them.* Why didn't you tell me?"

His dark eyes reflected the Aurora Borealis. "I didn't want it to destroy you if I couldn't get them out. If I was *wrong*. If they were . . ." He didn't say "dead." "How long have you known Silence and Night had them?"

She closed the medallion. She watched the natural magic that seemed to create a city of colors in the night sky. "I didn't. I just hoped. But when I saw Father Silence—he might have worn my dad's face when he murdered my mom and dad, but I recognized him because of his eyes. He had the eyes of the monster who ended my world."

"Evie . . . how long have you known about LFS?"

She answered reluctantly. "Since I remember my parents mentioning them. 'You can't quit La Fable Sombre.' La Fable Sombre. I loved that name. I pictured it as a fancy carousel. I was eight." She sighed. "I had to find the connection LFS had to the monster who killed my parents. But La Fable Sombre were all so young . . ."

"Your parents were LFS, once." He understood. "You connived your way into Mad, Dev, and Queenie's good graces. And Ciaran's . . . How did you know they'd be at the gala that night?"

"I'm entitled to some secrets." She drew her burning gaze down from the sky to meet his. She breathed out, scarcely believing it was finally happening. *They're alive . . . They're alive . . .* "Together, we can get my brother and sister back. We just need to find out where Silence and Night live. Which is a lot harder than I thought it would be."

He deleted the photograph from his phone. He rose. "Evie, to get them back . . ."

"I know." She looked away from him. "You'd better go before someone sees us."

"We'll find a way." Something shadowy and monstrous swept up around him. He vanished in a spiral of black smoke and a silver pentacle, the remains of which fell to the snow like liquid mercury. For an instant, Evie thought she glimpsed a rearing, equine silhouette with a horn spiraling from its brow.

A small shout of joy escaped her like a dagger flung at an enemy's heart. She curled up, her hands over her mouth. *Ezra. Juliet.* She had forgotten what their voices sounded like. Forgotten so many small moments in her quest to find them.

She straightened, wiping her face, ferocity moving through her. She would die for them.

She would kill for them.

—⁓—

Evie, spiky with anxiety, returned to the girls' suite to find Dev and Ciaran there, both somber. Mad and Queenie didn't look too happy either.

"Am I late?" Evie asked, wondering apprehensively if anyone had seen her with Jason. She sat on the floor with them, peered down at the map of the castle's grounds and the illustration of Pandora's jar . . . with an added inking of monsters pouring out of it. "Nice." She slid it around. "This your work, Dev?"

"Mad and I spoke to Priest tonight," Dev told her, and Evie realized they must have done so as she and Jason plotted. "The warnings were intense."

She didn't doubt it.

"He had ideas about the jar, how it might open." Mad lay back, staring at the ceiling painted with a mural of autumn leaves and stars. It was as if they sat beneath an enormous tree at night.

"How do you know *Silence and Night* don't have experts?" Evie challenged. "Who've told them how to open and use the *Bestiarum* and the jar?"

"I know who their experts are, and they aren't like Priest." Ciaran twirled around the sketch of Pandora's jar. "Mythical vessels won't break. Can't use a bottle opener. Or pop it like champagne. The *Bestiarum* was created by demons. The Anesidora

Pithos was made by divinities." Ciaran traced the illustration. "Unlike the *Bestiarum*, it can't be opened with a key object. Books are unlocked. Jars are unleashed."

"So that's very cryptic." Queenie leaned back on her arms.

"From what Priest told us"—Dev leaned forward—"the jar is unsealed by a prayer or a spell. I'm thinking we don't have to be concerned about it being opened."

"He said jars like that are tricky." Mad traced the sketch, the animal–human figures depicted on the jar. "Twist the lid one way, you let something out. Twist it another way—"

"You let something in." Evie sat with her knees drawn up beneath her chin. "Do all of you believe Silence and Night? When they say they're collecting dangerous artifacts to keep the world safe?"

"Why wouldn't we believe them?" Queenie frowned.

Evie met Ciaran's gaze and wanted to say, *Because they have a graveyard filled with your fellow thieves.* She didn't. La Fable Sombre couldn't mutiny now, not until she and Jason found out where Silence and Night lived. But how long would it take to gain Silence and Night's trust? How many heists?

"Don't be a cynic, blackbird." Ciaran rose and walked to the terrace doors, opened them. It was snowing outside. "You've got me for that."

Snow flurried past him in a strange whirlwind—toward Queenie. Each flake began to glow, hundreds of cold little lights. Dev breathed out an awestruck profanity as Mad, delighted, lifted a hand to catch the luminous snowflakes. Evie, rising, could feel the snow melt as it brushed her skin. She traced a finger against her wrist where the glowing remnants trickled.

"It's so pretty," Mad whispered.

Dev said carefully, watching Queenie, "But it can be used as a weapon, can't it?"

"Close the doors," Queenie snapped.

Ciaran did so. The illuminated snowflakes continued to dance around Queenie.

"Queenie," he began. "Did snowflakes like you so much before?"

"Before what? Before all of you? No."

"Oh, Queens," Mad said ruefully. "We're getting better."

Evie glanced at Ciaran and thought she saw shadows snake from his eyes. She said softly, "No . . . I think we're changing."

No one, not even Ciaran, dared to ask, *Into what?*

And Evie felt a sharp bite of fear for all of them.

———

As Evie moved through the House of One Thousand Nights with Mad and Queenie, she knew that certain people who preferred the shadows over the light weren't the unsanctioned Collectors but rogue thieves. Dressed in an ebony velvet cocktail dress and calf-high boots, she felt as slinky as they looked. Mad, in a sleek pin-striped suit, moved blithely beside her through the gathering. Her eyeshadow resembled glittering angel wings. Queenie was daggered royalty in dark blue silk, her hair elaborately braided.

Evie spotted Ciaran weaving through the elegant and the shady, his navy-blue Armani suit perfect for thieving a fortune in supernatural artifacts. The sight of him made Evie want to be daring, to take risks, to show him she wasn't a scared little mouse.

They had gone over the plan last night. For the third time. Ironing out all the kinks that might become potentially hazardous. Evie had an obligation now, to work with her crew, no matter her true motives. The better she was, the closer she'd get to Silence and Night. And, if Jason was right . . . she'd find Ez and Jules.

Dev appeared beside Evie. The bird-of-paradise flower he'd tucked behind his left ear matched his buzz cut fade. He wore a bridal-white suit. "Hey, pretty girls. Ready for some fun? Ciaran says we're to get to work. He can be such a killjoy."

Queenie drifted away from them to pretend-flirt with Ciaran. In the public eye, they were still playing at being strangers.

Evie and Mad followed Dev down a flight of stairs, passing security and a group of people in diamonds. Evie and Mad shrugged on their coats.

"All these lovely, wicked people." Dev swaggered, his cashmere coat billowing. "So many temptations."

Mad spun in place, hands in her coat pockets. "Get out. You're a romantic at heart."

"Don't tell anyone." Dev headed down another stairway. At the bottom was a door and a big man in a suit. He eyed them as they approached. Mad handed him a black card. The guard took it, ran it under an ultraviolet light, handed it back.

It was still snowing as they left the castle glowing with music and voices. The flakes drifted down in glimmering swathes, stained gold by the light spilling from the windows. There were other guests taking a walk in the beautiful night. Evie, Mad, and Dev didn't speak as they made their way down a path that curved around the statue of a man riding a horse.

Beyond the statue was a park blanketed in snow beneath the moon.

"Hand-holding time." Mad clasped one of Evie's hands, and Evie reached for Dev's. Evie called the veil to wrap around the three of them, felt it become almost threadbare in places. The supernatural voices seemed eerie and childlike, drifting around them.

"Here's what they don't want anyone to notice." Dev led them past statues with human bodies and animal heads. They deviated from the path, pushing through tangled, dead trees, up a path choked by firs. They stepped into a clearing.

Before them loomed a huge, curving stone wall patched with moss and engraved with running horses. As they followed the giant wall, they found a large gate set within. Beyond was a sort of stone maze, knotted with trees and vines.

"What is it?" Mad whispered. "A labyrinth?"

"An ancient horse-riding arena." Evie peered through the gate. The walls within, rising toward the night, were painted with faded frescoes. "It's a weird style. Enough room for two horses, side by side." She smiled. "This is it. This is where they'd put the vault, isn't it?"

"Why isn't there any security?" Dev looked around. "No guards."

"They don't want people to know. Security would draw attention, create conflict." Evie stepped back, gazing at the circular stone structure. "The security will be inside." She reached out. "Dev. Mad. Ready?"

Mad began to levitate. Evie *willed* invisibility over the other girl, as they'd practiced. It took a Herculean effort. Her eyes watered. She tasted blood in her mouth. It was as if threads of her body were being tugged free. Then there was a razor sensation, as if those threads had been severed. She bit down on a cry of pain, hunched over. Dev gripped her shoulder. "Eves?"

"I'm okay." She breathed. "It worked."

Veiled in shadows, Mad rose into the air. She seemed to vanish into the night above. Evie heard her voice in the earpiece: "No one around. *Go.*"

As Evie and Dev approached the arena, Evie saw a figure standing behind the gates. She halted, dragging Dev back.

"Someone's there," she whispered.

Vero Jordan emerged from the dark, wearing a white gown and red roses in her hair.

"Evie." Dev didn't even look at the phantom. "I don't see anyone."

"They'll seduce you." Vero's voice was a warning, strangely echoing. *Sepulchral.* "Then they'll leave you to die."

"What do you *want*?" Evie whispered.

Vero remained tangled in shadow like a puzzle of skin and bone.

"Evie?" Dev was bewildered. "Who're you talking to?"

An inky darkness trickled down the right side of Vero's face. Blood pooled from her head, over her gown. Evie backed away from the crimson slithering across the snow, toward her boots. Vero lifted her head, her eyes red. She opened her mouth and a sound like a horse's shrieking whinny escaped her.

Then she was gone, with nothing but the moon-flung shadows marking where she'd been.

Whatever engine had driven the supernatural faded. Evie shuddered. She was cold all through. Her teeth were chattering.

"I'm freezing," Dev whispered.

"Do you hear anything?" Evie glanced at him.

He shook his head as they approached the stone monolith of the arena. His light tone didn't match his expression of unease. "Keep us unseen, Invisible Girl."

Evie kept the skin of invisibility over them. It clung like a cold film of Otherness. The whispers seemed more distant now, but Evie flinched when she thought she felt phantom fingers drift across the nape of her neck.

The arena's gates were a piece of cake for Dev. After he'd opened them, they entered cautiously, moving down the vine-clotted labyrinth, its walls frescoed with abstract horses and wild-eyed figures, some of which didn't look human. *Spirit horses*, Evie thought. *And spirits.*

"Traps," Dev said, as if she needed to be reminded. "If your invisibility works the way we hope, we won't be sensed by anything."

A leaf swept down—and was instantly impaled by a spike that speared from a slot in the stone wall above their heads. Evie flinched. Dev swore.

Evie had to concentrate to keep the veil around them. Before them, a playful wind curled a tiny cyclone of leaves in the air—

Two spikes whooshed from the walls. Evie and Dev fell back. Dev whispered, "They *must* reset this every night."

Evie resisted the urge to turn and run. She forged on with Dev. She was perspiring in the winter chill. They turned a corner, careful not to disturb anything—

Dev accidentally kicked a pebble. They watched in mutual terror as it skittered across the ground before them.

A spike shot up from the stones. The pebble teetered on the point, fell, bounced. Another spike broke from the ground.

Evie sensed Mad far above.

When they reached the monument in the labyrinth's center, Evie thought it resembled a tomb of glossy black stone carved with images of animals. The absence of surveillance so close to the goal worried Evie, as did the monument's apparent lack of a door. She glanced at Dev. "Can you open it?"

"It'll take me a minute." He leaned forward, pressed his brow against the stone. He laid one hand on the carving of a man with a lion's head. "More than a minute. It looks old-fashioned, but it's not, yeah?" He stepped back, studying the carvings. He began to walk around the monument. "What d'you notice about the decorations?"

Evie peered at the animal friezes, some of which had human qualities. "There are five animals depicted—hawk, mongoose, bear, lion, and a beetle. A scarab."

"My guess is five people are needed to unlock it." Dev stood before the monument, rubbing a thumb against his chin.

Evie frowned. "We all need to be here?"

A wind swept toward them, swirling a veil of leaves and snow before it. There was a strange, whispering *hush*.

A herd of translucent horses with black eyes, manes flowing like cobwebs, glided silently around the bend. Evie and Dev slammed back against the wall. The wind that accompanied the phantom horses swept Evie's hair into her eyes. She turned her head toward Dev, terror shrieking through her.

Half of his face had become an animal skull, with a muzzle and a slit-pupiled golden eye. Her hair began to writhe around her head with an unnatural life of its own. Something snaky snapped at her temple, her chin. She screamed.

"Evie!" Dev shouted as the phantom horses passed them like a silent hurricane. "Don't panic!"

She closed her eyes, pressed against the wall. She took a few deep true-'til-deaths. Quiet fell.

She opened her eyes. The horses had gone. She reached up and touched the tendrils of her hair. No snakes. She looked around. "Did you see—"

"Ghost horses and you with snakes for hair? I did."

She lifted her head, waiting for Mad to make a pass in the air above them. When she sensed Mad, a silhouette against the clouds, Evie said into her mic, "Let Ciar and Queenie know they need to be here *now.*"

Their earpieces and mics would be out of range this far from the castle. But Mad had a cell phone. Dev had told Ciaran he and Evie were taking enough chances with the little bits of tech they carried. He hadn't wanted phones in the building near the strike, but Mad would be above it.

Mad descended and looked around. "Was there some kind of a ruckus?"

"Ghost horses and assorted nightmare fuel." Evie flashed a smile.

"Eves." Mad was serious. "Can you do it? Can you invisible all five of us back through this labyrinth?"

"I don't know." Evie began walking, willing the veil to continue wrapping around Dev and Mad. Holding hands, they wove past the triggered traps, the cloud light from above causing their shadows to writhe on the stone.

Dev whispered, "I'm beginning to feel a bit walled in again. I like that we're all holding hands though."

"Breathe, Devilmaycare," Mad instructed. "You don't see me getting squirrely because the world's in black and white and I'm hearing scary voices . . ." She turned to Evie. "This invisibility, I'm beginning to think, is from that place between Ciaran's Doors."

"That would be a good guess." Evie breathed out when she saw the gated entrance and Ciaran and Queenie standing behind it.

Dev flung the gates open and said, "We all need to hold hands."

As soon as Ciaran stepped through the gate, he gripped Dev's outstretched hand while holding Queenie's. He met Evie's gaze. "How are you doing, blackbird?"

She wanted to fall down and sleep for days. The veil of invisibility fluttered reluctantly over Ciaran and Queenie. "We're alive, aren't we?"

"It's wicked, getting through," Dev warned them. "Follow our steps *exactly*." He began to lead, the five of them moving in single file like kindergartners on a field trip.

Queenie looked around. "*What* is that whispering?"

"Ignore the voices," Evie and Dev said at the same time.

Evie's fingers and toes suddenly went numb. In the gloom swathing her, she caught shadows flitting like bats. She gasped when one of her feet sank into a patch of otherworldly black grass—the grass faded back to stone, back to reality. Mad looked over one shoulder and her fingers tightened around Evie's.

They halted before the vault, forming a crescent. Dev told them, "Each of us has to lay a hand on one of these animal carvings."

Evie slapped a hand on the mongoose. Ciaran, the bear. Mad, the hawk. Dev, the lion. Queenie, the scarab. As Dev whispered lovingly to whatever mechanism kept the vault locked, Evie fought to keep the veil around all of them. She began to feel as if she was being flayed, as if her *skin* were forming the threads of invisibility. She leaned against the stone, her breathing ragged.

There was a shrieking, grinding sound.

"Let go," Dev ordered. They stepped back as the stone wall began to slide open . . .

. . . revealing a circular door of titanium, like some steampunk puzzle. Evie whispered, shaking, "I can't . . . the veil . . ." The invisibility was fading around them.

Mad glanced worriedly at her. "Everyone, keep holding hands. It's easier for her to invisible us that way. Dev? Can you get in?"

"No fancy tech. No voice or retinal to hack. It's genius. It's a cipher lock. I've only ever seen two of these. They use symbols and only a few people know the combination to get in. All I have to do is convince it I've solved the cipher."

He leaned against the titanium door, whispering like a lover. This time, the vault's mechanisms clicked and hummed. The massive door swung slowly inward. Queenie shone a flashlight into the chamber beyond. The light hit a network of glowing laser beams. In the center were dozens of display cases containing jewelry and artifacts, each labeled with a gold plaque. Queenie waved her flashlight around. "I don't see any cameras."

"No. Only the *lasers*," Evie whispered. Mad's and Queenie's hands were keeping her upright.

"My turn to shine." Mad transferred Evie's hand to Ciaran. "Cover me, Eves."

Evie swayed on her feet but urged the tethered veil of the unseen to remain around Mad as the other girl glided into the vault, contorting around the lasers. She stopped at a display case containing a small jar shaped like a little black beast—the Anesidora Pithos. She lifted the display case and picked up the jar, tucked it into her backpack.

"It can't be that easy," Queenie said tautly.

The invisibility unraveled from Mad like cobwebs. She fell to the floor, missing a laser beam by an inch. Something fluttered around her. Evie inhaled sharply when she glimpsed an inhuman female face with a beak and black eyes, white feathers cascading in a kite tail behind it. Evie flinched back—and broke the connection.

As Mad lay, unmoving, Dev swore.

"Mad!" Queenie lunged into the vault.

Ciaran dragged her back. "Break the lasers and the alarms go off . . . it's *malachite* . . . the inside of the fucking vault is made of malachite . . ."

Dev crouched down, produced a switchblade, and scraped at the stone floor painted black. He swore. "That's malachite, all right."

Fear whipped through Evie as she remembered what she'd been told about malachite: *It stunts our powers.*

Ciaran stepped into the vault, into the trap, breaking Evie's veil. A burning flash swept through Evie like a sudden fever. The frightening sensation was followed by a cold that numbed her fingers and toes. Her knees cracked like ice. She fell to the floor, her outflung hand brushing one of the laser beams. She wanted to tell them to run but couldn't move.

If I keep lying here, I'll die. With a mighty effort supported by ram-horned panic, she dragged herself up. Ciaran was hauling Mad out of the malachite vault.

Four young men emerged from the darkness. One of them pistol-whipped Dev, who collapsed against the wall, blood beading across his nose. The other three closed in on Queenie and Evie. Evie chanted, "Don't see us. Don't see us."

"We see you, *milashka*." A young man with dark curls grinned. He and his comrades had those kohl-rimmed eyes. They were Batavi, the mercenaries Silence and Night had hired, now switched sides. Evie thought, *Greedy mother—*

The Batavi raised a gun and fear splintered her courage.

"Wait." Queenie's hair fell over her face as she leaned against Evie, holding up one hand. "Please. He *made* us do this."

"Who made you, *milashka*?" Curly didn't lower the revolver.

"Him." Queenie flung out a hand to point at Ciaran—and tossed crimson glitter into Curly's face. The Batavi stood as if frozen, his eyes wild.

Ciaran slammed into Curly. They continued to fight with savage violence as the remaining three Batavi aimed their revolvers at Queenie and Evie.

Mad, who had recovered now that she was out of the

malachite vault, twirled through the air. She kicked one of the young mercenaries in the jaw. He dropped the gun, staggering.

Dev, blood on his face, rose to confront the Batavi closest to him, his smile a threat and a promise. He coaxed, "You don't really want to hurt me, do you?" The Batavi stared at him. The gun fell from his hand. "Thanks, mate." Dev swept the gun up and disdainfully flung it away. To the Batavi, he said, "Sleep for me?" The Batavi dropped to the floor.

Mad had grabbed her Batavi and, levitating, was lifting him in the air by his collar. She let go. Something cracked as he hit the stone.

The last mercenary pointed his gun at Evie. He looked scarcely older than she was. "What are you?" He backed away.

"Just a girl." Evie walked toward him. She swept the veil around herself, refusing to believe a bullet might end her, shred through skin and bone and rupture a major organ.

The Batavi shook his head. "You're *monsters*."

A foot in a pink Nike knocked the gun from his hands. Mad, levitating, pirouetted and kicked him in the head. He fell.

Several more Batavi appeared. Mad somersaulted in midair, tossing the backpack containing Pandora's jar to Evie, who caught it. Mad shouted, "Go! We'll follow!"

There was a crack of gunfire. Evie cried out at a razor pain in her arm, saw blood blossom where a bullet had grazed her. Shock made her colder.

More Batavi appeared. As blood streamed from the graze in her arm, Evie *wished* invisibility—a force lashing from her body in an agonizing effort—over Dev, Ciaran, Queenie, and Mad. A tidal wave of darkness smoked over each of them, and Evie felt as if blood were gushing from her pores. She staggered. The world went a glacial black and white. She tasted copper.

The veil wouldn't last once she was gone.

She heard a gunshot.

Another body collided with hers. She fell, tangled in strong arms. She rolled, saw Ciaran crouching beside her, blood staining his shirt from where another bullet had grazed his collarbone. Everything went dark around him for a moment.

What Evie saw in that darkness that had been Ciaran was a black-and-silver python wrapped around a porcelain spine and rib cage. *What are you?* she thought, terrified.

The disturbing vision vanished. Ciaran stood. He yanked Evie up, shoving her in the direction of the exit. "Get invisible and *get out*."

She dragged the veil around herself and ran with Pandora's jar. If they lost the jar, all of this would be for nothing. She raced down the labyrinthine corridor, leaving a trail of blood drops. The veil trailed after her, leaving the others exposed.

Something smacked her in the head. She staggered, caught herself from falling. As she regained her balance, a girl with golden braids appeared, her black coat swirling, her fingers glinting as if laced with jewelry.

Evie, dazed, touched her temple and winced. It was as if she'd been *burned.*

Her eyes focused on the girl's hands—it wasn't jewelry that adorned her fingers . . . it was tiny sparks of *electricity.* Evie whispered, "Who are you?"

The girl smiled and spoke, voice edged with a Russian

accent. "Tsar crew's newest. Now hand that over. Silence and Night want *you* alive. The rest . . ." She shrugged.

Tsar crew? Evie backed away, drawing the invisibility around her.

The girl lunged, *seeing* her. Evie swung the leather backpack containing the jar. It struck the girl, who staggered, snarled, and grabbed Evie's wrist. A shock sizzled up Evie's arm. Her heart jumped with frightening power. She dropped to her knees in the snow as the blonde girl gripped her wrist harder. The electricity biting through Evie's body became vicious.

Something fanged and misty snaked from the veil around Evie and lunged at the blonde. The girl collapsed. Evie crawled to the backpack, pushed to her feet in the snow. She stared down at the girl, whose eyes had rolled back in her head and whose limbs had frozen in a grotesque spasm. She still breathed.

Dev and Mad came running out of the arena, Ciaran and Queenie following. Evie swallowed a shout of joy.

Together, they raced away from the arena, across the snow—

Evie ran into something and bounced back, crashing into Mad. They fell in a tangle. Ciaran's eyes narrowed as he scanned the wintery landscape. It had begun to snow in heavy swathes.

Dev lunged in the opposite direction, also hit an invisible barrier. He slammed a fist against it. *"What?"*

Evie watched the wind sweep snow from the pavement around them. Dismay nearly stole the last of her energy when she saw several circles of green stone beneath their feet. "Ciaran . . ."

He watched as she kicked the snow away from the swirling green stone. *"Malachite.* A trap."

"Nothing'll work now." Evie fought panic. Dev proceeded to swear.

A new group of Batavi appeared on the snowy landscape, moving toward them. Ciaran said, grim, "We're going to have fatalities."

Mad was frowning at the malachite beneath them. "Why does malachite *do* this to us?"

"I can transform the malachite." Queenie unslung her small backpack. "Malachite is copper carbonite hydroxide." She lifted a clear container of liquid. "Oil of vitriol."

"Sulfuric acid?" Evie glanced at her, away from the Batavi striding toward them. "You always bring that with you?"

"I'm the Alchemist, Invisible Girl."

"They're coming," Dev warned.

Evie rooted for her power, as fragile and wan as hope.

"Why aren't they shooting?" Mad wondered darkly.

Evie didn't want to tell her what the blonde Tsar girl had said . . . Silence and Night wanted Evie alive.

"Cover your noses and mouths," Queenie ordered, and carefully poured the viscous fluid over the malachite, creating a trail to the circle's perimeter. Evie heard a *pop* and thought a shot had been fired, but it was only air pressure, as the invisible barrier collapsed. Queenie stepped out of the circle. "Hoof it!"

"Seriously." Dev laughed as they ran. "I am proposing to you, Victoria Olanna Nuliajuk St. James!"

The Batavi gave chase. Evie again hurled the veil of unseen over herself and her companions, but it misted away. She had no more strength. As snow whipped into her mouth and eyes, she felt exhaustion claw through her. Her chest heaved. She hunched over, saw the splash of blood in the snow as it dripped from her nose.

Mad gripped one of Evie's shoulders. "Eves—"

Ciaran, Dev, and Queenie halted, turning. Ciaran said, "Queenie . . . the snow . . . can you do it?"

"I don't know . . ."

The approaching Batavi raised their revolvers. Evie slid to her knees, unable to summon any of that darkness to cloak her. It was as if something snaked through her, unhinging its jaws to bite her brain.

Dev and Mad stood their ground, hopelessness written on their faces.

Ciaran strode forward, arms raised in surrender, that wicked smile transforming him into a king of seduction. "Soldiers of fortune, a word with you."

Queenie lifted her arms slightly to either side. She closed her eyes. Her lips moved. Her hair twisted up in the whorls of snow. The flakes seemed to catch fire around her.

Evie watched, stunned, as the snow swept forward, a blizzard of tiny, glowing dots. It surged around Ciaran, past him.

The Batavi broke ranks and ran, their forms swiftly hidden by the wall of shimmering, weaponized snow.

Mad caught Queenie before she could collapse. Queenie's eyes were black, her lips blue. Evie saw a shadow sweep around her throat in the form of a black rabbit.

Ciaran walked back toward them. "We need to find a Door."

The gunshot that cracked the air; the bullet that went through him; the figure that blinked into existence behind him, a revolver pointed—all occurred in a heartbeat.

"Ciar!" Mad's voice tore with anguish. Evie instinctively lunged toward him, saw him clutching his midriff, blood like raspberry jam on the snow, something beautiful that was so ugly. She saw the figure with the gun—a young man in a chic pastel suit more appropriate for a Miami nightclub—grin. His hair was a crimson mohawk. Ciaran growled, *"Lycan."*

"That's right, asshole. Not dead." In a blink, Lycan stood behind Queenie, an arm around her throat, the muzzle of the revolver against her temple. "I'm here to kill—"

Behind him, Dev clamped a hand on his shoulder and said in a voice that made the air vibrate and Evie go momentarily deaf, *"STOP."*

The word was power, not an enchantment or a persuasion, but a tiger's roar before the kill.

And Lycan *stopped*. His eyes rolled back in his head. He dropped into the snow. As Dev stared down in horror, Evie and Mad hauled Ciaran up. "Is he *dead*?" Dev whispered.

"No." Ciaran, one hand pressed against his bleeding abdomen, picked up Lycan's fancy revolver. He used both hands to cock it, then aimed it at Lycan.

Evie flinched as two bullets punched into the corpse. Ciaran tossed the gun into the snow. "The Batavi killed him."

"He was a Traveler." Evie lifted her horrified gaze to Ciaran's, saw that he understood. Her voice cracked. "Like you."

"We need to find a Door. Now. Come on." Mad slid an arm around Ciaran's waist as Dev kept Queenie upright. Evie staggered after. They began to run through the snow.

A crescent of Batavi appeared from the drifting whiteness, moving toward them. Evie, her fingers numb, exhaustion devouring her, tugged the backpack from her shoulder. She was prepared to toss Pandora's jar now, so that they could all get away—

A bullet whined through the air, hit the snow near Queenie's feet. Only Queenie's obscuration of snow was shielding them now.

Mad caught Evie's hand and yanked her to a halt as the others continued running. "You got any more invisible in you, Eves? Because I can still fly. The two of us can do some damage if the Batavi can't see us."

Evie shook her head, sensing the power in her flickering like a dying firefly.

Ciaran, Dev, and Queenie had begun running back toward Evie and Mad.

A bullet tore past Mad, grazing her cheek.

An SUV came roaring across the snow. It swerved in a neat curve between La Fable Sombre and the Batavi, braking only inches from them. There was a weird sound in the air, as if a generator had just exploded.

Jason stuck his head out the driver's side window. "Let's go!"

Evie laughed and wanted to yell, *I love you!*

"I love you, Jason Ra!" Dev shouted.

Evie and Queenie slid into the back, Ciaran and Dev ducking in after. Mad, bleeding from the bullet that had grazed her, opened the passenger side door and got in.

The SUV peeled across the snow toward the pack of Batavi, who scrambled out of the way.

"Jason." Ciaran's velvety voice had a note of savagery beneath. He was clutching his side. The amount of blood was worrisome. "Welcome back."

Jason didn't reply, too busy avoiding trees and statues as he drove through the snow, away from the House of One Thousand Nights.

"We need a place with a door," Queenie said calmly.

Evie remembered her and Jason's clandestine meeting at the tower folly. "Take a left, here."

Jason met her gaze in the rearview mirror and twisted the wheel. Tires squealed. He drove across the snowy field. At the foot of the hill, he slammed on the brakes. Everyone got out and ran toward the fake tower.

"There's no door!" Queenie spun on Evie. "Ciar needs a door to get us out—"

"Jason can spirit us away." Mad turned to Jason.

He shook his head, grim. "I can only spirit away one person at a time. Without practice . . ."

"All I need is a door." Ciaran turned to Evie.

Evie pointed to the stairs inside the tower. Everyone ran up, with Evie and Jason trailing after. Jason said, "Evie."

"Thank you for the rescue." She reached out to clasp his hand, weaving her fingers through his.

"I'm sorry," he whispered. "I can't let you."

She stared at him. She tore herself from his grip. Reaching for her, he grabbed the strap of the backpack. It slid from her shoulder. The darkness twined around him.

He vanished with the backpack, the silvery pentacle fading in the air. She had seen the shock in his eyes—he'd meant to take her with him.

"Evie!" Ciaran leaned down over the railing above.

She ran up the stairs to find them all standing around the trap door. Ciaran asked, low, dangerous, "Where is he?"

"He left."

"And the jar?"

Evie had her fairy chess piece—she drew the small jar, with its intricate images of therianthropic figures, from a rucksack she carried within her coat. Ciaran breathed as if in love. "He didn't get it."

Queenie grinned. Dev laughed. Mad hugged her. In that moment, Evie loved them all.

Ciaran hunkered down and laid one hand on the trap door, asked Evie, "Where do you want to go, blackbird?"

Shivering and bleeding, she thought of sun and heat. She told him.

He opened the Door. As the others gathered around, Ciaran rose and clasped Evie's hand. She closed her eyes and made a wish.

They jumped.

Part III

L'obscurité Sauvage

Chapter Sixteen

Burned Sweetness

Evie fell through darkness into a world consisting entirely of water. It stung her nostrils, filled her lungs. Unable to reach air, she began to flail. She shed the coat, kept the rucksack with the jar in it—*Which way is up? Which way is up?*

Be calm, a voice ribboned through her brain. *Water. We love water. Water can't harm us.*

She relaxed, lips parting. The moment she calmed, the water became a helpful element, making her body light as air. She surged upward.

She broke the water's surface. Oxygen rushed through her lungs and she greedily inhaled. She realized there was sand beneath her feet. She stood, wavering. She spit out water—her mind had almost tricked her into believing she could inhale it. She was surrounded by sea. Above her was a night sky strewn with stars.

"Evie." Ciaran rose from the sea like a god and walked

toward her, soaked, his hair slicked back. His eyes seemed completely black in the night. Politely, he asked, "You said Greece, but were you thinking of the ocean when you jumped?"

"Kind of. This is where I learned how to swim. We came here on vacations when I was little." Her voice drifted. Pain stabbed through her bullet-torn arm. She had to bite her lip to keep from crying out. She looked at her arm and realized it was only a shallow laceration.

"There's the beach," Ciaran told her. "Come on."

They waded toward a beach that swept up into a grove of fig trees. Beyond was a temple fallen to ruin. Orange light flickered across it.

"Where are the others?" Evie twisted around, anxiously seeking the rest of La Fable Sombre.

Ciaran shed his blazer and shoes. He lifted his phone, which glistened like some sort of dark totem. "Mad texted me before my phone bit the dust. They ended up farther along the coast. Dev wants to know why you're trying to kill him. He can't swim. Queenie rescued him."

Evie gazed across the wild beach. She toed the pebbles beneath her feet and shivered. "You got shot." She indicated the blood.

"So did you." He tugged at the rip in his shirt, revealing a wound that still bled. "That's a nick."

"It wasn't a nick." She stared, apprehension fluttering in her brain. "How much blood are you planning to lose?" She drew the switchblade Mad had given her and cut a strip of silk from her slip.

"How sexy." He smiled as she wrapped the silk around his

midriff. Her fingers brushed his velvety skin and his muscles jumped. It was awkward and his closeness made her fumble the knot. She asked, "Is there a bullet in there somewhere?"

"Was. It went out the other side."

She winced. "So they didn't miss."

"I heal fast. Whenever I step between the Doors."

"That's something I didn't know. Doesn't that scare you?"

"Do I look like I'm ever scared?"

She doubted he'd ever been scared a moment in his life.

Tearing his sleeve, he said, "My turn." And he gently knotted the fine material around her bleeding arm. He took care while doing this, which made Evie aware of the muscles moving in his scarred arms, the wet curve of hair against his temple. "There." He smiled. "All patched up."

As they walked onto the sand, he tilted his head. "Listen."

She heard the bass thump of music, and voices beneath, coming from behind a hill of scraggly trees. The temple was painted with firelight. She and Ciaran hiked up the hill of pebbles and stunted trees. When they reached the summit, they found more beach below and a group of people around a bonfire. Nearby were several motor scooters. Ciaran said, "This is our story: our boat overturned."

"And mermaids shot at us?"

"There you are."

As she followed him toward the gathering on the beach, she ran her fingers through the tendrils of her hair, which felt as if it were writhing around her head. She felt invincible.

——

Of course, Ciaran spoke Greek. He interpreted for Evie as he sat drinking a bottle of beer and talking to the bearded youth in charge of the music. His name was Christos, and he and his boyfriend had offered to take them to the hospital. A first-aid kit from someone's Vespa had sufficed.

Evie and Ciaran sat a little apart from the others. Evie had accepted coffee. The thermos cup warmed her chilled hands. While their hosts chatted, Evie told Ciaran, "A girl tried to get Pandora's jar as I escaped the horse arena . . . she almost *electrocuted* me. She was like us, Ciaran. She said she was with Tsar crew. And then Lycan, a *Traveler,* shows up . . . Would Silence and Night ever want to replace us?"

"You're asking me a question I think you know the answer to." Ciaran watched her, his eyes dark. "I've got no proof. Queenie worships Night. Dev's in love with Night. And Mad . . . Mad is in awe of both Night *and* Silence. So, you see my problem?"

"Do you think Silence and Night sent Lycan to assassinate you?"

"Silence and Night found a Traveler to replace me, he tried to do something stupid, and now he's off the board." Ciaran spoke coolly. "Now, they have to play by our rules. Those extra powers they planted in the other crews will never be La Fable Sombre."

"What will we do?" Evie pushed her hands over her face. What would *she* do? She needed access to Silence and Night . . . "Priest didn't want Silence and Night to have Pandora's jar." She watched the rucksack set between them—she didn't want any lingering contact with the object inside. "Or the *Bestiarum.* He doesn't trust them. What do you think they're going to do with them?"

"Not much." He watched her with his usual mysterious amusement—as if he hadn't just, a little over an hour ago, shot a man. He drank the rest of his beer. He set the bottle down and rose. He held out a hand to her, fingers unfolding, skull ring flashing. "Come with me."

She took his hand, narrowing her eyes to let him know he'd better actually tell her something. He led her toward the temple, up the steps, past the statue of the Greek god Mercury, with wings on his head and on his sandals. The statue was a re-creation, the stone too new. Vines draped pillars and other broken statues. The firelight washed everything in crimson and gold, fringing the shadows.

Ciaran drew the black jar from the rucksack. The Anesidora Pithos radiated a vibe that was both alluring and repellent. The stopper was shaped like a girl's head with swirling hair. It was one of the most beautiful and sinister objects Evie had ever seen. Ciaran said, "Do you know the story of Pandora, Evie? She opened a vessel and let a plague of bad into the world. A host of sins. But I can feel what's in this jar, can't you?" He lifted it to her ear, leaned close, whispered, "*Listen.*"

It was like holding a conch shell to her ear. It began with a hollow sound. As when she traversed the darkness between Ciaran's Doors or drew the veil around her, she began to hear a hush of voices that weren't human. She drew back. "What's in it?"

"Whatever found us. Whatever is in us and whatever is in this jar come from the same place . . . the darkness between the skin of the worlds."

"What do Silence and Night want with it?" She stomped on a spark of cosmic terror.

"Control." He gazed down at the jar. "See these?" He traced a knotwork of sigils amid the figures on the jar. He tugged up his sleeve to reveal the dark knotwork of tattoos around one upper arm—the symbols were identical to the ones on the jar. "And the *Bestiarum* had the same sigils in the border illustrations. Come with me again."

As she returned the jar to the rucksack, he led her to an arch with a bronze door. He clasped her hand. "Make us invisible."

She wished the veil over them. Ciaran pushed the Door open.

Darkness bled through, along with a cold worse than that which presently smoked over their limbs from the veil. Evie's breath clotted in her lungs. She gazed in horror at a meadow of dark blue grass and bone-white trees like skeletal hands. In the center was a vast stairway of black basalt, its banisters twisting like huge serpents. Something sat on the stairway, something monstrous and beautiful. It began to stand. Beyond it, beneath one of the bone trees, something large and humanlike began to prowl on all fours, toward them.

Terror shivered through her.

"They can't see us," Ciaran reassured her. "Look at the stairs. You see those designs? Same ones in the *Bestiarum*. On the jar."

She backed out. She dragged him with her. The Door closed.

"What was that?" Evie whispered. "What did you just show me?"

He leaned in on her like a hooded cobra, his eyes as black as that alien stairway. "That, Evie, is the Wild Dark. That is where our powers come from."

He reached out and plucked something from her hair. She

flinched as he revealed a wasp of black glass with jewel-blue wings. It crumbled in his palm. He lifted his gaze to hers. "It's in us. What's there. Whatever wrote the *Bestiarum*. What's in that jar."

Evie wanted to open the Door and fling the jar into that terrifying landscape.

"Evie." He gently clasped her arm, frowning as he studied the wound she'd dabbed with gauze and antiseptic. "You are so brave. Have I told you that? Without you . . . I don't know where we'd be."

She was close enough that she could feel the heat of him through their still-damp clothes. She took a step closer because this insane night made her reckless. He cupped her face in both hands, his eyes gone dark. Desire swept through her with a burned sweetness she could taste on her tongue. He became an eclipse, drawing her against his body, serpentine muscles hard against her softness, his lips parting over hers with ruthless delicacy. When he slid to his knees, his brow pressed against her stomach, her heart rioted in its corset of muscle and bone. She folded down and fiercely kissed the lush mouth that had spoken seductive promises and dark secrets. He bunched up her dress as her hands dove beneath his shirt to grip the wings of his shoulder blades.

But something was bothering her, an unanswered question that needled through her desire. She drew back. "Why did you really poison Lila Pearce?"

"Because we have to do something before they replace us."

"You declared war on Silence and Night." She pulled back. He caught her hands, fingers twining with hers. She whispered, "*Why* are you giving them the jar? Why'd you give them the

Bestiarum?" She figured it out in a flash. "You're going to *steal them back*. You can track objects, you said, that carry a drop of your blood. You marked the *Bestiarum*. You're going to do the same with the jar . . ."

"Blackbird." There was no amusement in him now. "I'm going to find out where they live."

"You're going to kill them." The words left her like a curse. She pushed to her feet, stepped back as he rose, his face in shadow.

"Chaos is going to be our friend, Evie, and, in the midst of it, the king and queen will die. I'm killing Silence to take his place. I don't have an Oedipus complex, so I don't need Mother Night. I need *you*."

Her earlier theory returned to haunt her—that he'd been planning this mutiny for some time. "How do you know all the crews will follow you after you've offed Mom and Dad?"

"They'll follow me. And you, Evie. Imagine what you could do."

She did. She imagined finding out where Silence and Night lived. Where they had her siblings.

"I thought"—her voice was scratchy—"this was to protect our friends. Was it always about taking over?"

"Evie . . . just how do you think Silence and Night *became* Silence and Night?"

"That's not how it worked with other La Fable Sombres. But because Silence and Night assassinated the Dolls, they think that's how it'll go with them? No wonder they see us as a threat."

He leaned closer to her. "I want La Fable Sombre to rule. And I know you want the same."

That's not what she wanted. He was watching her, calculating. His voice vibrated through her, into the chambers of her rattlesnake heart.

"You also want your brother and sister, whom they stole. And this is the only way to get them back."

Shock tore through her. She heaved in a breath, let it out in an unsteady exhale. How long had he known about Ezra and Juliet? About Silence and Night having taken them? It was a gut punch. She hadn't been as clever as she'd hoped.

"Jase figured it out." Ciaran tilted his head. "Did you really think *I* wouldn't? Looks like we've both been keeping secrets."

"Sorry to interrupt." A bashful voice spoke.

Ciaran's gaze cut to Christos standing beside a pillar. Evie straightened her dress, burning and bewitched and terrified.

Christos pointed. "I think your friends are here?"

Evie heard motors. Grabbing the strap of the rucksack, attempting to breathe normally, she scanned the beach for any sight of the Vespas she could hear in the distance. She glanced at Ciaran, saw something snake through the silver pools of his eyes. She was reminded of what he was capable of. He distracted with charm, but there was that underlying menace—anyone who wasn't La Fable Sombre was the enemy. And Jason Ra proved how quickly those tables could turn. To Ciaran, charming the Greek partygoers or murdering them would all be the same to him. He'd shot Lycan at the House of One Thousand Nights. He'd poisoned Lila Pearce.

His hand dropped to his side, curling into a fist. He took a step closer to her. Gazing past her, he whispered in her ear, "Together, we will end Silence and Night."

The three Vespas roaring across the beach swerved to an impressive halt, as if choreographed. As Mad, Dev, and Queenie strode toward the temple, Ciaran descended to greet his crew with a smile and a question: "What the fuck took you so long?"

Evie stood alone, facing the ocean, remembering how she'd been so afraid of the water as a kid. Until her mom had told her, *When you're afraid of something, Evie, walk up to it and—grr! Make* it *afraid of* you.

She was afraid of Ciaran Argent.

———

Their Greek hosts departed, leaving the Dark Fable seated around the fire, generously bestowing upon them blankets and a cooler packed with snacks and beer. Ciaran was sprawled on the temple steps, staring out at the ocean. Queenie sat beside him, a beer bottle dangling between her fingers. Evie understood the somber mood. Queenie, Dev, and Mad had managed to polish themselves up, but they also had wounds, and their smiles vanished the moment the taillights from Christos's Vespa disappeared up the road.

All Evie wanted was to sleep on the beach beneath the sky scattered with constellations, beside the ocean, near an ancient temple strewn with the remnants of old gods. She was still in shock from Ciaran's revelation, not certain if his mutiny was a good circumstance or a bad one, considering her own scheme. She recalibrated in ten minutes, realizing with stomach-churning unease what she would have to do. If she could get him to help her find her siblings before he declared war on Silence and Night, she might just pull this off.

Unless he told the others. And they hated her. And she lost

them. Terror snapped through her. What would she be without the Dark Fable?

The ancient jar that might have belonged to a demigoddess seemed to hum in the rucksack, as if singing. Or maybe she was imagining it. She opened the rucksack and peered in, saw the reflection of her left eye on the jar's obsidian surface. A slithering tendril of darkness curled from her reflection's brow, opening its mouth to reveal tiny fangs.

"Evie."

She snapped the rucksack shut as Mad crouched beside her and said, "Can I see it?"

"Don't look at the jar's surface." Evie handed the object to her, watched as Mad held it so that the jar wouldn't catch her reflection.

"It's so small to be so dangerous," Mad whispered. "It's like it's singing." She handed the jar back to Evie. A laceration on her cheek had been neatly stitched up by Queenie.

Evie turned the jar and inadvertently faced its reflective surface toward Mad. She looked up to see Mad frozen, staring at her reflection as if what she saw horrified her. A worm of blood trickled from her left nostril.

"*Mad . . .*" Evie shoved the jar into the rucksack. "Are you okay?"

Mad wiped absently at her nose. "Don't worry about it." She rose and walked away to gaze out over the ocean.

"We're really going to sleep here?" Queenie moved down the temple steps, looking like a fallen monarch in her torn gown of burgundy silk.

"I think it's nice." Dev lay back in the sand, one tattooed arm over his eyes.

"How did that guy—Lycan—blink into existence?" Queenie demanded. "Aren't any of you worried about that?"

Mad spoke, her back turned to them. "He was a Traveler."

Evie told them, "A girl showed up when I was running out of the arena. She told me she was a new Tsar—she tried to get the jar. She did something weird with electricity."

"What happened?" Dev sat up, arms draped over his drawn-up knees.

"I knocked her out."

"You didn't kill her, then." Bitterness rooted in Dev's voice. "Good for you."

"Dev. Lycan had a gun pushed against my head." Queenie crouched beside Dev and laid a hand on one of his knees. "You did what needed to be done."

"You see a pattern yet?" Ciaran spoke. "Nara's newest recruit could see through Evie's veil at the Plaza La Mer. Lycan of the Fenrir was a Traveler. The Sirens mutinied after receiving their newest recruit. And three of those crews lost members this year. Through *accidents*." He leaned forward. "Silence and Night have found others like us—and set them in separate crews."

Dev's voice was edged with anger. "They're *replacing* us."

Ciaran was painted by firelight and shadow. "We used to be Mother and Father's favorites. But they have crews they can *control*. Who aren't a threat."

"And each of those crews now has someone like us," Queenie grimly stated.

Evie hated this. Hated that, now, Ciaran's scheming would help her. "That's why Circe and the Sirens mutinied—they found someone like us in their midst." She waited for Ciaran to mention the graveyard in the desert.

Ciaran lifted his head. "Silence and Night knew that Vero and Jason were planning to leave. I don't think Vero's murder was accidental. I think Mother and Father set Jason and Vero up on that strike with one of their Collectors, to be killed."

A stricken silence followed this revelation.

Mad's face was sharp and feral. "What are we going to do?"

Ciaran rose and walked toward them. "The jar and the book are the keys to the Kingdom. That's why Silence and Night kept them from the Collectors. Silence and Night aren't new to this game. Who knows what relics previous Father Silences and Mother Nights have found and stashed in that vault beneath Paris? The vault Mother and Father don't have the key to because they murdered their predecessors. If we let them keep the *Bestiarum Vocabulum*, hand over the Anesidora Pithos . . ."

"They'll have nukes," Evie finished, "to use against us."

"How are we going to *exist* if Silence and Night have been trying to *end* us?" Queenie asked with sharp anger and a little panic. "If they want us out of the game, we need to *vanish*."

"No." Ciaran told them. "We need to take their kingdom away from them. We are going to steal back the book—and the jar after we've given it to them. Silence has the *Bestiarum* in his house in Ireland. Night will spirit Pandora's jar to her house in France. I can track them with my blood."

Mad spoke quietly. "You want to kill Mother and Father."

"We'll blame Nara and Fenrir, who are ambitious enough." Ciaran hunkered down and cast his arsenic gaze over all of them. Evie felt a sense of finality, as if she'd fallen into a well and her last handhold had slipped. If they failed, Silence and Night would come after them with all their resources.

"Divide and conquer." Queenie tucked her hair behind her ears, probably to disguise her shaking hands.

Dev shook his head. His eyes were wide, tawny gold. "I don't know how we can pull this off."

Even Mad looked doubtful.

Evie exchanged a look with Ciaran—they were losing support for a mutiny that would save their lives—*and* her brother and sister. They all needed to be on board for Ciaran's brutal strategy. She said, carefully, "Jason Ra showed me a place in the desert where Silence and Night have buried people they've killed. And the last victim was Matthew Orion, the Siren."

Queenie swore. Dev groaned. Mad flung a look at Ciaran, one of betrayal. She whispered, "You know about that, Ciar?"

"Yeah." He didn't defend it. "I knew. And it's why I've been planning to get us out."

"We should just run," Queenie said, serious.

"We can't do that." Ciaran's gaze settled on Evie. "Tell them why, blackbird."

She stared at him.

"Go on, Evie," he coaxed, his beauty a mask over the cold, calculating darkness within. "Tell them how you schemed to get into La Fable Sombre. How you found the Queen Cobra in your parents' possessions and donated it as a lure. For us. Because someone told you your parents were in the last incarnation of La Fable Sombre and Silence and Night killed them. You held vigil at the petrol station at Silver Cove's highway entrance to keep an eye out for us. Took a stint at the country club full of wealthy targets, just in case we were tempted. Got another job as a caterer at the Plaza La Mer to lie in wait for us to grab that necklace. All for revenge."

Evie knew what he was doing as everyone looked at her—she saw hurt, astonishment, anger.

"*Evie?*" Mad sounded small and crushed.

Queenie regarded Evie with disdain. "I knew it. All those charming little chats with us . . . to learn about us, use our stories against us."

"No . . . I mean . . . yes, at first. But," Evie pleaded, "things changed."

"Tell us why." Dev sat up straight. He was all edges now, the soulful charmer armored in thorns, as if betrayal was something that might rip out his heart. He looked ready to snarl. "I'm sure you've a good reason for using us."

Mad gazed sorrowfully at Evie. "Your parents . . . Silence and Night—"

"Silence and Night murdered my parents and stole my little brother and sister." The secret and cruel hope she'd carried for so many years—that her siblings had been spirited away by a monster in human skin, yet had survived—spilled out like jewels and blood, beautiful and gruesome. "Jason's been looking for two missing kids that I hired his mentor to find a couple years back." She dropped her gaze to her hands, clenching and unclenching them. "He traced them to Silence and Night."

"You were using us to get closer to Silence and Night." Queenie stared at her. "Like we're nothing to you."

"I'm sorry," Evie whispered.

"Just a means to an end," Dev said, somber. "That all we were?"

Tears pricked Evie's eyes. "In the beginning. Not anymore." She knew they had only each other, La Fable Sombre; that her betrayal might be unforgiveable. If she lost them, she lost herself, not just the opportunity to locate Juliet and Ezra.

Dev gazed up at the sky. "I imagine your brother and sister don't recall much of their lives before . . . what happened."

"They were raised by two monsters from a fairy tale." Mad bowed her head, honey-gold hair veiling her face. "What if they don't remember you, Evie? How old were they when they were taken?"

"Six and four." Evie watched all of them, scarcely daring to hope. It would be a miracle if they didn't toss her out or abandon her for her deception.

But Ciaran had told them the truth for a reason. He had a strategy. "Evie is still one of us. Family. So, her brother and sister are family."

Queenie looked at Ciaran. "How many of us do you think Silence and Night have murdered?"

"As many as they needed to." Ciaran's voice sliced the air.

Mad sat very still. "How could we have just not known? What they were like?"

Evie figured Mad saw what she wanted to see.

Dev clasped one of Evie's hands, lacing his fingers with hers. "So, we break into Silence and Night's homes. Retrieve the book and the jar. Rescue Evie's siblings. Then what?"

"We'll come up with a plan back home." Ciaran met Evie's gaze across the flames. "We'll all get what we want."

I'll get Ezra and Juliet, Evie thought. *And you'll get the Kingdom.* She looked at Dev, Mad, and Queenie. Fiercely and silently, she promised, *I will always take care of you. I will always love you.*

CHAPTER SEVENTEEN

Poison

The next evening, Evie, Mad, Queenie, and Dev gathered to plot Mother Night and Father Silence's downfall. They sat on the floor in the main room of the lair, waiting for Ciaran. Mad's manic pixie dream girl persona had vanished, replaced by the wolf-eyed criminal who spoke ruthlessly. "Mother and Father have betrayed us—even more so than Evie. The evidence is damning—Evie saw Silence murder her parents. It's pretty obvious the two kids they have are her brother and sister. Vero and Jason, who were going to leave us, had a strike that ended with Vero dying. There's a freaking *graveyard* in the desert that we can all be sure isn't for those of us who've died of old age. And then there are the ringers with *abilities* planted in each crew."

"There is nothing circumstantial about any of that." Queenie's mouth twisted with bitterness.

"Are we really doing this?" Dev's tawny eyes flashed gold as he bowed his head. "I just think about how Mother loved to cook for us, how she taught me to waltz . . ." His voice softened. "How Father showed me how to box like a gentleman."

Queenie tugged at her hair. "Night got me my first Louboutins. She taught me French. She's the coolest person I know—well, aside from my grandparents. Silence gave me a first-edition copy of Isaac Newton's *Principia Mathematica,* helped me get money to my hometown, lay the groundwork for a STEM school . . . How are we going to *do* this?" she whispered, her voice breaking.

"Mother Night took me to get fitted for my first Versace gown." The ache in Mad's voice made Evie bite her lip. "Father Silence gave me my first switchblade, shaped like an owl. Night told me stories when I got sick last winter. Silence bought me the Aston Martin for my eighteenth birthday because he was proud of me." She looked up, her gaze fierce. "It's us or them. Don't think of them as our parents, don't you dare. They gave us *things.* Not love. It was all hollow. Just to control us."

They all stared at Mad, who was not typically a beacon of self-awareness.

Evie spoke with steely resolve. "I'll kill Night when the time comes. It isn't your vendetta. It's mine—"

"Eves . . ." Mad was staring at something over Evie's shoulder. The back of Evie's neck prickled, as if a door had opened onto a cold violet place with no sunlight. She stood, turning.

Like a moon god from an eclipse, Jason Ra, in a hooded coat, stepped from a silver-and-black pentacle. The immense shadow of something horned, equine, and vicious pooled before him.

Dev stood, an edge in his voice. "What are you doing here, mate?"

"Hey, Jase," Mad greeted, her golden hair swirling. "Glad you could join us."

"Why is *he* here?" Queenie was wary.

"Jase is going to help." Ciaran strolled into the room. "Nice to see you, bruv."

"Once this is done"—Jason spoke in a low voice—"*we* are done."

"Sure, Jase. That a promise?" Ciaran flashed a smile.

Jason didn't reply, his gaze flicking to Evie.

"I just need you to get them out," Evie told Jason. "Ezra and Juliet. Just get them to safety."

"You'll need to make sure they're outside." Jason looked at Ciaran. "We won't be able to use our powers in Silence and Night's homes—they'll have wards or protections, whatever they utilize at the Palm and the Lotus, on all the doors and windows."

"Malachite?" Evie asked. "Holy objects?"

Jason shook his head. "That would affect them too. Whatever they use to keep us out, it won't be something that dilutes *their* abilities."

"We're more than our tricks, Jase." Ciaran nodded to Evie. "So, you take her brother and sister somewhere safe while we do what we do best."

"Steal." Jason was watching Evie, who wouldn't look at him. "What else?"

"What do you think?" Ciaran's amiable demeanor didn't falter. "What do you think we have to do? You saw the graveyard in the desert."

Jason took a step toward Evie. "Evie . . ."

Mad slid in front of him, setting one hand on his chest, and Evie could almost imagine Mad leading Jason by his tie onto a dance floor in some nightclub. Mad said, "Jason. You want to help? Don't be a Galahad. Be your old self."

Jason didn't drop his gaze from Evie's. Beyond him, Ciaran watched, no longer smiling.

Evie swept a look over all of them. The ancient darkness nesting within her saw their fidgeting, uncertainty, and arrogance—with the exception of Jason, who stood among them like an icy beacon. And Ciaran, whose gaze settled upon Evie as if he were sizing up some nettlesome element.

"Fine." Jason's voice bit the air as he drew back. "Tell me my part and I'll do it." *And we'll deal with the fallout later* were the words he left unsaid.

"Right, then." Ciaran walked to the table and began sliding diagrams and illustrations from the envelope he carried. "Gather round, children, and let's plot two blind strikes in one night."

Evie walked toward Ciaran, avoiding Jason, but searingly aware of his anger. Ciaran had gotten another thing he'd wanted: Jason back.

Ciaran said, "Winter holiday ends in a week. Silence and Night will have Evie's siblings at their separate homes in Ireland and France. Our time is growing short as well—Silence and Night plan to end us and let our substitutes work with separate crews. No more LFS. Also, while they've the *Bestiarum* and the jar, it's now or never that we can scarper them." He cast a glance around the table. "First, as Jason said, it's a guarantee the doors and windows will be warded, so our tricks won't work inside."

"So, we do it the old-fashioned way," Jason told them. "With one trick."

"Your blood on those objects." Evie looked at Ciaran. "It'll lead us into the houses. But how do you use a Door if the houses are warded? And if you've never seen them before?"

Ciaran and Jason exchanged a look, and Evie realized how: "Jason will amplify your ability. And you've been to their houses before."

"That's right." Ciaran tapped the sketch of a general floor plan. "Silence's house will be first. We should end up in the same room as the *Bestiarum*. We nick the book. Separate. Search for your brother."

"And Silence," Mad said solemnly.

"I won't be a party to murder," Jason told them with a dark look at Ciaran.

"No problem, bruv. You won't have anything to do with it. You and Evie go looking for little brother."

Jason glanced at Evie, pleading.

"*Jason.*" It was Dev who spoke in a calm, hard voice. "If we don't do this terrible deed—tell us Silence and Night won't come after us once we screw them over."

Jason told them: "I can't tell you that."

"Jase," Ciaran said gently. "I'll be taking care of Silence. Then, we open a Door to retrieve Pandora's jar from Night's house in France. Once we have the jar, we separate to find Evie's sis."

"Ezra'll be with us?" Evie was doubtful.

"Yeah, we'll have to protect the kid, so . . . who ends Mother Night?" Queenie's voice was taut.

"I do." Mad jutted her chin, her eyes wide.

"No." Although Evie was terrified of Silence and Night—they all were, with the exception of Ciaran—she couldn't let Mad commit murder. "I do."

Jason shot her a look of fury and horror.

"You're not a killer, Evie." Mad kept her focus on Ciaran. "*I* am."

Evie didn't argue but sat back, troubled. Dev whispered, "Mad . . ."

Queenie held up both hands. "Is that what's going to happen? We're going to be killers?"

"Or be killed." Evie knew she spoke the terrifying truth.

"Madrigal." Jason gazed at her with regret. She ignored him.

"Once that's *done*"—Ciaran narrowed his eyes—"Jase and I open a Door back to the lair." Ciaran spread out photographs. "We need to look like Fenrir and Nara. We'll be wearing masks and Fenrir's atrocious wardrobe choices, then we change into Nara's style. We'll carry rappelling equipment to make it look like we got in the hard way; tasers, since Queenie's potions won't work; spray paint for any cameras; our Bluetooth devices for communication; and watches, because we'll be timing this. We all need to meet back at the starting point to get through the Door." Ciaran cast a warning look around at all of them. "We'll have thirty minutes to get in and out of each strike. We're going to be powerless and separate from one another." He let that sink in. "It's absolutely crucial we keep track of time and each other."

"Are you using my poison?" Queenie bowed her head, tattooed fingers knotted together. "For . . . *them*?"

"Your poison was made with a Wish of death, Queens.

Technically, it's a supernatural trick. No, I found something else that will work. Evie." Ciaran met her gaze. "Just to clarify for everyone"—he glanced meaningfully at Jason—"are you absolutely sure you remember the true face of the man who murdered your parents?"

"Yes." Evie hated this, hated the way Jason watched her as if she were drowning and he couldn't save her. "It was Silence. I knew it the minute I saw his eyes."

Ciaran nodded. "We'll need to be everything for this, without our tricks. Jase can't hold all of our hands and amplify what we do. The only reason I believe the Door will work is because it's a liminal space we'll be working in."

Evie could sense the terror in the room, the immensity of what they would be attempting, the fatal consequences. The odds of defeating two cold-blooded and supernaturally gifted people. And murdering them.

"We'll all be the Flaunt, the Eye, Tooth and Claw." Mad tilted her chin up. "We can do this."

Evie spoke softly, "We're La Fable Sombre."

"And what happens," Jason challenged, his cold gaze on Ciaran, "when this is finished? *You* rule the Kingdom?"

"No, bruv." Ciaran looked at Evie. "La Fable Sombre rules the Kingdom."

No, Evie thought. You *rule the kingdom.*

———

Jason left, led out by Mad. Dev and Queenie followed. Evie remained with Ciaran, who said, "Come with me, Evie."

They ascended to the roof, which Mad had decorated with

garden lights and antique furniture. Evie leaned against the low wall, imagining the night sky was a sea filled with stars that she could swim in. She breathed out. "This is going to be impossible."

"*We're* impossible." He draped himself against the wall beside her. A wind circled them, tugging at their hair and clothing, as if the spirits from Marseille, from Morocco, from St. Petersburg, had followed her here. She knew it was only a remnant of the Santa Ana.

"I don't want Mad to be a murderer." She gripped the stone wall.

"Evie . . . you know her story." Ciaran gently continued, "She already is."

"How do *I* end Mother Night?" She stubbornly ignored the reminder of Mad's past.

He took from his pocket a tiny box, the sort engagement rings were kept in. He opened it to reveal a silver ring decorated with a beautiful face surrounded by snakes. "Just a scratch. That's all it takes. The catch is here. The needle comes out. You'll be in no danger of poisoning yourself."

"Queenie made this?" She was horrified.

"Not Queenie. Someone else made this a long time ago."

How long had he been planning this? She stared at the poison ring. The ring stared back. His voice was gentle. "You can do this, Evie. Of us all, you are the most like me. Imagine it— you and your brother and sister, safe always."

Evie took the box containing the poison ring, closed the lid with a snap.

He reached out and cupped one of her hands, tracing the rings she wore. "Do these mean something?"

She had gotten each ring with a different foster parent. Some had been gifts, others found or nicked. "No, Ciaran. You don't get to ask me any more questions and learn my story when I haven't gotten one piece of yours." Even Mad didn't know. Mad's theory was that Ciaran was the son of a criminal mastermind who had murdered his wife, and Ciaran had turned to a life of crime to combat his father.

"All right." He rested his elbows on the wall. "What do you want to know? Anything, blackbird."

"Are you Silence and Night's son?"

He laughed and cast her a look of disbelief.

"Okay." She hunched her shoulders. "Who was your dad?"

"Nobody." Ciaran's casual tone belied the bitterness of his words. "He was a nobody."

Evie was troubled by this. "Your mom?"

"She was someone, unfortunately."

She glared at him. "You're being enigmatic, oblique, and elusive."

"Is it because I'm not bleeding all over you, like Jase does?" There wasn't even any jealousy in that statement. He stepped so close, their breath mingled. "Like I said, you'll need to know me a little bit longer, blackbird, before I tell you my story."

"Jase and Mad have known you for years, and you still keep your secrets close." She rested one palm on his chest, above his heart. She stared into eyes as gray as frost light on a mirror.

"Oh no you don't." He stepped back with a velvety laugh. "I'm not falling for *that*, blackbird. I'll see you in the morning."

He left her on the rooftop, with the wind tangled in her hair and the poison ring in one hand. She wrapped her fingers around the medallion of the maiden death, lifted it to her lips, whispered, "I'm alone. Rooftop."

She waited for an hour before realizing Jason wasn't going to return, that she wouldn't have anyone tonight to confide in, to offer reassurances, to fold the wings of comfort around her.

CHAPTER EIGHTEEN

Demons at Dinner

Evie was seated on her bed, the medallion cupped in her hands, when Mad and Queenie arrived. Mad wore strapless pink satin and a diamond tiara. She looked like another person. Queenie, in snow-white silk, had coiffed her hair elaborately with bone pins carved into seal shapes.

"Evie." Mad gently tugged Evie to her feet. "Have you even picked out what to wear?"

Evie felt as if she were bursting with secrets, like a solar-flaring sun. "We're going straight there?"

"We're taking a Door that will set us adjacent to the Palm and the Lotus." Queenie swept past her, to the closet where Evie had hung a few dresses. She drew out a black gown. Satin rustled as Mad walked to the sofa and slouched like a cast-off doll. Evie dropped beside her, watching Queenie critique her wardrobe. "All black? Really, Eves?" She held up a night-hued gown, its short sleeves ropes of onyx beads. "This'll do."

"I wanted to wear the black velvet." Evie began to level out with the normal conversation, as if they weren't about to stage a coup against two terrifying criminals.

And, if she didn't think about Ezra and Juliet, seeing them alive and safe, or losing them again, she wouldn't fall apart.

"This is Mother Night we're dining with, not some Victorian grand dame. Change." Queenie shoved the gown at Evie. "You pick your shoes. I can't even."

"Don't worry," Mad told Evie. "She bullied me too." She smoothed the pink satin of her gown. "But I chose this one. It makes me feel like Marilyn Monroe."

Queenie put her hands on her hips and demanded, "Is that the one Mother Night gave you?"

"I'm wearing it for sentimental reasons."

"What am I going to do with you, Mad?" Queenie sank down beside her.

Evie grabbed the gown and headed for the bathroom. "Give me a minute."

"Try not to betray us while you're in there," Queenie called out.

Evie winced. In the bathroom, she sank down on the tub's rim and fought waves of panic. Dinner with Mother Night, whom she was planning to kill.

—⁓—

A female Batavi with bleached hair, dressed in a white suit, waited for La Fable Sombre in the assigned place, a Marrakesh alley. As Ciaran's Door closed behind them, the Batavi didn't even blink. She ushered them to a Rolls-Royce and drove them to the Palm and the Lotus. It was a silent ride, bereft of the usual banter.

When they entered the Palm and the Lotus, the marble and

stone around them seemed to hold the echoes of their footsteps and hushed voices. Evie carried Pandora's jar in a bronze box etched with Greek designs. She could feel the jar humming inside the metal. She wanted to tell it to be quiet.

Ciaran began speaking to the Batavi, charming her into showing him her fancy revolver and giving him her name. They stepped into an elevator, a cage of curling metal, which took them to the penthouse.

The doors opened onto a palatial room of white rococo molding and sky-blue paint, with a domed ceiling and a hearth like a monster's mouth. Silver stag-head lamps illuminated a table displaying a dinner of roasted birds, vegetables and tabbouleh, and a tiered cake. Mother Night, in a silver gown patterned with lilies, leaned against a pillar. Diamonds frosted her collarbones, her fingers, her ears. Her raven hair spilled down her back. Father Silence sat at the head of the table.

Mother Night indicated the table. "It's time for a bit of a tête-à-tête."

Dev strolled over and pulled out a chair for Queenie. Mad, all wide-eyed innocence, sat near the cake. She took up the knife and began cutting herself a piece. Evie sat opposite, the bronze box in her lap. Ciaran swung a chair around and sat, turned slightly toward Father Silence.

Silence inclined his head and signaled to a serving man, who brought over a steaming pot of coffee and began pouring it into little cups. "It's Turkish. You'll be awake until the sun rises, but then we're all nocturnal, aren't we?"

Mother Night moved past Evie and sat in the chair at the other end of the table.

"Now." Father Silence set his hands on the table. "The Anesidora Pithos."

Evie lifted the bronze box and pushed it toward Mother Night, who was closest.

"Do you know how to open it?" Evie asked with what she hoped was convincing naivete.

Mother Night lifted out the jar, traced fingers along the stopper sealed with some sort of black metal. "We have people working on that. Tell us about this last strike."

Evie went still. Mad, delicately eating cake, shrugged. Dev twirled a butter knife. Queenie stared at the jar. Ciaran poured himself more coffee and said, "There was a fatality."

"Of course there was." Silence rose. He walked past Evie, around the table. "Go on."

"The Collectors or the thieves hired Batavi. *Someone* hired Batavi. The Batavi shot someone, a rogue thief—one of two who tried to steal Pandora's jar from us." Ciaran was speaking of Lycan and Electricity Girl, pretending he didn't know who they'd really been. "Word got out about that auction and what was in that vault." His movements as he cut his meat were economical, unconcerned. "There were a lot of Batavi."

"An army," Mad agreed.

Mother Night said, "So we were betrayed in St. Petersburg."

"It's a tragedy . . . betrayal." Silence's brogue was as cold as a blade across skin. "It makes one wonder if anyone can be trusted. In our profession, a betrayal most often occurs due to greed." He smiled as if mocking his own lust for wealth. "Or dissatisfaction. Are any of you greedy or dissatisfied?"

Evie tensed.

"I don't know, Father." Ciaran watched him. "We have

wealth. We're young. We can go anywhere we want. What else is there?"

"Power." Silence spoke with an almost paternal gentleness.

"We have that." Ciaran rolled his head as if his neck bothered him. Then his eyes went completely black. The lamps flickered. Evie saw a shadow twining around Ciaran like an enormous python. Her heart began to gallop.

Father Silence leaned forward. His face shifted and became a copy of Ciaran's. Queenie whispered a profanity. The doors separating the salon from the dining room slammed shut. The lights went out.

Something massive sat in Father Silence's chair, something with branching antlers—

The lights came back on, and Father Silence was gentle and handsome again. "We're not like them, the rest of humanity. But the power wanes, the older you get. They came to you when you most needed them."

"What are we?" Evie tossed the question into the air. She had asked it so many times.

"What are you?" The French in Mother Night's voice peaked with her amusement. "*Ma chérie*, how can you not have figured that out by now?" Her eyes were black as she met Evie's and said, "A terrible event occurred in each of your lives. You called on something, anything, not a god or a saint. On anything that would help you. You called on something without naming it."

The memory that Evie had so carefully avoided, despite Mad's and Jason's gentle nudging, began to seep like blood from beneath the floorboards of a home. A mirrored door opened . . .

An eight-year-old girl sat on the floor, happily fingerpainting on a huge swath of paper. It was raining, a thunderstorm that made her feel shivery and safe. Her parents were arguing, but the rain drowned that out. Juliet, only six, was using the fingerpaints on a doll. Ezra, four years old, was sleeping.

Then the thunder entered their house. Evie heard her mom cry out, her father yell. Another crack of thunder tore her breath away. She heard footsteps coming down the hallway. She scrambled up, breathless, watching the doorknob turn. She knew something terrible had happened. A monster had gotten into the house. She thought, desperately, Don't let it see us. Don't let it see us. Please.

The door opened. The monster wearing her father's face walked in, holding the gun. He slinked past Evie. He lifted up tiny Juliet and sleeping Ezra.

He walked out with her siblings. He glanced back. Evie saw his true face before the door fell shut.

The mirror on the back of the door revealed her reflection, facing away from her, a backward girl. Terror swept over her.

—m—

Her dad had killed her mom and himself. Only he hadn't. The murderer had been Father Silence, a monster wearing his face. And, when Evie had pleaded for help, a different monster had come out of the dark and gotten inside her. Not an imaginary friend. Not a helpful spirit, as Ava had told her. Not some Jungian, dark-side version of her psyche.

A demon. Her own thought, mired in fear.

Evie stared at Mother Night. "We're possessed."

Mad took another dainty bite of cake. "Mine speaks to me all the time, in my dreams. Her name is Strix. The Bone Mother. An owl spirit."

Dev spoke carefully, "What's inside of me. It makes me feel like biting people. It's feline, but not a cat. It's scarier. It's slinky and quiet and sly. Like a Bengal tiger."

"You're blessed," Mother Night gently told them. "As others have been, as every member of La Fable Sombre has been throughout history."

Evie's monster had always lingered in the shadows of her dreams: a beautiful girl in a gown of black silk, a girl with envy-green eyes and a halo of emerald snakes for hair. Evie had always thought her imaginary, a friend who had first appeared to her after all the light had left her world.

Queenie whispered, "I dream of a black hare. Her name is Pyewacket. She tells me the secrets of plants, how to make potions and poisons. In my dreams, she licks blood from a cut she makes in my thumb."

Evie met Mother Night's gaze. "In my dreams, mine hides in the shadows, in a pool. She has snakes for hair." The girl came out of that pool, sometimes, with gifts Evie never remembered.

Mad was watching Evie. "Yours is a gorgon? Like Medusa?" She lifted her hands to her head and wiggled her fingers.

Queenie was still processing. "I shouldn't have let her in."

"Everyone," Ciaran spoke sternly, "calm down."

Evie felt the world tilt into something she didn't recognize. The lights felt too harsh. The shadows were like malevolent things in the corners of the room.

Mother Night continued, "There's a fine line between the

demonic and the divine." She watched Mad, who had begun to cut another piece of cake. Mad laid the slice on her plate, the knife glinting in her hand. Evie reached out and took the knife from her.

"Can we get rid of them?" Dev asked carefully. "Can we exorcise them?"

Father Silence regarded Dev over his brimming wineglass. "Why would you want to? They are your allies, your *power*."

Mother Night said, "They made certain you didn't simply survive. Think about the good people in your lives—the handful of them that there are—and then you think about being powerless. You chose the power and will continue to do so, no matter what the price."

Evie couldn't imagine living without the creature she'd always pretended was her inner voice, the brave one, the wise one—even if it had been a horrific tragedy that had caused her to become host to an entity whose motivations were unclear. Jason had warned her: "*Whatever happened . . . that's how it got into you.*"

"No." Queenie shook her head. "Whatever they are, they're organisms of some kind, made of energy, or maybe dark matter? Symbiotic, not parasitic."

"That's right, Queens." Ciaran was watching Silence. "Only the superstitious would call them demons. Everyone who ever joined La Fable Sombre had a supernatural talent and a dark day."

"There are many theories about what they are, passed down from one La Fable Sombre to another. Unfortunately"—Father Silence glanced at Mother Night—"that knowledge is locked in the vault. Which brings me to the crux of our conversation."

Mother Night set down Pandora's jar, and it seemed to crouch malevolently on the table.

The crux of the conversation wasn't that we're possessed by demons? Evie was still unsettled, aware of every odd shadow in the chamber. Aware of the shadow within herself, like a spiritual virus.

"The key to the vault was stolen by one of our colleagues when our Mothers ended their lives." This sinister sentence from Mother Night made Evie glad, then, of her demon.

"The vault key." Ciaran was as mesmerized and ready to strike as that cobra he'd bewitched in the Marrakesh marketplace months ago. "You know where it is?"

"That is to be your first strike of the new year." Father Silence smiled. "Go to Istanbul and extract the key from the Basilisk."

Mad groaned and slumped in her seat. Queenie swore. Dev set aside his glass and swigged straight from the bottle. Evie met Ciaran's eyes, her own widening. She asked, "Just who is this Basilisk?"

"The devil," Dev replied at the same time Mad said, "A villain," and Queenie answered, "Psychotic."

"One caveat," Silence continued. "You will not be accompanying them, Evie. We need you for something else." His gaze passed over Dev, Queenie, Mad, and Ciaran. "You won't need her. You're clever enough."

Evie froze. She speculated there was no vault key in the Basilisk's possession. Silence and Night were sending La Fable Sombre to their death.

But not me? Why not me? She had to stop thinking and

pretend, pretend she didn't suspect treachery, that she wasn't ready to become treacherous as a result.

"If we do this . . . ," Ciaran asked idly, his gaze a challenge. Because, of course, he knew. ". . . and succeed, do we get to see what's in the vault?"

Quiet etched itself through the room, tucked itself into the corners of the frescoed ceiling, and swooped into the dark cavern of the hearth.

"You will succeed, and of course you may see what's in the vault." Mother Night, holding Pandora's jar as she sauntered to Father Silence, set it down before him, her back turned to all of them as she faced Silence, one hip curved against the table. Evie could imagine the look the two exchanged, and a chill ran up her vertebrae.

Evie asked, casually, "So . . . what will I be doing?"

"A small heist." Night turned her head and smiled, radiant. "Father and I have a strike of our own. We need you for that."

Father Silence sat back so that his face was in shadow. "You have two weeks. Enjoy your holidays, children."

Evie met Ciaran's gaze, reading the true meaning of Silence's words: *Enjoy the last days of your lives.*

CHAPTER NINETEEN

Bloodstained Armor

Madrigal Jones."

"That's my name. Evie Wilder."

"Mad . . . I'm sorry."

Mad looked away. "I'm not gonna lie—it really hurt me, knowing what you did. And Dev might not act like it, but he's angry. He goes real quiet when he's pissed. And Queenie . . . actually Queenie's just fascinated. Like, how could someone like *you* infiltrate *us*?"

"Hey." Evie protested gently. "I researched the psychology of covert agents, how they constantly reassessed their situation, absorbed information. I was so paranoid, I didn't dare even *think* about what I was doing."

"Are you going to tell me how you planned it all?"

"Someday."

Mad sighed. "How do you think Ciaran found out? About your brother and sister?"

"I don't know. Jason knew because, three years ago, I hired the PI he apprenticed with, to look for Ezra and Juliet. And Jason inherited that case."

"Yeah. Jase is clever." Softly, Mad asked, "When you get them back, are you going to leave us?"

It was the night of their planned strike against Silence and Night. Evie sat with Mad on the roof of the Silver Cove lair. It was starry and chilly, and Evie practically sparked with adrenaline. If she survived this, if she was able to rescue her siblings, she would leave La Fable Sombre. Take Ezra and Juliet and her substantial earnings and live somewhere they wouldn't be found. A whisper of regret trailed that plan, and her stomach dropped as if she were on a nosediving plane. To be without La Fable Sombre . . . without Dev, Queenie, Mad. And Ciaran. "I don't know."

"Evie." Mad lifted a ladybug from her bare arm. "We'll be okay. So we're ending Silence and Night. They betrayed us."

"Sometimes I wonder about you." Evie nudged her, refusing to surrender to the absolute terror of what they were about to attempt.

Mad turned her head. "It's either them or us. Ciaran gave you a poison ring for Mother? Give it to me." Evie identified the glint in Mad's eyes—LFS was Mad's only family. Without them, she felt she wouldn't be much. She truly *would* die for all of them.

"No. I told you, Mad. *I'm* going to do it. When we're in Night's house, I need you and Jason to look for Juliet." Evie kept her eyes fixed on a star far above. *I am going to kill someone to save my family.*

"Eves . . . it won't be easy." Mad drew her knees up to her chin. "Killing someone the first time."

"What do you mean, 'the first time'?" Evie's voice sharpened.

Mad gazed out over Silver Cove, at the boardwalk like a constellation with its Ferris wheel and rollercoaster. "The only one that I regret is the person I *didn't* kill."

Evie stared at Mad, alarmed, thinking she really didn't know the other girl at all. "I don't suppose you can clarify that?"

Mad kept her eyes averted. "In Los Angeles, before LFS, I was being chased by the cops. I thought it was the best thing ever . . . until the cop chasing me hit a wall and spun out. The officer driving ended up almost smashed to pieces, lost the ability to do almost everything . . . I *broke* a person." Her voice was brittle. "Her name was Lisa Rodriguez. She has two little kids." Remorse darkened her eyes.

Evie was startled by this confession, couldn't imagine being responsible for such damage. But it did explain Mad's reckless ways, her refusal to let anything bother her or weigh down her conscience. Mad already had something lodged in her psyche.

"This won't be the same." Evie twisted the Medusa ring on her right forefinger. Could she do it, poison Night in cold blood, watch her die? Live with that? "This is for our survival." She pictured her mom and her dad and thought of Ezra and Juliet growing up alone in boarding schools. All that she had lost . . . "How many people have been collateral damage to Silence and Night?"

"You're scary." Mad widened her eyes. Then she grinned

and rose, balancing on the wall without fear. "It's almost time. You ready?"

Evie nodded and slipped to her feet. Her heart was hammering. Her stomach was churning. "Let's go get my brother and sister."

———⁓———

In the dead of night, Ciaran attempted to open a Door with Jason's power amplifying his own, a silver pentacle imprinted on a swirling darkness. Ciaran worked blind, tracking the blood drop he'd let fall on the *Bestiarum*. He struggled this time, gripping the handle of a door to an abandoned shopfront and tugging at it. Jason also tried to open the door. Failed. He and Ciaran stepped back.

"Can we kick it in?" Mad asked seriously. They each wore wooden wolf masks. Evie, Mad, and Queenie had slicked back their hair and wore men's suits, Mad dashing in pinstripes. They were all posing as Fenrir, betraying their Father.

"I'd rather not," Dev told her.

"I'm going to need all of you to push with me," Ciaran ordered. "It's the wards Silence has on the other side preventing it from opening." Ciaran, Dev, and Jason put their shoulders against the door. Queenie, Mad, and Evie braced and pushed with hands flat against the wood.

The Door flew open onto a darkness fluttering with deeper shadows. In the distance was a square of light, an elegant room with a stag's head mounted over a fireplace. *Father Silence's house.*

"Hold hands." Ciaran folded a hand around one of Evie's.

"Keep your gaze straight ahead. Don't look into the darkness—and don't even *attempt* to use your abilities. Something in their houses will flag us if we do."

They plunged, single file, into the dark and the cold. Evie felt something pluck at her hair, heard a malevolent whisper against one ear. Jason, who held her other hand, tightened his grip. Finally, the cobweb shadows released them, and they stepped into a hallway with moonlight glowing through tall windows. The room with the mounted stag's head was at the end of the hall, scattered with hunting trophies and trophies of another sort—bizarre curios, antiques in display cases.

Ciaran led them into the room, to a pair of white metal doors. The door handles were made of iron twisted into patterns of animals that appeared to be attacking and devouring human figures. "It's in here. The *Bestiarum*. I can sense it."

"How do we get in?" Evie wanted to run out of there and find Ezra.

"That's our alchemist's job." Ciaran stepped back. "This needs to look like Fenrir did it. Keep your masks on."

Queenie came forward, removing a metal box from her backpack. She crouched before the door. She adjusted her mask—which, like the rest, came with filters to protect them from toxic fumes—and slid on heavy gloves. She removed two glass tubes from the metal box. "Usually, it's hydrochloric acid, but I've found something a bit better, like aqua regia, only for baser metals." She poured a blue liquid onto the lock. "And less dangerous."

The iron lock began to corrode. Fumes twisted upward in strange shapes and faded.

Queenie pushed open the doors.

The head of another enormous stag was mounted on the opposite wall of a round room. Moonlight spilled from a skylight. The heads of other animals—a boar, a tiger, an antelope—took up space on the walls, among antique weapons and paintings of beautiful women. There were three display cases. Evie saw a sword in one and a stone head in another. The third . . .

Dev approached the one containing the *Bestiarum Vocabulum*. He halted a short distance from it, glanced up at the stag head. Evie caught a glint in the stag's glass eyes. "Camera."

"I see it." Dev glided forward, dragged a chair over, and sprayed the stag's glass eyes—not before letting the cameras inside get a good look at his wolf mask. He stepped down from the chair.

Ciaran looked at Mad. "Your turn."

Queenie switched off the lights. A web of blue lasers surrounded the *Bestiarum* in its case.

Mad moved lithely through the web, performing some serious gymnastic moves without levitating. Dev whistled. Queenie laughed softly. Mad ballet-toed to the display case holding the *Bestiarum*. She broke the glass with a small mallet, reached in, and lifted out the book. She tucked it into her backpack.

They exited the room. As they hurried through the hall toward a window, Dev unslung his backpack and drew out the rappelling equipment they'd brought to further incriminate Fenrir. They set up the fake getaway, then stepped back.

"Now for Evie's brother." Ciaran tapped the Bluetooth communication device in his ear, identical to the one each of them wore. "Keep in touch, you beautiful devils."

Ciaran glided up the stairs with Dev and Queenie. Evie, Mad, and Jason headed down a black corridor lit by silver stag wall lamps. Evie was certain everyone could hear her beating heart.

"I'll take this side," Jason whispered, indicating another corridor, its shadows broken by splashes of blue illumination. "Remember the time."

Evie nodded. She and Mad hurried onward.

She yanked Mad back into a window alcove as two men in suits came around the corner. They weren't Batavi, but they had the cold and efficient look of capable killers. When they'd gone, Evie whispered, "I think I know where Ezra's room'll be."

She hurried up the stairs to the third floor, Mad trailing after. Ezra had always loved the sky. Even at four years old, he'd been amazed by the stars. He'd always wanted to be awake to watch the sun rise or to see the moon appear.

Evie produced a little switchblade with a built-in compass on the hilt and led Mad down a hallway, its windows facing east. When she saw a sign on one of the doors—Aliens Welcome, Humans Fuck Off—she pushed open the door, revealing a large bedroom hung with posters of indie musicians, neat with bookshelves and science gadgets.

"No one here." Mad shoved her mask up. She snarled like a wolf angel. "Where is he?"

Evie pushed the palms of her hands over her eyes. *Where is he?* She walked to the balcony doors and flung them open. The peppery ammonia fragrance of rain swept over her—*petrichor*. Her mom had told her the name for that particular scent, Greek for stone and the blood of the gods. She saw an expensive telescope pointed toward the stars, and a half-eaten hamburger on a plate. "He's here somewhere."

"Okay. You go left. I'll go right. Keep looking." Mad zipped from the room.

Evie moved stealthily down another corridor, hoping there were no more cameras. She was armed with a taser in one pocket and a can of spray paint in another.

She halted when she saw a pair of doors ajar, amber light glistening on the floor. In the room beyond, she glimpsed a wingback chair, a masculine hand holding a glass of liquor. She froze. *Silence.*

She didn't know what compelled her to step over the threshold, into a book-laden study with a fire snapping in the hearth. Everything was ebony, with silver and forest green accents. She approached the chair. The Medusa ring on her forefinger became ice cold, as if death itself rested within the metal. She saw, in the mirror over the hearth, that the man in the chair was asleep, head bowed. It was very disconcerting to find Father Silence in such a vulnerable position.

She moved around and stared at him. Reaching out, she set a hand on his left shoulder, the poison ring against his neck.

His eyes flew open, flickering with confusion. "Who—"

"The ring is poisonous," she told him, her voice icy. "Where is my brother?"

He moved so swiftly, she scarcely had time to snatch her hand back before he was up and lunging at her—

Ciaran slid between her and Silence. He slapped a hand against the side of Silence's neck. Silence staggered. Evie cried out, "No!"

Silence's eyes rolled up in his head. He clutched at a bar cart before collapsing in a crash of shattering bottles and spilled liquor. He jerked spasmodically. He went still, eyes staring, foam at the corners of his mouth. Evie turned away, sick, horrified.

"Come on, Evie." Ciaran's voice was too calm. "It's done."

"Ezra . . ." She couldn't believe she didn't have her brother.

"He's not here. They've searched the house. *Listen*."

She heard shouts, running footsteps. Ciaran continued, "They know we're here. We need to get back to the Door—"

"I'm not leaving until I find him!" She didn't look at Silence's body. She ran for the exit.

The door burst open. Dev stood there. "Come on! There's a small army headed up the stairs!"

Ciaran strode past Evie. "Your brother is probably with your sis at Night's. It's the holidays. Come on, blackbird."

Panic and anguish roiled within Evie as they ran down the hall to where they'd originally opened a Door. Mad and Queenie were waiting. As Dev locked the hall doors that were the only other entry point, Mad questioningly met Evie's gaze. Evie looked around. "Where is Jason?"

"He'll be here," Mad told her.

While the boys turned away politely, the girls shed their suits and straightened the Issey Miyake dresses they wore beneath. Queenie unzipped her backpack and distributed prim heels and ornate deer masks to Mad and Evie. They were to become Nara, all stealth and charm.

Ciaran set both hands on the closed Door. "He'd better get here soon. I need him to open this Door—"

The hall doors crashed open, revealing two men, who raised their guns.

A shadow appeared behind them, struck one guard in the head with a golf club. The other guard whirled, a bullet cracking out. Jason bashed the second thug in the gut with the golf club. As the man crumpled, Jason stepped into the room and kicked the doors shut. They all watched in awe—but for Ciaran, who was grinning—as Jason strode across the room. He set his hands on the Door. As darkness bled from Ciaran and Jason's silver pentacle shimmered over the wood, Ciaran said, "Nice to have you back, bruv."

Jason didn't reply but slid his gaze to Evie. When he nodded, she *knew* . . .

He'd found Ezra and gotten him out of the house. Away from the wards, Jason had spirited him to safety and returned. They hadn't dared communicate over the Bluetooth mics.

As security broke through the hall doors, Ciaran's Door opened. He led them through, into the darkness. Voices whispered. Something clammy brushed against Evie's lips. She shuddered. She could scarcely see the others in the clotted shadows. A field of inky grass and a gaping sky of absolute night surrounded them.

After too long, they stepped into a hallway carpeted in white, where lilies bloomed in alabaster jars on little tables. The Door shut. As the others prowled toward a salon with a snow-pale piano and blanched furniture, Jason caught Evie by one wrist, whispered, "Your brother's safe. I got him out."

Joy shattered through her. "Where—"

"Come on," Ciaran called back.

Evie moved forward with Jason, resisting the urge to throw her arms around him.

"Where's the jar?" Mad turned in a circle in the white room.

"It has to be close by." Ciaran began inspecting the pale walls. "I can sense it."

Dev walked toward a painting of a sphinx, reached up, lifted it to reveal a safe.

He got the safe open. There was no Pandora's jar inside . . . only a wooden cigar box painted with roses. He lifted out the box and raised the lid as Evie peered over his shoulder. In the box were Polaroids, hazy, gold-touched snapshots. Evie fanned these out on the bureau. Most of the photographs were of a striking blue-eyed teenage boy and a girl with black hair—Silence and Night. There were other photos, taken in exotic locations. Polaroids of the former members of La Fable Sombre from twenty years ago. Her parents were among them.

Evie met Ciaran's gaze. He said, "You, Jase, and Mad find your sister and brother. We'll find the jar."

Dev and Queenie looked grim when they glanced at Evie—Mother Night's future murder was left unspoken.

As Ciaran, Queenie, and Dev left the salon, Evie led Jason and Mad down a hallway.

Two female Batavi in white suits rounded the corner. Before they were seen, Mad twisted Evie into a deserted room, while Jason stepped into another. As Evie and Mad hid on either side of the doorway, glued to the wall, they waited tensely.

When the Batavi had gone, Jason found them. He whispered to Evie, "Where would your sister's room be?"

Juliet had loved David Bowie. She had been afraid of high places, and her room had overlooked their mother's garden.

"Her room'll be on the ground floor, near a garden." So, to the east again, where the sun rose to nourish plants.

"You take that hall, I'll take the other," Jason directed. "And we'll have searched this entire floor."

As Jason moved off, Evie and Mad strode down a hall of white doors, eerie in the moonlight flooding through the windows. Evie heard a thread of music—David Bowie.

She ran down another hall, shoved open a door to reveal a room with a veiled bed, rosy plush beanbag chairs, and posters on sun-yellow walls. The windows framed a view of a walled garden gone bare in winter but still lovely. Evie sank against the door frame. "She's not here."

"Give me that wicked ring," Mad demanded. "*I'll* find Night."

"No." Evie turned to her, desperate. "But I trust you, Mad, to find Juliet." She caught Mad's hand. "Even when she was six, she was a night owl. She loves gardens. Look for a conservatory or some kind of sunroom with plants."

Mad whispered, "Eves . . . you're not a killer."

"Mad. *Go.*"

As Mad moved down the hall, Evie turned to face the stairway. She began to ascend. The upper hall was a cloister of narrow windows, with elegant mirrors on the opposite wall. The effect created an unsettling illusion of limitless night.

Something was breathing at the end of that hall. What Evie had thought only a mass of darkness stirred. Moonlight glinted over huge eyes in a too-large face. A woman's voice whispered in a language that sounded Greek. Evie began backing away.

Mother Night emerged from the shadows, cradling the little black jar. "Evie. I've been expecting you."

Evie flinched. Night said, "Do you want to see Juliet again? Come with me." She walked down the hall. Evie had no other choice but to follow, the poison ring burning on her finger.

Night led Evie into a little conservatory. "This was your sister's favorite place." She trailed her fingers through purple blossoms. For a moment, regret flickered across her face. She held out Pandora's jar. "Don't touch that mic you're wearing. You will take this jar. We will let you 'escape.' When you are with Ciaran and the others, you will open the jar. All their demons will be drawn into it. Then you will bring me the Anesidora Pithos on the roof of the Plaza La Mer at midnight tomorrow. And we will return to you your brother and sister."

Night didn't know about Silence's death, Evie realized. She brushed a shaking hand across her face. Had Jason found Juliet? She had never felt so powerless, so alone. "You were going to send La Fable Sombre to the Basilisk. To their deaths. Why not me?"

Night smiled like the Madonna, all mystical benevolence. "You inherited your mother's useful demon. And your brother and sister have something waking within them, whispering in their minds. We *need* the three of you. You and the new ones we've chosen, scattered amongst the other crews."

"But you need a Traveler and Ciaran killed—" Evie stopped talking.

"Lycan was regrettable. Jason will follow you if you ask. Jason will be the Traveler we need. If you take their power away,

Dev, Mad, and Queenie will live." She didn't speak Ciaran's name. "I will not send them against the Basilisk. The key to the vault is lost forever."

"I don't want this." Evie let the plea bleed into her voice.

"Oh, *chérie*, do you think you have a choice?" Tenderness darkened Night's eyes as she tucked a stray lock of hair back behind Evie's right ear.

"I don't know how to open it," Evie lied. "The jar."

"Madrigal has a resource in ancient knowledge. You *do* know how to open it. And you won't do it now because I have one of these and it protects me from magic. Here." Mother Night handed Evie a bracelet of black beads shaped into tiny animals. "Blessed obsidian. It will keep *your* demon from being sucked into the jar." She tapped the jar. "I *will* know if you bring this to me empty."

Evie accepted the bracelet and the jar, whispered, "If you wanted me all along, why didn't you tell me about Ez and Juliet?"

"Because you would have come after us with a vengeance. We needed you to find your way first. To find out who you really are." A strange tenderness threaded through her words.

Evie whispered and heard another voice beneath her own, one of liquid malevolence. "You killed my mom and dad."

"We didn't kill your mother and father." Mother Night closed her eyes, and a massive darkness enveloped her with a sigh, its giant woman's face beautiful, its teeth sharp, its body leonine. "Run, Evie. This needs to be convincing."

Evie, now understanding the Gothic phrase "mad with terror," whirled and fled.

The shadow sphinx chased her. She glanced back, her

breathing hoarse with fear, saw the immense darkness loping down the hall, claws tearing the beautiful wallpaper. She continued to run, her heart bashing against her rib cage. She heard something hissing in Greek, clawed feet clicking against the marble floor—

She burst through a pair of doors to find four Batavi aiming guns at a Door, where Ciaran stood, bracing it open. His skin scrolled with black script and jewel-bright illustrations—he was using the *Bestiarum*'s power to keep the Door open. His gaze locked with Evie's.

The Batavi stood between them. All four Glocks swerved toward Evie. Ciaran shouted her name.

"*Go!*" Evie yelled at him. She twisted around and raced in the other direction. She heard Night shrieking at the Batavi. "*Don't shoot her!*"

Evie had to believe they had all gotten to safety.

And Jason . . .

She fled through a door, into the garden. Jason had to have gotten Juliet by now. She spoke into the medallion, breathless. "Jase. Garden. East. The woods. There's a big white tree . . ."

She continued running until she vanished into the night beneath the trees. He would find her. He had to find her. She sank down, her breath heaving, her heart ready to burst.

What seemed an unbearable hour later, Jason came walking through the trees. She rose, and he smiled. "Evie . . . she's safe."

She laughed in triumph and grabbed his hand. He spun her into the silver pentacle and the darkness beyond.

She landed on cement, skinning her knees as the jar tumbled from her arms. Rain lashed the air. She looked back into the black hole, the gateway, to see Jason stepping out, the hood of his jacket falling back. She swept up Pandora's jar and rose, cradling it. "Jase."

She didn't believe the enormous black serpent that unfurled behind him, eyes sulfur gold, fangs ivory hooks, spiky scales razored with crimson. She screamed his name as the horror clamped fangs into Jason's left shoulder. Blood spattered, its ruby brilliance obscene, across his face. *No.* Terror ripped through Evie. She lunged forward as he reached out. Their fingers brushed—

"Zeppelin," he said, his eyes black with desperation, before he was dragged into the night between the worlds. The black hole sealed itself with a howl.

Evie felt the world tilt. Everything was moving too fast. Her throat closed, and all sounds ceased in a crashing silence. And, in that vacuum, she fell to her knees. She didn't know how to use the creature within her, the gorgon hissing and spitting, to fix this. She touched her face, Jason's blood still warm on her cold skin. *This can't be happening.*

Dead. He is dead.

She clutched her belly as if her insides had been ripped out.

Eventually, she rose. She turned and saw the neon coquette curved around a grinning crescent moon—the Blue Moon Motel. With Jason's sky-blue Chevy Bel Air parked in front of his room. She sobbed once, a torn gasp.

She ran toward the motel, bashed her fists against the door. It fell open. The lights were on.

"Ezra! Juliet!" She dashed in.

The room was deserted in that dull fashion that only motel

rooms could be. But it was worse because she'd expected her brother and sister to be here.

Where are they? She crumpled, curling wretchedly around Pandora's jar.

Jason was gone. And she still had a terrible thing to do.

———

Evie had never learned to drive, but she managed to steer the Bel Air down Silver Cove's main avenue, toward the warehouse district and La Fable Sombre's lair. She had stopped shaking, but an occasional shudder wracked her body. Jason's blood was still sticky on her skin. She glared at the night through strands of damp hair. She knew who was responsible for Jason's death.

She parked in front of the esoteric bookshop beneath her apartment. She could traverse the maze of hallways to the main room and hope La Fable Sombre were all there.

She glanced down at the little black jar that would end them. She carefully picked it up.

The bookshop was still open, topaz lights hazy in the windows as dusk darkened the air. She hurried up the stairs. Inside, she made her way down the corridors, to the main room. The doors were closed. She heard them arguing beyond.

"What is that blood from, mate?" Dev sounded angry. "Is that hers? Did our Evie get shot?"

"We left her there." Queenie's voice swept over everyone else's. "We just left her."

"We have to go *back*." Mad.

Ciaran's calm, deep voice followed. "Jason will save her. Or she'll save herself, more like. If she's not here soon, I'll track the jar and find her."

In the corridor outside, Evie sank against a wall, cradling Pandora's jar. She wore the bracelet of obsidian beads Night had given her. She remembered the despair in Jason's eyes, the blood . . . Tears slipped from beneath her lashes as she thought of every time he'd risked himself for her.

She straightened. If she didn't do what Night had asked her to . . . Night would come after them.

If she did this, she would lose a second family. If she didn't do this, she would lose her first family. Again. And she didn't know where Jason had taken Juliet and Ezra.

She closed her eyes. She pictured that last day on the beach with her parents, with Ezra and Juliet. Her father had been strumming a guitar as dusk stained the sky. The ocean had reflected golden rays from the setting sun. Her mom, in a scarlet swimsuit, had been whirling with little Ezra and Juliet. It had been the best day of Evie's childhood, even with gray storm clouds on the horizon.

She pushed one hand over her face and silently screamed. Anguish tore through her. Jason's violent, possible death had created more emptiness inside her, an emptiness she knew was making room for whatever entity had slithered into her, pretending to be a water-born girl with snakes for hair and a stone for a heart. *Jason* . . . His rare smile flickered in her memory. She raked nails down one arm, felt the satisfying beading of blood.

When she glimpsed a massive shadow stirring in a corner, she went very still. She stared as it billowed and grew.

The Wild Dark moved toward her in a graceful, terrifying form. Cold and darkness folded over her, making her invisible. Then she was alone, veiled by the unseen.

She heard Ciaran and Mad arguing. She carefully opened the door to the lair and slid in.

La Fable Sombre mirrored the elemental colors of her last day with her family on the beach. Dev, his buzz cut glowing dusk red, sat on the pool table, glowering. Queenie, smoldering in a scarlet kimono, sat on the spiral stair. Mad stood on the windowsill, leaning against the frame and gazing out at the courtyard, the strands of her golden hair like sun rays flaming around her head. Ciaran, a stormy darkness amid his crew, stood facing away from all of them, in front of the fireplace, a liquor bottle dangling from his fingers. His demon was different from theirs. *Python, Dweller on the Threshold,* the voice of her own demon whispered in her head. The Wild Dark between the Doors healed Ciaran. He was tattooed with symbols from that place. He'd been able to overcome Silence and Night's wards to open Doors in their houses.

Veiled, she moved silently into the room. No one looked at her. No one saw her. The lights flickered.

"She'll be coming for us," Queenie insisted. "Night. When she finds out about Silence . . ."

"I have a plan," Ciaran said, his voice idle, cold. He took a swig from the bottle. He set the bottle down on the floor. He turned and lifted the *Bestiarum Vocabulum.* "We fight if Night comes. If she doesn't . . . we'll know Evie did what she had to."

Mad whispered. "We need to go back."

Queenie rose. "Use that thing to open a Door, Ciar."

Dev's face hardened. "Let's get Evie."

"No," Ciaran told them. "We wait. Have a little faith in our blackbird."

The jar in Evie's hands began to hum, the sound making the hair rise on the back of her neck. She touched the lid of the jar sealed in metal, asked the creature crouched within her: *How?* The girl-thing whispered an ancient language, and Evie understood, repeated it, the vowels like razored runes on her tongue.

"What's that?" Dev looked around.

The jar's metal seal melted, beading down the obsidian surface. Evie remembered the directions Mad had gotten from Priest: turn the lid one way to release whatever was in the jar; turn the lid the other way to trap something inside of it. But which way? She went with what her dad had taught her whenever she'd clumsily "helped" him around the house, eight years old and eager to be like him. *Right to tighten. Left to loosen.* She took a shuddering breath, realizing she had to betray the four people she had come to love to save the two she had always loved.

She twisted the lid to the right and opened Pandora's jar. Nothing happened. Evie waited, tangled in barbed-wire tension.

Queenie shivered, glanced around. Dev slouched, rubbing at his temples. Mad stiffened as light began to thread from her skin. She whirled, wolf eyes wide. She whispered, *"Evie?"*

"Ciaran..." A substance like black ink trickled from Queenie's eyes and nose. As a rabbitlike darkness swept from Queenie, twining toward the jar in Evie's hands, Evie slammed back against a wall.

Dev hunched over, shuddering, blood beading on his skin,

swirling upward, becoming a crimson tiger that swept into the jar.

Mad curled forward with a cry. A huge translucent owl with a woman's face arched from her, winging toward Evie, who shut her eyes and held out the jar to catch it.

"Evie." The voice that spoke her name was a guttural snarl. She opened her eyes.

Something massive and glittering black swept from Ciaran, a shape with enormous eyes containing nothing but malice. Evie backed away as its hooded head arched over Ciaran's. Ciaran's eyes were night-dark. He said, "I see you, Evie."

She spun and ran. The serpentine spirit followed. She felt cold scales scrape her neck—

The massive darkness twined over her and into the jar. She clutched the jar, shoved the stopper in as she raced down the stairs. She slammed the button to open the automatic doors. As they slid apart, she halted.

Three black cars had arrived, producing an army of Batavi, who moved with ruthless efficiency.

Father Silence, cold-eyed, slid from a Mercedes. Evie's stomach lurched. *How was he not dead?* Anger burned through her, followed by a wraith of terror. She kept very still as Silence gazed at the warehouse, straightening his blazer. His gaze passed over her, not seeing her. He told the Batavi, "Kill everyone you see."

The Batavi stalked forward, grim reapers unholstering shiny guns.

Kill everyone you see.

Evie turned and ran back into the lair. Still invisible, she flung open the doors to the main room. Ciaran stood in the center, the rest of La Fable Sombre behind him.

Evie *wished* the unseen over Dev, Mad, Queenie, and Ciaran. It left her in a tidal wave, a sonic boom, the force of which flung her backward. Yet she was cushioned by the sheer power of the web of invisibility as it swept forward and wrapped around La Fable Sombre.

She caught herself against the wall, clutching the jar.

Silence and his men stormed into the lair, Silence's gaze flickering around, narrowing.

"Where is everyone?" one of the killers asked, revolver pointing as La Fable Sombre quietly separated in their tendrils of invisibility. Queenie selected a fireplace poker. Dev twirled a pool stick. Mad had taken a baseball bat from the memorabilia wall.

They closed in on Silence and his men, soundlessly, unseen.

Silence's gaze swept around.

"*Ciaran.* I'm finding it difficult to keep up with all your tricks. And you can't keep up with mine—I can shapeshift others when I need to . . . like that poor sod you stuck with your little needle because you thought he was me. Evie can't hold this for long. The veil will drop. We'll see you. Then I'm going to kill one of your girls. Very slowly. Not Evie, of course. You're going to tell me where everything is that you've stolen from me. Because I know you've begun a collection of your own, boyo. You'll tell me, or I'll cut up another girl."

So much for "Father," Evie thought contemptuously.

Mad was sneaking up behind Silence, her wolf eyes luminous with rage.

340

Ciaran tilted his head to one side. "Whatever would Mother say?"

Silence raised a revolver. Ciaran shook his head. "So . . . I'm guessing the Basilisk doesn't have that vault key after all?"

Silence smiled and aimed. "Farewell, Ciaran. You are a disappoint—"

Mad swung the bat. As it struck him, Silence swore and dropped the gun. The rest of La Fable Sombre moved, swinging and stabbing. Gun shots cracked out. Silence's men shouted. When a revolver skidded to Evie, she crouched down and slid the gun back across the floor, toward Queenie, who snatched it up. The skin of invisibility ribboned from Queenie as she undid the safety from the gun and aimed it at Silence.

Silence lunged, slamming into Ciaran. Another man pointed his revolver at Queenie.

Evie swung a statuette against the man's head and became visible as her power wavered.

Dev clobbered one thug with the pool stick, bent back to avoid being stabbed. Mad swung the bat at another man's head.

Silence smashed a fist into Ciaran's jaw. Ciaran staggered. Silence, his shadow on the floor massive, antlered, shoved Ciaran against a wall, one arm across his throat to crush his windpipe.

Evie shouted, "Ciaran! His bracelet!"

Ciaran and Silence both looked at her.

Ciaran ripped the bracelet of sigil beads from Silence's wrist.

Evie opened Pandora's jar.

Cold swept through the room. Silence's antlered shadow raced over the wall, the ceiling, toward Pandora's jar. As his demon was sucked in, Silence staggered.

Ciaran straightened, blood swathing the lower half of his face. He looked demonic. He stepped toward Silence and clapped one hand, the skull ring glinting, against Silence's neck.

Silence was stunned.

He collapsed.

As Ciaran was tackled by another thug, Silence dragged himself toward Evie. She backed away, shocked by the suddenness of his downfall. He smiled with blood-stained teeth. "Did you know? All this time? Oh, you are definitely ours." He spat blood. He sprawled on the floor, convulsed once. He stared sightlessly up at the skylight depicting the shadowy beast in its background of bloodred.

Evie gazed down at the man who had so brutally and monstrously ended her world. She should have felt something—triumph, satisfaction. There was only emptiness. In the end, Silence hadn't mattered.

Evie fled. She didn't look back. La Fable Sombre could handle themselves. Even without their powers.

CHAPTER TWENTY

Night

At the Plaza La Mer, Evie slid from Jason's car. A suffocating dread made her light-headed, her steps uneven.

She was alone now.

You're not alone, a girl's voice whispered, and Evie felt strength pour into her, glimpsed threads of shadow drifting from her fingertips. As she stepped into the lobby elevator, cradling the jar containing La Fable Sombre's demons, she thought about her options. She decided she could prick Night with the poison ring now.

When the doors slid open, four young women in white suits, eyes rimmed in designs of black kohl, stood on the roof, revolvers pointed at Evie. Around them, the roof was decorated like an estate garden, with pillars and little statues on pedestals.

Mother Night moved into view. She wore a white gown, like a Greek goddess, her black hair coiled up. "Evie." She indicated her guards. "These are Nouveau, Hawk Eye, Magpie, and Scarlet. You can't win this."

Evie couldn't see any way out. She wondered why Night didn't just snatch the jar from her.

"You're wondering why I don't take the jar from you?" Night stepped forward and reached out.

An invisible force shoved the woman back so hard, she slammed into two of her Batavi, who kept her from falling. As Evie stared down at the jar, Mother Night straightened. "If it's being held, it has to be given willingly."

"You don't have my sister," Evie whispered, despair etching her heart.

"But I can find her. And your brother." Mother Night held out her hands. "We need you, Evie."

The elevator pinged. Everyone turned, the four Batavi raising their revolvers.

The elevator doors slid open.

Wearing their bruises and blood like badges, Ciaran and Dev stepped out with Queenie and Mad. Ciaran met Mother Night's cold gaze. "You tried to kill us, Mother."

"And I'm not in love with you anymore." Dev had never looked more dangerous.

Mad said disdainfully, "You made Evie sacrifice us, you bitch."

Queenie lifted a middle finger. "Mother Night."

Mother Night smiled. "It doesn't matter. I have replacements."

Ciaran told her, "Father is dead."

Evie flinched as Night's face changed, the monster beneath her skin shifting upward with her rage. She showed her teeth. "An eye for an eye." She flicked a finger.

The scarlet-haired Batavi swept toward Mad, a blade glinting in her hand.

Dev tackled the Batavi. Mad and Queenie went for the others.

Ciaran walked toward Evie. One of the Batavi shot at him. He hooked an arm around another Batavi, using her as a shield.

Evie drew invisibility around herself and turned toward Night, dreading what she needed to do to save them all.

Night shouted at her Batavi as, cloaked by the unseen, Evie moved toward her, the poison ring burning on her finger. She halted.

She realized she couldn't do it after all.

A darkness flickered before her, became a girl in a wet black gown, her hair writhing, her eyes burning green. Evie knew what the demon wanted her to do. As the gauzy darkness whispered and clung to her skin, and La Fable Sombre's skirmish against the Batavi whirled around her, Evie continued toward Mother Night.

Night whirled, darkness twisting around her, sparkling with tiny bits of purple energy. Her eyes were as black as holes in the universe. *"I see you, Evie."* She reached out to grab Evie, to spirit her away—

Evie smashed Pandora's jar into Night's beautiful face. Night screamed, blood running from her broken nose as she collapsed.

As the fight between La Fable Sombre and the Batavi continued, a Batavi with the cold eyes of a hawk raised her gun and pointed it at Evie.

Mad said, her voice carrying, "How I wish I could fly."

Evie twisted the lid to the left and opened the jar.

Four phantoms of black, white, dark green, and copper swirled from the jar, gliding toward their original hosts. Other shadows escaped, twisting into the night like terrifying, ephemeral mockeries of animals.

The Batavi hesitated, struck with awe and terror, as La Fable Sombre, eyes glowing, faced them.

His eyes tiger-gold, Dev swaggered toward one of the girls, smiled, and said persuasively, "You don't want to hurt me, do you?"

The girl with the crimson braids lowered her gun, her expression one of adoration. Dev gently took the gun from her.

The Batavi called Hawk Eye spun, gun aimed, as Mad levitated like a ballerina in the air. She kicked Hawk Eye in the face. The Batavi fell, the Glock spinning from her grip.

At the same time, another Batavi lashed at Queenie with a knife. Queenie slid back, reached into a pocket of her coat, and flung a handful of pink glitter at her attacker. Inhaling, the Batavi was struck by a fit of coughing. She dropped to her knees. Queenie clonked her on the head with a little statue from a nearby pedestal and the girl crumpled.

Evie saw Ciaran holding two revolvers on the remaining Batavi—Hawk Eye, who staggered up, and the other Batavi, a white-haired girl.

Mother Night was back on her feet, aiming a Glock at Mad.

Everyone froze, Ciaran looking torn between aiming his snatched revolvers at the two Batavi or turning one of the guns on Night.

"Here." Evie set down the jar, stepped back. "Take it."

Night met Mad's gaze, lowered the revolver. Relief replaced the fear on Mad's face.

Night raised the revolver and shot.

Mad fell.

Ciaran shot Night. She staggered, shocked, clutching at her bloody midriff. She began to change, darkness looming behind her, an immense face forming, a shadowy lion's body with razor claws taking shape around her. Evie stared in horror at the emerging monstrosity.

Mad pushed up, blood blooming on her coat, and lunged at Night, carrying them both off the roof.

Evie screamed, *"Mad!"*

Mad turned in the air with Night, the darkness swirling around them.

Mad let go, her arms wide, her golden hair twisting.

Night's fading scream ended abruptly.

Evie looked away, shaking so badly, she felt as if her skeleton were rattling.

The two Batavi left standing fled.

"Evie!" Ciaran yelled.

Something monstrous and black, a winged lion with a woman's face, swept upward, from where Mother Night had fallen, toward Evie. Evie saw death. Standing her ground, confronting it, cold night fell over her, a raptor wind tearing at her hair and her clothes. She saw talons reaching down for her like scythes, a pair of enormous silver eyes glowing. Rage ripped through Evie. *This* had taken her world away.

Something reared up in Evie, something equally monstrous, causing tendrils of writhing shadows to snake from her. She raised Pandora's jar. The winged sphinx reared back—and spun into the jar like a small tornado. Evie slammed the lid down on whatever had left Mother Night's body.

As they all stood where the battle had ended, Mad glided back to the roof, examined her wound. She shrugged. "It's just a scratch." She turned to Evie, her wolf eyes iridescent. "Where's Jason?"

Evie looked at Ciaran. "Do you want to tell them? Or should I?" Anguish bled away her adrenaline.

Ciaran set the revolvers down on a table. His gaze never dropped from hers. He said, "Evie. We've won."

To the others, Evie said, "Something dragged Jason into the dark and bit out his throat. Something like a giant python."

Mad, Queenie, and Dev stared at Ciaran. Queenie whispered, "You were delayed getting out of the Door . . . we thought you were staying for Evie."

Dev's brows slanted. "And whose blood was on you?"

"You were in that place between the Doors. The Wild Dark." Mad sauntered toward Ciaran, golden and feral. "Weren't you? Jase's pentacle trick takes him there. *What did you do?*" She slammed her fists against Ciaran's chest.

He caught her wrists and said, eyes flashing, "Power needs a sacrifice."

Dev swore brokenly. Her eyes on Ciaran, Queenie began to edge toward a fallen revolver.

Mad tore away from Ciaran's grip. "*Who else have you sacrificed?*"

"Vero," Evie said quietly, still cradling Pandora's jar. "Ciaran told Silence and Night she and Jason were going to leave—he needed Vero's, and Jason's, deaths to convince the rest of you to turn against Silence and Night."

"*Vero?*" Dev whispered, one hand drifting to the tigereye pin Vero had given him.

There was a *click*. Queenie had the revolver in one hand, pointed at Ciaran.

Ciaran looked around at all of them, his gaze finally coming to rest on Evie. The twist of anguish in his voice was a master stroke. "Vero wasn't supposed to die."

"You're a liar." Evie twisted the lid on Pandora's jar.

Ciaran lunged, swift as a snake, and grabbed her, slamming them against the stairway door—through a *Door*.

They fell into darkness. Ciaran hauled her past clinging shadows. Sharp spines or thorns or nails grazed her skin, tore the dress from her as if skinning her false personality away. She lost her shoes in the hurtling journey between the Doors.

Light burst over them. Evie caught herself against a railing of wrought-iron curlicues. She and Ciaran stood in an interior of iron girders surrounded by night sky. She could hear traffic below. She recognized the steampunk glamour even as vertigo threatened. "Are we . . . ?"

"The Eiffel Tower." Ciaran watched her. "You've always wanted to come here. Because of your mum. She was Night's bestie. Did you know?"

Evie, barefoot and flimsily dressed in her black slip, confronted Ciaran's blood-stained elegance, resenting her vulnerability. Yet she still held Pandora's jar. "Do you think I should be grateful you helped end Silence and Night?"

He leaned close, whispered, "You faked it so well, making us work to get you, our little snake in the nest. You used us, Evie. You used me."

She laughed in disbelief and shoved him. "You used *us*. For your goddamn power grab. And I can't believe you . . ." She could scarcely say the words. The sentence left her as a wail of regret and grief. *"You killed Jason!"*

"Blackbird—"

"Don't call me that."

He said, voice low and cutting, "It was you who used him, didn't you, to spirit your siblings away because you didn't trust me."

Evie felt as if she'd been kicked in the stomach. She whispered brokenly, "I didn't . . . I . . ." The word "love" became impossible because she scarcely understood it anymore. And it was too late. "Jason was your *friend*. And Vero . . . did you even care about her?"

Darkness drew around him, slithered across his tattooed arms. Most of his face was in shadow but for a stripe of light over his eyes. "Give me the jar, Evie."

The Anesidora Pithos had to be given. It couldn't be taken from someone else's hands.

The wind swept around them, thieving something nameless from Evie, maybe the cruel element that was hope. She couldn't let Ciaran get the jar. She saw in his eyes the vicious darkness that matched hers. He would do what he did best—use his gorgeousness and charisma to convince her that a demon soul was better than a human one. *And, really,* she thought, desperate and conflicted, *why wasn't it?*

"Evie." Ciaran spoke tenderly. "I destroyed Silence and Night for you. We're free. Your brother and sister—Jason got them out. And Mad, Queenie, and Dev are La Fable Sombre again. *Safe.*"

Evie whispered, "Not with you around."

He reached out, brushed one thumb across her jaw. "When did we become enemies?"

"When I saw the light leaving Jason's eyes." She realized she'd backed up to the metal railing with its dizzying drop beyond.

He laughed, bitter and sharp. He shoved his hands though his perfect hair. "Even dead, Ra is fucking up my life."

He surged forward to grip her by the throat. She felt his skull ring cold against her carotid. "I'm right vexed with you, Evie. But I can forgive you."

"Forgive me?" She choked on another laugh.

"I'll give Queenie and Dev a second chance. And Mad—I'll forgive her for anything. I won't hurt your brother and sister. They'll be as protected as if they were my own."

She lifted her gaze to his and knew he was lying. Mad, Dev, and Queenie had turned against him. He didn't need them. He would find others, recruit other lost boys and girls possessed by demons. Ciaran Argent was beautiful. He had no origin story that was true. Whatever had gotten inside of him had devoured whoever he'd been. *That's* what she was talking to, something cunning and ancient—like the snaky-haired creature who'd kept Evie safe all these years.

"Now," he continued, coaxing. "Just give me the jar."

She made herself invisible. She began to lift the jar's stopper.

He struck her so hard, she slid to one knee, tasting blood in her mouth. She caught herself against the metal railing, still clutching the jar. While her brain resettled in her skull, she stared through strands of her hair at his shiny shoes.

He could *see* her.

She pushed to her feet, sweeping up the hand gleaming with the poison ring he'd given her for Mother Night. He caught her by the wrist and twisted the ring off. He yanked her close, whispered, "Don't make me do this. What the fuck are you fighting me for? Silence and Night are gone. *We* are La Fable Sombre."

She spat blood. "There *is* no more La Fable Sombre."

"There is, Evie. And you've inherited it. Do you know why?" He stepped back, his gaze cruel, amused. "Because you're their kid."

She couldn't speak. She couldn't understand what he was saying.

"That's right," he continued, relentless, circling her. "Two kids in boarding schools—your brother and sister—and one more, born in a Paris hospital. A girl. Why do you think they wouldn't kill you?"

I remember Night being as round as a moon, Priest had told Jason. Mother Night had wanted Evie to take over La Fable Sombre. All the coded conversations Evie had shared with Silence and Night flooded back to her. She pressed one hand over her mouth to hold in a scream.

"Your other 'parents,' the ones they killed, took you, blackbird, because . . . well, I don't know, but isn't that ironic?" He smiled. "You were stolen by the two people you loved. You helped end the two people who you were stolen from."

Something shifted in the shadows behind him. When she saw what wove through the pillars, she stood straight, letting the awful revelation fall away. She would deal with that wreckage later.

Ciaran slammed a hand against her neck. When she felt the prick from his skull ring, terror spiked through her. As he whispered, "Sorry, blackbird," the poison moved sluggishly into her bloodstream. He stepped back, waiting for her to die so he could take the jar. She remained upright, cradling the jar, clutching at the railing behind her as a deadly languor swept over her. She lifted her head with an effort. As the poison swarmed through her, she focused on the darkness prowling across the floor behind Ciaran.

She whispered, "You said you'd die for them."

She collapsed, hit the metal floor hard, cried out as Pandora's jar slid from her grip and rolled off the lip of the walkway. Vanishing into the darkness below.

The big shadow stalking toward Ciaran leaped.

Evie stared at the obsidian horn that speared through Ciaran's chest. Blood whipped out. She whispered, "Hello, Zeppelin." She saw fury and anguish flood Ciaran's eyes as the black unicorn dragged him backward into the glimmering pentacle and the Wild Dark beyond.

The pentacle faded in silver beads.

Just like that, Ciaran Argent was gone. His blood glistened with a sickening ruby brilliance on the floor.

Evie dragged herself up, fighting the fatal, poisonous splinters of ice and darkness that ripped through her. She doubled over, blood spilling from her nostrils. The poison was turning her to stone. As she slid to her knees, fighting to breathe, she felt the girl gorgon slither from her and whispered raggedly, *"No . . . don't leave me . . ."*

A shadow galloped toward her, reared to a halt a short distance from her, its horn spiraled with silver runes. Jason's demon, which, out of some vestigial loyalty, had protected her, spit something at her feet—Ciaran's skull ring.

Evie closed her eyes and welcomed Zeppelin as it guided her into a pentacle of silver and black.

—◇◇—

Evie fell to the floor in Queenie's apartment. The antidote to the poison was here, somewhere. *The red cabinet . . .*

She struggled to rise, her legs numb. Inside her, Zeppelin twisted and licked at the poison in her blood but faltered. The demon phantomed out of her . . .

Demons wouldn't remain in dying or aging bodies.

Evie focused on the red cabinet, only five steps away. She fell again. Her hands were icy. She began to crawl. She reached out, her fingertips brushing the cabinet door. *Please. I don't want to die . . .*

The apartment door slammed open.

"Evie!" Queenie and Dev were suddenly there, dragging her into a sitting position, their arms unbelievably warm, their voices like sun rays. Evie, death crawling around the edges of her vision, whispered, "Hey."

Mad slid to her knees beside Evie. "Queens . . ."

Queenie and Dev scrambled to the cabinet. Evie, fading, heard them arguing. Then they were back.

"Where?" Mad asked calmly.

Evie could feel her heart straining. Queenie said, "Heart. I don't think I can—"

Mad took the needle from Queenie. Without hesitation, she plunged the needle into Evie's heart. The pain made Evie black out for a second. Then warmth rushed through her, tingling through her fingers and toes. Her brain was no longer mush. Her heartbeat steadied. A small cry of relief escaped her.

"There she is." Dev's smile was radiant.

Mad shed her pink bomber jacket and tucked Evie into it.

"I knew he'd do it." Queenie sat back on her heels. "I knew he'd use my poison."

"And I figured you'd charm Jase's demon." Dev's gaze was serious. "That's how you got here?"

"Zeppelin," Evie whispered.

"*I* was the one who said she'd come here." Mad solemnly told Evie, "Now, you really need to go."

Evie heard sirens and raised her head. "Why?"

"Someone saw Night fall," Dev explained. "And Mad drove here like a lunatic in Jason's car, breaking all sorts of laws, so . . . yeah, we need to go."

Mad looked at Dev and Queenie. "Get her out of here. Take my car. Keys are in the ignition."

Queenie and Dev hauled Evie to her feet. As she reeled, she said, "Mad, we can't leave you."

"We're *not* leaving you." Queenie looked desperate.

Outside, tires screeched and doors slammed. A voice deepened by a bullhorn blared orders.

Mad looked over one shoulder and smiled sweetly. "You think I can't get out of this?"

"Madrigal," Dev pleaded.

"See you in a while, crocodile." Mad loped out of the room.

Evie swore as Dev and Queenie helped her through the greenhouse, down the rickety stairs, through the maze that led to Mad's apartment and the alley below, where Mad had parked her Aston Martin.

As Queenie drove the car onto the main road, Evie looked back and saw the red and blue lights surrounding the lair.

"Mad," she whispered, and thought of a little girl learning to fly because she'd wanted so desperately to live.

Chapter Twenty-one

Unicorn

Evie found Jason standing before the jewel-hued medieval tapestries of *The Hunt of the Unicorn*. He stood straight and true in a dark blue cashmere coat and nice threads.

Evie halted beside him and gazed at the huge work of art.

"You never visit me." He didn't take his gaze from the tapestry.

"I didn't know where you were." Evie turned to him, her heart twisting. "Do you want Zeppelin back?"

"He won't do me any good where I am." He looked at her. "Don't try to find me. This is just a dream."

She woke up in a hotel room to find the serpent-haired girl in the slinky black gown crouched at the foot of her bed. Evie said to her, "So, you came crawling back."

Chapter Twenty-two

Queen of the Clouds

Madrigal Jones walked between two orderlies down a corridor of St. Lazarus Hospital, a white art deco building behind ten-foot-tall iron fencing. Everything here was white: her loose clothes, the band on her wrists. Most of the other patients genuinely belonged here, but others . . . well, they just had that fizzy familiar feeling. There was a boy whose eyes flashed venom-green in a certain light. And a girl whose shadow sometimes seemed to slink along the walls.

No one had come to visit Mad. These bastards wouldn't even allow her a phone call. One of the orderlies had told her he'd help her if she was *nice*, so she'd blithely broken his nose. She'd been here a month, lying, charming, threatening. Not once had she used her talent—she wasn't stupid.

She hadn't had a chance to ask Evie what had happened to Ciaran. But she knew because he, like Jason Ra, haunted her dreams.

Today, she had visitors. As she ambled between the two female orderlies, she wondered if it was a trick. When they reached the room with the Plexiglass and the phones, she halted.

The girl who sat in a chair behind the glass wore all black but for a pink bomber jacket. Her hair was a halo of dark tendrils. Mad walked slowly over and sat. She tossed one of her two braids back and daintily picked up the phone. A male security guard stood nearby, facing away from them.

"Hey, Evie." Mad smiled.

"Hey." Evie smiled in that crooked fashion that Mad understood. "You lied."

Sadness ghosted through Mad, but she chased it away. "Yeah. I got caught. You gonna tell me how you did all this? Took Silence and Night and Ciaran down?"

"I'm sorry, Mad."

"Just tell me how you did it, doll." Mad leaned forward. "The whole double cross. I gotta know. You owe me a story."

Evie breathed out. "My dad used to talk about La Fable Sombre, how it would find us someday. That he and my mom hadn't gotten away from it. That pretending to be other people wouldn't last forever. Then they were killed. A murder-suicide. I started hearing about La Fable Sombre when I was fourteen. When I was eighteen, I found a metal plaque inscribed with Greek writing inside my favorite rag doll. I brought it to antique shops and dealers to find out what it was. Turns out, it was a codex that had belonged to Cleopatra the alchemist. Someone who had eyes and ears in those circles found me. He wanted the codex. He asked me weird questions: *Did people ignore me? Did*

I sometimes steal things? He said he had known my parents. I told him I knew about La Fable Sombre."

Realization dawned in Mad's eyes. *"Priest.* Priest was in on it?"

"I said I'd give him the codex if he helped me find a way into LFS. He agreed, warning me that I couldn't let on that I knew what La Fable Sombre were or that my parents had once belonged. He told me to play hard to get. In my mom's belongings, I also found the Queen Cobra that had belonged to the other Cleopatra, the Egyptian one—my mom had a thing for Cleopatras. I didn't know what it was, but I figured it was something. I used it as a lure and donated it to the Silver Cove Museum fundraiser—Silence and Night knew my parents had taken the Cobra. They sent all of you after me."

Mad whistled, low.

"When I saw Father Silence in Morocco, Mad . . . I remembered him in my house that night. When I found out he could look like other people, that his murders were meant to mimic suicides . . . It wasn't a monster who had opened my bedroom door when I was a kid—it was Silence, wearing my father's face."

"Evie . . ." Mad wanted to reach through the Plexiglass.

"I joined La Fable Sombre, learned your strengths and weaknesses, your patterns like fractals, complex and beautiful. I gamed the outcome." Evie continued with longing in her voice, "I loved my mom and dad. My dad could spin illusions, miniature unicorns and glowing hummingbirds. My mom made up stories that made me feel brave. Juliet and Ezra . . . I was their big sister. I was supposed to protect them. They were beautiful. And Silence and Night stole all of that from me."

"Eves . . . Your brother and sister . . ."

"Zeppelin knows where they are. It took me a while to find out. So, Mad, I have a question for you." Evie's smile made her look so young. "Can you still fly?"

Mad's heart began beating so fast, she thought everyone could hear it.

The security guard turned, and it was *Dev*. He winked.

Evie dropped the phone and vanished.

Mad turned her head. A moment later, she saw the window across the room slowly open outward.

She whirled to her feet. She sprinted past the orderlies. They shouted, lunging for her. One of the nurses lifted her head, revealing herself to be Queenie. She raised a hand and blew glittery red pollen at the two orderlies. They collapsed.

Mad stretched out a hand toward the window.

A hand grasped hers as she leaped onto the sill, into a veil of invisibility, of rustling shadows and whispers.

Standing on the sill, Evie met her gaze. "We're trusting you, Mad."

Queenie and Dev jumped up onto the sill and clasped their hands. Evie's veil concealed all of them. Mad laughed. "Ready? Hold tight."

They stepped into the air.

CHAPTER TWENTY-THREE

I Love Paris

Evie had one more trip to make.

A few days later, Zeppelin spirited Evie, Queenie, Mad, and Dev through the darkness and left them in a fading silver pentacle in a courtyard of flourishing greenery and Greek statues. Evie walked to the wrought-iron gate and opened it and stepped out with the others onto the Avenue de Camoens, the Eiffel Tower looming at its end.

When she saw the two teenagers seated at a table in front of a café, she stood very still. The lean boy with the tousled pompadour and the curvy girl with the fall of brunette hair were perfect. She clutched the maiden death medallion, the one that held the photograph of her brother and sister when they'd been little.

She looked over her shoulder. As chic as Parisians themselves, Mad with an arm on Dev's shoulder and Queenie leaning against Mad, they watched, smiling.

"Family's everything," Queenie told her with a shrug.

"Well, go on then," Dev encouraged. "Let's have our happy ending."

Evie turned and walked swiftly toward the boy and the girl who, seeing her, rose, their faces radiant. Evie felt the darkness fall from her, the daggers slipping out of her heart. As Ezra's and Juliet's arms folded around her, she sighed.

Her world had finally been returned to her.

—◆—

In the deserted building that had once been La Fable Sombre's lair, a metal door rattled. A jagged line appeared in the floor, widening with a loud crack. The door flew open. Darkness congealed beyond, whispering. Obsidian eyes opened in a face of shadows.

Former La Fable Sombres

Medieval Paris: The Trinity

Ismail Ameziana, a student of medicine and son of
a Moorish ambassador with an extraordinary
ability to heal

Bruno Zincalos: A highwayman, a supernaturally
gifted tracker and marksman

Mariette Chevalier: A disgraced aristocrat's daughter and
a courtesan, could convince anyone of anything

Renaissance Italy: The Lovers

Niccolo Leone: Italian jewel thief who could tame any beast

Julian Aguirre: Basque apothecary who could appear
to be anyone

The French Revolution: The Sisters

Antoinette Paquet: Daughter of an infamous female thief
in Paris. Could mimic voices

Claire Paquet: Could scale any buildings with
acrobatic ease

The Victorian Era: The Mystics

Marie Laveau: herbalist, hairdresser, and practitioner of Voudou. Could charm people into telling secrets

Matthew Byrd: A divinity student from New England who could create illusions

The Wild West: The Tricksters

Wild Bill Hickok: A Texas sharpshooter. Could make people see what wasn't there

Gemma Algernon: A saloon girl from Ireland who could make herself unseen

The Gilded Age: The Elegants

Oruko Musa: A musician from Nigeria who could con people with his voice

Astrid Ehrling: A girl acrobat from Denmark who could predict people's actions

The Roaring Twenties: The Stars

Kaden Idrissi: A movie star from Morocco. Unusual strength and reflexes

Zoe Becker: From Chicago. A flapper. Contortionist

Depression Era: The Grifters

Cal Jensen: A bank robber from California who could find precious objects

Ida Kimura: A Japanese typist and thief who could move faster than the eye could see

World War II: The Rebels

Mae Starr: A girl pilot from Idaho who could see the luckiest outcome

Luis Castillo: An archaeology student from Mexico City who could speak to the dead

The Fifties: The Hunters

Ava Dubrowska: A pianist from Poland. Could convince anyone with a song

Alexander Abernathy: Ex-soldier turned thief who had unusual strength and reflexes

The Sixties: The Songbirds

Chey Dodge: A Navajo musician from Nevada who could levitate

Thalia Khatun: A girl guitarist from Bangladesh who could weave illusions

The Seventies: The Rogues

Vergil Tucker: A boy from Michigan who could shapeshift

Grace Flores: A girl from Paris, studied anthropology, could create illusions

The Eighties: The Misfits

Cassie Anders: A girl from Texas with supernatural reflexes

Deo Torres: A boy from Colombia gifted with telekinesis

The Nineties: The Dolls

Ruby Ndlovu: A girl from Somalia, a London Goth. Used mirrors to Travel

Annabelle Chalabaj: A girl from India who could transform objects

The 2000s: The Sovereigns

Michael Quinn: A boy from Ireland who can appear to be other people

Camille Chevalier: A girl from France who can spirit people away

Acknowledgments

I would like to thank my agent, Thao Le, for her fierce belief in this book from its first draft, and her absolute confidence in me as a writer.

I would like to thank my writing group: Val, Carol, Roy, Amyrah, and Colin, who were my patient beta listeners, even when I didn't do the accents.

And thank you to my fabulous beta readers, whose contributions strengthened my family of thieves so that they have history and heart beneath the pathos.

Thank you also to those generous small press editors of fantasy and horror magazines, whose advice and coaching throughout many years were the best teachers a writer could ask for.

And thank you to my wonderful team of editors at Bloomsbury, to Mary Kate Castellani and Kei Nakatsuka, to my proofreaders and copy editors, who made this a story I can read and be proud of.